# DISHONOUR

Helen Black was brought up in a mining town in West Yorkshire. She moved to London in her twenties and trained to be a commercial lawyer. On qualification she shifted lanes and has practised criminal and family law for over ten years. She specialises in representing children in the care system. She now lives in Bedfordshire with her husband and young children.

For further information on Helen Black, visit her website at www.hblack.co.uk.
Helen Black blogs at StrictlyWriting.

Praise for Helen Black's books:

'A fantastic first novel.'
> Jane Elliott, author of *The Little Prisoner*
> and *Sadie*

'A dark and gripping read that will have you on the edge of your seat . . . this terrific debut novel is full of intrigue and a real page-turner.' *Closer*

By the same author:

*Damaged Goods*
*A Place of Safety*

# HELEN BLACK

## *Dishonour*

**AVON**

AVON

A division of HarperCollins*Publishers*
77–85 Fulham Palace Road,
London W6 8JB

www.harpercollins.co.uk

A Paperback Original

1

First published in Great Britain by
HarperCollins*Publishers* 2009

Copyright © Helen Black 2009

Helen Black asserts the moral right to
be identified as the author of this work

A catalogue record for this book is
available from the British Library

ISBN: 978-0-00792-612-1

Set in Minion by Palimpsest Book Production Limited,
Grangemouth, Stirlingshire

Printed and bound in Great Britain by
Clays Ltd, St Ives plc

I can't believe this is my third book. The time has raced away in a haze of drafting and editing.

Once again I must thank those who have given generously of their time, energy and support. First up, the Buckman posse, who unfailingly smile at my plans for world domination.

Then of course there is everyone at Avon, particularly Sammia Rafique, who helped with cultural inconsistencies. Salaams, girlfriend.

To the boys at HUG I send a salute. Keep on keeping on, comrades.

Last but by no means least I want to thank my fabulous family. Living with a writer can't be easy but you guys take it in your stride. Every day I count myself lucky that I am able to do what I love, surrounded by the people I love.

To Dad. We miss you.

# Prologue

I watch Yasmeen sleep, her breath shallow, her mouth slightly parted.

She is so beautiful.

Wherever she goes people stare at those eyes, heavy-lidded, flecked with amber.

At mosque, when she takes her usual place, her hijab secured tightly under her chin, I can see her lips move. They are garnet red as she murmurs her prayers.

Here, on the bed, I am dazzled by her all over again and I nearly change my mind. There's still time. I could call an ambulance and they would inject her with drugs, attach her to machines.

I pull out my phone and my finger hovers over the number nine.

But no. I have made up my mind.

There was a time when I would have done anything for this girl and she would have done the same for me. In this cruel world we stood shoulder to shoulder against those who would torment us. When I lost hope she held my face in her hands.

'God will provide.'

I wonder then why she has chosen to wreck everything. To bring this family to its knees. To crush me like a can.

Her chest rattles and I picture myself sitting here in Yasmeen's bedroom, watching this girl I have loved so well. Watching her die.

Do I still love her?

With all my heart.

Yet I am immobile as her life creeps away.

She lets out a tiny gasp and a pink bubble forms on her lips.

When it bursts I know it is over and through my tears I whisper the words she cannot say for herself.

'I bear witness that there is no God but Allah.'

# *Chapter One*

May 2009

'Un-bloody-believable.'

Lilly Valentine leaned against the wall and sighed. 'I paid for all this to be up and running last week and I still can't make outgoing calls.'

The telephone engineer was lying on the floor, unscrewing a socket. 'There must be a glitch in your system,' he said.

'A glitch?'

'That's right. There are often problems with the fibre optics.'

'Listen, mate, I'm trying to run a law firm, not sit for a degree in telecommunications.' Lilly heaved her backside into a chair. 'Can you fix it?'

'I'll need a new circuit board,' said the engineer. 'Can I come back tomorrow?'

Lilly shook her head in despair.

'Try not to worry,' the man laughed. 'Teething troubles are routine.'

Lilly smoothed her hand over her pregnant belly and

3

looked around at the new offices of Valentine & Co. Unopened post was spewed across the doormat, files littered every seat, the espresso machine still in its box and the potted plant had already died.

'Trust me,' she said. 'Nothing in my life is ever routine.'

As the engineer stood to leave Lilly leaned over and opened a box of headed notepaper. The smell of fresh ink escaped.

The engineer looked over Lilly's shoulder. '"Valerian and Co,"' he read. 'Ain't that a type of sleeping pill?'

Lilly closed her eyes tight and hoped this was all a bad dream. When she opened them everything was exactly the same.

'Un-bloody-believable.'

The heat of the smoke makes Ryan's lungs sting but he holds it in and counts to five.

Only girls can't take their weed. And batty boys.

Lailla wags her finger. 'You gonna get caught with that.'

Ryan laughs in a cloud of grey. 'You worried about me?'

'I think you a big enough boy to be looking after yourself, Ryan Sanders,' she winks.

Naz and some of the other boys whistle but Ryan knows Lailla is only messing. She flirts with all the boys at school but everyone knows she's going with Sonny. He's eighteen and picks Lailla up in a black Merc. Personalised reg plate and everything. Respect to him 'cos Lailla's well fit.

Ryan, Lailla and their friends meet here every lunchtime, on the grass between the lower school playground and the boundary wall. The headmistress calls it the Orchard Green but there ain't no trees or nothing. There used to be a climbing frame but someone fell off and broke his shoulder so they took it down. It gets muddy sometimes but it's the furthest point from the classrooms that they can get without breaking the rules. Not that Ryan gives a shit about rules, but some of the others are a bunch of pussies, innit.

The girls giggle and apply lip gloss while the boys smoke and chat them up. Ryan sometimes deals a few baggies. Nothing major.

'Who's your friend?' asks Ryan, nodding at a girl hovering in the background.

He's seen her around school, though she's not in any of his sets, except in art. She's got long shiny hair to her waist and a shy smile. He tries to catch her eye but she's looking anywhere but at him. She don't seem like the type to hang with Lailla, to be honest, and he wonders why she ain't indoors revising or some shit.

Lailla grins, showing her sharp white teeth. 'Why you asking?'

'You know me,' says Ryan, 'I like to get to know all the pretty girls, innit.'

Lailla smiles again but her eyes narrow. She don't like anyone else to get the attention. Likes to be top dog, she does.

'Aasha,' she pulls the girl by the arm, 'come say hi to Ryan.'

The girl flushes and checks the ground.

'So you can't speak now?' Lailla laughs. 'Can't look a boy in the eye?'

There's something cruel in Lailla's voice, like she enjoys her friend's embarrassment. Girls are like that, though, thick as thieves one minute, bitching about each other the next.

Aasha lifts her chin as though it were made of concrete or something. When she finally, painfully, meets his gaze he can see his reflection in her eyes. 'Hi.'

'She's a good Muslim girl,' Lailla tells him, 'so don't be getting no ideas.'

Ryan laughs. A good Muslim girl. He's heard that like, what, a million times before.

At least half the kids at school are Muslim, and yeah, they can chat in Urdu or whatever and they don't make a big thing of Christmas, but they ain't that different. Sometimes there's trouble, like that time the Mehmet brothers got the school play stopped, but Ryan stays out of it. You can't judge a person on whether they're white, black, brown or fucking green, can you? And girls are girls, whether they cover their heads or not, innit.

'A good Muslim girl,' Ryan makes a face at Lailla. 'Is that what you are in the back of Sonny's car?'

Lailla gives him a playful slap. 'Be nice.'

He approaches Aasha, his head cocked to one side. 'I'm always nice.'

Where else would one tombola ticket cost five pounds? Lilly shook her head. Only at Manor Park, her son's prep school, would such a thing be considered reasonable.

'How many do you need?' asked Penny Van Huysan, one of the mothers running the stall.

6

Penny, like most of the Manor Park parents, was minted. Her idea of budgeting was to cut down the housekeeper to four days a week.

'Who's in charge of the tea tent?' asked Lilly. 'Ronnie Biggs?'

Penny rolled her eyes. She and Lilly were long-standing friends. Despite the Yummy Mummy appearance and her addiction to Harvey Nicks, Penny was kind and honest, and often provided respite care to disabled children whose own parents were on the brink of collapse.

'Have you seen the prizes?'

Lilly scanned the table. Diptyque Candles, a Cartier fountain pen, vouchers for dinner at The Ivy.

'Very nice,' Lilly nodded, 'but nothing I need as much as five quid in my purse.'

'Every penny goes to disadvantaged children.'

Lilly patted her stomach. 'Which is exactly what this one will be if I chuck away my hard-earned cash.'

Lilly felt strong arms circling her waist and smelled the familiar mix of lemon and leather that meant Jack was near.

'Is this one giving you grief?' Jack asked Penny.

'Pleading poverty as usual,' said Penny.

Lilly leaned into Jack's embrace. 'We can't all be married to millionaires.'

'In my next life I'm coming back as a hedge fund manager,' said Jack.

Lilly nuzzled his neck. 'Don't you bloody dare.'

He touched her pregnant belly gently. 'How's Frank?'

'Frank?' Penny raised an eyebrow.

'Don't go there,' Lilly warned.

Jack had spent weeks trying to engage her in naming discussions. Lilly flatly refused.

'Then I'll choose myself,' he'd said.

'Not interested,' Lilly had replied.

'Frank,' he'd declared. 'A good solid name.'

'The only Frank I ever knew ended up doing a five stretch for attacking his neighbour with an axe.'

'I thought you weren't interested,' he'd retorted.

'Come on, Jack.' Penny waved a book of tickets. 'You must have the luck of the Irish.'

Jack laughed. 'That's the lot from the Emerald Isle. Trust me, there's nothing lucky about Belfast.'

'You managed to tie Lilly down, didn't you?' said Penny. 'You must be doing something right.'

Jack kissed Lilly's cheek, winked at Penny and pulled out his wallet. 'Och, give us a couple then.'

'You didn't have to do that,' said Lilly as she and Jack wandered around the May Fayre.

The school grounds lent themselves to the resolute Englishness of the celebrations, children streaking across the extensive lawns, gobbling ice creams. Blossom blew in the spring breeze like confetti. A white marquee seemed at home next to the immaculate cricket pitch.

Jack shrugged. 'A copper's wage may not be six figures but I'm above the breadline.'

'Unlike this struggling solicitor,' Lilly laughed.

'We'll get by.'

'We'll have to,' said Lilly. 'I can't even get the sodding phones to work.'

'Good,' said Jack.

'Good?'

'Haven't I been saying all along that you should wait until after the baby's born to set up shop?'

Lilly rolled her eyes.

Jack had made his feelings abundantly clear. *Ad nauseam.*

But she wasn't some chicken on an egg. As much as she wanted this baby, and imagined little fingers curled around her own, she couldn't be expected to sit around all day incubating.

'I worked right up to the week before I had Sam,' she said.

'You weren't forty then,' Jack replied.

Lilly gave him a playful punch on the arm and anticipated one in return when she felt Jack stiffen. She followed his eye line and saw Sam and his dad walking towards them. Things had been tricky in the past between Jack and David. Hell, things had been tricky between Lilly and David. Her ex-husband had a talent for winding everyone up.

'Hey big man,' Lilly called to her ten-year-old son.

Sam was wearing a straw hat garlanded with flowers and ribbons.

'I'm loving that look,' said Jack.

'It's for morris dancing,' said David.

'And there was me thinking it was his rugby kit,' said Jack.

Lilly kicked Jack's ankle. For Sam's sake, a truce had been called and they had each agreed to be as civil as possible.

'It looks great, Sam,' she said.

'It looks totally lame,' Sam scowled. He glanced at another group of boys in similar attire. 'People will think I'm with those dorks.'

'Still, you've a good chance of being crowned May Queen,' said Jack.

Sam put up a fist but couldn't resist a laugh.

'Can Sam have tea with you, David?' Lilly asked. 'I've got to see a man about a phone.'

He shook his head. 'Sorry. I've got to collect Cara and Fleur from baby massage.'

Lilly felt heat rising up her neck. David's girlfriend, Cara, and their child always seemed to take priority and it infuriated her. Truce or not, she opened her mouth to remind David that he had two children.

'I'll take him back to the cottage with me,' said Jack. 'You're cool with that, aren't you, Sam?'

Lilly mouthed her thanks.

'Can we call at the shop for crisps?' asked Sam.

'Sure,' said Jack.

'And in the baker's for a cake?'

'Why not?'

David pointed to Lilly's bump. 'I suspect you won't be following the school of firm parenting, Jack.'

Lilly gave her ex-husband a cold stare. 'I'll settle for the school of just being around.'

Aasha knows she should be listening to Mr Markson. Maths is her worst subject. She'll definitely get As in everything else. Maybe even A*s in geography and art. But maths has always puzzled her. Who really cares how you work out the average score on dice? And why would you ever need to calculate the average speed of a train from London to Inverness? She'd been to Scotland once for a cousin's wedding and it had taken eight hours in the car to get there. She and her brothers had bickered most of the way, and she'd been sick in a lay-by near Birmingham, but no one had asked her to work out their average speed.

But as her dad is constantly reminding her, she needs to get at least a B.

'Or no good university will even look at you, and what then?'

What then, indeed.

She tries to drag her attention back to the lesson but in seconds it's wandered back to where it was before. Ryan Sanders.

Aasha can't believe she's giving him head space. He's such a loser, in the bottom sets for everything. He'll be lucky to scrape any GCSEs, never mind a good grade in maths. The only thing he's any good at is art, and then he doesn't turn up most of the time. Not that she's noticed him. Or even cares.

'An ASBO kid,' her dad would call him.

Not that Ryan has an ASBO, or at least not one that Aasha knows about. But he's that type. A bad boy.

'Bet I know who you're thinking about,' whispers Lailla.

Aasha feels the heat creep around the base of her throat. 'I'm not thinking about anyone.'

Lailla giggles. 'So why are you writing his name all over your notebook?'

Aasha looks down and gasps. She's doodled Ryan's name all down the margin.

'Your brothers will kill you,' says Lailla.

Aasha turns over the page and smooths it down. 'Shut up, Lailla.'

She forces her eyes back to the white board but she can still hear Lailla laughing – just like she can still see Ryan's name through the paper.

'Any chance of a coffee?'

The engineer was once again prone on the brand-new carpet in Lilly's office, ferreting about in the socket and squinting like Popeye.

Lilly indicated her espresso maker still in its box, and turned her attention to the printer. She lifted the lid and rooted around. Where the hell did you put the ink?

'You ain't really cut out for this,' the engineer observed.

Lilly bristled. 'Just fix my phone.'

But he was right. Of all the people best suited to organising things, Lilly had to be at the bottom of the list. She was a litigator, a case lawyer, a court-room brawler.

She pulled out her mobile and called her old boss.

'Rupes, it's me.'

Rupinder laughed. 'How's it going?'

Lilly poked suspiciously at her printer. 'It's a bloody nightmare.'

Rupinder gasped. 'Is something wrong with the baby?'

'Oh, that.' Lilly patted her bump. 'No, everything's fine.'

'So what's the matter?'

'I just don't know how you did it.' Lilly looked mournfully around the office. 'How did you run everything so efficiently?'

'Ah,' Rupinder caught her meaning. 'Well, for one thing, I had help.'

Lilly nodded. When she'd worked for Rupes there'd been three partners, a handful of secretaries and the old bulldog on reception, Sheila. Lilly never thought the day would come when she missed the interfering old battleaxe, but at least she could work the photocopier.

'I can't afford to hire anyone,' Lilly said. 'Not until I'm up and running.'

'And how will you manage that on your own?'

Rupinder's voice was, as always, the epitome of calm. Lilly wished she were still around, that they could work together.

'I miss you, Rupes.'

'I miss you too.' Her words were like balm. 'But you still won't manage on your own.'

Lilly pushed out her lip. 'I'll just have to.'

Sam licked the sugar off his fingers and eyed the last doughnut.

'Are you eating that?' he asked.

Jack patted his six-pack. Since the enormity of becoming a dad had hit him, he'd decided the very least he could do was try to stay alive. He'd started slowly, refusing the odd takeaway curry. He'd curbed the beer and upped the running. Before long he began to enjoy his new regime and now ate no wheat, sugar or dairy. It drove Lilly insane.

'Fill your boots.'

He watched Sam devour it, enjoying the pale sunshine streaming in through the kitchen windows.

'What?' Sam spoke through a mouthful of jam and grease.

'You're just like your mum,' said Jack.

Sam frowned. 'Thanks a bunch.'

'Your mother's a fine woman.'

'Whatever.'

Jack shook his head. When had Sam turned from wide-eyed boy to grunter?

'She always does her best for you.'

Sam rolled his eyes. 'I barely see her.'

'All that's going to change,' said Jack. 'What with the baby coming, she's promised to take her foot off the pedal.'

Sam raised an eyebrow.

'Mark my words,' Jack promised, 'things will be different.'

Sam wiped his sticky lips with the back of his hand and stood to leave the room. When he got to the door he turned.

'Just because you want it to be true, Jack, doesn't mean it is.'

When the engineer had finally left, Lilly put her feet up on her desk. Her ankles were swollen to elephantine proportions. She felt like an overstuffed cushion, all lumpy and uncomfortable. She didn't remember being like this when she was pregnant with Sam. Then again, that was over ten years ago and she hadn't yet hit thirty.

When the door opened she remained in the same undignified position. What the hell did the phone guy need now?

'Are you open?'

A young Asian man looked at her doughy toes.

'Not exactly,' said Lilly, and struggled to get upright.

'Oh,' he said, but didn't move.

'Can I make an appointment for you?'

Lilly scrabbled around for the diary she'd bought especially. It was leather-bound with gold lettering and had a whole page for each day. Her plan was to colour-code clients. She'd promised herself faithfully to avoid criminal and childcare cases: there was no money in either. Red for family, green for property. It was her first step to getting organised. Now, where had she put the damn thing?

She grabbed a biro and a ticket for the dry cleaner's.

'Next Tuesday?' she asked.

The young man stroked his goatee. Lilly could see now that he was in his late teens, nineteen at most. A boy really.

'Thing is, I've got my mum in the car,' he said, 'and we really need to talk to someone.'

'I don't want to be unhelpful,' Lilly smiled, and opened her arms to encompass the chaos, 'but as you can see we're not quite up to speed.'

He ignored the telephone wires that crisscrossed the floor and levelled Lilly in his gaze.

'My sister killed herself and we need to know what to say to the police.'

Lilly watched the woman sitting opposite. Her body was frail, lost in the folds of her plain brown shalwar-kameez. Her eyes were downcast to arthritic fingers that lay gnarled and motionless in her lap.

'I'm so sorry for your loss.'

The other woman didn't acknowledge Lilly's words but continued staring down at her hands.

Lilly moved two phone directories, a box of manila envelopes and a broken laptop from her desk.

'Sorry for the mess,' she muttered. 'Like I said, we're not really open yet.'

The boy gave a perfunctory nod and drew himself up. Lilly could see he was barely able to contain his tears.

She opened a drawer for a legal pad. Amazingly there was one inside.

'Can I start with your name?'

'Anwar Khan,' he said.

'And your mum?'

Anwar's eyes darted towards the woman beside him. She looked old enough to his grandmother. Strings of thin grey hair escaped from the woollen shawl draped loosely over her head. Her face was lined and worn.

'Deema Khan,' he said.

Even at her name Mrs Khan remained impassive. Lilly assumed she must be in shock.

'And you say your sister died recently?'

'Yes . . .' Anwar coughed to clear his throat. 'She took an overdose.'

'I'm sorry.'

Anwar took a deep breath as if to steady himself. 'It's very important to us that she's buried as soon as possible.'

'I see,' said Lilly.

'Mum is devastated.'

Lilly cast a glance at Mrs Khan, who continued to contemplate her lap. If it were Lilly, and her son had topped himself, she was sure she'd be screaming and

16

wailing. But then grief did strange things to people, didn't it?

'And what can I do to help?' asked Lilly.

Anwar cleared his throat again. Lilly's heart went out to this young man, so evidently forced to take control of what must be a terrible situation.

'The police still have Yasmeen.' He paused. 'You know, her body.'

'When did she die?' Lilly asked.

'Two days ago.'

Lilly smiled kindly. Two days wasn't very long in the circumstances, though she understood it must seem like for ever to the family.

'Have they given you any indication when they will release it?'

Anwar shook his head. 'That's why we're here. We want someone to speak to them, make them understand how important this is.'

Lilly looked from Anwar's poor stricken face to his mother, who seemed oblivious to her surroundings. Her heart sank. She had promised Jack that there would be no more stress. No more clients needing to lean on her. She had to think of the baby.

'I'm not sure you actually need a solicitor,' said Lilly. 'Can another family member not help?'

Anwar pushed the heels of his hands into his forehead. 'Mum can't deal with this, Miss Valentine.'

A cursory glance told Lilly he was right. Deema Khan was nothing more than a shell.

'What about your father?'

'He's dead,' said Anwar. 'I'm the head of the family

17

so it falls to me to ensure my sister has a proper Islamic funeral.'

Lilly saw that the burden of responsibility was physically weighing the boy down, and sighed.

'Give me the officer's details and I'll see what I can do.'

Lilly parked in a side road and walked towards the police station, wondering why the Khans hadn't chosen a local solicitor. Perhaps they thought she might have more sway with the police. The idea made her laugh out loud. Still, there were plenty of others she could have redirected them to.

She swallowed down her guilt, telling herself this wasn't going to be a difficult case. It wasn't even a proper case. Just a chat with a copper. Absolutely nothing stressful. She knew Jack wouldn't be pleased but if he'd seen the look on Anwar's face he'd understand.

The High Street in Bury Park was throbbing with shoppers laden with carrier bags and trolleys. Grocers piled their stalls high with melons, oranges and custard apples, their skins covered with indentations like a thousand dirty fingerprints. Lilly stopped to smell a plastic container of lemons, their leaves still attached.

'A pound a bowl,' the shopkeeper called from inside.

A woman reached past Lilly for a handful of okra. She was enshrouded in black, even her eyes covered. Only her toes were naked, brown and soft, peeping out from under her burka, in leather flip-flops.

Behind her, a girl of about sixteen rattled into her phone in Urdu. The startling cerise of her hijab matched her nail varnish and handbag. She handed over a pound and took her fruit without stopping for breath.

The traffic crawled to a standstill as drivers stopped on double yellow lines to collect waiting relatives or chat to friends in the street. The smell of incense wafted through the air.

After the stuffy environment of Manor Park it made Lilly smile. It made her feel alive.

'Saag, very good for baby,' the shopkeeper shouted, waving a bunch of spinach at Lilly.

He wore a beige Afghan-style hat that Lilly was sure he didn't need in the May sunshine.

'How can I resist charm like that?' Lilly laughed.

By the time she arrived at the station she had spinach, ginger, a can of coconut water and an interesting fruit called a pow pow. And it had taken a lot of willpower not to buy a jewelled sari in peacock blue.

At the front desk she looked at the notes she had taken during her meeting with Anwar and pressed the buzzer.

A blonde WPC came into the reception. Her shirt was tucked neatly into her trousers and displayed a tiny waist and flat stomach. Lilly stood as near to the counter as her own pumpkin-sized belly would allow.

The WPC's eyes couldn't resist a flicker towards Lilly's girth. It was quick but Lilly clocked it. When she'd been pregnant with Sam she'd bloomed. The apples of her cheeks had a rosy glow and she'd worn her jeans until the sixth month. This time, she felt like the bloated corpse of a humpback whale.

'Can I help you?' The WPC's smile was as perky as her chest.

'I'd like to speak to DI Bell,' said Lilly.

'Is he expecting you?'

Lilly tried a smile. 'I called to say I was on my way.'

The policewoman nodded and skipped away. Lilly lowered herself into one of the metal-framed seats. She could feel the steel tubes tattooing their pattern onto her bum.

At last the WPC returned and ushered Lilly through. She gave a puzzled look at Lilly's shopping, shrugged and led her through the corridors at such a sprightly pace Lilly could barely keep up. When they arrived at the foot of a steep staircase Lilly let out a groan. Plastic bag in one hand, she grabbed the banister and hauled herself up. By the time she arrived at the inspector's room she was gasping for air.

'Good grief,' said DI Bell, leading Lilly to a chair, 'are you OK?'

Lilly took a deep breath. 'The stairs . . .'

The DI frowned at the WPC. 'Why on earth didn't you show Miss Valentine to the lift?'

'I didn't think.'

DI Bell waved her away with an impatient flap of his hand. 'Young people these days can't put themselves in anyone else's shoes, can they?'

He didn't wait for Lilly's reply but turned instead to pour her a glass of water.

Despite the fact that it was her own wellbeing in discussion, Lilly didn't like his tone with the young woman and gave her an apologetic smile as she left. Everyone had been young once, hadn't they?

'So . . .' DI Bell smiled and displayed perfect, even, white teeth. 'What can I do for you?'

Lilly clamped her lips over her own crooked teeth and wished her mother had made her wear a brace as a child. Sam and all his friends sported matching train tracks; some even had the hugely expensive 'invisible' ones that turned a disgusting brown when they drank Coke. When they came off they would all troop back to their dentists for the obligatory bleaching.

'I understand you're overseeing the death of Yasmeen Khan,' she said.

DI Bell nodded and handed her the glass. His fingers were surprisingly small, the nails clean and buffed.

'I've been instructed by the family to ascertain when you intend to release the body.' Lilly sipped her water. 'I'm sure you understand that they are very keen to bury their loved one.'

DI Bell nodded again. 'It's natural for any family to want to make arrangements.'

His accent was public school. In the past this might have grated, but Sam sounded exactly the same.

'And as Muslims, they would be expected to carry out the necessary prayers and ablutions as soon as possible,' she said.

DI Bell raised an eyebrow. 'And as a police officer I would be expected to carry out an investigation into any death for as long as necessary.'

'I'm not suggesting otherwise,' Lilly smiled. 'I'm just asking you to take into account the family's religion.'

'I will of course take that into account,' DI Bell

straightened his back, 'whilst continuing with my investigation.'

Lilly gathered her patience. She was tired and uncomfortable. Her feet were bursting out of her shoes. Why did coppers have to turn everything into a row?

'The girl killed herself. What exactly is it you need to investigate?'

'I simply want to assure myself that this matter is as cut and dried as it seems,' said DI Bell. 'And I would assume Yasmeen's family would want the same. Whatever their religious affiliations.'

Lilly levelled the man in her sights. Now she listened carefully, his voice was all wrong – too stilted, trying much too hard. He said all the right things but it was as if he were reading from a script.

'Why don't we speak again in two days?' she said. 'I'm sure that will give you ample time.'

The plate of pakora smelled so delicious Lilly's stomach lurched. She could almost taste the chilli and coriander.

'Please,' said Anwar, and gestured for her to take one.

Lilly's smile was rueful. 'Spicy food is a bit of a problem at the moment.'

This was an understatement. A month ago, when Lilly had cracked and had a takeaway delivered, she had barely swallowed three spoonfuls of chicken korma and a nibble of chapatti when the heartburn kicked in and she'd been up all night chugging on a bottle of Gaviscon.

Anwar gave a polite smile and passed the plate back to his mother to be returned to the kitchen.

After a momentary rattling of crockery and cupboard doors she resumed her place next to her son. On a chair to the side of the room sat a man in his early fifties. He wore white cotton kurta pyjamas and kufi cap. He scowled at Lilly from behind a long grey beard.

'This is my uncle,' said Anwar.

Lilly held out her hand. 'Pleased to meet you.'

The man looked from Lilly's face to her hand and back again before finally taking it in his. 'Mohamed Aziz.'

Lilly cringed at the sweat on his palm and surreptitiously wiped her hand against her leg.

'Have you spoken to the police?' asked Anwar.

'Yes,' said Lilly, 'I met with the officer in the case about half an hour ago.'

'"Officer in the case"?' Mohamed sneered. 'The sad passing of Yasmeen is not a case.'

'It's a figure of speech,' said Lilly. 'The officer who has been assigned to look into Yasmeen's death.'

Mohamed shook his head, clearly dissatisfied with Lilly's explanation.

Then the the door burst open and a teenage boy and girl burst in.

Anwar jumped to his feet. 'What are you two doing back here?' he said. 'I told you to stay at Auntie's for the afternoon.'

The girl straightened her hijab. 'She felt ill so we came home.'

'OK then,' Anwar was still on his feet, 'why don't you go upstairs?'

The girl looked at Lilly and knitted her brow.

'Listen to your brother,' said Mohamed.

23

The girl frowned but turned as if she might head for the stairs.

The boy, however, was not so easily persuaded. He squared his shoulders, openly aggressive. 'Who's this?'

'We'll talk about it later,' said Anwar.

The boy folded his arms across his chest. 'I want to talk about it now.'

Anwar pursed his lips but Lilly caught his glance towards his uncle, who gave an almost imperceptible nod. Evidently, Anwar did not make all the decisions for the family.

'Fine. This is Miss Valentine,' said Anwar. 'A solicitor.' He turned to Lilly. 'This is my brother, Raffique Khan.'

'Pleased to meet you,' said Lilly, and held out her hand.

Much like his uncle, the boy looked at her hand as if there was nothing he would less like to do than shake it. But Lilly had dealt with stroppier teenagers than this in her fifteen years of practice and she held fast, her arm outstretched. Eventually he had no option.

'Why do we need a solicitor?' Raffique asked.

'You know perfectly well.' Anwar sat down heavily. 'We need the police to release Yasmeen's body.'

'The police are racist scum,' the younger brother spat. 'They will do whatever they can to make us suffer.'

Anwar sighed. 'Don't start all that, Raffy.'

Raffy kissed his teeth. 'So why is my sister's body still in their morgue?'

Anwar looked at Lilly, his eyes pleading for some help.

Lilly cleared her throat. 'As I was trying to explain to your uncle, the police will not close this matter until they have assured themselves that Yasmeen's death was either suicide or accidental.'

'And how long will that take?' asked Mohamed.

'I've given them two days to review the matter and get back to me.'

Raffy threw his arms in the air. 'I can't believe we're just gonna sit here and agree to that.'

'So what do you suggest?' asked Anwar.

'That we sort this out ourselves,' Raffy shouted. 'Do you honestly think that if it were one of us Yasmeen would just hang around chatting with solicitors?'

Anwar rolled his eyes. 'OK, Raffy, let's go down there and storm the place.'

'Why not, man? Better than leaving everything up to her.' He jabbed a finger at Lilly. 'She's probably in on it with them.'

Anwar groaned. 'She's a lawyer.'

'She's *fakir*.'

Lilly had had enough. In situations like this, feelings ran high – of course they did. She was a past master at letting clients get it all out of their systems. Vulnerable kids often covered their fears with swearing fits and throwing chairs, and who could blame them? The lawyers that represented them knew when to take cover and wait but they also knew when to call a halt to the hysteria.

'Why don't you call them?' she asked.

Raffy's eyes flashed. 'Call who?'

'The police.' Lilly pulled out her mobile and laid it on the table. 'I'm sure they'll be only too happy to tell you what a pain I am. That I am most definitely not in on *anything* with them.'

Raffy glowered at her but Lilly held his gaze. 'Sadly, there's no love lost between me and Her Majesty's constabulary.'

At last Raffy looked away. 'I still don't see why we can't use one of our own.'

'Do we really want someone local sticking their noses into our business?' asked the girl, who Lilly had almost forgotten was there. 'Hasn't Mum suffered enough?'

The girl rubbed her mother's arm and Deema's hand fluttered upwards as if she might touch her daughter. Eventually it just sank back into her lap as if she were incapable of giving or receiving comfort.

'Saira is right,' said Anwar. 'We need to keep this as quiet as possible.'

'Absolutely,' said Mohamed.

Finally, Raffy's shoulders loosened and he let his head drop. 'Fine,' he muttered, 'whatever.'

DI Bell straightened his tie. His appearance mattered to him very much. Being slightly shorter than average he struggled to get shirts and suits off the peg.

He watched the chief superintendent pacing his office and wondered if the Force had the higher ranks' uniforms especially made. When his own time came he would pay his tailor to run one up, just in case.

'I don't have to tell you,' the chief super stalked to the window, 'that the country is in the grip of racial tension.'

'I'm well aware of that, sir,' said DI Bell.

'Then I don't have to tell you how tricky things are in Luton in particular.'

Bell nodded. The local Muslim community was one

of the most disadvantaged in Britain. A feeding ground for the young, the disenchanted and the angry. It was no coincidence that the 7/7 bombers had begun their fateful train journeys from Luton. The redtops had nick-named Bury Park 'Al-Qaeda Street'.

'You're too young to remember the last serious race riots.' The chief super wagged his finger. 'But I was a sergeant in Brixton in 'eighty-one. I saw at first hand what happens when positions become polarised.'

Bell stifled a yawn. 'That must have been tough, sir.'

'Forty-eight hours of pitched battle. Petrol bombs raining down on us, for the most part.'

Bell promised himself that when he wore the stripes on his shoulder he would never bore junior officers with tales of distant heroism. Sure, he would start a few rumours, let Chinese whispers do their job, but he would remain dignified in his silence.

'Your father was there, of course,' said the chief super.

Bell nodded impassively, like he always did when the old man's name came up.

'One of his team took a direct hit,' the chief continued. 'He would have been burned alive if your father hadn't reacted as quickly as he did.'

Bell's face remained impassive but inside his mouth he bit his cheek.

'There were no paramedics, of course – far too dangerous,' said the chief – 'so your father took off his own jacket and rolled the man in it. Left himself completely open, of course.'

Bell imagined the burly silhouette of the old man, the burning skies of South London behind him.

'It was absolute chaos, and I don't mind telling you that the rest of us were struggling,' the chief pointed at Bell, 'but not your father.'

Time to change the subject.

'So what is it you want me to do about the Khan girl?' he asked.

The chief super was a flinty pragmatist, but even he wouldn't actually order the release of Yasmeen's body. Would he?

'I don't want you to do anything.'

DI Bell felt a stab of disappointment in the other man. His lack of conviction made him look weak. Something else he would never allow. As the old man never ceased to point out, you had to show the lower orders that you were a man of iron.

'What I want,' the chief super continued, 'is an assurance from you that the current situation is absolutely necessary.'

So that was it. The old bugger wanted something to say if the shit hit the fan. An excuse.

'All I can tell you, sir, is that I'm not entirely convinced that the girl killed herself. Something about it is all wrong and I think it's only right we look into it.'

'Quite so,' said the chief super. 'But we don't want to open ourselves up to accusations of racism.'

DI Bell knew exactly what to say. 'Don't you think it would be more racist not to follow up the death of a young Asian woman? I mean, sir, if she were white we wouldn't just leave it, would we?'

The chief super closed his eyes, evidently weighing up the rock and the hard place.

'Fine. Continue the investigation,' he said, 'but be ready to give a decision and release that body as soon as possible.'

'Their lawyer wants an update in two days,' said Bell.

The chief super raised his eyebrows. 'They've instructed a solicitor?'

'She came to see me earlier today,' said Bell. 'A Lilly Valentine.'

The chief super groaned.

'You know her, then, sir?'

'We've had several dealings in the past,' said the chief super, 'and none has been what you would describe as a pleasure.'

'She seemed pretty harmless.'

'Do not underestimate that woman,' the chief super warned. 'If Luton is a tinderbox then Valentine is just the type to light a bloody match.'

At least one day a week they have biryani for supper. Somehow Mum always manages to pick the day when she has the most homework.

'You don't like my food now, missy?'

Aasha sighs. Of course she likes her mother's food. Biryani is one of her favourites, especially when there are crispy fried onions crumbled into it. The problem is the clearing up. There's the dish the meat has been in, the bowl the rice has soaked in, the onion pan and then the cooking pot itself, caked and hard with slow-baked spices. And because it's their mid-week treat her father will insist it is served with the maximum ceremony of side dishes.

She rinses the third pickle dish under the tap and checks her watch. Seven thirty. She can hear her brothers in the sitting room, laughing at some comedy with Catherine Tate. It annoys her that they don't offer to help.

Mum would never let them, of course, but they could at least ask.

'There,' says Mum, and puts away the last spoon. 'Finished.'

'What about the floor?' asks Aasha.

Her mother insists on 'doing the mop' after every meal.

'I'll do it,' says Mum. 'You get on with your school work.'

Aasha watches her mum bend down for the bucket. She seems much older than her forty years. A lifetime of looking after her husband and sons has wrung her dry.

Aasha grabs the mop. 'Go sit down, Mum.'

'What about your maths?'

'I got it done at lunchtime,' Aasha lies.

An hour later Aasha is tucked up in her room. It's the smallest one in the house. The boxroom, as English people call it. There's hardly enough room for her single bed and wardrobe. There's certainly not enough space for a desk like her brothers have.

'Aasha can use the dining table,' her father says.

Fat chance. It's always covered in letters from Pakistan, her brothers' self-defence magazines and piles of clothes for ironing. This week Dad has been dismantling an old radio and the parts are scattered across it.

Anyway, Aasha prefers to spread her books out on her bed. That way she can be sure of some peace without anyone telling her what to do or what to think. Here in her ill-lit cupboard she is mistress.

She logs on to her laptop and looks at her maths homework. Algebra. She'll be in for a tough one tonight.

After twenty long minutes trying to work out how Y can possibly equal X, a box pops up in instant messenger.

Lailla says: *I've been very naughty.*

Aasha laughs and types her reply: Aasha says: *What have u done now?*

She waits for the answer, imagining her friend's candy-pink fingernails dancing across the keyboard.

Lailla says: *I've told Ryan u fancy him and he should msn u.*

Aasha is about to send a stinging response when another box pops up.

*Ryan wants to be your friend.*

Aasha chews her lip. She knows full well what her dad thinks about her having anything to do with boys. And as for a boy like Ryan, well, he'd send her 'back home' on the next plane in forty-two pieces.

'No nice doctor or lawyer will want to marry a girl who's been running around the town with every Tom, Dick and Henry.'

And he's right. Take Lailla. It doesn't matter how many times she insists that she and Sonny have never gone all the way, no one believes her. So even if it's true, which Aasha very much doubts, no boy will want her afterwards.

Then again, messaging isn't exactly the same, is it? It's not real life. No one can say you've done anything wrong, can they?

The box pops up. Another message from Lailla.

Lailla says: *PMSL at u angsting over what to do!!!*

Aasha doesn't know whether she's more cross at Lailla for knowing exactly how she'd react or herself for being so predictable.

Well, not this time. This time she'll live a little. If you could call it that in virtual reality. With a nod to her own courage she accepts Ryan as her friend. Almost immediately she regrets her decision.

Ryan says: *Hi beautiful.*

Aasha says: *Hi.*

Ryan says: *What u doing tonite?*

Aasha says: *Not much. U?*

Ryan says: *U gotta guess. Is it a. thinking about Lindsay Lohan or b. thinking about Aasha Hassan?*

Aasha says: *c. doing ur maths homework.*

Ryan: *Ha ha. Ur a funny grrl.*

Aasha is breathless and pink and doesn't know what to say next. Fortunately Ryan sends another message.

Ryan says: *Will u meet me after school tomoro?*

Aasha says: *I don't think I should.*

Ryan says: *Come on. I'm nowhere near as bad as everyone says.*

Aasha considers what to say next and almost squeals at her own daring.

Aasha says: *That's very disappointing.*

# Chapter Two

'Our words are dead until we give them life with our blood.'

I'm frozen in my place in front of the television, the breath literally sucked out of me.

The man on the screen is so angry, as if he can barely control it. His eyes shine with fury, not fear, despite the fact that he filmed himself making this speech just hours before he strapped explosives to himself and led the most devastating attack upon London since the Second World War.

The newspapers have spent every day since 7 July reviling this man: evil, murderous, insane. Now his picture stares out from every broadsheet, every tabloid. His words ring out from every TV and radio station.

He is dressed in an Arab keffiyeh, an AK-47 slung, almost casually, over his shoulder. He spits his death message out, each syllable a poisonous bullet.

'Until you stop the bombing, gassing, imprisonment and torture of my people, we will not stop this fight.'

But it's not what he is saying that cuts me to the quick

but his accent. Thick and strong, as Yorkshire as coal dust. This is a lad from Leeds. Born in this country. Died in this country.

Yet each toss of his head, each challenge in his face, tells me this man did not consider himself British. He is a stranger here. Unloved. Unwelcome.

His words ring so true, he could be me. It feels like coming home.

'You've got to be having a laugh.'

Lilly pointed at Sam's plate piled high with chocolate digestives.

'What?' he asked.

'That is not a proper breakfast,' said Lilly. 'Get some cereal.'

'I don't want cereal.'

Lilly raised an eyebrow. She hadn't slept well and her feet were still swollen. 'I don't have the energy to fight, big man.'

'Then don't.'

She reached for a packet of Cheerios. 'For me?'

He licked the chocolate from a biscuit.

'Just a few spoonfuls for your poor old mother.'

Sam ignored her.

'Your poor old *pregnant* mother?' She emptied a handful into a bowl. 'A mother who worries about her son all day if he hasn't a decent meal inside of him.'

Sam poked the box. 'That's hardly a decent meal.'

'Better than that.' She nodded to the biscuits.

Sam grabbed the bowl, the dry hoops rattling around the bottom, then yanked the milk from the fridge.

'You, Sam Valentine, are an angel,' Lilly laughed.

'Whatever.'

Something was going on with Sam. He was sullen and uncooperative. The child whom every school report described as 'sunny' had morphed into a shadow.

When his face first darkened, Lilly had assumed it was the baby troubling him and had taken every opportunity to assure him that he wouldn't be pushed out.

'There'll still be lots of time for you,' she'd said.

'There's no time now,' he'd moaned.

Lilly had acknowledged the truth of this. She was always busy, pushed for time, trying to juggle everything. Poor Sam often got pushed to the sidelines.

And yet something told her now that it wasn't the arrival of a new baby brother or sister that was bothering him.

'Is everything all right at school?' she fished.

Sam rolled his eyes theatrically.

'If there were any problems, you know I'd go straight up there,' she said.

'Everything's fine,' he mumbled.

She watched her son drag himself and his breakfast up the stairs. She certainly didn't have the strength to follow up the 'no eating in the bedrooms' rule. No doubt she'd find the remnants stuck to the windowsill, the discarded bowl making a perfect white circle on the freshly glossed wood.

After a fire in the cottage had left every room blackened by smoke, the insurance company had agreed to cover the cost of redecoration. For three weeks two handsome Polish men filled the cottage with their indecipherable chatter and the smell of undercoat.

The place hadn't looked this good in years. The walls were still uneven and the hall filled with bags for recycling, but everything seemed much less shabby. Although Lilly had been terrified by the fire she had to admit that there had been this one small silver lining.

Penny had suggested she invite some of the Manor Park mums over for a coffee morning. 'Show the place off,' she said.

Hmm. The lining wasn't that bloody metallic.

Lilly fingered her new kitchen curtains. They were gingham and wonderfully kitch. They made her smile.

'I never took you for a woman so interested in soft furnishings.'

Lilly turned to Jack, who had slipped into a chair.

'Think of the hours you could while away in John Lewis picking some cushions to match,' he said.

Lilly threw a dishcloth at him. It landed on his lap with a wet thump.

'And there was me going to make you a bacon butty,' she said. 'But you can whistle for it now.'

Jack laughed and threw the cloth back. It hit the window behind her.

'Fried pig,' he patted his stomach, 'I don't think so.'

Lilly had to admit that Jack's current regime of running ten clicks a day had paid off and he *was* looking pretty buff, but his refusal to eat anything remotely bad for him was bloody irritating. She had always loved to cook and he had always loved to eat. A match made in heaven. Now all he would countenance was salad and soup.

He grabbed a banana and kissed her on the cheek. 'Get plenty of rest today.'

Lilly waved him away. His healthy lifestyle was unattractive enough without his constant worrying.

'I'm not ill, Jack.'

'Don't be so defensive, woman. I just thought that since you've no work to do you may as well put your feet up.' He peered at them, spilling over the sides of her slippers. 'They look like they need it.'

She knew full well he was just trying to be nice but as she watched Jack peel the banana and take a bite, her annoyance rose.

'I do have work to do,' she said.

'Is that right?' Jack's mouth was full of fruit.

'The family in Luton I told you about want me to pursue matters with the police.'

Jack swallowed hard, his Adam's apple dancing. 'I thought you said they just wanted a bit of advice.'

'They did,' said Lilly, 'and now they need some more.'

Before Jack could give his opinion Lilly picked up the phone and dialled.

'I'll be going then,' he said, and left the room.

When Lilly heard the front door slam she felt a pang of guilt. She'd been hard on Jack and she knew it. She was the one making difficulties, refusing to play happy families. He was making her brain hurt at the moment – but he meant well, so why was she railing against him? She considered going after him but on the fifth ring, DI Bell answered.

'It's Lilly Valentine here,' she said, 'the Khans' solicitor.'

'Ah,' he said.

'We agreed to review the situation in two days.'

'I recall that's what you said, not necessarily what we agreed.'

Lilly gave a polite laugh. 'So can I tell the family you'll release the body today?'

Bell paused. Lilly had been around enough barristers, judges and senior police officers to know that they liked to milk the moment. She knew that the best way to get what she wanted was to allow them their dramatic tension. But the baby was lying heavily on her pelvis and she desperately needed to pee.

'DI Bell?' she prodded.

He gave a small humph, disappointed not to be allowed his moment in the sun. 'I'm afraid not,' he said.

Lilly crossed her legs. 'Oh, come on, Inspector, you've had enough time to make a decision.'

'Yes I have.'

'What?'

'You're absolutely right, I've come to a decision,' he said.

'Then you have to give this girl back to her poor family.'

'I'm afraid I don't.'

Lilly shook her head. What was he going on about? He may be a pretentious jobsworth but he wouldn't risk a legal action against him, would he? Unless . . . Lilly felt a heaviness settle on her. She gulped.

'And the reason?'

DI Bell cleared his throat. Lilly could almost see

him straightening himself up to full height. 'It is my considered opinion that Yasmeen Khan was murdered.'

Jack's desk was buried in paperwork: forms to be filled, statements to be drafted, information to be forwarded to the courts.

He flicked one of the larger piles with his nail. Being a copper these days was like being a civil servant.

He took a violent gulp of coffee and checked his email.

**To: Sergeant Jack McNally**
**From : The desk of the Chief Superintendent**
**Subject : A Meeting**
**Please see me at your earliest convenience.**

Jack scowled. The super was a total prat. He couldn't just pick up the phone, could he? No doubt he wanted to go over a list of dead cases for archiving or review the latest figures for youth offending. Ticking boxes was something the man revelled in.

Jack refused to hightail it up to the super's office. He'd finish his coffee first.

To be fair, Jack knew full well it wasn't the email that was making him cranky. It was Lilly. The woman was beyond infuriating.

He'd be the first to admit that her pregnancy had come as a bit of a shock. Becoming a dad was never something he'd wanted. He couldn't look after himself, never mind a kid. All those years living alone and he still never managed to have fresh milk in the fridge or pay his gas bill on time. How on earth would he remember all the stuff you had to do for a baby? The poor wee fella would probably starve if it were left to Jack. But after a couple of months he'd settled into the idea. The two of them, with Sam and now a baby, seemed somehow right. A family.

It should be a time of joy, shouldn't it? Anticipating the big day, buying prams, choosing a crib. He'd even bought one of those baby names books. So why was Lilly so determined to carry on as usual?

Setting up a new office, taking on cases, were not what women ought to be doing at a time like this. She should be taking care of herself, letting *him* take care of her. Maybe he didn't put it across well but he only ever wanted to look out for her.

He took another sip of his now cold decaf and pulled out his phone to call her.

'It's Jack,' he said.

'Right.' She sounded distracted.

'Are you OK?'

'Mmm,' she said. 'Just right in the middle of something.'

'Sounds important.'

'Yes,' she said.

Jack knew he should leave it there but he just couldn't help himself.

'Have you taken your folic acid?'

'What?'

'Have you taken your folic acid? It's very important for a growing baby.'

There was a small silence.

'I put the tablets next to the kettle,' he said. When she didn't answer he added, 'In the kitchen.'

'I know where the kettle is, Jack.'

'Of course you do. I'm just saying.'

Lilly heaved a sigh down the phone. 'I have to go.'

Jack stared at the phone for a few seconds after Lilly hung up. He could picture the brown bottle of tablets, untouched, exactly where he'd left them. Lilly couldn't possibly have missed them. He slapped his mobile back in his pocket. It made him so angry that Lilly wasn't prepared to do such a small thing for their child.

Today was not looking good and a meeting with the biggest penpusher of them all would just about finish him off. Sometimes he was tempted to walk out of the door and never come back.


'Take a seat, Jack.' The chief super pointed to the chair at the opposite side of the desk.

Jack slipped silently into his place. Something about the chief super's office, with its clean lines and heavy paperweights, made Jack uncomfortable. Every visit increased his discomfort.

'I won't beat around the bush,' said the chief super.

That'll be a first, thought Jack.

'You'll have heard about the death of Yasmeen Khan.'

Of course Jack had heard about it. Every copper in Luton knew there were rumblings that the girl's suicide wasn't all it seemed. A short-arse called Bell had been swanning around making sure everyone knew just how big this was going to be.

'I understand DI Bell is heading the investigation,' said Jack.

The chief super nodded. 'I'd hoped – well, we'd all hoped – that this could be sorted out.'

'And can't it?'

'It seems not.' The chief super steepled his fingers. 'It seems that the girl was murdered.'

Jack raised his eyebrows. 'Who's in the frame?'

'I'm not at liberty to divulge that at this stage, Jack,' said the chief super, 'but believe me when I say this situation is going to need to be handled with the upmost care.'

Jack nodded. He thought the tragic death of any young woman merited the upmost care, whatever the current political situation, but he knew this was not something the senior officer wanted to hear.

'And this is where you come in, Jack.'

Jack was stunned. The chief super wanted him to assist on a murder case. He'd been involved in only one other – when a young girl in care was accused of killing her mother. That case hadn't exactly gone to plan. Still, he couldn't help feel a warm glow of satisfaction. Perhaps his talents were being recognised after all these years.

'I'll do whatever I can to help,' he said.

The chief super touched the bridge of his nose with his forefingers. 'What's needed here is someone with a delicate touch. We can't go stamping around with size tens.'

'You can count on me,' Jack beamed.

'Excellent.'

The chief super tapped his keyboard and the printer

sprung into life. He motioned for Jack to collect the printed document. Jack read it.

> Bury Park Community High
> Denleigh Secondary
> Lealands
> St Joseph's Roman Catholic High.

It was a list of the local secondary schools. Jack nodded in what he hoped looked like a thoughtful way.

'Didn't the Khan girl attend Beech Hall?'

'Two of her siblings still do,' said the chief super.

'It's not on the list,' Jack pointed out.

'Like I say, Jack, this is all very sensitive. Which is why you need to steer clear, for the present time at least.'

Jack wasn't so sure. If he was being tasked to talk to people who knew Yasmeen then Beech Hall was the obvious place to start. He didn't want to argue with the chief but wasn't convinced the other schools would prove anywhere near as useful.

'I wouldn't want to leave it too long, sir,' he ventured.

'A couple of months should do it.'

'A couple of months?' Jack couldn't disguise his surprise. 'That would normally be considered far too late in the day to start gathering evidence.'

The chief super frowned. 'What evidence?'

'It's difficult to say, sir.' Jack shrugged. 'Maybe her fellow pupils know something. Maybe she said something to her friends.'

The chief super pursed his lips. 'I have no idea what you're talking about, Jack.'

Jack felt heat seep around his collar in embarrass-ment. He didn't consider himself the most articulate of men, he wouldn't win a debate with Stephen Fry, but most people could understand him.

'I think, sir, that in a murder case it would be fairly standard procedure to speak to everyone who came into regular contact with the victim,' said Jack, 'and in this instance that would be the pupils and teachers at Beech Hall.'

The light of recognition came on in the chief super's face. 'Of course, of course.'

Jack heaved a secret sigh of relief. He was beginning to think he was going mad.

'DI Bell and his team have already got that underway,' said the chief. 'The Head has already set up an impromptu interviewing room in one of the science labs.'

'I see,' said Jack, but he didn't.

If they didn't want him to gather evidence in the schools then what on earth did they want him to do? He didn't want to flag up his lack of experience in serious offences but he needed some help here.

'And you want me to do the same at these other schools?'

'Good God, man, no. We don't have the manpower to do that,' said the chief super. 'Can you imagine the expense?'

'I hadn't given it much thought, to be fair,' said Jack.

The chief super's smile was nothing short of patro-nising. 'Which is why you're so good at the sort of thing I'm talking about.'

Jack reread the list of schools. He had no alternative but to admit defeat.

'And what sort of thing is it I'm good at, sir? What is it you actually want me to do?'

The chief opened his arms as if the answer were obvious. 'I need you to visit those schools and chat with the staff.'

'To find out what?'

'Nothing in particular, Jack,' said the chief. 'What we need at this delicate time is a calm and friendly presence among the young Asian community.'

It hit Jack like a truck on the M1.

'You're asking me to be a schools liaison officer.'

'Oh, nothing as official as that, Jack. For one thing we can't afford to create an actual post,' said the chief. 'A one-off visit to a couple of schools with a high proportion of Asian students should suffice.'

Jack felt disappointment swell in his chest, crushing his ribcage.

'You don't want me on the murder team.'

The chief super looked embarrassed. 'Best to leave that to the detectives, don't you think?'

Jack didn't answer.

'Anyway,' said the chief, 'you have a huge conflict of interests.'

'I do?'

'Lilly Valentine,' answered the chief. 'She's representing the Khan family.'

Lilly chewed her lip. She headed over to Bury Park with the intention of telling the Khans what DI Bell had said. Their beautiful daughter and sister had not killed herself. Someone had murdered her.

45

She couldn't imagine how they would react.

She'd been racing over in her Mini Cooper when Jack had called to moan about some vitamin or other. The man had no sense that there was anything else going on in the world apart from her pregnancy. She knew she should be flattered, grateful even, but she just couldn't stand it. She could well guess what his reaction would be to the current turn of events and so she'd hung up. Getting involved with Raffy Khan would be seen as foolishness. Like forgetting those bloody pills. Right now she just didn't have the time to explain things to him; to make him understand.

She pulled up outside the Khans' house and rang the bell.

Deema opened the door. She held her shawl against one cheek, dark circles under her eyes.

'Mrs Khan,' said Lilly, 'may I come in?'

The older woman didn't answer but looked over her shoulder to her elder son, who was hurrying down the hallway, wiping his hands on a piece of kitchen roll.

'Thank goodness it's you.' Anwar ushered Lilly through to the living room. 'Mum's been desperate for news.'

Lilly cast a glance at Deema. She seemed devoid of any emotion, let alone desperation.

'We've all been very anxious.' Anwar was gabbling, his hands shaking as he dried between his fingers furiously. 'I'm sure you can imagine.'

Lilly smiled calmly, determined not to be infected by Anwar's anxiety. She needed to deliver her news in a composed manner.

When he opened the sitting-room door she was greeted by a sea of faces. The Khans had already congregated. Raffy sat at one end of the sofa, his legs apart, his arms folded. Mohamed had taken one of the chairs and was tapping the arm with his thumbnail. Deema slid into the other like a trickle of water.

Saira appeared from the kitchen. 'Can I get you some tea, Miss Valentine?'

'Thank you, no,' said Lilly.

Saira nodded and took her place on the sofa next to Raffy. She tucked her feet under her.

Anwar pulled over a kitchen chair and beckoned Lilly to sit. He stood at his mother's side.

They were all waiting expectantly. Lilly gulped down her panic.

'I thought the younger members of the family might be in school.'

Raffy tossed his head like an angry colt. 'We ain't kids, you know. Saira's seventeen and I'm fifteen.'

Lilly made the mental calculation. If Anwar was nineteen and Yasmeen had been sixteen, Mrs Khan had had her gaggle of children one after the other.

Her eyes flicked to a family photograph taking pride of place on the wall. The young Khans smiled up at their handsome father. Anwar's hair was neatly parted at the side and Raffy's front teeth were missing. Even Deema had a lightness to her and held Saira and Yasmeen close. The girls were laughing, sharing a private joke.

Anwar followed Lilly's eye line to the photo.

'Happier days,' he said. 'Eid, two thousand.'

'Two thousand and one,' Saira corrected him. 'Just before Dad died.'

Anwar nodded sadly.

'Yasmeen was very beautiful,' said Lilly.

'Oh, yes, everybody said so,' Anwar agreed. 'She had the reddest lips I've ever seen.'

'I can see that,' said Lilly.

'When you two have finished your little chat maybe we could get back to the important stuff,' Raffy snarled. 'Like our sister being dead and the police harassing us.'

'Please remain civilised, Raffy,' said Anwar. 'Miss Valentine is our guest.'

'Guests are people we invite over, brother.' He pointed at Lilly. 'She works for us.'

Lilly gave a tight smile. 'Well, I'm glad you're all here because I have some important information.'

'Don't tell me,' said Raffy, 'you found the police station.'

Anwar ignored his younger brother and leaned towards Lilly like an excited puppy. 'They're sending Yasmeen home to us?'

Lilly looked into his expectant face. How was this man-child going to cope with what she was about to say? She put her hand over his.

'I'm so sorry, Anwar, but that's not going to happen.'

Lilly didn't know which was worse, the cacophony of abuse from Raffy or the look of quiet horror in Anwar's eyes.

'I told you we should have instructed one of our own.' Raffy leaped to his feet. 'What does someone like her care for a bunch of Pakis?'

Lilly snapped back her hand from Anwar and

whipped her head towards Raffy. 'Oh, sit down, you stupid boy.'

Raffy was momentarily silenced but he remained standing. 'What did you say to me?'

Lilly hauled herself to her feet and looked the teenager straight in the eye. 'I told you to sit down.' Her voice was ice.

Raffy opened his mouth to speak but Lilly waved away the words before they had the chance to leave his brain.

'What I'm about to say is pretty shocking so I'd prefer it if everyone in this room behaved with dignity.'

At last Raffy snorted his disgust and flopped back onto the sofa.

'As you know, I agreed with DI Bell that he would have until today to conclude his investigations,' said Lilly.

'You've spoken to him?' asked Anwar.

'That's why I'm here. I'm afraid the police won't release Yasmeen's body because they believe she was murdered.'

There were a few seconds' silence punctuated by the sound of Lilly's pulse in her ears.

'Murdered?' Anwar whispered.

Lilly nodded. 'That's what they believe.'

There was more silence until Raffy let out a shocking roar. He pulled back his leg and kicked over the coffee table. Cups, plates and books scattered across the carpet. Saira screamed.

'That can't be right.' Mohamed was also on his feet.

'Of course it's not right, Uncle,' Raffy shouted. 'Those racist bastards just want to torture us.'

Anwar had his head in his hands. 'This cannot be happening.'

'Wake up, brother,' Raffy screamed. 'They hate us.'

Saira had begun to weep, deep racking sobs from the depths of her belly.

'You can't let them get away with this,' Mohamed said to Lilly.

'I can't stop a murder investigation,' she replied.

'Look at what they're doing to this family.' Mohamed opened his arms to encompass all the Khans.

Lilly looked around her. Raffy was stalking from one end of the room to the other, crunching through the broken crockery. Saira continued to sob. Anwar sat with his face in his hands. Only Deema remained unmoved and untouched by the chaos around her.

'I don't understand,' said Anwar, tears coursing down his cheeks. 'Why would they do this to us?'

'Because we are Muslims,' screamed Raffy. 'We're the enemy.'

Saira, still sobbing, got down on her knees and began to collect up the pieces of broken china.

'For goodness' sake, leave that, sis,' said Raffy.

'Someone might hurt themselves,' she murmured, and continued to clear the shards.

'I said fucking leave it,' he snapped.

Lilly tried to clear her head. This was all wrong. She'd feared the family would be devastated but not like this.

'I truly don't believe your religion has any bearing on this matter,' she said.

'Religion has a bearing on every matter,' said Mohamed, a dangerous darkness in his tone.

'Miss Valentine's correct, of course.'

Everyone turned to see a man in the doorway, his waspish frame incongruous in a charcoal pinstripe suit.

He held out his police badge in front of him. 'DI Bell,' he said. 'I don't think you could hear me knocking.'

Anwar stood to offer his hand. 'I'm sorry for that.'

'Don't apologise to him,' spat Raffy.

DI Bell slid his badge into his breast pocket and looked Raffy up and down. A lone wolf, eyeing up his supper.

'How can we help you, Inspector?' asked Anwar.

'I came to inform you that Yasmeen was murdered but I see Miss Valentine got here first.'

'How can you be so sure?' Mohamed asked Bell.

'The only thing he's sure of is that he wants to make our lives a misery,' said Raffy.

Bell's lips formed a slight smile. 'I can't go into the evidence at this time.'

'Because you don't have any,' said Raffy.

Lilly could see that Raffy was pushing it too far. *She* might be able to excuse an angry grieving young man but DI Bell would not. If she didn't defuse the situation he might get himself arrested for threatening behaviour.

'Do you have a suspect?' she asked.

The inspector turned to her with unconcealed satisfaction. 'Indeed I do.'

'Who?' demanded Raffy.

DI Bell licked his lips, the proverbial cat who had got the cream.

'Raffique Khan, I am arresting you for the murder of Yasmeen Khan. You do not have to say anything but it

51

may harm your defence if you do not mention when questioned something you later rely on in court . . .'

Jack parked outside Denleigh Secondary School. He drained a bottle of Evian and threw the empty plastic bottle over his shoulder. It landed on the back seat of his car amid fourteen others. Lilly kept nagging him to recycle them.

He snorted. Lilly recycled everything. Bottles, tins, cereal packets – you couldn't get into the cottage for bags and boxes of the stuff piled up in the hallway.

'It's like one of those strikes in the seventies,' he'd complained one evening when he'd nearly broken his ankle trying to leap over a month's worth of newspapers.

'I'm just trying to make sure this baby has a planet left to live on,' she'd said, pointing at her swelling belly.

He'd laughed, like he always did. Said she was right, like he always did.

He thought about all those Coke cans, milk cartons and unwanted Christmas cards being collected, crushed, cleaned and used again. Maybe more than once, maybe lots of times. Maybe the same tin got used again and again and again, each time filled with something different, last time beans, this time peas, next time, who knows? But it was the same tin going round and round.

He knew how it felt. He'd been doing the same job for over ten years, living in the same flat, drinking in the same pubs. It was like Groundhog Day.

He had tried so hard to change things and thought Lilly's pregnancy might be just the catalyst. A fresh start for them both, a proper relationship. But no. He and Lilly were dancing the same dance they had always done.

He'd met her years ago, when one of her clients had been caught nicking tins of sweets in Woolies. He'd thought she was gorgeous and had impressed her by giving the lad a fiver and letting him go. Her smile had been worth the bollocking he'd got from the shop manager and it had kept him warm throughout a Christmas dinner of beans on toast. Lilly's admiration of Jack seemed to have gone the same way as Woolworths since then.

She did what she felt she had to do, regardless of the consequences to him or his career. He wasn't so stupid to think that if it wasn't for Lilly he'd be in the murder team now, but she hadn't helped.

During his last review, which had taken place, unhelpfully, a week after he and Lilly had 'lost' one of her clients on the way to the immigration authorities, the chief super had confirmed what Jack already knew.

'Your choice of girlfriend is not especially helpful.'

And here they were again.

Jack scratched his scalp and tried to remind himself that Lilly's commitment to her work was one of the things that he had always admired. The children she represented had no one else. Often she was all that stood between them and Armageddon. A lone voice in the chaos. Had he really thought she'd stay quiet just because she was pregnant?

He looked up at the sign at the school gate.

No man is an Island.
Together we are strong

'Try telling that to Lilly bloody Valentine,' he said aloud.

The secretary's hair was cropped so short, Jack could see patches of pink scalp peeping through. In fact, the hairs on her chin were longer.

'Sign, here, here and here.' She pointed at three spidery crosses.

'Jesus,' said Jack, 'you've more security than the nick.'

'We had a lot of trouble a year ago.'

'Oh, aye?'

She leaned towards Jack so that her beard was inches from his nose. 'Some of the Asian pupils have difficult family members.'

'Difficult how?'

'Storming into the classrooms, dragging the girls out of their lessons,' said the secretary.

Jack scratched his signature across the form. 'That doesn't sound good.'

A voice came from behind. 'Ancient history.'

The secretary blushed and filed her paperwork.

Jack turned and got to his feet.

A tall blonde with long tanned legs strode towards him.

'Mara Blake,' she smiled. 'Head Teacher.' Her accent was South African, clipped.

Jack smiled back. Jesus, teachers had never looked this good when he was at school.

'Sergeant Jack McNally,' he said. 'I made an appointment to discuss race relations.'

'Indeed you did. Shall we walk while we talk?' She had already set off, leaving Jack to trot after her firm thighs.

The corridors were strewn with rucksacks and footballs but Mara picked her way through in dangerously high heels without a second's pause.

'We pride ourselves on discipline,' she said. 'You get caught with drugs, you're out. The same goes for weapons.'

Jack stifled a laugh. Zero tolerance or not, he would bet that a random spot check of the students' pockets would furnish enough flick knives and bags of weed to send the *Daily Mail* into meltdown.

'The children are here to learn and they know it,' she said.

Again Jack smiled. Denleigh Secondary School had one of the worst academic records in the country. In the League Tables the government insisted on publishing each year it usually came somewhere between West Brom and Sunderland.

Mara gave him a hard look. 'I know what you're thinking.'

'You do?'

'That our results are terrible.'

Jack shrugged. He could scarcely deny it.

'Just bear in mind that some of these children are incredibly disadvantaged. Over a quarter don't have English as their first language, the rate of divorce within families is high, as is unemployment,' she said.

He passed through to the art rooms and was hit by the familiar smell of acrylic paint. He scanned the walls covered in batik prints of Chinese dragons.

'We try to incorporate as many cultures as possible

into the curriculum,' said Mara. 'Art is a great way to express mutual respect.'

Jack hovered next to a particularly well-crafted design. The dragon's eyes narrowed menacingly, his teeth appeared ready to bite.

'Over half the kids here are Muslim, right?'

Mara joined him with a smile. 'At least.'

'Is there any racial tension?' Jack asked.

She rattled her answer like a gun. 'We don't tolerate any form of discrimination.'

Jack put up his hand. 'I know the policy. What I'm asking is if there's an undercurrent. Your secretary mentioned some problems with parents.'

Mara sighed, her breath escaping in a minty rush. 'Not parents so much,' she said. 'Older brothers.'

Jack raised an eyebrow for her to continue.

'We tried to put on a musical last year, *Grease*.'

'Don't tell me,' said Jack, 'there were riots over who was going to play Sandy.'

Mara laughed and put her hand on his arm. 'I wish. To begin with none of the Asian pupils would take part and we knew we couldn't go ahead with half the school unrepresented in the cast.'

'So what did you do?' asked Jack.

'We had a chat with some of the more integrated students, made them see how great it would be.'

'Something tells me it didn't end up being that great.'

Mara removed her hand from his arm. It immediately felt cold.

'Two of the girls involved didn't tell their families and when they found out they were not happy,' she said.

'Certain brothers and uncles arrived en masse and made a scene.'

'Did you call the police?'

Mara shook her head. 'To be honest, I felt we'd caused the girls involved enough stress without making matters official.'

'And no more musicals?'

Mara laughed again. 'Definitely not.'

'Something funny, miss?' A boy had entered the studio. He was in his mid-teens, his trainers muddy.

Mara nodded at the batik dragon. 'We were just admiring your work, Ryan.'

Ryan bounced back and forth on his heels. 'It's alright, innit?'

Jack traced the dragon's tail with his finger. 'It's excellent.'

'You can buy it for a tenner,' said Ryan.

'Don't you need it for your assessment?' asked Mara.

Ryan shrugged. 'I'd rather have the tenner.'

'I'll tell you what,' said Jack, 'do me another just like it and you can have the cash.'

Ryan watched Jack, his slits of eyes mirroring his dragon. 'You're on,' he said, and headed for the door.

'Don't you want to know where to find Mr McNally?' asked Mara.

Ryan gave her a pitying look. 'Down the nick, innit?'

'Am I that transparent?' asked Jack.

Ryan laughed and closed the door behind him.

Jack took a last look at the print. The fire and rage seemed even stronger now he had met the artist.

'The boy has a real talent.'

Mara smiled but there was a sadness to it.

'Problem?' asked Jack.

'He's easily our most talented student,' she said. 'He should apply for a scholarship to art school.'

'But he won't?'

She shook her head. 'He's often absent, always scruffy. His attitude will let him down.'

'Teenagers, eh? They're all cocky little so-and-sos.'

'It's more than that,' she said. 'He's a very angry young man.'

'What's the family like?'

'They've never set foot in the place, not even for parents' evening,' she sighed. 'I fear it's going to end badly for Ryan.'

'What a waste.'

'I don't know what else to do,' said Mara.

'If you're worried, I could make a few enquiries,' said Jack, 'discreetly, of course.'

Mara's face lit up. 'That's very, very kind of you.'

Jack nodded. It was totally beyond his remit, but what was the good of being a copper if you could only stick to the script? Jesus, you may as well work for the Inland Revenue.

DI Bell's office was extraordinarily tidy. Lilly wondered how people did that – put things away, kept papers in files. Every office she had ever worked in ended up like a homeless person's squat. Her old boss, Rupinder, had occasionally ordered a clear-up on the grounds of health and safety.

Lilly looked down at her scribbled notes. 'Is that it?'

DI Bell showed his open palms. 'What more do you need?'

'How about some evidence?' she said.

'You'll find plenty of evidence in what I've told you,' he said.

She threw her notebook on the table in disgust. 'You say Yasmeen died from an overdose of OxyContin and Perocet.'

Bell nodded. 'The pills were ground down and placed in a can of Coke to hide the taste. The can was found by Yasmeen's bed. The dregs showed traces of both drugs.'

'Enough to kill her?'

Bell nodded. 'Even small amounts can prove fatal. Perocet should never be taken with other drugs and OxyContin should never be ground down.'

'Because?'

'They're designed for slow release; crushing them makes the effects far too strong.'

'Maybe she did that herself.'

DI Bell folded his arms. 'Why on earth would she do that?'

'Maybe she didn't like the taste. Who knows what goes on in someone's mind before they take their own life?'

'There was no suicide note and no suggestion that anything was wrong.' He eyed Lilly coolly. 'She didn't kill herself.'

Lilly waved him away with her hand. 'Perhaps it was an accident.'

'There's no evidence she had either drug in her possession,' said Bell. 'She wasn't in receipt of a prescription.'

'I'll bet you can buy them on the net,' said Lilly.

'Indeed you can. But there's no record that Yasmeen ever did that and no packaging was found in her room.'

Lilly had to admit it didn't sound like suicide.

'That still doesn't mean that Raffy had anything to do with it,' she said.

'There were two sets of prints on that can. Yasmeen's and your client's.'

'That only means he touched the can, not that he put the drugs inside it.'

DI Bell licked his lips. 'We obtained a warrant to search your client's school locker and guess what we found?'

Lilly watched Bell open his drawer and pull out a clear evidence bag. Inside were two small boxes. Even before Bell put them on the table between them, Lilly could read the word 'OxyContin'. Her heart sank.

'When were you going to tell me about this?' she asked. 'Or were you going to spring it on us in the interview?'

DI Bell dazzled Lilly with the whiteness of his smile. 'I'm telling you now.'

'Because I'm warning you,' Lilly pointed at him, 'I will bring a halt to it if you try any more tricks like this.'

Bell narrowed his eyes but didn't reply.

'And think about it,' said Lilly. 'If Raffy was guilty, why wouldn't he cover his tracks, throw the packets away? Why on earth would he put them in his locker?'

DI Bell's eyes were two dark slits. 'Who knows what goes on in someone's mind after they've murdered their sister?'

\*　　\*　　\*

Raffy sat upright in his chair and stared at the wall. Lilly wondered if he was frightened. He certainly was not prepared to show it.

'The police believe you killed Yasmeen,' she said.

He didn't look at her. 'I'd worked that out myself.'

Lilly glanced at Anwar, who had agreed to attend as his brother's appropriate adult. Anwar seemed much more frightened than his younger brother and chewed his bottom lip.

Lilly took a deep breath. 'They say you put Perocet and OxyContin in her drink.'

'Is that right?' said Raffy, his eyes locked on the wall behind her.

'Do you know anything about those drugs?'

'Nope.'

'The police searched your school locker,' she said.

Raffy's eyes darted to Lilly, then returned to their spot behind her. 'And?'

'And they found packets of those drugs.'

Raffy shrugged. 'Planted.'

Lilly nodded. It was not unheard of for the police conveniently to find evidence, but it was not as common as her clients would have her believe.

'Right then, let's do it.' Lilly stood to let herself out.

'Is that it?' asked Raffy. 'Is that all you've got to say?'

'What were you expecting?' Lilly's hand hovered on the door handle. 'A preprepared statement?'

Raffy grimaced. 'Some advice might be helpful.'

'You don't seem to want my help, Raffy.'

The boy gave a low snort in his throat.

'Just keep your answers short, say as little as

possible.' She opened the door. 'Don't give them any ammunition.'

The interview room was silent as DI Bell ensured the video equipment was working. He was deliberately checking and rechecking the plug, the leads, the angle of the camera, letting the tension ratchet. Certainly Lilly could feel the terror emanating from Anwar but the old police tactic wasn't working on Raffy, whose every pore radiated unalloyed resentment.

'OK then,' said DI Bell, and took his seat.

Raffy lifted his chin and stared at the ceiling.

DI Bell placed his suit jacket on the back of his chair. In just his shirt Lilly could see how slight the man was, his frame almost boyish. Still he puffed out his chest like a robin, enjoying his position.

He cleared his throat. 'For the sake of the tape let me introduce myself as DI Bell. Also present is Miss Valentine, the suspect's solicitor.'

'Correct,' Lilly nodded.

'We also have Anwar Khan, the suspect's brother, acting as his appropriate adult,' said DI Bell.

Anwar mumbled something.

'I'm sorry,' said DI Bell, 'you'll have to speak up.'

'Sorry,' Anwar coughed, 'sorry.'

Lilly passed him a glass of water, which he gulped loudly.

'Thank you,' he whispered. 'It's just that I've never been in a police station before and I'm very nervous.'

'That's perfectly understandable,' said DI Bell. 'Take your time.'

Anwar set the empty glass down carefully in front of him.

'I just wanted to confirm that I'm Raffy's brother.'

DI Bell was a study in calm. 'Excellent. Now everyone's been introduced I want to remind Raffique that he's still under caution. Do you know what that means?'

'I'm not stupid,' said Raffy.

Lilly cringed. The last thing anyone should be in an interview was cocky. Frightened, yes. Angry, possibly. Cocky, never. While Lilly understood that bravado was often the refuge of the terrified child, juries imagined only those with lots of experience of the criminal justice system would have the temerity to be cocky.

DI Bell smiled. Lilly wasn't the only one in the room who knew how juries thought.

She put her hand on Raffy's thigh hoping to remind him of her advice to say as little as possible; not to give them any ammunition.

'Do you know why you're here?' asked DI Bell.

'Like I said, I'm not stupid.'

Lilly sighed. Her client was doing nothing except harming his own chances of getting out of here.

'Then humour me,' said DI Bell. 'Tell me in your own words why you've been arrested.'

Raffy laughed, the noise travelling upwards.

'Is something funny?' asked the inspector.

'Not really.'

'Then why don't you tell me why you've been brought here, unless you want to share the joke?'

Raffy licked his lips and nodded. 'OK then, I'll tell you what I think.'

DI Bell's smile stayed in place, his hands crossed on his lap.

'I think there's a war going on,' said Raffy.

'In Iraq?'

'In Iraq, Afghanistan, Palestine, you name it.'

Anwar put a hand on Raffy's shoulder. 'This is not the time or place.'

'Brother, this is exactly the place,' he shrugged Anwar's hand away, 'and this is definitely the time.'

'Powerful is he who controls himself in anger,' said Anwar.

DI Bell leaned back in his chair, clearly enjoying the show. Lilly's mind began to whirr. If she stopped the tape it would look as if she were preventing her client from incriminating himself. If she let him carry on he might alienate everyone who ever saw and heard this tape.

Did Raffy realise he was digging a deep hole for himself? Did he care?

'Most of all there's a war going on right here, and you,' Raffy pointed at DI Bell, 'are on one side and we are on the other.'

'Do you see yourself as a soldier then?' asked Bell.

Lilly had to do something. She couldn't let Raffy condone any sort of violence. His outburst was as much about Yasmeen as a conflict thousands of miles away. Or at least in any juror's mind it would be.

'Could we move away from politics and stick to the matter in hand?' she said. 'I suggest you stop playing games, Inspector, and put the charge to my client.'

DI Bell's disappointment darkened his face. 'This isn't

a game,' he said. 'I just wanted to hear what Raffique had to say for himself.'

Lilly gave the policeman a hard stare. 'Then put the charge to him.'

Bell paused. No doubt he was hoping the loose cannon opposite would fill the silence. Lilly tightened her grip on Raffy's thigh, held her breath and hoped it would restrain him.

At last the inspector continued, 'Raffique, it is my belief that you poisoned your sister. Is that true?'

'Nope.'

'So you didn't crush Perocet and OxyContin tablets and put them in her drink?'

'Nope.'

'You didn't leave Yasmeen to die?'

'What do you think?'

'I think you're a strict Muslim, Raffique,' said DI Bell.

Raffy shrugged. 'Not particularly.'

'You sounded fairly extreme a few moments ago.'

'There's nothing extreme about my politics. Every Muslim feels the same.'

'I don't believe that.'

Raffy sneered at the police officer. 'And how many Muslims do you actually know?'

They stared hard at one another. Lilly was surprised it was Bell who was the first to look away.

'I think you expect your sisters to be good Muslim girls,' he said.

'My sisters *are* good Muslim girls,' Raffy snapped.

'I think you discovered Yasmeen had a boyfriend.'

Raffy shook his head furiously. 'She did not have a boyfriend.'

'And I think you decided to teach her a lesson.'

'That's rubbish.'

'I think your family honour needed to be avenged,' said Bell.

Raffy shrugged towards Anwar and laughed. 'You've met my brother. Do you think he gives a shit about family honour?'

'I can't speak for Anwar but I think you care very much,' Bell replied. 'I think it matters to you that other people see you first and foremost as a Muslim. And your sister carrying on with her boyfriend just didn't fit.'

'Why don't you stop chatting this crap and listen?' Raffy jabbed his ear. 'My sister didn't have no boyfriend.'

DI Bell let the satisfaction slide across his features. What did he know that they didn't? Lilly tensed her muscles, waiting.

'Well, I'm not a Catholic, Raffy, and I don't believe in the Immaculate Conception.'

Raffy pursed his brows but alarm bells were already sounding in Lilly's brain.

DI Bell slid a folder across the desk to her. 'Autopsy report,' he said. 'It says Yasmeen was ten weeks pregnant.'

Aasha calls in at a café on the way home from school. She tells herself that she's thirsty and orders some chai but she knows it's a delaying tactic. She doesn't want to get home before five when starvation will force her brothers to swallow their pride and help themselves to whatever Mum's left for them to eat.

66

Honestly, those boys are going to make terrible husbands. Whenever her mum and dad go out her mum leaves a pan of dahl or something in the fridge. They only have to bung it in the microwave but they moan about that.

'Aasha will get everything ready,' her mother assures them.

Well, not tonight. Tonight they can do it themselves.

She takes one of the plastic orange seats in the window and blows over the rim of her mug. She feels satisfied by the small stand she is making.

'Hello, beautiful.'

Aasha nearly spills her drink when Ryan sits in the chair opposite.

'Hi,' she says, hoping she hasn't turned completely beetroot.

'What you doing here?' he asks.

Aasha nods at her mug. 'Take a guess.'

She immediately regrets her tone. She was trying to be funny but it came out all sarcastic and wrong.

She needn't have worried because Ryan just laughs. That's one of the nice things about him, actually: he doesn't take offence. He's always easy-going.

When Lailla calls her a geek and laughs at her, Aasha wants to punch her in the face and grinds her teeth to make the feeling go away. Ryan's not like that. Sometimes, during art, Lailla says horrible things to him about his clothes being scruffy or cheap or whatever, and he just makes a joke of it. Aasha wishes she could do that. One time he drew a cartoon of Lailla's face and stuck it onto the body of some porn star.

He'd got into masses of trouble for that, but it *had* been funny.

'So what are you doing here?' she asks.

'Following you, innit.'

Before Aasha can work out if he's teasing her, he grabs the plastic menu and casts his eye along the list of specials.

'There ain't no sausage and chips,' he says.

Aasha giggles and points to the stamp certifying that all meat sold on the premises is halal.

'So why can't I get halal sausages?' he asks.

She shakes her head at him as he orders a doner kebab roll, chips and a can of Lilt. When the heaving plate arrives Ryan pushes the lettuce and tomato into a napkin and tosses it to the other side of the table. He takes an enormous bite of his roll and grins.

'They don't feed you at home?' asks Aasha.

Ryan frowns and she worries she's offended him but he barks out another laugh.

'My mum can't cook for shit.'

Aasha tries to imagine what would happen if her mum couldn't cook. Her father and brothers would have to fend for themselves. Unthinkable. That's something else she likes about Ryan, his independence.

Ryan offers her a chip. She isn't hungry but she takes one all the same and nibbles the end.

'So what you up to after this?' Ryan asks.

'I've got to finish my history assignment,' she says.

He sucks in his breath. 'Living dangerously.'

'Shut up,' she laughs.

He finishes every last scrap of his food and licks ketchup from his fingers.

'You need to have some fun,' he says.

'I have plenty of fun,' says Aasha.

'Like what?'

'Like ...' Aasha smoothes back her ponytail, tucking stray strands of hair behind her ears, 'well, I'm not going to tell you, am I?'

Ryan wipes the back of his hand across his mouth and closes it over hers. She can see the greasy streak gleam.

'Why don't we do something really bad?' he says.

Aasha gulps. Her throat feels like she's swallowed his dirty plate whole. She knows Ryan has had a lot of girlfriends and maybe this is how it is with other girls. Maybe they just speak freely about stuff like sex. She swallows down the dregs of her tea where the sugar has settled. It's sweet and grainy in her mouth.

He leans in towards her so she can smell the lamb on his breath. 'Let's do a runner,' he says.

'What?'

'Let's have it away on our toes without paying.'

'Oh.' She can feel sweat starting to prickle in her armpits. 'I thought you meant ...'

He cocks his head and half closes one of his eyes. 'You've got a dirty mind.'

Aasha feels embarrassment open every pore in her body and she jumps up to leave. There is only one thought in her mind: escape.

'Come on then,' she stutters, and heads for the door. She can feel Ryan following closely behind.

'Where do you think you're going?' shouts the owner from behind his counter.

Aasha looks back, hesitates, but Ryan pushes her outside.

'Run,' he shouts.

She dashes across the road, hearing the blare of a horn, the screech of brakes and her feet pounding down the pavement. Three Polish girls block her path, chatting and smoking as they compare the waistbands of their skinny jeans. Aasha bursts through them, knocking them sideways in their plastic high heels. They shout after her but she doesn't miss a beat.

She streaks past Bangla Groceries, the skips outside overflowing with stinking vegetables and bubble-wrap. A group of old men have gathered outside the Holiday Shop next door, pointing at the special offers on flights to Kashmir advertised in the window. They stare as she races past them but she doesn't care.

She keeps on going, her strides long, until she reaches the other side of Sainsbury's car park. She pauses at the trolley station, her chest heaving. Ryan arrives seconds later and sinks to a crouch to catch his breath.

'What kept you?' she asks.

Ryan is still panting but laughs. 'I've just eaten, you cheeky cow.'

'Maybe you should change your diet,' she says.

Ryan stands and pushes his hair out of the sweat on his forehead. 'Maybe I should kiss you,' he says.

She looks at him, crippled by embarrassment. She has no idea what to do next.

Ryan cocks his head to one side. 'So you going to let me then?'

'OK,' she says slowly.

Ryan smiles, his eyes greedy.

'But you'll have to catch me first.' Aasha laughs and sets off at a run.

Raffy banged his head against the cell wall.

'Stop,' Lilly said.

He didn't register that she was there, let alone that she had spoken. Instead he continued to headbutt the wall with frightening ferocity.

'Raffy,' Lilly shouted, and pulled him by the shoulders.

The grey plaster was smeared with blood, Raffy's forehead grazed and angry.

'You need to listen to me.' Lilly held his shoulders tightly.

His eyes were blurry, his face contorted.

'They are going to charge you with murder,' she said. 'Do you understand?'

Raffy didn't answer. A drop of blood trickled between his eyes.

'You must not say anything else,' she said.

She led Raffy from his cell to the custody sergeant's desk, where DI Bell was hovering.

The sarge nodded at Raffy's head. 'Is that one of them bindi things?'

'No,' Lilly sighed. 'It's a cut.'

'How did that happen?' asked the sarge.

'Don't ask.'

The sarge shrugged. If the boy's solicitor wasn't worried that was clearly good enough for him.

'Raffique Khan,' he said, 'I am charging you with the murder of Yasmeen Khan.'

He read out the caution and looked towards Lilly. 'Does your client have any reply?'

She shook her head and was about to sign the documentation when Raffy stuck out his chin.

'I do not accept the jurisdiction of British law,' he said.

'Say what?' the sarge laughed.

Raffy's nostrils flared. 'You asked me if I had anything to say and I replied that I do not accept the jurisdiction of British law.'

Lilly couldn't believe it. She had advised Raffy to say nothing at all. Didn't he realise that his answer to the caution was on the record?

'I am a Muslim and I do not bow to your rules of evidence,' Raffy continued.

Lilly closed her eyes. This was an utter disaster.

'Are you having me on?' asked the sarge.

'Just write it down,' Bell instructed, rubbing his hands together.

Smoke hung in the air. Lilly coughed and felt her way down the office stairs to the old cellar where the fuse box was located.

After her hideous day she had decided to set up the espresso machine for a coffee. Jack had stopped drinking caffeine, said that she should try it, that her energy levels and concentration would increase tenfold. Maybe he was right, but Raffy's performance at the nick had left her with no willpower. A tiny, brutishly strong espresso with at least two sugars was definitely in order. No doubt the pregnancy police would be up in arms but millions of Italian women survived, didn't they?

Instead there was a fizz, a bang, the fishy smell of wires burning, then the office had been plunged into darkness.

Lilly patted her hand along the cold plaster of the cellar wall. It felt moist and crumbly to the touch. Rising damp. Fantastic. There wasn't enough money in the kitty to decorate, let alone deal with mould.

Her fingers searched for the control board, hoping against hope that she had simply overloaded the system and tripped it. When she finally found the row of switches she crossed her toes and flicked.

The lights came on.

'There is a God,' she muttered and ambled back to the stairs, studiously ignoring the dark wet patches that scaled the cellar walls and the telltale lines of mice droppings that littered the carpet.

Back in the reception she surveyed the complete disarray. What had she been thinking of, setting up her own firm? She had never been any good at organisation. The only reason Rupinder hadn't sacked her was that she admired Lilly's unwavering commitment to her clients. And in the end, even that had proved too much, leading to chaos and disaster for all concerned.

When Rupinder retired due to ill health there was no question of the other partners allowing Lilly to continue and she had been left with the choice of getting another job or working for herself.

Now her decision was beginning to look somewhat rash.

She had promised both Jack and Sam that things were going to be different, that she would stay well away from any children who happened to find themselves in the centre of terrible crimes. Hell, she had promised herself that she would no longer put herself on the line. The emotional fallout was simply too great let alone the danger that she seemed to attract.

Yet here she was again with another fifteen-year-old charged with murder. But what was she supposed to do? The kid had no father, and his mother wasn't exactly a rock. Could she really turn her back so easily?

Lilly sank into a chair, exhausted. What Raffy had said in answer to that charge played through her mind on a loop. Any jury that heard it would conjure up, not a frightened boy devastated by the loss of his sibling, but a cold and arrogant youth, capable of committing a terrible act to uphold his family's honour. Perhaps that was exactly what he was. In which case he was hardly the vulnerable child she was painting him.

Then there was Bell. Ambition radiated from him and Raffy was fuelling his fantasies. Did Lilly really want to get into a fight with him?

Lilly poked at the unopened post. How on earth could she take on a high-profile and difficult case when she was incapable of even the smallest of tasks?

'Impossible,' she muttered to herself.

'I was brought up to believe everything is possible.'

Lilly turned to the voice. In the doorway was the face of an angel.

'Sorry,' said Lilly, 'we're not open.'

The angel smiled. Her caramel skin was so even it was as if she had been dipped in liquid silk. Her features were so perfect, so timeless, it seemed the most natural thing in the world that they were framed by a circle of black chiffon.

'I can see you're in a bit of a muddle,' she said.

Lilly laughed. 'There are ship wrecks tidier than this place.'

'You need help,' said the woman.

'Have you been talking to my shrink?'

The angel smiled again, her eyes twinkling. She stepped into the reception and Lilly could see she was tiny, no more than five feet. Even the jacket of her black trouser suit, which fell past her thighs, couldn't disguise her doll-like frame. Not even an angel then, but a cherub.

She looked around the room and nodded as if unpacked boxes were commonplace in solicitors' offices.

'You really do need an assistant,' she said.

She let a surprisingly long finger slide across the pile of envelopes.

'My name is Taslima.' She handed her CV to Lilly. 'I have a degree in law.'

As tempting as it would be to have anyone, let alone this beautiful young woman, helping out, Lilly knew there was no way she could afford another member of staff.

'I'm in no position to hire anyone,' she said, and popped the CV in her bag.

'I can answer the phone and use a computer.'

Lilly shook her head. 'I'm sorry.'

Taslima gestured to the espresso machine. 'I could get that working in a jiffy.'

'I think I broke it,' said Lilly.

'Not at all. You've just overloaded this adaptor plug.'

Lilly frowned and tapped the plug. 'I followed the instructions.'

'Electrics can be tricky,' said Taslima.

'You're telling me.' Lilly pushed the adaptor away in disgust.

The office was once again plunged into darkness.

'Oh dear,' said Taslima, her voice honey in the shadows.

Lilly took a deep breath. Hadn't Rupinder said she wouldn't be able to do everything on her own?

'When can you start?' she asked.

Taslima stabbed the button for the lift.

There was no response. It was out of action. Again.

She took a deep breath, picked up her heavy bag and began the six-floor ascent.

She pinched her nose against the smell of urine in the stairwells and tried to ignore the graffiti.

*Pakis Go Home.*

Taslima shook her head. 'I'd love to.'

Home. Taslima tried not to think about the house where she grew up on a tree-lined street in West London with a breakfast room where the sun streamed in and a study where the walls were shelved floor to ceiling with books. As a child she would sneak in to sit at her mother's feet while she prepared her lecture notes, the smell of all those dusty pages filling the air.

She deliberately quickened her pace. All that was behind her. This was her home now.

When she got to her landing the next-door neighbour was waiting for her and scowled. Whoever said

Jamaicans were laid-back had never met Evelyn Roberts.

'You get a job today?'

Taslima smiled and nodded. She was about to give details but Mrs Roberts had already turned away, her ample bottom sashaying down her hall to the kitchen.

Taslima followed her, her heart pumping as she crossed the threshold.

The kitchen was filled with steam as an oversized pan of rice bubbled on the gas ring. Taslima's stomach growled.

'How much they going to be paying you?' asked Mrs Roberts.

'I don't know yet,' Taslima admitted.

Mrs Roberts kissed her teeth.

'It should be pretty good,' said Taslima. 'I'll be working in a solicitor's office.'

In fact she hadn't discussed money but Lilly Valentine had come across as a decent woman. Dizzy and disorganised, but decent.

Mrs Roberts seemed unimpressed.

'I'll pay back everything I owe,' said Taslima.

Mrs Roberts didn't answer but took a pinch of salt from a bowl and tossed it into the pan.

Taslima could see the white rice studded with kidney beans like glossy, mahogany jewels. She smelled the air appreciatively.

Mrs Roberts pointed an accusing finger at Taslima. 'You look half starved.'

'I didn't get time for lunch,' Taslima lied.

Mrs Roberts narrowed her eyes. 'You want some?'

Taslima nodded. 'Please.'

Mrs Roberts ladled rice and peas into one Tupperware box, curried ackee into another. Taslima could almost taste the spices on her tongue. Mrs Roberts wrapped the boxes of food in a clean tea towel and handed them to Taslima.

'Things are on the up, Mrs R.' Taslima gratefully took the boxes. 'This time they really are.'


Aasha washes the plates without a sigh. The dahl is stuck to the edges like grey cement and she has to pick at it with the edge of her thumbnail. Her brothers have been told a thousand times to run them under the tap when they've finished but why should they bother?

As soon as Aasha put her key in the door they were on her case. Why wasn't she wearing a hijab? Why was she so late?

Aasha could feel her heart in her chest. Had they noticed her sweaty shirt? Her dirty shoes? Her brothers seem to know everyone in Luton, perhaps the owner of the café has called them, told them what she did?

She told them she'd been kept late at school. Described the extra maths session in detail. Even offered to show them her notes. It was a surprise how easily the lies slipped off her tongue. Her brothers soon drifted away to the television, leaving her to the dishes. They don't care about her life as long as it doesn't affect theirs.

As she rinses the last plate, Aasha wonders what it would be like to be a boy. She'd be able to come and go freely without anyone checking up on her. She'd sit with

Imran and Ismail, have a laugh with them. They'd have to listen to what she has to say. Notice her.

Because they don't do that. They don't actually look at her. Aasha is sure that if someone asked them what colour her eyes were, they wouldn't even know.

Ryan knows. He says they're beautiful.

She checks her reflection in the back of a spoon.

He says he likes the way they sparkle in the sun, and her long black lashes.

'What are you smiling about?'

Aasha looks from the spoon to see Imran, leaning lazily against the counter. His hands are in his back pockets, pulling his jeans down so she can see not only the elastic of his Calvin Kleins but most of his hipbone.

Dad is always on about it. 'Do you need to display your backside?' he says. 'Are you a gorilla?' But he doesn't actually do anything about it, does he?

Aasha can just imagine what would happen if she went about showing her pants. She's not even allowed hipsters or skinny jeans.

'Make us a cup of tea, Ash?' Imran says.

'I have to do my homework,' she sighs.

'It'll take you ten seconds.'

Aasha shakes her head but is already filling the kettle. She wishes she could just tell him no. One day she will. One day soon.

'Me too,' Ismail calls from the other room.

She makes the chai and takes refuge in her room. As she logs on to her computer she already knows that her English assignment can wait and eagerly dives into MSN.

Within seconds a message arrives.

Ryan says: *Are you in training or wot?*

Aasha laughs and types her answer.

Aasha says: *I've always been fast.*

She bites her lip as she waits for his next message.

Ryan says: *Why did you run away?*

Aasha doesn't want to admit how nervous she was in his company. The thrill of being with him made her heart beat faster than not paying for their food. But she's not going to just tell him that, is she?

Aasha says: *I had to get home.*

Ryan says: *You won't get away from me so easily next time.*

She bites her lip so hard it hurts.

Aasha says: *Maybe I don't want to.*

# Chapter Three

December 2005

'Merry fucking Christmas.'

A middle-aged man pushes past me to get off the bus. His breath smells of beer and cigarettes. He's wearing felt reindeer antlers with bells that tinkle annoyingly.

I hate this time of year. It's cold and dark, and if you venture out of Bury Park everyone is pissed. English people have given up even pretending they're celebrating the birth of their saviour. Christmas for them is an orgy of eating, drinking and buying plastic tat from China.

I watch the man stagger off the bus and vomit in a shop doorway. Revulsion washes over me.

On the back seat a group of boys are getting rowdy. Fuelled by testosterone and cheap cider, they throw chips at some of the other passengers' heads. I scowl at the ringleader. His pasty face is liberally scattered with spots. I'd say he's fond of glue as well as White Lightning.

If even one chip hits me I'll punch his ugly face. The Prophet Mohammed, praise be upon him, did not

81

advocate violence, probably wouldn't approve. But he didn't live in Luton.

I'm glad to get off in Browning Street, I can walk from here.

A freezing wind has got up and the Christmas lights strung across the street by the council wave and shake as if desperate to be free. I remember reading about some argument over them in the local rag, whether we Muslims would be offended by them. As if we care about a few lights.

I put my head down and walk to the mosque.

This is not my local one where the family go for prayers, where my father's body was taken when he died and where the imam tells me I have to be strong for my mother.

I have to cross town to get to this one, two buses full of *kuffar*.

Despite that I still come as often as I can. I love it.

My mother doesn't approve.

'It has a reputation,' she says.

She's right.

Tonight there is a discussion about the imminent elections in Palestine and I've spent all week doing research on the internet. I can't wait to join in, to feel part of it.

When I finally enter the great wooden door and slip off my shoes I feel a sense of calm wash over me. It is a wonderful sensation. At last, I am free.


'Sexy or what?'

Lilly thrust a bloated foot in Jack's direction. The flesh was so engorged the ankle bone had disappeared.

Jack didn't look up from his breakfast.

'Okaaaay,' said Lilly, and slid two slices of bread into the toaster.

She waited in silence for them to pop and looked out of the kitchen window. The garden had been a tangle of weeds and overgrown bushes but since Jack had moved in he'd tamed the mess, hacking back dead wood and clearing long-lost flowerbeds. Lilly could see flower heads beginning to peep through, shy of the changing season.

She slicked butter over the golden crusts and sat down to eat.

'Want some?' She proffered her plate to Jack.

He shook his head and sipped what he called his 'breakfast infusion'. Hot water with a squeeze of lemon.

The silence stretched between them, punctuated by the sound of Lilly chewing. She knew he must have heard down the nick that she was representing Raffy and that he'd be bloody furious She waited for him to bring it up.

'So how long do I get?' she asked.

Jack pursed his brow.

'The silent treatment,' said Lilly. 'An hour, a day, a week?'

He didn't answer.

'Even the worst villains get a tariff,' she said.

Jack put down his cup. 'It's not meant to be a punishment.'

'No?'

'I just don't have anything to say.'

Lilly swallowed and waited. She had known Jack a

long time – years before they started dating – and she had never known him short of words.

'The thing is, Lilly . . .'

'Ha!' She gulped down the last of her food with a triumphant smile. 'I knew you couldn't do it.'

Jack went to the sink and rinsed his cup.

'It's not a bloody game, woman.'

'Then don't act like a child,' she said. 'Whatever's on your mind, just spit it out.'

'What's the point?'

'Because you're dying to tell me.' She pointed a greasy finger at him. 'You can't help yourself.'

Jack put his cup to drain and headed for the door.

'Where are you going?' she asked.

'For a run.'

'Without a word?'

'Like I said,' his shoulders slumped, 'no point.'


The gear crunched as Lilly tried to depress the clutch. With her feet in this state, driving was a very bad idea but asking Jack for a lift to work was not an option.

She'd known he'd be pissed about her taking on Raffy's case but the silent treatment was unbearable. Why could men never just say whatever they were thinking and move on?

Yes, she had said she would take it easy, but she was a solicitor, for God's sake. Should she really turn down murder cases?

Jack wouldn't be happy unless she was tucked up in bed until she gave birth, everything safe and sound.

She loved Jack very much and wanted to make a life

with him, but she was starting to suspect that she couldn't do what was necessary to keep him happy. He wanted her to give up the work with children. The work she loved. Even Sam, who seemed to lose out so often in terms of her time, had never said that.

She'd agreed while she was pregnant to avoid the stresses and strains of certain work, and to be fair, when Anwar first walked into her office she couldn't have guessed she'd be plunged into a murder case. But to turn her back on the Khans now just wasn't an option. At least not for Lilly.

Jack wanted to change her and at this moment she couldn't bear to think what that might mean for them.

The journey to work was a nightmare of jerking and grinding as her foot slipped off the clutch. She was relieved to arrive outside her office. From her car she waved at Taslima, who was waiting outside, today's jewelled hijab twinkling in the sun.

No doubt that would be something else Jack would complain about: taking on staff she could ill afford.

When Lilly tried to apply the brake, her foot simply would not bend and she overshot her parking spot by three yards, hitting the kerb and a litter bin.

'Shit.' She yanked on the handbrake.

Taslima ran to the car, her face full of concern.

'Are you OK?'

Lilly pulled herself out, letting the car door take her weight.

'Can you drive?'

Taslima had never been to court before and excitement clenched her stomach into a knot.

After university she'd intended to go to bar school but then she'd been introduced to Kaden by a friend. He had pursued her with an intensity that enchanted Taslima and within months they were engaged. Her mother had warned her to wait, to finish her education before marriage, but Taslima was sure she knew best. In her mind she could have it all, the handsome husband and glittering career.

Once their vows were exchanged Kaden wanted to start a family. He begged with the same intensity he had used when they first met. Bar school could wait, he reasoned. After all, she could reapply later when they were settled.

Taslima had been swept along with it like a good wife. She should have known better. She should have listened to her mother. She'd be qualified now, earning her own living, instead of being forced to go cap in hand to Mrs Roberts.

But there was no point wasting time on regrets. Today was what mattered, and at least she had a job. She was moving forward. The past was exactly that, and there was no reason anyone need ever know about it. A fresh start.

Lilly led them into the Youth Court at Luton, pointing the way through the crowds of teenagers that shouted to one another across the foyer. Groups of boys, baseball caps pulled down past their eyebrows, jostled each other with their elbows. The atmosphere, though good-natured, felt rowdy; as if it could change.

'All right, miss?' a young black boy, the hood of both his jacket and his jumper pulled tight over his cap, stood in Lilly's way.

'You working undercover, Jermaine?' she asked.

He formed his fingers into the shape of a gun and pretended to shoot Lilly.

'I'd fall down dead, Jermaine,' Lilly patted her bump, 'but I don't think I could get back up again.'

'Who's the baby's father, miss?'

'Brad Pitt.'

'Good one,' he laughed.

'Never mind me, what are you doing here?' Lilly asked. 'Tell me you haven't been nicked again.'

The boy stepped back in mock horror and spoke directly to Taslima.

'She's so suspicious, ain't she?'

'Given where we are, it's a fair question,' Taslima said.

He shook his head at them both. 'Women. You always got to be so negative.'

'Years of experience have worn me down,' said Lilly, and gestured to Taslima that they should move along.

Taslima was bowled over by Lilly's easy rapport with the boy. She could never do that.

'Client?' she asked.

'On and off.'

'Not today?'

Lilly opened a door marked 'Crown Prosecution Service' and ushered Taslima inside.

'He's not in court for a case today,' she told Taslima. 'At least I hope not.'

'So why on earth is he here?'

'To hang with his mates,' Lilly said. 'A day out.'

Taslima assumed she was joking until the woman at the table in the middle of the room spoke up.

'They treat this place like a bloody youth club,' she said.

Not a joke then.

The woman, who Taslima assumed was the prosecutor, sat in a sea of files.

'Nice to see you, Kerry,' said Lilly. 'You've lost weight.'

Taslima had to swallow a gasp. Lilly was irreverent but surely that was a jibe too far, considering Kerry was at least fourteen stones, her thighs spreading across the plastic chair, the fat melting over the sides.

'Another ten pounds,' said Kerry.

Ah, a diet.

Lilly nodded to her own feet, which were almost square with water retention. 'I think you're giving it all to me.'

Kerry laughed but Taslima was no stranger to animosity and could feel it hovering in the background. This woman was clearly no fan of her new boss.

'So who are you here for?' Kerry asked.

'Raffique Khan,' Lilly answered.

Kerry laughed, but again there was no warmth in it. 'I should have known you'd be involved in the biggest case of the year,' she said.

'I'd hardly call it that,' said Lilly.

Kerry got out of her chair, the flesh of her bottom making a small sucking sound as it was prised away. She walked to the window and looked outside.

'Being a prosecutor in Luton is not a great job,' she said, 'but even I'm getting excited by an honour killing.'

Taslima too, was excited. On the drive to court Lilly had told her about Yasmeen Khan. At first her family

88

thought she'd committed suicide, which would have been terrible enough, then the police discovered it was murder. Taslima hadn't been able to speak for fear of showing how inexperienced she was. A murder. It was like something on the telly. And she could imagine how the poor mother was feeling. Not only had she lost her daughter, but now her son had been accused by the police. Unspeakable.

Lilly joined Kerry at the window. From where Taslima was standing she couldn't see the view but she knew it would be grey.

'I'm going for bail,' said Lilly.

Kerry frowned. 'On a case like this?'

'I can't see any harm in making the application,' Lilly shrugged.

Kerry tapped the glass with her sausage fingers. 'Lilly Valentine, you never do anything the easy way, do you?'

'I'm guessing she's not your biggest fan,' said Taslima with a smile.

Lilly felt relieved. On the way to court her new assistant had been so unforthcoming Lilly was beginning to worry that she'd made a mistake in hiring her. Quiet was fine, uptight was not. When she'd told her about Raffy, the younger woman hadn't even asked any questions. She just bit her lip.

Lilly hoped Taslima's joke was evidence that she wasn't going to turn out to be some sensitive soul. In this game you couldn't afford to be.

'Kerry and I have history,' she said.

'And not at a book club.'

Lilly laughed. 'There was a case last year that turned into a serious scrap.'

'Isn't that all part of the territory?'

'You'd think so,' said Lilly.

'So why did she take it personally?'

Lilly paused, unsure how much she should say. Now they were back on an even keel she didn't want to shock Taslima again.

'Let's just say she doesn't like my style.'

She led Taslima down to the basement and rapped at the iron door.

'Ever been in a cell?'

The younger woman shook her head again, biting her lip, and Lilly was reminded that she was young and inexperienced. It was easy to forget, given how cool and unflappable Taslima always seemed. Lilly remembered the first time she'd visited a client in the cells. He was a heroin addict with one of his front teeth missing. Lilly had not been cool and hadn't been able to take her eyes off his track marks. His name was Jason and he died a year later, the needle still in his arm.

The sound of clanking locks accompanied the opening of the gaol and Lilly saw a shiver pass through Taslima's body.

'Don't worry,' Lilly put a hand on Taslima's shoulder, 'it's nothing like on the telly.'

Jack kicked off his sweaty running clothes and trainers. They hit the bedroom wall, leaving a mark on the fresh cream paint.

Lilly wouldn't be happy. After the fire she'd spent time

choosing paint colours and curtain patterns and she protected her handiwork like a tigress. Jack had offered to help, but she'd refused, preferring instead to hole up with Penny over interior design magazines and glasses of wine. He should have realised then that, even after he'd moved all his stuff in, she'd never see him as more than a lodger.

Jack snapped on the shower and stood under the cold stream of water.

That was the trouble with Lilly: the woman had no patience. She wanted to live her life at a pace better suited to a teenager. If something absorbed her she went at it full pelt. He used to find it endearing but it was beginning to seem irresponsible.

From the other side of the room he heard his mobile ring and, cursing, he grabbed a towel.

'Hello.' Water dripped down his face and pooled under his chin.

'Sergeant McNally?'

'Speaking.'

'It's Mara Blake here.' The voice at the other end softened. 'I hope you don't mind me calling you.'

Jack felt his cold, damp skin burn. 'Not at all.'

'I'm not interrupting anything?'

'I'm not working today,' he said. As an afterthought he added, 'I've been running.'

'I could tell you were a man who liked to keep yourself fit.'

Jack checked his reflection in the bathroom mirror. The daily workouts were making a difference.

'It's important to stay in shape,' he said.

Mara giggled. 'You look in great shape to me.'

For a second that seemed to stretch like elastic Jack could think of absolutely nothing to say. He could hear Mara breathing.

'So what can I do for you?' he asked at last.

'I just wondered if you'd had any chance to find out about Ryan's family,' she said.

'Not just yet,' he said.

'Oh.'

If Jack didn't know better, he might have thought Mara was simply finding an excuse to call him. But he wasn't that much of an eejit.

'But I thought I might pay his mother a visit later this morning,' he said.

'Not on your day off, surely.'

He *had* planned to go over to Lilly's new office, help with the unpacking. But she'd be at court on her new case. So.

'I'm not doing anything else,' he said.

'This is very good of you, Jack.' She paused. 'Do you mind me calling you Jack?'

'Of course not.'

Jack looked at the graze on the wall from his trainers. He probably should try to clean it off. Instead he slipped on some clean clothes and headed for the door.


Aasha checks the school notice board, her rucksack clutched to her chest. One of the teachers has pinned up a notice for a new after-school club. It's called the Debating Society and they'll meet once a week. This week's debate: 'Women are equal to men'.

She'd love to go but it's set in stone that she'll help mum.

As she scans the other posters someone comes in close behind her.

'Boo!'

Aasha jumps and drops her rucksack, her books escaping across the floor.

Ryan laughs, his eyes twinkling.

'You scared me.' Aasha bends to collect her things.

Ryan bends beside her, so close that she can smell the soap he uses. 'You up for something really naughty?' he asks.

Aasha pretends to play it cool and busies herself with her books. 'What you got in mind?'

'Follow me.'

He leads her through the school and out into the Orchard Green. When he gets to the far wall he clasps his hands together.

'Come on, I'll give you a leg up.'

Aasha frowns. 'We can't just leave school.'

'Why not?'

'Because,' she doesn't know what to say. Because it's against the rules, because we might get caught. It all makes her sound so lame.

He gives her one of his irresistible lop-sided grins and she pushes her foot into his hands.

She waits at the other side of the wall for Ryan to scramble over. When he lands with a thump her heart makes the same sound. What now? Will he suggest they go back to his house? Aasha's mouth feels dry at the thought of it.

She likes Ryan. Likes him a lot. But she doesn't know if she's ready for anything physical.

'On a beautiful day like today a beautiful girl like you didn't ought to be cooped up in school,' he smiles.

'No?'

He takes her hand. It's soft and warm in his.

'Nah.' He pulls her along.

She's been a bit flirty with him on MSN so does he just assume they'll have sex? Is that how it works? Even as the pleasure of his fingers entwined with hers runs through her body, she can feel the panic rising in equal measure.

'Where are we going?' Her voice sounds small.

He raises his eyebrows as if it were obvious. He licks his lips as if they were delicious. They probably are, and Aasha would love to find out – but she's not ready. She's made a total idiot of herself and Ryan will be cross because she's led him on. He'll tell everyone what she's done and call her a prick tease.

'Let's go to the park,' he says.

'Bags, please, ladies,' the security guard beamed at Lilly and Taslima.

Lilly plonked her battered briefcase on the desk and let him rifle through. He pulled out a blackened banana that Jack had forced on her weeks ago and Taslima's CV, which had chewing gum stuck to it.

'It's a bleeding health hazard in there,' he said.

Lilly rolled her eyes. 'They get very bored down here, Taslima.'

Taslima offered her own bag for inspection. Lilly could

see the contents were immaculate. No half-eaten KitKats or chewed biros.

'You a drug dealer?' the guard laughed.

Taslima blushed deep crimson.

'Two mobiles,' said the guard.

'I keep an old one,' Taslima spluttered, 'for emergencies.'

Lilly pulled Taslima away by the sleeve. 'Ignore him.'

'I'm going to try to get you out of here.'

Lilly sat down next to Raffy on the hard wooden bench in his cell. The concrete floor felt cool beneath her poor swollen feet. Taslima stood rod-straight by the door.

'It's not going to be easy,' she continued, 'but the evidence isn't overwhelming and of course your age will go in your favour.'

Raffy didn't answer.

'Do you understand what I'm telling you?' said Lilly. 'I'm going to apply for bail.'

Raffy shrugged.

Lilly groaned inwardly and struggled to her feet. A sudden yet overwhelming urge to get out of the drab cell had taken control.

'I'm beginning to think you have a problem with women, Raffy.'

He shot a glance at Taslima. 'I have nothing but respect for my Muslim sisters.'

'Tell that to the magistrate,' Lilly rapped on the door to be let out, 'the white female magistrate.'

Lilly hauled herself back up the stairs and Taslima fell in alongside.

'What pisses me off,' said Lilly, 'is that my partner really didn't want me to take this case.'

'Business partner?' asked Taslima.

'God, no.' Lilly patted her bump. 'Boyfriend.'

'Ah.'

'He wants me to stay at home, look after myself. But, oh no, I insist on coming here supposedly to help him.' She pointed her thumb downwards in the rough direction of the cells.

Something flashed across Taslima's face. 'A husband should support his wife's work.'

'That's what I told him, apart from the wife bit, but to be honest I don't know why I bothered.' Lilly leaned heavily on the handrail. 'Raffy obviously doesn't want to be helped.'

Taslima went ahead and opened the door at the top. The shouting from inside the foyer hit Lilly like a hot wind.

'He might not want our help,' said Taslima, 'but he certainly needs it.'

Lilly raised her eyebrows.

'He agreed to see you,' Taslima pointed out. 'He didn't send you away.'

'Probably because I came with my *Muslim sister*,' said Lilly.

Taslima wrinkled her nose, making three neat lines under each eye. 'Ignore all that Islamist stuff.'

'You reckon?'

'If he were a boy from the estates spouting all that bling-bling gangster rapper rubbish what would you do?' Taslima asked.

Lilly laughed. Most of the kids she had represented talked a load of old rubbish.

'I wouldn't pay any attention,' she said.

'Same thing,' said Taslima. 'Underneath that hot air is a frightened boy.'

'The difference is, Raffy sounded like he knew what he was talking about,' said Lilly. 'He sounded like he meant it.'

'Do you think he meant it?' Taslima asked.

Lilly shook her head. 'It doesn't matter what I think, courts take these things seriously.'

'Of course it matters what you think,' said Taslima. 'If you don't believe in Raffy, then what has he got?'

Lilly regarded Taslima with fresh eyes. 'There was me thinking you'd rather I wasn't involved in this case.'

'Whatever made you think that?'

'This and that.' Lilly shrugged. 'You wouldn't be alone. Not many of us enjoy getting down and dirty in the cells.'

Taslima shook her head. 'We have to help him.'

From the other side of the foyer Lilly saw Anwar. He was wearing a suit, the knot of his tie small and uncomfortable. The newspaper under his arm hadn't been opened.

Lilly waved and he immediately darted towards her.

'Miss Valentine,' his words fell out in a breathless tumble, 'I know it looks bad for Raffy, but he's just a frightened boy.'

Lilly gestured to Taslima. 'Are you two in league?'

Anwar seemed terrified that he had missed something. 'Our family is falling apart,' he said. 'Everything I've

97

done has been to keep it together, to do what my father would have done.'

'I understand that,' said Lilly.

Anwar closed his eyes. 'Everything is falling apart.'

Lilly put her hand on his arm. 'Don't worry,' she said. 'I'm going to do everything I can.'

Lilly took her place at the long table in the centre of the courtroom. She at one end, Kerry at the other. To accommodate her girth the other woman usually pushed the bench so far back that Lilly could barely reach her papers but today she was glad to have enough room to squash her own stomach into the gap. DI Bell slid in next to Kerry.

The magistrate, Mrs Lucinda Holmes, sat opposite, at a table at the head of the courtroom.

Taslima led Anwar to sit at the back of the court. As they waited for Raffy to be brought from the cells he picked at the cuffs of his shirt.

Lilly wondered where Mrs Khan was. She had clearly been suffering from the shock of her daughter's death at their previous meetings but Lilly couldn't imagine anything keeping her away from court if Sam got himself into trouble.

As the side door opened everyone craned their neck to look. A security guard entered, his greying hair cut short. Not a skinhead, but not far off. He led Raffy into the courtroom and grunted an instruction to him to take the chair next to Lilly. The hatred in his eye was as obvious as the scar that ran through his eyebrow, leaving a unpleasant pink track.

Raffy slumped into the chair, his head resting cockily to one side. Only a slight tremor in his hands betrayed his fear. Lilly went to touch them but Raffy snatched them away from her and sat on them.

'Don't say anything unless I tell you,' Lilly whispered. 'OK?'

Raffy's nod was barely there but Lilly caught it.

Taslima and Anwar were right: for all his bravado this was a child, and a terrified one at that.

Kerry was the first to speak. 'I'm sure you have already seen from the docket that the defendant, Raffique Khan, is charged with murder.'

She didn't stand since this was the Youth Court, but her sheer bulk lent her a formidable presence and the enormity of the crime was lost on no one.

Mrs Holmes nodded. There was nothing she needed to say.

'The prosecution say that the defendant poisoned his sister Yasmeen with a combination of prescription drugs.'

Lilly felt Raffy tense beside her but he remained silent. Perhaps he was finally beginning to understand that he needed to take Lilly's advice. She prayed that was the case.

'He ground the tablets down,' Kerry continued, 'and hid the powder in a can of cola.'

'Given the magnitude of the offence and the defendant's age, I shall transfer this case to the Crown Court.' Mrs Holmes removed the lid of her fountain pen. 'I shall also ensure that it is listed for directions as a matter of expediency.'

She began to write the order and the security guard moved towards Raffy.

'Madam,' Lilly held up a finger to the guard, 'I should like to make an application for bail.'

Mrs Holmes put down her pen. Lilly thought she could see a smile playing around the edge of her mouth.

'Do the prosecution object?' she asked.

'I would be extraordinarily surprised if they didn't,' said Lilly.

Mrs Holmes turned to Kerry. 'Have you anything to say, Miss Thomson?'

Kerry shifted on the bench. 'This case could not be more serious, madam,' she said. 'It is not only one of murder but the murder of a young girl. The punishment attached will be long and hard, something the defendant must be aware of.'

Mrs Holmes nodded. 'Even you can't deny that, Miss Valentine.'

'Of course not,' said Lilly.

'Then you must also accept that the defendant is a flight risk,' said Kerry. 'The temptation to abscond is overwhelming.'

'If he had killed his sister he could have run away then,' said Lilly, 'but he didn't.'

'He didn't think he'd get caught,' said Kerry.

'But where would he go?' Lilly opened her arms. 'He's fifteen, he still lives with his mum.'

'Children go missing every day of the week,' said Kerry.

'Not children from stable homes,' said Lilly. 'Not children with warm loving families.'

Mrs Holmes frowned. She had years of experience in these courts and Lilly would need to offer some strong backup.

'We'll sign on at the police station,' said Lilly. 'Every morning and evening, if you want. That way the police will know exactly where he is.'

DI Bell leaned towards Kerry and whispered in her ear.

'The defendant has family in Pakistan,' said Kerry.

'As does every Muslim kid in Luton.'

'He could easily go there,' said Kerry. 'We'd struggle to get him back.'

Lilly didn't miss a beat. 'We'll hand his passport to the Court.'

DI Bell exhaled loudly, showing the magistrate what he thought of Lilly's argument.

'I know it's a hard thing to ask,' said Lilly, 'but Raffy is a young boy who has everything going for him. He has no social problems and is doing well at school.'

She could see Mrs Holmes wavering.

'If he spends the next God-knows-how-many months in custody awaiting trial his life will be ruined.' She paused for good measure. 'Everyone in here is well aware of what prison is like and what it does to people. Let's not fool ourselves into thinking that if Raffy is acquitted he'll be able to put the experience behind him.'

Mrs Holmes rolled her pen back and forth with her index finger.

'You'd give us the passport and sign on every day?'

'We'll chuck in a curfew, if that would help,' said Lilly.

DI Bell groaned. He could see as well as Lilly which way the hearing was going. Lilly bit back a smile.

'Raffique,' Mrs Holmes addressed him directly, 'would you agree to those conditions?'

Raffy got to his feet.

'You don't have to stand,' said Lilly, taking his elbow.

Raffy slapped away her hand with a ferocity that startled her.

'I do not accept your British laws.' He pointed at Mrs Holmes. 'And I do not accept the legality of your courts.'

It was Lilly's turn to groan.

'I beg your pardon?' asked Mrs Holmes.

Raffy threw back his shoulders. 'You have no jurisdiction over me.'

Anwar jumped to his feet. 'Don't listen to him. He doesn't know what he's saying.'

'Everyone sit down, now,' ordered Mrs Holmes.

'Raffy, please.' Anwar stumbled towards his brother. 'Tell her you didn't mean it.'

'I said sit down,' Mrs Holmes's voice was steely.

The guard moved towards Anwar and grabbed his shoulder, the sleeve of his uniform riding up to reveal a bulldog tattoo. He clutched the material of Anwar's new suit. The force knocked Anwar off his feet and he grasped at the advocates' desk for ballast, knocking papers and files across the courtroom before falling to the floor.

Raffy sprang over the bench and stood between his brother and the guard. 'Don't you touch him.'

A smile spread across the guard's face as if he couldn't believe his luck. 'You want some, do you?' he snarled.

Raffy didn't reply but his body language was challenge enough.

The guard took a lunge at him but Raffy dodged backwards. The guard grunted and his nostrils flared.

Fearing her client was about to receive the worst beating of his life, Lilly slid her arm in front of him.

'Stop this right now.'

'He started it,' shouted Raffy, still every inch the petulant teenager, so different from the posturing extremist of moments ago.

'I don't care,' said Lilly. 'Just move aside now.'

She could feel the muscles of his chest like stone, every sinew taut, against the flimsy barrier of her arm.

'You,' she glared at the guard, 'need to calm down.'

She could see a vein in the man's thick neck throbbing and his jaw clenched rhythmically She held her breath until the guard took one small step back. Her arm was beginning to ache as she pushed it against her client.

Raffy looked at the guard, a tiny smile playing at the corner of his lips. Don't you bloody dare, she thought. He muttered something under his breath but Lilly caught it.

'Pussy.'

The guard heard it too and swung back his arm. Lilly tried to move out of the way. Too late. The punch, aimed at Raffy, glanced off her shoulder and sent her spiralling to the ground.

Raffy took one look at his solicitor and head-butted the guard. His brow connected with the bigger man's nose with a wet crunch.

The guard collapsed, out cold.


'Is it always this boring?' Taslima held a wet tissue against Lilly's cheek.

Lilly attempted a smile. 'Ow.'

They were sitting in the magistrates' chambers, the

room behind court, waiting with Kerry and DI Bell for Mrs Holmes.

'You'll find that Lilly attracts excitement,' Kerry advised Taslima.

Lilly wanted to argue but her face hurt. She had caught it on the corner of the table as she fell and it was swollen and hot. God knows what Jack would say when he saw it. If she were a better liar she'd make something up, anything to avoid a scene that would rival the one they'd just had in court.

'What about junior?' Taslima gestured to Lilly's pregnant bump. 'OK?'

Lilly nodded. 'I think all the excitement has woken him up. My ribs hurt almost as much as my face.'

Mrs Holmes bustled into the room and took a seat.

'The ambulance has taken the security guard to the hospital,' she said. 'His nose is broken.'

'Couldn't happen to a nicer person,' said Lilly.

Mrs Holmes gave a disapproving look.

'I'm sorry,' said Lilly, 'but the man is a thug.'

'I admit his handling of the situation could have been better,' said Mrs Holmes.

Lilly turned to Bell. 'You should nick him for assault.'

Mrs Holmes spread her hands flat on the table. Her nails were short but perfectly smooth.

'I'll deal with him,' she said. 'And in the meantime I suggest you go home and put an ice pack on that.'

Lilly waved the concern away. 'We didn't sort out Raffy's bail.'

'You cannot be serious,' said Kerry.

Lilly ignored her and spoke directly to Mrs Holmes.

'You seemed to accept my argument that a child should not spend time on remand if it can be avoided.'

'Perhaps,' said Mrs Holmes.

'Then we can't let an incident that was not of my client's making override that,' said Lilly.

She could hear the snorts of derision coming from her left but she refused even to acknowledge them. She kept her eyes trained on Mrs Holmes and willed her to grant bail.

'You seem to be forgetting what precipitated all this,' said Mrs Holmes.

Lilly shrugged.

'The defendant's little outburst about not being subject to the law,' said Mrs Holmes.

'Silly nonsense from a young boy,' she dismissed it.

Mrs Holmes raised her eyebrows. 'He's fifteen, Miss Valentine – and he sounded as if he knew exactly what he was saying.' She let the words hang in the air until they were an established detail with which Lilly could not argue.

'The fact remains,' said Lilly, 'that a child should not be in prison.'

'The fact also remains,' countered Mrs Holmes, 'that I cannot release someone who refuses to even recognise the conditions of his bail.'

Lilly let out a long breath. Raffy had backed Mrs Holmes into an impossible corner. There was no chance of bail and her cheek hurt.

Kerry leaned over and patted Taslima's arm. 'With Lilly, there's never a dull moment.'

* * *

The Clayhill Estate was a shithole.

Jack had spent over ten years in Child Protection in Luton and had visited every tower block more times than he could remember. The Clayhill had to be the worst.

He parked outside a children's playground, the swings long since abandoned by young mums. Every year the council would spend thousands clearing away the smashed glass and used condoms. A new roundabout would be installed and cheery footprints painted on the ground but days later the low-life would creep back in.

He double-checked his car was locked and headed towards the nearest block of flats. The group of boys huddled at the foot of the slide didn't glance his way, but mumbled into their freezer bags of glue. Jack knew he should get their names, send them on their way, but what was the point? They'd be back before he had time to input their details on the police computer. These kids didn't go to school, would never work, might be dead before they were thirty. Christ, it was all so depressing.

He pushed on to the address Mara had given him. Ryan Sanders lived in the very heart of this cesspit.

As Jack entered the walkway to Ryan's floor he put his hand over his mouth to avoid the stench. Even through the thick rubber soles of his boots he could feel the sticky mess of vomit. How could people live like this?

Of course, Jack knew the answer: they had no fecking choice. And for kids like Ryan, who grew up thinking this was perfectly normal, there was no reason to change it.

But Ryan could change things – for himself, at least.

He had a talent and, in Mara, someone who cared enough to watch out for him. That was far more than most. Though the boy probably couldn't see it, he was bloody lucky.

Jack knocked on the door and waited. When no one answered he knocked again. He could hear muffled sounds from within, someone moving around. Still no answer.

Jack bent to the letter box and peered inside.

'Mrs Sanders,' he called, 'it's the police.'

He heard an exchange of voices in a distant room, one definitely male and angry.

'Come to the door, Mrs Sanders,' Jack shouted.

At last he saw a slight figure shuffle towards him. The door was unbolted in almost slow motion and at last it was pulled ajar.

The woman standing in the sliver of light was painfully thin, her skeleton protruding violently through her clothes. She gripped the side of the door with shockingly white fingers, her nails ragged and bloody.

'Mrs Sanders?' Jack asked.

The woman didn't look at him, but nodded.

'Can I come in?' he asked.

'Why?' Her voice was tiny, childlike.

'I'd like a word with you about Ryan.'

Mrs Sanders threw a nervous glance over her shoulder.

'Give me a second,' she whispered, and shut the door.

Jack waited outside the door, listening to another exchange, the male's voice becoming increasingly angry. When the door finally reopened Mrs Sanders was visibly shaking and her son stood behind her, his face a study in fury.

'Hello, Ryan,' said Jack. 'We met at school, remember?'

Ryan glowered at Jack. 'I ain't got Alzheimer's.'

'He wants to come in,' said Mrs Sanders.

'Has he got a warrant?' asked Ryan.

Mrs Sanders' fingers flew to her mouth. 'I didn't ask him.'

'How many times have I told you?' Ryan shouted. 'Do not let them in without a warrant.'

Mrs Sanders ran her cuticle across her front teeth. It was so raw Jack was certain it must hurt.

'So,' Ryan spat at Jack, 'have you got a warrant?'

Jack ignored him and smiled gently at Mrs Sanders. 'I just want a chat.'

'Tell him, Mum,' said Ryan.

Mrs Sanders bit the ragged skin until a fresh drop of blood rose like a crimson flower.

'Tell him,' repeated Ryan.

'You're not welcome here,' she said, and slammed the door in Jack's face.

For a second Jack remained outside the flat. He wasn't shocked. Coppers were well used to a less than enthusiastic welcome, especially on estates like the Clayhill, but usually the venom came in equal measure from adults and children alike. Mrs Sanders hadn't reacted like that.

He put his ear to the door, pretty sure he could hear crying.

Mrs Sanders wouldn't be the first parent to be afraid of her teenage son.

Aasha puts up her hand and asks to be excused. This is the third time she's pretended she needs the toilet so she can check the art rooms on the way. She scuttles through the corridor but Ryan is nowhere to be seen.

As soon as the bell goes for break she grabs her phone and checks her messages.

'I don't know why you're so stressed.' Lailla applies a fresh coat of mascara to her long lashes. 'That boy is always bunking off.'

True enough, Ryan has hardly done a full week all term.

'I just want to know he's all right,' says Aasha.

Lailla looks at her through heavily blackened lids.

'It's not like you're going together, Ash,' she says. 'Not like me and Sonny.'

'I know that,' Aasha gulps, 'but he does like me.'

Lailla returns to her reflection, leaving Aasha to call Ryan's number. Again.

Aasha can't remember when she's last been as happy as she was this morning with Ryan in the May sunshine.

It had been wrong, of course, to truant like that, and her dad would kill her if he found out, but just the way Ryan looked at her was enough to make her forget all that.

They strolled through the park, hand in hand, until Ryan stopped.

'You going to let me kiss you then, or what?'

Aasha blushed. She wished he hadn't asked, wished he'd just gone and done it.

'OK,' she said at last.

So he pulled her to him and pressed his lips against hers. Then he'd pushed his tongue into her mouth, which had startled her so much it had made her gasp.

'See, that wasn't so bad, was it?' he laughed.

Aasha didn't trust herself to answer. Bad? It had been absolutely fantastic.

Then two junkies had wandered over, whistling at Aasha. Ryan put his arm around her waist.

'Piss off,' he growled.

'Why did you do that?' she whispered.

'You're my girl, innit.'

Aahsa was about to ask him what exactly that meant when someone called Ryan on his mobile and he'd had to rush off, leaving Aasha to sneak back into school herself. Now she didn't know what to think.

Ryan's number rings twice, then he answers. 'Yeah?'

'It's Aasha.' Her words tumble out.

'I know.'

'I just wondered why you weren't at school.'

'Things to do, innit.'

There's no laughter in his voice. He sounds distant and cold.

'I thought you might be sick or something,' she says.

'Nah.'

She doesn't know what else to say but he saves her the trouble.

'I gotta go.'

He hangs up.

Aasha closes her phone carefully and slides it back into her bag. Lailla leans on her shoulder so that Aasha can barely breathe for the smell of Charlie Pink.

Lailla giggles. 'Looks like you've been dumped.'

\* \* \*

110

Lilly limped out of court. Her cheek throbbed and she felt completely wrung dry. Taslima, carrying the bags and files, followed her to the car.

Lilly nodded to the Leg of Lamb, a dingy pub with peeling paint and a welcome mat sprinkled with dog-ends. 'Don't suppose you fancy a drink?'

Taslima wrinkled her nose.

'I've been sticking to five units a week,' Lilly said, 'but it has been a bugger of a day.'

Taslima looked at the ground. 'I don't drink alcohol.'

'Oh?'

'I'm a Muslim . . .' Taslima's words trailed away.

Lilly felt her face redden. 'I did know that, I just didn't think.'

Taslima smiled. 'There's no reason why you should.'

They slipped into the car and Taslima drove them back to the office. In minutes Taslima had fixed the coffee machine and placed a steaming mug in front of Lilly.

'Have you never been tempted,' Lilly asked, 'by just a small glass of wine?'

Taslima laughed. 'Of course. I'm a Muslim, not a saint.'

'I don't know about that.' Lilly raised her coffee in salutation.

Taslima waved the praise away and plonked a huge pile of papers in front of her boss. Lilly raised an eyebrow.

'It's the prosecution evidence against Raffy,' said Taslima. 'We need to know how they intend to fight Raffy's case.'

'Why bother?' said Lilly. 'The stupid boy will do it for them.'

Taslima pursed her lips.

'I know you think it's just noise,' said Lilly, 'but he sounded pretty convincing in court.'

'He's too young to understand what it all means.'

'The magistrate didn't think so and neither will a jury,' said Lilly.

Taslima split the pile in two and handed one fat wad to Lilly. 'Then you'll just have to convince them otherwise.'

'What makes you think he even wants me to represent him?' asked Lilly.

Taslima picked up a red pen and began making notes. 'He didn't sack you, did he?'

When he got back to his car Jack pulled out his mobile and dialled Lilly's number. He wanted to run the situation with Ryan past her. She had good instincts with kids and would know instantly if Jack was reading things correctly.

When she answered, the fatigue was palpable in her voice and concern rose in his chest.

'Are you all right?' he asked.

'Shit morning at court,' she said.

Jack tried to bite his tongue but couldn't. 'You shouldn't be working.'

'Did you call to have a go at me?'

'Of course not.' Jesus, was that how she saw him? 'I just get worried.'

She didn't reply, and in her silence he knew exactly how she saw him. A nag. A moaning old nag. 'Actually,' he said, 'I wanted to ask your advice.'

'What about?'

'A boy I'm working with,' said Jack, 'and whether he could be abusing his mother.'

Lilly sighed. 'How could I possibly know that, Jack?'

'I just wondered what your gut reaction would be.'

'My gut reaction,' said Lilly, 'is that you're finding reasons to call and check up on me.'

'For God's sake, woman, I called to run something past you.'

'So how did we get onto the subject of whether or not I should work?' she asked, clearly not persuaded.

'Because you sound terrible,' he was shouting now, 'and because you said you had a shit morning at court. Am I supposed to just ignore that?'

There was more silence.

'Lilly?'

'Have you finished?' she asked.

'Yes.'

'Then let me get on with my work.'

When she hung up he threw his phone onto the passenger seat in disgust. He was still smarting when it rang. If it was Lilly calling to apologise she would have to do some Olympic grovelling.

'Jack?' Mara's breathy voice tingled in his ear.

'Hello.'

'There's a meeting tonight at school about certain racial issues,' she said. 'Police harassment will almost certainly come up.'

'Oh?'

'Some of our more radical parents are questioning your presence at school yesterday.'

'Who bloody told them I'd been?' Jack asked.

'Some of my students can spot a policeman at forty paces.' She coughed. 'I thought you might like to come.'

Jack thought for a second. He'd said he would be home for dinner – but then again, Lilly was doing everything in her power to avoid him.

'I'll be there,' he said.

It was nearly ten and Taslima was exhausted. The neighbours had been arguing for hours, their drunken screams ever increasing. She jumped at the sound of something hitting the wall and prayed it wasn't a head.

She glanced at the thick pile of papers she had brought home, intending to work her way through, but she couldn't concentrate. At this rate she'd still be up reading them at midnight. She closed her eyes and tried to drown out the noise. At times like this, when she felt all alone in this horrible place, she questioned whether she had done the right thing.

She'd given up everything. Home and family. Was it worth it? She missed her mother so much it hurt.

'You had no choice,' she said to herself, and picked up her pen.

At last the howling calmed to an insistent sobbing and she began to work. She had barely read the first paragraph when there was shouting outside. What now? She went to the curtains and peeped outside.

In the car park below two youths sat on the bonnet of an ancient BMW smoking cigarettes and knocking off each other's baseball caps. They could have been any teenagers larking about until the arrival of a skinny white girl, scuttling like a beetle towards them, confirmed what they were. Dealers. Bold as you like.

Though she had lost a lot of weight and her hair was now scraped back in an unflattering ponytail, Taslima recognised the white girl as a noisy resident of one of the ground-floor flats.

When Taslima had first moved in she'd asked Amber to stop throwing used nappies out of her window. It was a health hazard and the bins were only at the end of the walkway.

The white girl had spat at Taslima's feet and called her a 'rag head'.

The nappy throwing had stopped a few weeks ago.

'The social done take them kids away,' said Mrs Roberts. 'And not before time.'

Taslima felt a stab of sympathy as she watched the girl grasp something from the teenage boys and totter unsteadily back to her flat. They laughed openly at her but she didn't seem to care. Where was her self-respect? Did she hate herself so much?

Once again Taslima gave thanks that she knew how much God loved her and how much she was cherished. With that understanding everything else was easy. And if not easy, then at least bearable.

She went back to the sofa to work. As she reached for the first statement her mobile rang and she snatched it up.

Lilly held the phone in the crook of her neck as she hovered over the evidence she had spread across the kitchen table. Jack was working late so she'd been able to take the place over.

'Hello?' Taslima's voice was barely above a whisper.

'Sorry to call so late,' said Lilly, 'but I've just finished reading my stack of paperwork.'

'I'm nearly there too.'

'Great,' said Lilly. 'Anything interesting?'

'I'm not really qualified to decide that,' said Taslima.

'Fair enough,' Lilly laughed.

There was a low wail in the background.

'Is that crying?' asked Lilly. She could hear Taslima moving about and closing doors.

'No.'

'Is everything OK?' asked Lilly.

There was a pause.

'Everything's fine,' Taslima laughed. 'It's the baby next door.'

'Blimey, your walls must be thin.'

'Like paper. So did you find anything interesting?'

'Yes, I did.' Lilly searched for the document she'd marked with a highlighter. 'I've checked through the telephone records for Yasmeen's mobile and on the day of her death she made a lot of calls.'

'To who?' Taslima asked.

Lilly scanned the list. 'Friends, her mum, her uncle, her sister, Saira, Anwar.'

'Any to Raffy?' asked Taslima.

'One,' said Lilly.

'That's good,' said Taslima. 'She wouldn't have called him if he was at home.'

'I see where you're going but this was in the morning. He would still have had plenty of time to make his way over there and bring his sister a can of Coke.'

'What was the last call she made?' Taslima asked.

'That's the interesting thing. About an hour before she died she called a women's centre in Luton. The Free Voice Collective.'

'We'd better find out why she got in touch.'

'You bet,' said Lilly. 'Which is why we're paying them a visit first thing in the morning.'


The old man lifted his finger skyward, his voice reverberating around the school gym.

'Make no mistake,' he told the assembled parents and teachers, 'the Muslims in this community will no longer nod their heads while the police and the education authority tell us how to behave.'

There was a mumbled assent.

'We do not believe in drinking, dancing and *Celebrity Big Brother*,' the old man spat out.

'No one is saying that any Muslim should take part in those things,' said Mara, with a tight smile, 'but it is my responsibility to ensure that all the pupils in this school have equal opportunities.'

The old man sneered at her. 'The opportunity to do what? Run around the town taking drugs and having sex? Excuse us if we don't want that for *our* girls.'

'Nothing I have suggested includes drugs or sex,' Mara replied. 'I'm simply trying to introduce a broader curriculum. Philosophy, debating, music. Nothing untoward.'

'Muslim girls have no interest in your broader curriculum.' The old man waved his hand dismissively.

'Whatever free time they have should be spent with their families.'

Jack had heard enough. The smell of stale trainers – coupled with bigotry dressed up as religious belief – sickened him. He left the gym.

Throughout the seventies and eighties, every two-bit bully in Belfast had declared themselves on the side of God. Masked gunmen had fired rounds of bullets into the air at weddings and funerals. Every religious festival was hijacked by the politicians and the bombers. And he'd had a gutful of it.

Mara slipped outside into the cool night air.

'I thought you'd deserted me.'

'I just can't stand your man in there pretending he's some defender of the faith,' said Jack.

Mara's eyes twinkled. 'Mohamed Aziz is the bane of my life. He doesn't even have any children at this school.'

'Oh, yeah?'

'Remember the trouble over the school play?' said Mara. 'He was one of the main instigators.'

Jack gave a hollow laugh. 'Why does that not surprise me.'

The doors to the gym opened and the old man came out surrounded by younger men all patting him on the back. Clearly they approved of his rhetoric and clearly he enjoyed the attention.

'Did you have a chance to catch up with Ryan?' Mara asked. 'He wasn't at school today.'

Jack looked at her and she smiled. 'Are you trying to change the subject?' he asked.

Her smile turned to a laugh. 'Am I that transparent?'

'Ryan's at home with his mother,' said Jack.

'You met them both?' Mara sounded impressed. 'I haven't managed to get a single meeting with that family.'

Jack thought of the door slamming in his face. 'Just part of my job.'

'Well, you must be bloody good at it,' Mara giggled. 'Pardon my French.'

Jack couldn't resist a smile. 'Things are not what they seem in the Sanders household,' he said, serious again.

'Is there anything I can do to help?' Mara asked.

Jack considered for a moment. He pictured Mrs Sanders' fear, how her hands shook, how her son had menaced her.

'We might have to reassess exactly who it is that needs the help,' he said.

'Why don't we sit down and discuss it?' Mara checked her watch. 'There's still time to grab a bite to eat if you're hungry.'

Jack had no idea how to respond.

'Oh dear,' said Mara, 'I didn't mean as in a date.'

Now he felt ridiculous. What had he been thinking? Of course she hadn't meant a date. She cared about Ryan and just wanted to talk things through, like he had wanted to with Lilly.

'I'm sorry,' said Mara. 'I expect you have other plans.'

'No plans at all,' said Jack. 'Dinner would be lovely.'

# Chapter Four

June 2007

'The Jews are the enemy of God and mankind.'

The visiting teacher holds his finger in the air as if he is balancing this dreadful truth. I haven't heard him speak before and have been breathless with anticipation about this meeting.

Every Islamist forum describes him as one of the most fierce politicians in the UK, and the mosque is packed with supporters who have travelled from mosques in Birmingham and Leeds. We sit, cross-legged, our feet tucked under us, our knees touching, and wait for him to continue.

'Make no mistake that they wish to dominate not only the Middle East but the world.' He pauses again and nods gently. 'They worship only power and money.'

A murmur of assent passes through the crowd.

'And who will stop them?' He opens his arms. 'America, Britain?' He lets the question dance before him. 'The West will do nothing but stand on the sidelines and smile while Israeli soldiers kill every man, woman and child in Palestine.'

He points to a young boy at the front, no more than twelve, his cap slightly askew. 'Do you know what they will do when their tanks have flattened Gaza?'

The boy shakes his head.

'They will turn their sights on another poor Muslim country that cannot defend itself.'

The boy's eyes are as round as an owl's. 'We must stop them.'

The teacher lets a slow smile spread across his cheeks. 'Indeed we must.'

He rubs his cheek with his right hand, the stump where his thumb should be obvious to us all. He is too modest to admit it but it is common knowledge that he lost it saving a brother in Chechnya.

'Indeed we shall stop them,' he says.

When he has finished and the crowd begins to disperse I sidle over to the corner where he is deep in conversation with the imam of the mosque.

'Excuse me.' My nerves swallow the words in my throat. I cough. 'Excuse me, I have a question.'

The imam frowns at me and waves me away. 'Can't you see the teacher is tired?'

I'm about to apologise but he smiles at me.

'The Prophet Mohammed, peace be upon him, bade us to answer where we can.'

The imam tuts but the teacher is still smiling so I take my chance.

'I just wondered what you thought about the Iranian president saying Israel should be wiped off the map. Is that not haram?'

The teacher cocks his head. 'What do you think?'

'I don't know,' I admit. 'The Koran tells us we can use force to defend our Muslim brothers but we must treat our enemies with mercy.'

The imam snorts but the teacher presses a hand upon his shoulder so I can see the stump of his thumb up close, how it ends brutally above his knuckle.

'Should not every right-thinking person ask themselves what is a sin and what is not?' the teacher asks him. He turns to me. 'It is an excellent point.'

I blush with satisfaction.

'Now Hamas have won the election in Gaza you think Israel will be forced to negotiate with them?' he asks.

I nod vehemently.

'And if peace can be achieved we must leave Israel alone?' he asks.

'Perhaps,' I say. 'Is that not what the Koran tells us?'

The teacher is still smiling but a shadow of sadness passes across his eyes. 'Israel will not negotiate with Hamas.'

I am shocked. 'But they're elected. It's a democracy, a government.'

'I have been to Gaza many times,' he says, 'and seen the great work they do building hospitals, setting up schools. These are not terrorists, as the Jews would have us believe.'

'Then Israel will have to negotiate.'

'No.' The teacher's voice is firm. 'Instead they will bomb those hospitals and schools.'

I am incensed. 'They couldn't.'

'By winter the ceasefire will be broken and Israeli rockets will murder Palestinian children in their beds.'

His words are so certain I have no reply.

'This is why President Ahmadinejad said what he did.' He nods with a conviction so final I am rooted to the spot. 'Israel will not rest until every good Muslim is annihilated, and to allow them to continue, now that would be haram.'

Lilly emerged from her bed to the smell of burned bread. When she got to the kitchen a low fog of black smoke hung in the air. She gritted her teeth at the thought of her freshly glossed woodwork.

Sam scraped the charred surface of a slice of toast into the sink, scattering charcoal crumbs across the work tops.

'You know you have to watch that toaster,' she said.

Like every other piece of electrical equipment in Lilly's life, it worked against her.

'What's the point in a toaster you have to watch?' he growled.

'Well, it still miraculously transforms bread into toast,' Lilly pointed out.

Sam scowled at her. 'The other day you were moaning at me to eat breakfast. Now I'm doing it and you're still moaning.'

Lilly bit back a retort. Sam was right. She was having a go and he was only trying to help. Not unlike Jack.

She reached into the breadbin and pulled out two fresh slices of wholemeal.

'I am glad you're eating,' she said as she slid them into the toaster. 'So let's start again, shall we?'

'Breakfast, or this conversation?'

'Both.'

'What did you do to your face?' he asked.

Lilly's hand flew to her cheek. The swelling had gone down but a violent purple bruise had formed during the night. She'd attempted a camouflage job with the lacklustre contents of her make-up bag, but evidently to no avail.

'Accident,' she said, and popped up his toast.

'Jack's not gonna be happy,' said Sam.

'No shit, Sherlock.'

'You are a terrible role model.' Sam waved his knife at her.

Lilly passed him the butter and jam, and watched him slowly chew.

'Penny will be here in five minutes,' she said.

Penny collected Sam and took him to school each morning. She'd offered when Lilly had been bogged down in another difficult murder case and the routine had stuck.

'I feel a bit sick,' said Sam.

Lilly cocked her head to one side. He looked perfectly fine.

'Can I stay at home?' he wheedled.

Lilly paused. Sam was no skiver but there was clearly nothing wrong with him. She touched his forehead to be sure and his skin was perfectly cool.

'Go in this morning,' she said, 'and get Matron to call me if you get any worse.'

He was about to argue when they heard the telltale sound of Jack's key in the door, followed by the thump of his trainers on the hall floorboards. He was back from his morning run.

'Here we go,' said Sam. 'Prepare to take cover.'

'Morning,' said Jack, and padded into the kitchen.

Lilly kept her back to him and busied herself making tea. She knew she was merely putting off the inevitable.

At last she turned to face him. 'Morning.'

Jack reached out to touch her face. 'What on earth?'

'It's nothing,' she shrugged. 'A bit of a bump.'

Jack sighed and dropped into a chair.

'I'm absolutely fine,' said Lilly.

'Is the baby OK?'

'He's absolutely fine.'

'Why didn't you tell me?' he asked. 'Or were you hoping I wouldn't notice?'

That was of course what she had hoped.

'Don't be daft,' she said. 'You were working late last night so I didn't get a chance.'

Jack looked down and reddened. Only Jack could feel bad about working while his girlfriend was pregnant. He was ludicrously over-protective and it was driving her potty, but his heart, as always, was in the right place.

She came close behind him and nuzzled the top of his head, tasting the salt lick of his sweat.

'A woman can't help it if her fella stays out till all hours,' she teased. 'What's she supposed to do? Stay up to give him all her news?'

His face fell. 'I'm so sorry, Lilly.'

She slid around him until she was perched on his knee. 'Now you really are being daft.' She kissed him on each cheek and then on the mouth.

'Bloody hell!' Penny waltzed into the kitchen. 'Get a room.'

Lilly looked up at her friend and Penny's face dropped.

'What in God's name happened to you?'

'It's nothing,' said Lilly.

'You look like you went two rounds with Amir Khan.'

Raffy Khan, thought Lilly.

'She shouldn't be working,' said Jack, his voice heavy with resignation that she would not listen to his wise words.

Lilly ushered Penny out of the kitchen before the conversation could go further. They went to stand by her car, waiting for Sam to get his school bag. The May trees were in full blossom, their boughs impossibly heavy.

'Have you noticed anything odd about Sam?' Lilly asked.

Penny frowned.

'He seems very touchy and he doesn't want to go to school,' said Lilly.

'I heard on the grapevine that some of the older boys had been picking on some of the younger ones,' said Penny.

'Bullying?'

Penny nodded.

'Should I call the Head?' Lilly asked.

She was no helicopter parent and hated the way some of his classmates were fussed over like bone china, but she would not stand for bullying.

For all the right reasons, Lilly's mother, Elsa, had insisted she attend a Catholic girls' school, two bus rides away from the sink estate where they lived. For all its supposed Christian ethos the pupils had taken great pleasure in deriding Lilly's clothes and accent.

The parents were worse. In seven years Lilly had not received one invite to tea, as if poverty were a contagious disease.

Penny put her hand on Lilly's shoulder. 'I think you need to get to the bottom of it.'

Aasha has been crying all night, hiding her sobs under her pillow.

She hasn't felt this sad since her Grandpa died and even that wasn't this awful because he was, like, eighty and hadn't been able to get out of bed to go to the toilet.

She knows she's being silly. Ryan and she have spent hardly any time together. And yet she feels as if he is the only person in the world who listens to what she has to say. He likes her for herself, not whatever he thinks she should be, like her parents, her brothers or her teachers do.

She slumps into the kitchen, her face puffy, her head throbbing.

'Are you all right?' asks Mum.

Aasha shakes her head and bursts into a fresh batch of tears. 'I feel awful.'

'Back to bed.' Mum shoos her out of the room. 'I'll bring you a cup of tea.'

Aasha wipes her nose on her pyjama sleeve and slides back under her duvet.

'So,' Mum puts a steaming mug on Aasha's bedside table, 'where does it hurt?'

Aasha chokes back a sob. 'Everywhere.'

Mum smooths a cool hand over Aasha's temples and Aasha aches to tell her about Ryan.

'Shall I call Dr Farouk?' asks Mum.

Aasha doesn't think there's much he can do. Is there even a cure for a broken heart?

'I just want to sleep,' she says.

Mum smiles and traces a finger over each of Aasha's eyelids until they shut. 'Then you do just that,' she says.

Ryan is completely stressed.

Since that copper came round he cannot relax. He stayed up all night playing Grand Theft Auto and smoking weed and his head is mashed.

His mum is a stupid, stupid, stupid bitch. Why the fuck did she even answer the door? It's not like she was expecting a friend or something. She don't know nobody.

He throws the console across the room. If that copper comes back, sticking his nose in, Ryan will be carted off and then she'll really be sorry, innit.

He can hear her scratching about in her room like some rat. She ain't come out all night. Too scared.

Lilly parked outside the Free Voice Collective in a dingy sideroad behind Luton Social Services. Sandwiched between a Polish convenience store and Blockbuster's it vied for attention between lopsided posters of cheese pastries and cherry jam and a life-size cut-out of Heath Ledger as the Joker.

'Is this it?' asked Taslima.

Lilly peered in at the window, obscured by layers of grime and frayed lace curtains. It was impossible to see whether anyone was there.

'Doesn't look too promising, does it?'

There was a buzzer hanging off the wall by the door, the electric wires bared to the elements. Rather than touch it, Lilly chose to thump the door with the side of her fist. The wood, though peeling, was solid beneath her hand.

They waited a few seconds before Taslima bent down and opened the letter box. It was filled with stiff bristles to prevent people posting junk mail. Or worse.

At last the edge of the curtain twitched and a woman peeked out. She looked from Lilly to Taslima and gestured to the door.

When it opened, Lilly was confronted by a gangly woman in her mid-twenties, her hair cropped, extravagant silver earrings dangling past her jawline.

'Yes?' Her tone was friendly yet brisk.

'Can we talk to you about Yasmeen Khan?' Lilly asked.

'And you are?'

'I'm the lawyer instructed by her family.'

The woman looked at Taslima, a green jewel glinting on her nostril. 'And you?'

'I'm Robin,' said Taslima. 'To her Batman.'

The woman smiled politely, though not warmly. 'You'd better come in.'

She led them through a corridor, the woodchip wallpaper dotted with notice boards. Lilly scanned the announcements. Meetings with the Anti-Nazi League and discussion groups with the Black Sisterhood. She felt a pang of nostalgia for her days at university when she and the rest of the Women's Committee had chained themselves to the car of a Tory MP who had presented a bill to the House of Commons aiming to criminalise abortion.

In due course the police had brought bolt cutters and slung them in the cells for the night where they had driven everyone on duty to the brink of insanity with their tuneless chorus of 'I Will Survive'. A few weeks later the MP had been caught with a rent boy by the *News of the World*. Heady days.

The room at the end was an office-cum-meeting room, one end covered floor to ceiling by books, the centre dominated by a desk piled high with files and boxes of pamphlets. An outsized computer with an incongruously tiny screen was perched precariously on the end. It looked twenty years old and heavy enough to break a foot if it fell.

The woman gestured to the hard plastic chairs. 'I'm Kash.'

Lilly lowered herself down. 'I'm Lilly and this is Taslima.'

'So what can I do for you?' asked Kash.

'We understand Yasmeen called this centre on the day she died,' said Lilly.

Kash's face was non-committal.

'Could you tell us what the call was about?' said Lilly.

Kash shook her head and her earrings danced. 'I didn't speak to her.'

'Do you know who she did speak to?' asked Lilly.

Kash reached over to a drawer and took out a small tube of lip balm, which she squeezed onto her little finger.

'Not off the top of my head, no.'

Lilly watched the woman smooth the cream first across her top lip, then her bottom lip. Deliberately, she replaced the top on the tube and returned it to the drawer.

'Could you find out?' asked Lilly.

Kash waved distractedly at the numerous files on her desk. 'We're not very good at keeping records.'

'Give me a break,' Lilly was surprised to hear Taslima chip in. 'You don't have a staff of hundreds. You know full well who spoke to Yasmeen.'

Kash raised her eyebrows but said nothing.

'All we want to know is what was discussed,' said Taslima. 'Is that such a big thing to ask?'

'Women call here when they are in trouble and they have nowhere else to turn.' Kash leaned forward and frowned. 'They know everything they say, everything they tell us, is confidential. If we can't offer that then, yes, it is a very *big thing.*'

'We understand that,' said Lilly, 'but Yasmeen is dead.'

'All the more reason not to collaborate with those that were involved in her death.'

'How can you be so sure her brother killed her?' asked Taslima.

'A Muslim girl contacts us.' Kash clapped her hands. 'Then she's gone.'

'It could be coincidence,' said Taslima.

'Get real,' said Kash. 'Honour killings are a problem in this community.'

Taslima flared up. 'Honour killings are unislamic.'

'Tell that to the fathers, brothers and uncles out there.'

Taslima shook her head. 'The Prophet, peace be upon him, tells us women are to be cherished.'

Kash banged her fist on the desk. 'I know exactly what he said, but wake up and smell the coffee, girlfriend. Women are being beaten and bullied and forced into marriage. When they won't comply they're murdered.'

'Do you think that's what happened to Yasmeen?' asked Lilly.

'To Yasmeen – and lots more like her.'

'Did you know she was pregnant?' asked Lilly.

Kash let out a slow puff of air. 'I didn't, but that just confirms my suspicions that she was murdered.'

'You don't know that,' said Taslima.

'You're not listening, sister.' Kash jabbed the palm of her left hand with the forefinger of her right. 'Systematic punishment is being meted out.'

'You make it sound organised,' said Lilly.

'It is,' said Kash. 'Have you heard of the PTF?'

Lilly shook her head.

'The Purity Task Force,' said Taslima. 'A militia group that polices the women in Afghanistan.'

'I'm impressed,' said Lilly.

Taslima shrugged. 'I like to know what's happening to my sisters around the world.'

'So this PTF,' Lilly looked from Kash to Taslima, 'what's their deal?'

'They patrol the streets, making sure women are properly dressed, not out unaccompanied,' said Taslima. 'If they hear about any behaviour they disapprove of, the PTF punish the woman involved.'

'I'm assuming you don't mean a good telling-off,' said Lilly. 'They sound dangerous.'

'And brought by popular demand to a street in Luton near you,' said Kash.

'You're kidding me,' said Lilly.

Kash stared hard at Lilly. 'Do I sound like I'm joking?'

'Do you think the PTF were involved in Yasmeen's death?' asked Taslima.

'Ask her brother.'

Back in the car, Lilly pulled out her laptop and went straight to her search engine.

'Purity – what-was-it?'

'Purity Task Force,' said Taslima.

At least twenty entries appeared.

'Popular little buggers,' said Lilly, and clicked on Wikipedia.

'"The Purity Task Force are the religious police based in Afghanistan,"' she read aloud, '"similar in function to the Mutaween in Saudi Arabia."'

Taslima nodded. 'They wander about in groups making sure the women are covered properly and chaperoned by male relatives.'

Lilly continued to read. '"The name Purity Task Force or PTF has been adopted by many groups enforcing Sharia law."'

There were links to articles from all over the world – Iran, Jordan, Malaysia . . . Lilly clicked onto Oman.

The lead photograph showed a group of frightened young women being bundled into a minibus by bearded men wielding sticks.

'"On 15 April scores of teenagers and girls were rounded up at a city shopping centre and arrested by the PTF,' Lilly read.

Taslima nodded. 'There are crackdowns from time to time.'

'"Horrified onlookers could do nothing as the girls were beaten and taken away for daring to walk the streets unaccompanied."'

Lilly had to look away. The treatment of children in the UK was often unpalatable but this was barbaric.

She went back to the screen and clicked the link to an article in the *Birmingham Observer*.

*Honour Attack linked to the PTF*
*A Muslim woman was blinded yesterday when acid was thrown in her face.*
*Relatives, who did not wish to be named, confirmed that the assault coincided with her decision not to marry her elderly fiancé from Bangladesh.*
*The woman's father has been arrested along with her uncle, both of whom are members of a local vigilante group calling itself the Purity Task Force.*

'Bloody Hell,' said Lilly.

As they sped towards Arlington, Lilly stole a glance at Taslima. She hadn't spoken since they had left Luton and was looking straight ahead.

'Do you think Raffy could be involved with this gang?' Lilly asked.

Taslima kept her eyes dead ahead. 'The PTF's not a gang, it's much more dangerous than that.'

Lilly tried to ease the tension. 'At least you'll be OK.'

'What?'

Lilly gestured to Taslima's headscarf. 'No one can accuse you of bending the rules.'

'The hijab gives me the freedom to make my own decisions.' Taslima's eyes sparkled. 'I wear it out of respect for myself, not because a man tells me I should.'

Lilly was sceptical. Surely Taslima dressed as she was expected?

'Is it really your choice?' she asked. 'Isn't it just part of how you were brought up?'

'Of course not.' Taslima straightened her back. 'My mother and sister don't cover their heads except in the mosque.'

'So why do you want to wear it all the time?'

'I don't wish to be seen as trivial or vain.' Taslima seemed to grow two inches. 'I wish to be taken seriously.'

Lilly glanced down at her maternity trousers with their sweaty elastic waistband. 'No one ever takes me seriously.'

A smile spread across Taslima's face. 'You are so funny.'

'It wasn't a joke.'

'You're a lawyer, Lilly, you make decisions that affect children's lives every day of the week,' said Taslima. 'Of course people take you seriously.'

Lilly checked her reflection in the mirror. She was developing a double chin.

'Maybe it's just me, then.'

Lilly pulled into the car park of Arlington YOI.

'This is a prison!' Taslima exclaimed.

Lilly looked up at the twenty-foot fence topped with razor wire that stood between them and the monolithic concrete block casting huge shadows into the distance.

'What were you expecting?' she asked.

'I'm not sure.' Taslima shook her head. 'But not this.'

Institutions for young offenders were supposed to be different from adult prisons. The website for Arlington promised education and programmes devised to produce law-abiding citizens. Activities ranged from catering to ceramic design. Buzz words littered the home page: 're-habilitation', 'specialist support'. In reality it was a prison.

They locked the Mini Cooper and headed to reception where a guard checked their identification. His pot belly was squeezed into a navy sweatshirt emblazoned with the word 'Securitas'.

'Don't they wear proper uniforms?' Taslima whispered.

Lilly placed her hand in the print scanner. 'The place is run by a private security company.'

'To make it less austere?' Taslima asked.

'To make it cheaper,' Lilly replied.

They passed along a grey corridor lit entirely by fluorescent strips that winked ominously. There were no windows and a strong smell of disinfectant.

'How many boys are here?' asked Taslima.

'About four hundred.'

Taslima stopped in her tracks and cocked her head. 'Where are they all?'

'In their cells.'

'But it's the middle of the day.'

'Twenty-three hours' bang-up,' said Lilly. 'Welcome to the Tenth Circle of Hell.'

Jack rubbed his forehead. He could feel the furrows beneath his fingers. When had he got so old? This morning he'd noticed a couple of renegade whiskers sprouting from his ears. And grey ones at that.

He looked at his desk, covered in paperwork and empty paper cups, like every other desk in the room.

Nothing ever changed, from the ugly décor to the piss-taking banter. His life seemed to be stuck on pause.

Even he and Lilly were stuck in a rigid knitting pattern of fight, fight, kiss, fight, fight, kiss. They were stale, like week-old bread, not even fit for toast.

His mobile bleeped with an incoming text. Expecting to hear from Lilly, Jack felt a jolt of surprise at the sight of Mara's number.

*Thank you very much for last night.*

They'd met up in a cosy Thai place where the doll-like waitresses wore full-length sarongs and remembered their order without writing anything down.

'I love it here,' Mara said, dipping a cracker into a sticky red sauce and nibbling gracefully.

She told him how she'd spent a year teaching English in Bangkok before travelling on to Vietnam and India. How the journey from Jaipur to Delhi had taken days, and each night she'd slept on the bus, not because she had no money for a hotel but because she wanted to.

She showed him a beautiful ring with a square green stone that she'd bought in Chiang Mai for thirty pounds.

'They said it was jade,' she laughed, 'but I'd bet my arse it's not.'

As Jack slurped his Tom Kah Kai he was ashamed to admit he'd never been further than the Costa del Sol,

when he and a mate had spent the week fighting hang-
overs and sunstroke.

When he told Mara his theory about Ryan and his
mother she put her hand to her mouth.

'That's awful.'

'I could be wrong, of course,' he said. 'She didn't
actually tell me he was abusing her.'

Mara shook her head. 'I guessed there was something
wrong there, but not this.'

'Like I say, I could be wrong.'

'I'm sure you're spot on, Jack,' Mara said. 'I saw what
I wanted to see, I'm afraid, whereas you're used to seeing
things from every angle.'

He took another mouthful of soup, secretly pleased
that she had such faith in his abilities.

'Is there anything that I can do?' she asked.

'Difficult, unless she makes a complaint.'

Mara dabbed her mouth, her scarlet nails perfect
against the white of the napkin. 'Maybe I should speak
to him,' she said; 'try to get through to him.'

The image of Ryan's contorted face flashed through
Jack's mind, how he'd growled at his mother, the menace
in his voice.

'Absolutely not,' he said. 'I'll tackle the lad.'

Then she smiled at him and put her hand on his knee.
'I am so very grateful.'

Once again he rubbed his face. He had to admit to
being very flattered at how appreciative Mara was. It
made him feel useful and he hadn't felt that way in a
long time. If there was even the tiniest bubble of guilt
rising to the surface, Jack pressed it firmly down.

He tapped the keys on his phone and pressed Send.
*It was a pleasure.*

'Tell me about the PTF.'

Lilly slapped her papers on the table between herself and Raffy. The legal visits room was full and hot. More than twenty inmates bent over documents with their lawyers.

Raffy glared at her. 'I don't know what you're talking about.'

'An organisation that attacks Muslim girls for stepping out of line.' Lilly held his stare. 'Are you a member?'

Raffy laughed. 'You are totally crazy.'

Another Asian boy swaggered past the table. Raffy held out his fist. 'All right, brother.'

The boy touched the fist with his own and slouched towards a middle-aged man in slip-on shoes and a comb-over.

A white boy in the far corner got to his feet and began to grunt. He had a skin head and swastika tattoos fought for space amid the acne on his neck. He brought his hands to his armpits and imitated a monkey.

Raffy jumped to his feet. 'You want to start something?'

The skinhead just laughed and threw a pen at the other Asian boy.

'You are going to get your head mashed,' Raffy shouted.

The guard dragged the skinhead out of the room and Raffy slumped back into his chair.

'Fucking pussy.'

Lilly sighed. 'My advice is to keep well out of any racial stuff.'

'Did I ask for your advice?'

'Nope, but I'm paid to give it,' she said. 'When it kicks off in here it's not safe.'

Raffy shrugged. 'Me and my brothers are perfectly safe.'

'When are you going to get it into your head that Lilly is trying to help you?' Taslima's words were quiet but clear.

'I don't need no help from a *kafir*,' he said.

'Do you put your trust in Allah?' she asked.

'Of course.'

'Well, how do you know he hasn't sent Lilly to help?'

Raffy sneered at his lawyer. 'Allah has sent me a white woman?'

'Allah intended that women are equal to men,' said Taslima.

'I don't have a problem with women,' said Raffy. 'My sisters are the sword of the Prophet.'

Taslima cocked her thumb at Lilly. 'Then show this sister some respect. Unless you and your brethren are enjoying yourselves so much you don't want to get out.'

Raffy's shoulders slumped. 'Fine.'

'Fine,' said Taslima.

Lilly nodded. 'Fine.'

'Let's start again,' said Lilly. 'Are you a member of the Purity Task Force?'

'I've never even heard of them,' said Raffy.

Aasha feels sick. She's slept on and off throughout the day but now she feels as though her stomach is pushing up into her mouth. She needs something to eat and drags herself to the kitchen.

Imran looks up from his iphone. 'You look like shit.'

She ignores him and opens the fridge, searching for something bland and starchy. She pulls out a bowl of cold rice from the bottom shelf, punctures the cling film with a spoon and shovels it into her mouth.

Imran scowls. 'Gross.'

She doesn't even look up at him but takes both the bowl and the spoon and heads back to her bedroom.

'I need to use your laptop,' he calls after her.

'No,' she says over her shoulder.

'What did you say to me?'

Aasha walks away.

Back in her own space, she takes a gulp from the mug of tea that has sat by her bedside all day, then propels another mouthful of rice down her throat. She gags a little but manages to keep it down. She takes another swig of cold tea and makes a decision: she won't sit around any longer feeling sorry for herself. She'll go over to see him and ask him outright what it is exactly that she has done wrong.

She's in the middle of pulling on her trainers when there's a knock at her door. Imran opens it before Aasha can answer.

She carries on tying her laces. 'What do you want?'

'You are acting very weird.'

He's right, she is acting weird. Well, not weird exactly, but definitely out of character. He's used to her bowing and scraping to him, just like Mum, but not any more.

She stands up and smooths her shirt down over her hips. It could do with an iron but she doesn't much care how she looks.

'I thought you were ill,' says Imran.

'I am,' she replies, and grabs her jacket.

'Mum's not going to like your attitude,' he says.

'Mum's not here.'

He blocks the doorway. 'I don't like it either.'

She doesn't answer, but pushes past him. At first he resists and for a moment she wonders if he will physically stop her from leaving. They tussle for a few seconds but he soon relaxes and lets her past.

'I don't know what you think you're up to,' he says, 'but you're bringing a whole heap of shit down on your head.'

She does up the buttons on her jacket and slams the door behind her.


Aasha knows from Lailla that Ryan lives in a bad part of town but she's still shocked. Bury Park isn't exactly Hollywood but the Clayhill Estate is horrible. There are smashed bottles and dog turds everywhere. The Spar is already closed even though it's only seven. Its iron grille has been pulled down and locked.

Imagine living here. Poor Ryan, no wonder he's a bit loony sometimes.

She strides to his door with her chin in the air but when she finally gets there she panics. What does she think she's doing? What on earth is she going to say?

She thinks she might just slink back home, forget all about it. But then what? She can never go back to who she was before all this started. Ryan has changed her – whether he meant to or not.

She knocks gingerly at the door, hoping no one's at

home, but if she's honest she can hear the TV blaring inside. She knocks again.

A figure comes to the door. It could be Ryan. What can she possibly say to him that won't make her sound totally lame? She doesn't want him to think she's some mad stalker but how else can she explain why she's standing on his doorstep?

She flicks a glance over her shoulder. If she runs away now, would she get to the walkway before he had a chance to see it was her? Maybe. But Ryan's just the sort to get pissed off by that and chase her. If he caught her she'd look even more stupid.

Perhaps she should act all angry with him? She could tell him that she's vexed, ask him what the hell he thinks he's doing messing her around. If he didn't want to be with her any more than why not just say so? It's not like they're kids or anything. Can he not just grow up or whatever?

She's seen Lailla giving Sonny a complete mouthful when he hasn't been able to pick her up from school or cancelled her at the last minute.

'If you're bored with me, Sonny, then just let me know,' she tells him, ''cos I can easily hook up with another boy who might enjoy my company. You get me?'

Then she hangs up on him and refuses to take his calls until he comes running, usually with a box of chocolates or a CD for her.

Aasha puts her hands on her hips and prepares to cuss Ryan out.

When the door swings open and it's a woman, Aasha's lost for words.

The woman is beyond thin and is wearing an ancient

Comic Relief T-shirt, which seems a bit odd because she's not even smiling.

'Yes?' the woman whispers.

Aasha opens and shuts her mouth, slides her hands to her sides. 'Is Ryan there?'

The woman's hands shoot up to her mouth and she presses her lips shut. Aasha sometimes does that when she wants to scream at her brothers but she knows she can't.

They stand like that for a minute, Aasha rocking uncomfortably, the woman shaking, her mouth sealed.

At last Aasha feels compelled to speak. 'Is he out?'

Relief floods the woman's eyes and she nods.

'OK,' Aasha stutters, and heads away. When she hears the door close she sprints to the walkway and takes the stairs two at a time.

'Make us a cuppa.'

Lilly plonked heavily onto the sofa next to Sam. She had changed into some of Jack's old pyjamas but the bottom three buttons didn't reach and her bump poked out like a football.

'You are so fat,' said Sam.

'And you are Prince Charming.'

Sam rolled his eyes but headed to the kitchen and began clattering for tea bags. Lilly padded after him.

'Where's Jack?' asked Sam.

Lilly shrugged. 'Working, I expect.'

'He's pissed with you for taking on that case.'

'Don't swear,' said Lilly, 'or if you must, don't use American slang.'

Sam pulled a face and poured boiling water into a mug.

It amazed her how that tiny boy who couldn't sleep through the night without SuperTed was now so capable. Time had passed too quickly.

'I love you,' she said.

Sam pulled another unreadable face.

'Anyway,' said Lilly, 'Jack's fine with me working.'

'That's a lie and we both know it,' Sam sighed. 'But he's going to have to suck it up, like everyone else.'

Sam reached into a cupboard for the biscuit tin. Lord, he didn't even need the chair.

'Is there anything you want to talk to me about?' Lilly asked.

'Don't start, Mum.'

'I'm not starting,' she said. 'I just want to know if there's anything or anyone on your mind.'

'I'm fine,' he said, unconvincingly.

Lilly was annoyed with herself that she'd let the day run away with her and hadn't made the call to Manor Park. She'd do it first thing tomorrow.

'So is your client guilty?' he asked, cramming a Hobnob into his mouth.

'That is the million-dollar question.' Lilly took a handful. 'My assistant doesn't think so.'

Sam spat out a mouthful of oats and chocolate chips. 'Since when do you have an assistant?'

'Since Taslima talked me into hiring her,' Lilly smiled.

'Taslima?' Sam rolled the name around his tongue. 'Weird.'

Lilly thought about the young woman with her black outfits and her earnest expression.

'Weird she's not.'

Then she remembered her smile and her quiet dignity, the way she had taken Raffy to task.

'She's different.'

'Well, you two should get along then,' said Sam.

Lilly laughed. Their companionable chat reminded her just how much she enjoyed Sam's company. He might be growing up fast, but he was still the same little boy underneath.

'Actually, we do get along.'

Sam reached for another biscuit, dunked it in Lilly's tea and brought it to his lips. Lilly was about to comment when a light flashed across the kitchen window.

Her heart hammered in her chest. 'What was that?'

Sam shrugged. 'What was what?'

Lilly pulled herself up and peered out of the window. In the gloom she could only just make out where the garden ended and the field beyond began.

There it was again. Definitely a light.

'Someone's out there with a torch,' she stammered.

'Chill out, Mum.' Sam joined her at the window. 'It'll be the farmer walking his dog.'

Lilly craned her neck, her pulse still racing.

'You're right,' she smiled weakly. 'Since the fire I'm getting paranoid.'

Mark Cormack jumped back in his Ford Mondeo and reached for a packet of Benson & Hedges. He thumbed the packet lovingly. He was trying to quit but couldn't resist.

He plugged a fag into his mouth and sparked it up, exhaling a long stream of smoke out of his nose.

He checked his brief and scribbled a note. He hadn't liked this job from the off.

He avoided Pakis whenever he could: they were bad payers, always arguing the toss. Arabs were the same. What did they think? That he was running a charity?

As soon as this pair showed up in his tatty offices he'd demanded five hundred quid up front, expecting they'd haggle like old women at a market stall. But they'd paid on the nose. And in cash.

Now he'd found who they were looking for, and he didn't feel great about himself and the trouble it would cause when he passed on her details.

But beggars couldn't afford to be choosers. He was the wrong side of fifty, divorced and had a passion for the gee-gees. He dealt in information. What other folk did with it was down to them.

# Chapter Five

October 2007

'Tahira Begum is getting married.'

Yasmeen and I are in the New Muslim Book and Gift Shop on Crompton Street. She's rifling through a pile of bonnet caps when she tells me about Tahira.

'She must be very happy,' I say.

Yasmeen seesaws her hand. 'She wanted to go to college and make something of her life.'

'Service to the family is service to Allah,' I say.

She picks out an ivory-coloured bonnet cap and matching hijab in the Egyptian style. The colour will suit her skin.

'I just hope her husband is good to her,' she says.

'En sh'Allah,' I reply.

She tries on the headwear, first tucking her thick hair into the tight cap, then laying the hijab on top and tucking it under her chin. She checks her appearance in the small hand mirror provided.

'Good?'

I cock my head to one side. She knows I prefer my sisters

to wear black. The Koran is very clear about how women should not seek to draw attention to themselves, something all Muslim women would do well to keep in mind.

Yasmeen sticks out her tongue.

I wander over to the books and pull out a favourite. *One True Religion.*

'Haven't you read that?' asks Yasmeen, the hijab draped over her arm.

'Yes,' I say. 'I thought I might get a copy for you.'

She rolls her eyes at me.

'Don't you want to expand your mind?' I ask.

'And end up like you?' she laughs. 'No, thanks.'

'What do you mean?'

'You're not exactly a barrel of laughs any more, are you?' she says. 'You're either at the mosque or you've got your nose squashed in one of your books.'

'I take my duty to Islam seriously.'

'So do I,' she replies.

I shake my head. 'You don't have any interest in your brothers and sisters around the world.'

'Yes I do.'

'OK then,' I say, 'tell me what's happening in Gaza right now.'

'Like duh.' She rolls her eyes again. 'The Israelis have set up a blockade.'

'And what does that actually mean, Yasmeen? What is actually happening to Palestinians as we speak?'

She sighs. 'Well, I don't know all the details, do I?'

I turn back to the books.

She nudges me with her elbow. 'So what is happening? You know, right now.'

'Innocent men, women and children are dying. They have no food, no water, no electricity. The hospitals have run out of medical supplies and the schools have had to close.'

'Is that what you talk about at those meetings you go to?' she asks.

'Of course,' I say, 'and the plight of Muslims all over the world.'

We make our way to the till and she hands over the money for her hijab.

'You should come along,' I say.

'Maybe I will.'


The keys rattled in the lock as Lilly opened the office. When she stepped into the reception she couldn't contain a smile. The transformation was unbelievable. In a few short days Taslima had cleared away the files, boxes and post so that the area now looked clean and efficient. She'd even worked her magic on the dying plant, which was now shooting fresh green leaves.

Lilly smiled and walked through to her own room where the photograph of Sam had been dusted and a Twix had been placed on her desk.

Her new assistant was a wonder.

In an attempt not to scoff the chocolate she tossed it in her drawer – she'd had two croissants for breakfast and didn't need the calories. Eating for two was one thing, but Lilly found herself scoffing enough food for five.

She picked up the phone and called Manor Park, determined to find out what exactly was troubling Sam.

The sound of Mrs Baraclough's voice made Lilly cringe. The mono-browed secretary of the head teacher was notoriously difficult. The other mums called her the Gatekeeper.

'It's Miss Valentine,' said Lilly. 'I'd like a word with Mr Latimer.'

The tone she used was ridiculously breezy. It didn't fool the Gatekeeper.

'He's in a meeting.'

'What time will he finish?' Lilly asked.

'I couldn't say. He's very busy all day.'

Lilly bit her tongue before she was tempted to mention the fifteen grand a year she handed over in school fees.

'Perhaps you could call back tomorrow.' Mrs Baraclough's voice made it clear this was an order, not a suggestion.

Under normal circumstances Lilly would have capitulated, but guilt at having already wasted time galvanised her.

'I really do need to speak to him today.'

'As I say, he's very busy,' Mrs Baraclough snapped. 'It's a full-time job running a school, you know.'

A full time job? thought Lilly. Well, bully for him. Didn't every normal person have a full-time job?

'He can't be busy all day,' she tried to argue.

'He is.'

'Not every second of every minute of every hour,' said Lilly.

Mrs Baraclough was, for the first time, speechless.

'He must stop for lunch, or at the very least a cup of tea,' Lilly continued. 'And even he needs to use the loo.'

'I beg your pardon?'

'Granted.' Lilly was on a roll. 'Just get him to call me.'

She hung up, feeling unstoppable, and pulled out a legal pad. Full-time job? The man didn't know he was born.

She made two columns. The first set out all the evidence that pointed to the fact that Raffy had murdered his sister.

1. His fingerprints were found on the can.
2. A box of OxyContin was found in his locker.
3. He spoke to Yasmeen on the day she died.
4. He refuses to explain himself to the police, the court or even me.
5. He would have been furious to discover his sister was in a sexual relationship – a motive.

She sighed. Things were starting to stack up pretty high.

Chewing the end of the biro, she tried to fill the second column: evidence that pointed to Raffy's innocence.

1. He said he didn't do it.

Not much to go on.

She reached into the drawer and retrieved the chocolate bar. She would eat just the one stick and save the other for later.

'Hello, Boss.' Taslima stuck her head round the door. 'You're in early.'

Lilly looked up. 'I wanted to make a start on building our defence.'

'And?'

Lilly pointed to the near-empty second column. 'Not what I'd call watertight.'

'I don't think he's guilty,' said Taslima.

Lilly laughed. 'I don't think a jury's going to take your word for it.'

'Then we need to show them he couldn't have done it.'

'No alibi, I'm afraid.'

'Then we need to show them who *did* do it.'

'A soddi,' said Lilly.

'Excuse me?'

'A soddi. Some other dude did it.' She wagged a chocolatey finger. 'You know for a rookie, you're pretty good.'

Taslima blushed.

Lilly reached for the second stick of Twix. At this rate she would soon look like a sumo wrestler.

'Actually the police haven't looked at anyone else,' she said. 'If we could at least show there was a possibility that someone else was involved . . .'

'We'd have reasonable doubt.'

'See, you're a natural.'

Taslima waved off Lilly's praise as ridiculous and busied herself with more filing. It was not her way to show pride but Lilly could tell Taslima was pleased by the compliment.

'So if not Raffy, then who is most likely to be our man?' said Lilly.

'Obvious choice would be the boyfriend,' said Taslima.

Lilly nodded, picked up the phone and dialled the CPS.

\* \* \*

Kerry put a baton of raw carrot between her fingers like a cigarette. She was eating around two kilos of them a day and could barely face putting it in her mouth.

Each evening she peeled and cut them for the next day. Then first thing in the morning she would grab her Tupperware box and run out of the house before her resolve weakened.

The phone rang and she grabbed it, grateful for the diversion.

'Hi, Kerry, how are you?'

'Lilly Valentine.' Kerry's voice was deadpan.

Lilly's voice was like an annoying budgie. Cheep, cheep. 'Are you still on a diet?' she trilled. 'You looked great at court the other day.'

Kerry sighed. 'What do you want?'

'I just wondered if the police had managed to track down the father of Yasmeen's baby.'

'Not that I know of,' said Kerry.

'Could you check for me?' Lilly asked. 'I just want to know what steps have been taken to locate him.'

Lilly's tone might sound friendly but both she and Kerry knew that the police would probably have done nothing whatsoever to ascertain either his identity or his whereabouts. They had their man, and therefore the investigation was complete.

'I'll chase it up for you,' said Kerry, and hung up.

She didn't know why, but she hated Lilly Valentine. Actually, she did know why. Lilly had always been irritating, with her soft curls and cleavage. She propagated an image that was cute and ditzy but Kerry had been trounced by her in court enough times to know that she was not all she seemed.

Lilly had graduated from figure of low-level annoyance to dart board material during their last murder trial when the prosecution barrister, Jez Stafford, had mooned after her like a love-struck teen. He'd laughed at her pathetic jokes and skipped in her wake. Kerry couldn't understand it. He was handsome, clever, successful. What the hell did he see in Lilly Valentine? To top it off, Lilly didn't even reciprocate his affections, instead choosing some scruffy copper to get her up the duff.

Whatever the reason, a cold, hard jealousy had begun to fester in Kerry's gut.

She took a fistful of carrot, stuffed them into her mouth and picked up the phone. It was answered on one ring.

'DI Bell.'

Kerry swallowed down the carrot. 'Kerry Thomson.'

'Are you all right?' asked the DI.

Kerry coughed as shards of vegetable caught in her throat.

'Fine. Look I've just had contact from Raffique Khan's lawyer.'

The DI groaned. 'Lilly Valentine.'

'Imprinted on your brain, is she?' Kerry smirked.

'Not an easy woman to forget.'

Kerry wiped her lips with the back of her hand and inspected the orange stain.

'What did she want?' asked the DI.

'To know whether you've located the victim's boy-friend.'

The DI laughed but sounded pissed off. 'Trying to pin it on him, is she?'

'I should think so,' said Kerry.

'Well, whoever he is, he's gone AWOL,' said the DI. 'None of the dead girl's friends or family even knew she *had* a boyfriend, never mind who he was.'

'You need to find out,' said Kerry.

'The investigation is over,' said the DI.

'Trust me, you should pursue this.' Kerry reached into her mouth with her pinky and scraped at a molar. 'Valentine will.'

She extracted a piece of carrot and flicked it away. She had covered all her bases.

DI Bell breathed in through his nose and out through his mouth, forcing himself to unclench his teeth and buttocks.

He absolutely would not allow Lilly Valentine – or any other defence lawyer, for that matter – to dictate the agenda. This was his case and he was in control. Raffique Khan had killed his sister, end of story. The case would go to court and the overwhelming evidence would secure his conviction. Bell would be lauded for his single-minded approach.

'It was difficult,' he would tell reporters, 'but justice must prevail, whatever the sex or race of the victim.'

He would pause at this point, make sure the cameras got his best side.

'I will not rest until these so-called honour attacks are a thing of the past.'

He smiled, imagining the headlines describing him as the, 'Honour Killings Tsar.'

They'd mention the old man, of course, detailing his meteoric rise through the ranks. His commendations for bravery would be listed and they would note how he had been set to become the youngest Chief of Police in history before his tragic death. But the final line would be saved for Bell himself, and how he superseded his father's illustrious career.

He stopped his reverie in its tracks. Kerry Thomson had been very sure that Valentine would pursue the boyfriend angle. What if she were able to sow even a tiny seed of doubt in the minds of the jurors? Or worse, what if she were able to criticise Bell for not investigating?

He frowned. People these days were so woolly and liberal, always so quick to find fault with the Force. A not guilty verdict in a case like this would do irreparable harm to his plans.

He nodded to himself, as it became clear what to do. He would head Valentine off at the pass.

**To: Dr Cheney**
**From: DI Bell**
**R V Raffique Khan**
**I note from your autopsy report that Yasmeen Khan was pregnant at the time of her death. We are keen to discover the identity of the father.**

**Could you please conduct a DNA test and run the results through the data base for a potential match.**

**This is a long shot, and I don't expect a match, but we must cover all bases on this one.**

\*   \*   \*

Aasha packs her school rucksack, throws it over her shoulder and starts to clatter down the stairs. She's got five minutes to catch the bus. She doesn't want to go to school but can't face another day in bed.

Imran appears at the bottom. 'Where did you go last night?'

'Nowhere.'

'Stop messing me about, Ash,' he snarls. 'Where did you go?'

Aasha stands her ground, halfway down the stairs, but she's nervous. She can see her brother's naked aggression. If Mum were here, she would defuse his anger. But she's not, is she? Everyone is out, leaving just Aasha and Imran's fury.

'Nowhere,' she repeats mechanically.

Out of the blue, Imran punches the wall and Aasha flinches.

'Tell me where you went,' he shouts.

Aasha's heart is pounding. Her brothers have never hurt her but she's never disobeyed them. Looking now at Imran's teeth, bared like a dog's, she feels frightened.

'I went to Lailla's,' she whispers. 'I needed to catch up on what I missed yesterday.'

'You'd better not be lying to me.'

Aasha gulps back her panic. 'I'm not lying.'

'What's her number?' He whips out his phone from his back pocket. 'I'll call her right now.'

Aasha can hardly breathe. Will Lailla cover for her?

'I don't remember her number.'

He jerks his head towards her rucksack. 'It'll be on your mobile.'

Aasha doesn't know what to do. If she gives him Lailla's number she can't be sure what Lailla will say. Lailla might be many things, but quick-witted isn't one of them.

'It's not on my mobile,' she says.

He holds out his hand. 'Just give it to me.'

She can't hand it over. What if he checks it? He'll find Ryan in her contacts, his number marked with a little heart.

'It's on my laptop,' she says.

'What?'

'I transferred all my contacts to the address book on my laptop.' If she gives him a moment to think about it he will realise this is a ridiculous lie. Instead she sprints back up to her room. 'I'll get it,' she calls over her shoulder.

Once in her room she shuts the door and leans her back against it. She feels sick with fear. How long does she have before Imran comes barging in?

Tears sting Aasha's eyes. It's all so unfair. She's done nothing wrong. She's a good girl.

'I'm warning you, Ash,' Imran's voice is sharp, 'don't vex me.'

She bites her knuckle to keep back a sob. She has to get out of there.

She runs to her window and looks wildly out. Her room is directly above the porch, its roof ten feet below. She can jump onto it and then down to the garden. Her hands shake as she opens the window. If she slips she might break her leg. Or worse.

'Ash,' Imran barks, 'don't make me come up there.'

She leans out. It seems such a long way and the porch roof is narrow.

She hears her brother swear, then the steady plod of his footfall as he ascends the stairs.

What scares her most? Her brother, or falling to the ground? Imran's footsteps are near the top. Definitely her brother.

She swings her legs over her windowsill so she is sitting on the ledge.

He's at her door. 'You are so going to regret this.'

She lets herself drop.

Her stomach rises to meet her mouth as she falls, but nausea gives way to terror as she lands on the porch roof and lurches forward. She throws out her hand to steady herself, trying desperately to gain her balance.

When she feels steady on her feet she gulps a lungful of air and wills herself to take the next step. The patio looks hard. She's been to enough science lessons to know she could kill herself if she lands badly.

'What the fuck?'

Aasha looks up. Imran is leaning out of the window, his face contorted by disbelief and venom.

'Are you mental?' he shouts.

She looks down at the patio, back up to Imran. Maybe she is mental. She certainly feels it.

She jumps.

The concrete rushes up to meet her and she jars her knees as she lands. Her hands are pushed forward, the skin scraping away. She groans in pain but knows she has no time to stop. She jumps to her feet and races across the lawn to the road. It will take her brother only seconds to leap downstairs and out of the house so she tears away, her hair flying behind her like banners.

She whips down the road, her mind whirling as fast as her feet. Where should she go?

Panting, she checks behind her. She can see Imran in the distance. He's a long way behind, but if she can see him, then he can see her. And he's fast. And fit. All those hours in the gym with Ismail and their mates.

She can't keep running much longer. Where should she go?

At the top of the street a bus pulls into the stop. The last passenger, some old man shuffling in his socks and sandals, clutching a Lidl carrier bag, climbs on. The driver puts on his indicator.

Aasha digs deep and finds enough energy to propel herself towards the bus. The automatic doors are just closing with an airy hiss when she slams her body into them. She glances behind her. Imran is gaining on her – she can see the look of pure hatred on his face.

She beats on the door with both palms. 'Please,' she shrieks, 'let me on.'

The driver rolls his eyes.

'Please.'

He opens the doors and Aasha falls inside.

'I wish mine were as keen to get to school,' he laughs.

She feels in her trousers for her bus pass, waves it at him and flees to the back seat.

Aasha looks out of the window for Imran. He is less than fifty metres away when the bus pulls out. Their eyes lock and he mouths something.

She doesn't catch the words but she knows exactly what he means.

Lilly glugged a mouthful of Gaviscon straight from the bottle. It was thick, sweet and chalky, like cold school-dinner custard. She tried not to gag and berated herself for wolfing chocolate so soon after a breakfast most people would consider greedy. She rubbed her breast-bone and took another swig.

'I've been thinking,' said Taslima.

Lilly burped unhappily. 'Thank God one of us still has a brain that functions.'

'Yasmeen's killer doesn't have to be the boyfriend,' said Taslima.

'Statistically murders are committed by those close to the victim,' said Lilly. 'And we know the killer not only got in the house without a struggle, but managed to poison Yasmeen's drink without arousing suspicion.'

'But someone else could easily have done both those things,' said Taslima.

Lilly nodded. 'Someone like Raffy.'

'Or any other member of her family.'

Lilly thought for a second. If this was an honour killing, like everyone seemed to think, then why did it have to be Raffy?

'I see where you're coming from,' she said. 'But Anwar doesn't seem likely.'

'Why? Because he's quiet and well spoken?' Taslima asked. 'That doesn't mean he isn't backwardly traditional.'

Lilly considered for a second. 'I suppose he is the head of the family since his father died.'

'And he seems to take that responsibility very seriously, no?'

'Yes, he does,' Lilly agreed, 'but I don't know whether that would stretch to murder.'

'Didn't you say there was an uncle?' asked Taslima. 'Would he be capable of something like this?'

Lilly had to admit she had been uncomfortable around Mohamed Aziz from the word go. His involvement with the Khans seemed to go far beyond avuncular duty, and he was domineering and bombastic. His demands to have Yasmeen's body returned seemed nothing to do with religion.

'There was something about him I didn't like,' said Lilly. 'His attitude to women seemed disturbing.'

Taslima clapped her hands.

'Hold on,' said Lilly. 'It's still far more likely to be Raffy or the boyfriend.'

'But we should check the uncle out, right?'

Lilly threw her car keys at Taslima. 'Saddle up, Tonto.'


Ryan's head is about to explode. He covers his ears with his hands but the ringing of the doorbell continues.

At first he tried to ignore it but someone has their finger on it and won't take it off. His mum wouldn't dare answer it but it looks like he's going to have to.

If it's that fucking copper he can jog on. He'll have to come back with a whole army, 'cos there's no way he's getting in, warrant or no warrant.

Whoever it is they're now hammering with their fist as well as ringing.

By the time he gets to the door he's seething with

163

fury, ready to punch the face of whoever it is outside. He's never been one to carry a shank, which is a good job, because he'd be tempted to cut whoever it is right there on the doorstep.

He yanks the door open and it hits the wall behind, sending plaster into the air.

'What the fuck do you want?'

When he sees who's standing there, and the state she's in, he's floored.

'Aasha?'

Tears are pouring down her cheeks and her shoulders jerk up and down between sobs. Her hands are covered in blood and dirt.

'What's happened?' he asked.

'I'm sorry,' her voice is raw, 'I didn't know where else to go.'

Ryan can feel panic starting in his stomach. There's no way he can let her in.

'What do you want?' he asks.

She shakes her head, sort of wild and out of control. 'I don't know.'

'Why are you here?'

'My brother's going to kill me,' she says.

Ryan's heard enough from Lailla about Aasha's brothers to know this might be true.

Aasha puts her hands on her knees and bows her head. 'I think I'm going to be sick.'

Ryan's heart is beating fast, like he's coming up on a pill. He doesn't know what to do.

Aasha, still bent forward, looks up at him, her eyes huge and sad. 'Please let me in, Ryan.'

What can he do? What can he say?

'I'm a bit busy,' is all he can offer.

'Please,' she whispers.

He grunts and pulls her inside. He takes her through to the kitchen and she flops into one of the chairs. He lets the tap run cold and fills a cup for her. She takes it in both hands and sips it.

He hopes he can calm her down a bit and send her on her way.

She takes another sip.

'You can't stay here,' he says.

Suddenly her shoulders bunch up and she puts her hand to her mouth. Sick seeps through her fingers and there's that horrible acidic smell in the air.

'Fuck's sake,' Ryan growls, and pushes Aasha to the bathroom.

He stands outside and listens to her throw up. This is total shit.

He can feel the anger rising in him, burning him from the inside out. What does she think she's doing, coming to his yard, banging on the door, puking all over the place?

'You done?' he shouts.

At last she opens the door, her eyes still wide and full of tears.

'Ryan,' her voice is all wobbly.

'Yeah.'

'Why is there blood in the bathroom?'

'What?'

'There's loads of blood and tissues all over the bathroom,' says Aasha.

They stare at each other, neither of them moving.

'Ryan?' she murmurs.

He shoves Aasha out of the way. There are splashes of blood all over the sink and bath.

'No, no, no.' His head is spinning. He races to his mum's bedroom. Aasha is running after him but he doesn't look at her.

The bedroom is in darkness but he can smell it. He bangs on the light switch with his fist and hears Aasha's scream behind him. His mum is curled, face down, on the bed, naked. The sheets under her are covered in blood.

'Mum,' he howls, and drags her onto her back.

There are cuts across her stomach, at least five of them.

'I'll call an ambulance,' Aasha says.

'No.' Ryan puts up his hand. 'It's not as bad as it looks.'

'What are you talking about, Ryan?' says Aasha. 'She needs a doctor.'

Ryan shakes his head. 'This happens all the time.'

Then he gets to work.

An hour later, Ryan's cleaned up his mum, dressed the cuts and put her to bed.

He shoves the sodden sheets in the washing machine and slams the door. He daren't look at Aasha.

'How long has this been going on?' she asks.

He still doesn't look at her; can't look at her.

'Ryan?' She takes his hand.

'I dunno,' he shrugs. 'Since my dad left.'

She still has his hand in hers. It feels surprisingly firm.

'You look after her?' Aasha asks incredulously.

'There ain't no one else.'

'Why did you never tell anyone?' she says. 'Ask for some help?'

He flashes her an angry look. 'From who?'

'School, social services, anyone.'

He snatches back his hand. 'They'd say she's not fit to look after me, stick me in care.'

'You could have told me.' Aasha takes a step towards him.

Ryan bites his lip, afraid he might cry.

She takes another step nearer and he can smell her lotion, like a Bounty or something. Then she puts her arms around his waist and pulls him against her. He breathes her in, leaning into her, resting his head on her shoulder.

'I'm just so tired of it,' he says.

'Shush,' she whispers into his hair. 'I'm here now.'


Lilly and Taslima navigated the High Street in Bury Park and pulled over outside Paradise Halal Butchers.

Orange nets of onions were piled high beside the doorway, together with cardboard boxes filled with knobbly roots of ginger and wicked-looking green chillies.

They followed a delivery man inside, his tray of chicken breasts quivering like pink jellyfish.

Mohamed Aziz wiped his hands down his stiff white apron and rattled a gunfire of orders in Urdu. The delivery man tried to respond but Mohamed let off another volley.

Mohamed Aziz was every bit as unpleasant as Lilly remembered.

As they waited for him to finish Lilly tried not to breathe in the flesh stench of row upon row of dead carcasses. Instead she distracted herself with the packets of spices lined upon a shelf. The rust red of paprika and the sulphur yellow of turmeric screamed for attention among the burnt-brown cumin seeds.

'Miss Valentine,' Mohamed greeted her at last, 'what can I do for you?'

'We'd like to speak to you about your relationship with Yasmeen,' she said.

'Relationship?' Mohamed spoke quickly. Too quickly. 'What are you implying?'

Lilly opened her palms. 'Only that between uncle and niece.'

Mohamed appraised Lilly openly, taking in every inch of her.

'Follow me,' he muttered, and disappeared into the back of the shop.

Taslima leaned in to Lilly and whispered, 'A regular happy camper.'

They followed Mohamed into a room at the rear. He closed the door behind them, sealing in the smell of raw meat that clung to his skin and clothes.

'What is it you want to know?'

'I just wondered how close you were to Yasmeen,' Lilly smiled.

Mohamed didn't smile back. 'She was a member of my family.'

Lilly nodded and kept her body language relaxed.

'And what exactly is your relationship with the Khans? Are you Mrs Khan's brother?'

Something flitted across Mohamed's eyes. Anger? Suspicion?

'As I'm sure your colleague will tell you,' he gestured to Taslima, 'Asian families include extended members.'

'So you're not actually their uncle?' Lilly asked.

Mohamed narrowed his eyes. 'I was a close friend of their late father.'

'So no relation at all, then?'

'Does this have anything at all to do with Raffique's defence?' Mohamed snapped.

'Absolutely,' Lilly replied.

Their eyes locked together and Lilly tried to read everything she could. She had been close enough to touch murderers before, to taste their depravity. She could sense Mohamed's distaste for her, his fury at her questions, but did that make him a killer?

'One last thing,' Lilly said. 'Did you speak to Yasmeen on the day she died?'

Mohamed didn't miss a beat. 'No.'

He led them back to the shop floor and picked up a meat cleaver, which he wielded over a leg of lamb. Clearly Lilly and Taslima were to show themselves out.

When they got to the door, Lilly spun on her heel.

'Are you sure Yasmeen didn't call you on the day she died?'

The cleaver hovered inches from Mohamed's face. Lilly watched the blade glint.

'I'm sure the telephone records show that she did,' she added.

Mohamed brought the cleaver down with a violent, yet precise stroke, which cut through the flesh and the bone cleanly.

'I remember now,' he said. 'She wanted to know if I had any work for her in the shop.'

Once outside, Lilly gratefully took a gulp of fresh air.

There was something very wrong about Mohamed Aziz.

Jack kicked the leg of his desk and scanned his inbox once more. He was restless and couldn't settle to anything. He checked his mobile, gave a theatrical huff and sauntered over to the kettle.

A PC with more forehead than face poured boiling water over a Pot Noodle. The air filled with the salt breeze of dried pork.

'That stuff will kill you,' said Jack.

The PC ripped the plastic packet of sauce with his teeth and stirred it through until every noodle was coated with MSG.

'We've all got to die sometime,' he said.

Jack popped a teabag into his mug. Green tea with lemon peel. Packed with antioxidants.

The PC wagged his fork. 'Now that really will kill you.'

Jack ignored him and sipped his tea.

A sergeant poked his head around the door. 'Who's free?' he asked.

The PC wiped his greasy lips. 'I'm having my lunch, Serg.'

'Tough. There's a family here, saying their daughter's done a runner.'

The PC groaned. 'Have they checked with her mates?'

'No one's seen her,' said the sergeant. 'They think she might be with some scrote called Ryan Sanders.'

Jack spat out his tea.

'I told you that stuff was lethal,' said the PC.

Jack patted him on the back. 'Enjoy your gourmet meal for one. I'll deal with this.'

Mrs Hassan handed Jack a plate of carrot halwa, so sticky just the sight of it made his teeth ache. He smiled politely and put it down.

Her eyes flitted to the window and back again. Her husband's foot tapped restlessly, his face etched with worry. In contrast, their teenaged sons slumped on the sofa, their legs hanging over the ends.

'You say Aasha's never done anything like this before?' asked Jack.

Mrs Hassan rubbed her nose with a tissue and shook her head.

'She's a very good girl,' said Mr Hassan.

The older of the two boys kissed his teeth.

Mr Hassan frowned at him. 'She goes to school and comes home.'

Jack nodded, wondering what sort of fifteen-year-old girl didn't hang out with friends.

'The report mentioned something about Ryan Sanders,' said Jack.

Mr Hassan threw up his hands. 'We've never even heard of him.'

'So what makes you think Aasha might be with him?' asked Jack.

'My sons checked her laptop,' Mr Hassan's voice dropped, 'and it seems she has been in regular contact with him.'

'Boyfriend?' asked Jack.

Mr Hassan narrowed his eyes. 'Aasha is not allowed boyfriends.'

The older boy gave a low grunt. Clearly there were differences of opinion in the Hassan household.

Jack imagined the sweet, beautiful girl smiling out at him from the school photograph they had given him with one of the nastiest little toerags he had met in a long time. The girl was obviously very sheltered, easily taken in by someone with street smarts like Ryan. It made Jack's blood boil.

'You must go to this Ryan Sanders and bring her home,' said Mr Hassan.

'It's not that straightforward,' said Jack.

'Surely you can go to your police data base and find out where he lives.'

Jack gave a tight-lipped smile.

'I told them that you wouldn't do anything,' the older boy sneered at Jack from the sofa. 'I said we should sort this ourselves.'

Jack's back straightened. 'I wouldn't recommend that.'

The boys looked at one another.

'Taking the law into your own hands will only result in trouble,' said Jack.

Mrs Hassan let out a low moan and buried her face in her tissue.

'No-one is taking the law into their hands,' Mr Hassan spoke as much to his sons as to Jack.

They stared at their father, the challenge dancing in their eyes.

'Am I the head of this household?' he asked.

Time seemed to stretch until the elder nodded and the younger returned to swinging his leg.

Mr Hassan turned to Jack. 'Just bring my daughter back.'

'I'll do my best,' said Jack.


'Why are these young men so angry?' Lilly asked Taslima as they drove back to her office.

They had been to Arlington on another legal visit and though Raffy managed to rein in his rudeness to Lilly, he was hardly co-operative.

When she'd told him the plan to try to pin Yasmeen's murder on someone else he had snorted in derision.

'It's a cut-and-dried case as far as the police are concerned.'

'Lucky for you I don't work for the police,' said Lilly.

He'd shaken his head as if she didn't understand, could never hope to understand.

'We think whoever did kill your sister must have been very close to her,' Lilly ventured. 'Maybe her boyfriend.'

Raffy visibly cringed at the mere mention of his existence.

'Or a family member,' she added.

Raffy became motionless, listening intently.

'Someone could have found out about her relationship,' she said.

Raffy remained still, appearing not even to breathe. What was he thinking? That she might be right?

'So we wondered if your uncle Mohamed could have had anything to do with it.'

Lilly watched her client intensely. He blinked slowly, as if turning the idea over in his mind.

'Could he have had anything to do with the PTF?' asked Lilly.

Raffy roared with laughter. 'Uncle Mo?' he spluttered. 'A hard-line radical?'

'He strikes me as very traditional,' said Lilly.

Raffy stopped laughing as quickly as he started and anger re-established itself.

'He's a pussy.'

She had been about to argue that during her own discussions with him, the old man had been anything but a pussy, when the skinhead boy from the previous visit sauntered into the room. His body language was loose, shoulders relaxed, head bobbing, and he whistled as he searched for his solicitor. Raffy bristled.

When the skinhead was about to take his seat he grinned at Raffy.

'Ignore him,' said Lilly.

Raffy nodded but didn't take his eyes off the other boy.

Lilly pressed her hand on his. 'He's not worth the aggravation.'

The skinhead lifted his arm to wave at them but at the last second straightened and turned it into a *Sieg Heil*.

Raffy jumped to his feet, his chair clattering behind him.

'You're a dead man,' he screamed. 'You understand me?'

The skinhead laughed at him.

After that Raffy had been unable to concentrate on anything other than his rage. Lilly had ended the visit early.

'I just don't understand,' she said to Taslima, 'where all the hatred comes from?'

'People can only be tolerant of being called a Paki for so long,' Taslima answered. 'You get to a point when you need to fight back.'

'Do you feel that way?' asked Lilly.

'Sometimes.' Taslima shrugged. 'I get tired of justifying myself. When people stare at my hijab I want to ask them if they'd rather see me in a cropped top and a belly ring.'

'Trust me,' said Lilly, 'I haven't put my belly on public display since I was ten.'

Taslima laughed and nodded at Lilly's bump. 'I can see more than enough, thank you.'

Lilly was about to feign a wounded expression when her mobile rang.

'Mrs Valentine?'

'Miss,' said Lilly.

The caller was a man, his accent clipped. 'That's right, you don't use your married name.'

'That's because I'm not married,' said Lilly. 'Look, who is this please?'

'Mr Latimer,' he said. 'I believe you wanted to speak to me urgently.'

Realisation dawned. It was Sam's head teacher.

'That's right,' she said. 'I'm worried about my son.'

'Indeed?'

'Yes, he seems tense,' she said. 'I understand there has been some bullying at school.'

'I'm not fond of that word,' said Mr Latimer, 'but there have been some recent problems.'

'And Sam's involved?'

'It would appear so.'

Lilly's heart thumped. Sam was being picked on by older boys. What were they doing? Pushing him around, stealing his lunch? Calling him vile names? Whatever it was it was enough to put Sam off going in at all.

'What do you plan to do?' she asked.

'I think you should come in to see me,' said Mr Latimer.

Taslima pulled up outside the office. 'What on earth is he up to?' She pointed at a man peering in the office window, taking photographs with a small camera.

Lilly frowned. 'I have to go, Mr Latimer. I'll call in tomorrow.'

She wound down her window. 'Can I ask what you're doing?' she called to the potential intruder.

The man turned to the Mini and slid his camera into the breast pocket of his jacket. Lilly could see his cuffs were grubby and worn.

'Do I need to call the police?' she asked.

The man smiled at her, revealing the brown, uneven teeth of a heavy smoker. 'I don't think that's necessary,' he wheezed.

'Then answer my first question,' said Lilly. 'What are you doing?'

He leered at Lilly. 'The estate agents sent me to take a few pictures.'

'What estate agent?' Lilly narrowed her eyes.

The man waved vaguely down the road. 'On the High Street.'

'I don't know anything about it,' said Lilly.

'I can see that,' the man chuckled. 'Truth be told, I thought I might have the wrong place when I saw it was all locked up.'

Lilly stared at him.

'No harm done,' he said. 'I'll be on my way.'

Lilly watched him meander away, telling herself that it was just as the man said, a misunderstanding. She had nothing to worry about. She was being paranoid.

Mark Cormack waited ten minutes before returning to his car. When the solicitor caught him he'd come out with a load of old rubbish and she hadn't bought a word of it.

He didn't want her noting down his number plate and getting some contact at the DVLA working out who he was.

They were like that, these legal types, friends in high places and all that.

When he was sure the women were gone he pulled out his packet of Benson & Hedges. Some muppet had told him that having fags with him would help him give up. Something about craving what you couldn't have. It was bollocks. If you had 'em, you smoked 'em. Simple as. He lit one up and took a deep, appreciative lungful of smoke before driving back to his office.

Now he knew where the woman lived and worked. Job done.

* * *

177

Ryan lies next to Aasha and watches her sleep. He daren't move a muscle in case he disturbs her, which is quite an achievement on his single bed.

Her chest lifts up and down as she breathes and Ryan copies her, taking in the air at the exact same time as her, then letting it out again.

Their hands are entwined. His white, hers lush brown. They could be on some sort of poster. He'll paint it one day and sell, like, a million copies. Then he and his mum can move out of the Clayhill and he'll pay someone to do the cooking and washing and that.

Ryan smiles. He hasn't felt this calm for the longest time. Probably not since his dad said he was going for a packet of fags and never came back. Before that, his mum had always been a bit edgy, hardly ever leaving the flat, taking to her bed on bad days. Ryan hadn't worried about it too much. He'd left it to his dad and done what other kids do: went to school; played football. Once it was just the two of them, his mum went downhill fast. Ryan doesn't play football any more. He keeps a baseball bat by his bed but it's not for a game with his mates.

If he goes out she won't eat or get washed, just waits for him to get back. Sometimes he has to, like for school and stuff, but then he just spends the whole time wondering what he'll be coming home to. When she goes through phases of cutting he just bunks off and stays indoors, bricking it that one day she'll cut too deep.

Some days he feels like going to the shops and never coming back, but then he'd be just as much of a cunt as his dad.

Aasha thinks he should tell someone at school about his mum. She says they'll help him and that at his age they won't put him in care.

'And if they did you'd just get the bus home.'

She knows he's scared but she doesn't take the piss. Instead she says she'll go with him, that they can talk to Mrs Blake together.

He leans over Aasha's face. Her skin is totally clear, no spots, not even any freckles. It's like a mirror or one of the blank canvases he loves. Sometimes he nicks paper from school so he can draw at home. He thinks Miss Black might know but she don't seem to care. When he puts them on the table they're completely fresh, waiting to suck up his imagination.

He looks at her lips and would love to kiss her, but he's afraid to wake her and spoil this fantastic moment. It'd be like breaking some spell. He wonders if he just grazes her lips with his own, she might sleep through it.

He hovers over her, his mouth millimetres from hers.

When the doorbell sounds he jumps back like a kid caught stealing biscuits. Aasha stirs but doesn't wake, so he prises away his hand as gently as he can and sprints for the door. This had better be fucking urgent.

When he sees the copper standing there Ryan could cheerfully smack him one. Why is this man in his face again?

'What do you want?' he asks.

'Nice to see you too.'

The copper has some weird accent, like maybe he's Scottish or something. He's wearing some Sean John jeans and Timberlands, thinking they make him look young.

'My mum ain't in,' says Ryan.

'No worries,' the copper says. 'I'm looking for a girl.'

'Perv.'

The copper gives a small laugh through his nose to show he's got a sense of humour. They all do it. They think it makes them seem friendly, or whatever. Like they're a mate. Pathetic, really.

'Her name's Aasha Hassan,' he says.

Ryan feels a small shockwave in his stomach. How has he worked out she's here?

'I ain't seen her,' he says.

The copper nods slowly but doesn't take his eyes off Ryan's face. He's trying to work out if he's telling the truth. Ryan doesn't blink. He knows how to lie.

'If you see her be sure to tell her to get in touch,' the copper says.

'I'll do that,' says Ryan, and closes the door.

The little shit was lying, of that Jack was certain. He knew exactly where the girl was hiding. She might even be inside the flat.

He needed to speak to the chief super and get permission to enter. There was nothing stopping him doing it off his own bat right now. He surely had reasonable suspicion. But there was no way Ryan would let him in and kicking the door off its hinges, only to discover Aasha wasn't there, didn't appeal. Ryan was just the type to start a case against him, say he was traumatised. Kids like that knew the law inside and out and they could smell a claim for compensation a mile away.

No, this one would need the belt-and-braces approach with the nod from a senior officer.

Jack looked at his watch. The chief would still be at the nick and might be prepared to deal with this over the phone. If backup came quickly they could have the girl home for supper.

She might even drop Ryan in it, give Jack cause to nab him. Now wouldn't that finish the day off beautifully?

He was salivating at the thought of sticking the little shit in a cell when his mobile rang.

'Hello, Jack.'

Jack was pleased to hear Mara's voice. The way things were working out with Ryan wasn't exactly what she'd planned but Jack was sure she'd understand. They'd tried to give the kid a hand but he'd refused to take it. This mess was entirely of his own making.

'I'm afraid there've been some developments,' he said.

'Oh dear,' she breathed. 'Should we meet to discuss it?'

Jack looked at his watch again. Come to think of it, the chief super would be on his way out and wouldn't welcome a half-cocked request. Far better if Jack went to his office in person, first thing in the morning, and set out the situation in detail.

'That would be really helpful,' he said.

'Why don't I make you some supper?' Mara suggested.

Jack paused. Enjoying Mara's attention was one thing, but going to her home was another. Lilly was an easy-going kind of woman but he was sure she'd draw the line at a cosy night in. And with a baby on the way shouldn't Jack be spending all his free time trying to patch things up with Lilly, not making them worse?

Then again, Lilly didn't seem to care too much these days whatever Jack said or did. She fought him at every turn.

'Jack?'

Supper at Mara's house was stepping over the line.

'That would be grand,' he said.

# Chapter Six

January 2009

'From the river to the sea, Palestine will be free.'

The crowd chants the same words over and over, the effect intoxicating.

I smile at Yasmeen and we join in.

When she asked if she could come to the demonstration I resisted. These events are small but hard core. I'm known as a radical, an uncompromising Islamist, and I don't want my reputation spoiled by association with some giggling girl.

We walk up Kensington High Street to the Israeli Embassy and I nod at a sister from the East London Mosque. She is pushing a buggy, the baby smiling out under his I ♥ Al-Qaeda bonnet.

There are rumours that her husband has gone to Gaza to help with the struggle.

'*Assalamu alaikum*,' she says.

I swell with pride that she has deigned to speak to me. '*Wa alaikum assalaam*, sister.'

She moves ahead to catch up with a group of women

in full burka and they unfurl a ten-foot banner declaring, 'We are all Hezbollah.'

I can tell Yasmeen is impressed by the way she adjusts her hijab. I smile secretly. She is learning.

When we reach Palace Green we form a ragged crowd and a group of young men wearing long linen tunics over their jeans and trainers push to the front where they begin to pile up wooden boxes.

'What are they doing?' Yasmeen whispers.

'Erecting a stand,' I say, 'then we'll take it in turns to speak.'

Yasmeen looks shocked. 'Will you speak?'

'I might.'

In truth I stand up at most meetings I attend at the mosque but I've never had the courage to do it on a demo. I worry that my mind will go blank.

When the makeshift platform is ready, one of the men climbs up. He puts a loud hailer to his mouth.

'The State of Israel has turned into the new Nazis,' he shouts.

The crowd claps.

Someone passes up a Palestinian flag and he waves it in exaggerated strokes. Over the green, white and black stripes someone has stitched a swastika and a Star of David.

'Bomb, bomb, USA,' he chants. 'Bomb, bomb, UK.'

We soon take it up.

'Can they hear us inside?' Yasmeen asks.

'*En sh' Allah*,' I answer.

The young men take their turns with the megaphone until it becomes clear that people have begun to talk among themselves.

'Morning, Comrades.'

Yasmeen and I turn to a white man with unbrushed hair and an earring. He's wearing a T-shirt depicting George Bush in a skull cap. I've seen him before selling copies of *Socialism Today*.

I wave away his offer of a leaflet but he presses it into Yasmeen's hand with what he no doubt believes is a cheeky grin.

'Thank you,' she smiles back at him.

'The pleasure is mine,' he says.

I stare hard at him, making it clear his presence is not welcome, until he moves on.

Yasmeen takes a glance at the leaflet.

'Bin it,' I say.

'Why?'

'It's communist progaganda.'

Yasmeen frowns. 'But isn't everyone here on the same side?'

I smile patiently. She still has a lot to learn.

'The hard left support us because they think we are the victims of racism and capitalist oppression.'

'Aren't we?'

'Yes,' I say, 'but the answer is not to turn the whole world into an atheist state.'

Yasmeen pouts. I can tell she's finding this hard to follow.

'So what is the answer?' she asks.

'That we turn our face to Allah,' I say, 'and accept the one true religion.'

\* \* \*

Lilly heaped two spoons of coffee into a mug, then added another.

She'd barely slept all night, snatching twenty minutes here and there between long periods of staring out into the night.

Despite her efforts to reassure herself, the man taking photos of her office had spooked her and she was beginning to wonder if it was more than a coincidence that she'd also seen someone creeping around the cottage with a torch.

Her mother, Elsa, had been a fond of sayings, some traditional, some entirely of her own making. Lilly recalled one of her favourites: 'Just because you're paranoid doesn't mean they're not after you.'

Though a firm pragmatist, Elsa taught her daughter to watch her back.

Lilly replayed the moment when her cottage was firebombed over and over in her mind. She could still see the flash of orange, still smell the smoke.

When Jack finally came home in the early hours he'd slid between the sheets and fallen instantly into a deep sleep.

She was glad he was getting stuck into his work again. He habitually went through periods when he questioned whether there was any point to what he did. And she loathed that.

At these low points it wasn't just the cynicism she balked at but the fact that since she told him she was pregnant Jack redirected all his energy towards her. Lilly just wasn't used to that level of attention and found its glare uncomfortable. She certainly wouldn't confess her unease to Jack or his attention would refocus in a nanosecond.

She stirred her coffee and sipped, watching morning unfold in her garden. The rabbits were out in force, nibbling and crapping, like a scene from *Watership Down*, and a little chaffinch tapped rhythmically on the window with his beak.

She needed to be in court in an hour and a half, and certainly needed a shower beforehand, but she couldn't summon enough energy to rush.

Jack strode into the kitchen, a heady purpose in his step. If he noticed the dark circles under Lilly's eyes he didn't comment.

'Shouldn't you be getting ready?' he asked.

Lilly leaned against the counter. 'I'm psyching myself up.'

'Right.'

He whistled as he poured hot water over a slice of lemon.

Lilly watched him over the rim of her mug.

'I've got to go into school today,' she said. 'Mr Latimer wants to speak to me about Sam.'

'Right,' he repeated.

Was he not going to ask why?

Jack drained his cup and headed to the door. 'See you.'

Obviously not.

Too late she noticed his mobile lying on the counter. It skipped through her mind that she should run after him, but she didn't. She knew her response was linked to his lack of interest.

She wasn't sure exactly how she felt. Though grateful not to be the target of his all encompassing anxiety, she would have liked a small enquiry as to her health. She *was* pregnant, after all. And although Sam wasn't Jack's son, he'd always looked out for him, so his indifference was unsettling. She was being utterly irrational and she knew it. She could put it down to hormones but hadn't she always been this way? She fingered the keys on his phone. He'd probably come back for it.

The chaffinch came knocking again. He hovered briefly, then tap, tap, tap.

Sam had once told Lilly that birds saw their own reflection in the glass and thought it was an interloper.

Lilly knew how they felt: she was a past master at fighting with herself.


Ismail Hassan was nervous. There was a sick feeling in the pit of his stomach, like just before an exam. Or even worse, just before the teacher gave you the results.

He and his elder brother, Imran, were meeting some men in this café on the High Street. They called themselves the PTF and were supposed to be some sort of religious group.

'Are you sure this is a good idea?' Ismail asked.

Imran shook his head, his disgust obvious. 'Do you want to get Aasha back or not?'

Ismail let his arms drop to his sides. Mum had already spoken to Jack McNally – the policeman who came to the house yesterday – and he hadn't even managed to speak to Aasha, let alone bring her home.

Mum had been crying all morning.

Two men arrived and Imran shook their hands.

'*Assalamu alaikum*, brother,' they said in turn.

'*Wa alaikum assalaam*,' Imran responded.

Ismail wondered if he should greet them but the words caught in his throat.

They took the seats across the table and waited. One was much larger than the other, his neck thick, his chest bursting out of his polo shirt. He folded his hands in front of him and Ismail could see scratches crisscrossing his knuckles. The smaller one had a wiry intensity, and a nervous tic in his left eye.

'You want our help?' the bigger man asked.

'We've tried the official route,' said Imran, 'but the police don't want to know.'

The man nodded. 'Why should they care if a Muslim girl disobeys her family?'

Ismail couldn't help think that they didn't seem religious. They looked more like those men you saw outside pubs. Bouncers. He had a very bad feeling about getting them involved.

'They did say they're looking into it,' he ventured.

The man grunted. 'And how long will that take? A week? A month?'

'They didn't say.'

'And in the meantime you're being dishonoured.' The man splayed his fingers on the table. 'We need to deal with this matter ourselves, before she makes a laughing stock of you.'

Imran gave one short nod and the men left.

'I still think we should leave this to the police,' said Ismail.

'You're a fool,' said Imran.

'What if they hurt her?' Ismail asked. 'She's not a bad girl, she's just made a stupid mistake.'

Imran had always expected Aasha to do exactly what he told her and didn't stand for any backchat, but surely he still cared about her. She was their sister, after all.

Imran didn't look at Ismail. 'She needs to be taught a lesson.'

Lilly met Taslima outside court one in Luton Crown Court.

'Looking good,' Taslima grinned.

Lilly glanced down at the buttons of her white shirt straining over her bump. She tried to cover it with her gown but the ends wouldn't meet.

'At least I don't have to wear a wig for full comedy effect.' Her hands went to her hair where a ponytail was disintegrating, tangles of curls escaping on all sides. 'On second thoughts.'

Taslima tapped her hijab. 'Never a bad hair day for us Muslim sisters.'

Lilly laughed until the sight of Kerry Thomson thundering towards them cut her short.

'What are the defence asking for?' she snapped.

'Good morning to you too,' said Lilly.

Kerry wrinkled her nose.

Lilly sighed. 'I want all the unused material.'

'You have it.'

'Are you sure about that?' Lilly asked.

Kerry rolled her eyes and went into court.

Lilly followed and found Saira Khan sitting patiently

at the back of the room, her hands resting neatly in her lap.

'Anwar couldn't come,' she explained, 'and Mum isn't well.'

Lilly smiled kindly. 'It's fine, Saira. I'm sure Raffy will be very glad to see you here.'

Saira gave a stiff nod as if she remained unconvinced.

Lilly felt a wave of sympathy for the girl and her elder brother, both forced to act as unofficial parents.

Judge Francis Chance glided in. He was newly appointed and new to Luton. Lilly hoped that he wouldn't be trying to make a name for himself. Bell's ambition and Kerry's animosity were more than enough to contend with. Lilly shuffled to her place.

'Good morning,' he smiled.

'Good morning,' Lilly smiled back.

'By all means take a seat, Miss Valentine.' The judge waved at her bump.

Excellent. Not only was he reasonable but thoughtful into the bargain. This should be painless.

Kerry made a tutting sound. 'Your Honour, I would like to set this matter down for trial at the Court's earliest opportunity.'

The judge put up his finger. 'Indeed, Miss Thomson, but first I wish to speak to the defendant.'

He took off his glasses. It was an affected gesture, reminiscent of a hundred ITV dramas. But the judge was new so Lilly wouldn't hold it against him.

'Young man,' he frowned at Raffy, 'you should know that this is not the youth court and I will not tolerate any outbursts from you.'

'I didn't say nothing,' said Raffy.

'You do not speak to me except through your solicitor, and if you do not show this Court the respect it deserves I will have you taken back down, do you understand?'

Raffy didn't respond.

'Do you understand, young man?'

Lilly coughed. 'Your Honour just told the defendant not to speak directly.'

'Don't play semantics with me,' the judge ordered. 'Now does your client understand what has been said to him or not?'

Lilly sighed. Her hopes of a reasonable judge had been well and truly dashed. She nodded at Raffy in the dock.

'Fine,' he said, 'I understand.'

'Then let's get on,' said the judge. 'Are there any applications?'

Lilly got to her feet. Somehow it didn't seem appropriate to remain relaxed with Judge Chance. 'I'd like an order for the unused material,' she said.

'Your Honour, she has it,' Kerry sighed.

The judge scowled at Lilly. 'I would encourage you to check all the paperwork beforehand.'

'Naturally I've done that, Your Honour,' she said, biting back a retort.

'Then you'll know it's there,' said Judge Chance. 'I've seen the list myself.'

Lilly took a deep breath. 'Then Your Honour will know that there is no information about any other lines of enquiry.'

'Perhaps there was none,' said the judge.

Lilly shook her head. 'I want to know who else was considered a suspect, who was interviewed.'

'Read my lips, Miss Valentine,' said the judge. 'Perhaps there were no other suspects.'

'Then I want confirmation here and now from the Prosecution that the police made no other investigations.'

The judge glared at her but she wouldn't back down. At last he turned to Kerry.

'Miss Thomson, can you give Miss Valentine the assurances she wants?'

'Not at this very second,' said Kerry. 'I'll get back to her as soon as possible.'

'Not good enough,' said Lilly.

The judge banged his gavel. Another gesture stolen from gritty Sunday night telly and wholly unnecessary in the circumstances.

'I will decide what is and what is not good enough.' He nodded to Kerry. 'Miss Thomson, you have a week.'

Lilly and Taslima descended to the gaol.

'You were good out there,' said Raffy.

'I am good,' said Lilly. 'Bloody good.'

'What do you want it for anyway?' he asked. 'This unused stuff?'

Lilly smiled. 'I want to prove that the police didn't bother looking in to the boyfriend or anyone else because they had already made up their minds.'

'How will that help?'

'I want to show the jury that the police jumped on the latest bandwagon. A Muslim woman was killed so it had to be her brother,' she said. 'They made the evidence fit their theory rather than the other way round.'

Raffy grunted with what could have been appreciation.

'I will do everything in my power to help you,' said Lilly, 'but you have to help yourself.'

'I'll try,' he replied.

She nodded at some cuts on his knuckles. 'So tell me you haven't been fighting.'

He gave a lopsided smile, the first she had ever seen on his face. 'I haven't been fighting.'

Jack hadn't felt this chirpy for as long as he could remember. Dinner at Mara's had been great. Just a simple salmon steak and salad.

'I don't like a heavy meal at night,' she'd said.

Jack couldn't agree more. The pasta frenzies Lilly put together were indigestible after eight. No wonder she was up half the night with heartburn.

They'd discussed Ryan, though he had to admit not for long, then Mara had put on some music. She loved jazz and spoke passionately about Louis Armstrong and Jelly Roll Morton.

When he fell into bed in the early hours, Lilly was fast asleep. Of course, he'd felt guilty but that had soon dissipated this morning at the sight of her sour face. A text from Mara had sealed the deal.

*I enjoyed last night so much. U?*

He bought a fresh fruit salad in Marks and Spencer's and skipped to his desk. He picked out and ate all the mango before dialling the chief super's office to ask for permission to enter Ryan's flat.

'McNally,' the chief barked.

'Could you spare a moment, sir?' asked Jack.

'I can spare ten,' said the chief super. 'Get up here now.'

Jack had expected to have to make his case over the phone. Doing it in person was a bonus. He took the stairs two at a time and rapped on the Chief's door.

'I'm grateful for the time, sir,' he said, but stopped when he saw DI Bell standing at the window. 'Sorry, I'll wait outside.'

The chief beckoned him in. 'For God's sake, man, I've been calling your mobile all morning.'

Jack patted his breast pocket for his phone. It was conspicuous by its absence.

The chief's nostrils flared. 'Tell me what's going on with the Asian girl that disappeared yesterday.'

Jack couldn't imagine how the chief had got to know about it or why a detective on another case needed to be there.

He spoke slowly, not at all sure where this was leading. 'I think she may have run away from home.'

'Do you know where she is now?'

Jack's throat felt dry. 'I have an idea.'

The chief leaned over his desk and glared at Jack. 'And have you acted on this idea of yours?' he asked.

'I went round there, sir,' Jack answered, 'but nothing doing.'

'Then what? You went to the pub and forgot all about it?'

Jack blushed, not least because that adequately summed up his evening.

'I thought it was too late last night, sir, that it would be better to discuss it with you first thing this morning.'

The chief rapped a stubby finger against his watch. 'But it's not first thing, is it?'

Jack thought about the mango with a stab of regret.

'Is an hour going to make that much difference, sir?' he asked.

The chief super threw his hands up in exasperation. 'Can you get through to this idiot?' he asked DI Bell.

DI Bell straightened his silver cufflinks. The word around the nick was that Bell had been transferred from Nottingham under a cloud. He'd been promoted to DI because of his father but he hadn't been able to cut it and had been shunted sideways to Luton.

Jack preferred to give other coppers the benefit of the doubt – he hoped he was right to do so this morning.

'The trouble is, Jack, the girl's family have already been in touch asking what exactly we've been doing,' said Bell.

'I'll speak to them,' said Jack. 'Explain where we're at.'

'I think they already know where we're at,' said DI Bell.

'Bloody nowhere, that's where,' the chief super grunted.

'You can see how this looks,' said DI Bell. 'Particularly given our involvement in the Khan case.'

Jack was lost. 'I don't see the connection.'

The chief super pushed back his chair. It freewheeled away until it crashed into the wall behind.

'Then you're a bloody fool.'

Jack wasn't about to disagree.

'We've been getting criticism for arresting Raffique Khan,' said DI Bell. 'There have been mutterings from some quarters that we failed to check other avenues because the defendant is a Muslim.'

The chief pointed at Jack. 'I should add that those quarters include your girlfriend.'

Jack felt a flush rise up the back of his neck.

'Our CPS rep just had an uncomfortable hour in court with Miss Valentine,' said DI Bell.

The sweat glands on Jack's back began to prickle. 'I don't have any control over what Lilly does or says with regards to her work.'

'That much is obvious,' the chief snapped.

'The point is we cannot be seen to pursue the Muslim community on one hand whilst ignoring their concerns on the other,' said DI Bell.

'I'll call Aasha's parents right now,' Jack blustered. 'Tell them I'm on to it.'

'And then,' the chief bellowed, 'you will go and get their daughter.'

'Do I have permission to enter the property in question?' Jack asked.

The chief was scarlet with temper. 'You're supposed to be a copper, not a bloody schoolboy.'

'Yes, sir,' said Jack, and made a hasty retreat.

He considered popping home for his mobile but decided that would be a very bad idea indeed.

Aasha rinses the cutlery under the cold tap and smiles at Ryan.

At home she feels like Cinderella having to do all the chores and she swallows her resentment as she clears away the table. But this morning she feels only too glad to help.

Ryan has carried a terrible burden for a long time.

His mum is called Carrie and she's mentally ill. She can't look after herself, let alone her son.

Aasha remembers a neighbour who had to be hospitalised after her third baby. People said she tried to smother it but Aasha doesn't think that can be true because she was never put in prison or anything.

Instead they took her to a clinic called Meadowlands and gave her lots of medicine. Imran said everyone there was crazy, that they screamed all night and ate their own turds, but Imran was always saying horrible things. He'd never actually been there.

Aasha wonders if Ryan's mum could get better if the doctors gave her a lot of medicine. Ryan says she's tried every drug in the chemist's but they soon wear off.

This morning Aasha made everyone buttered toast. She took a slice and a cup of tea in to Carrie and laid it gently on her bedside table, just the way her own mum had done for her two days before.

'Are you OK?,' Aasha gestured to Carrie's stomach where she had slashed herself. 'Do you need anything?'

Carrie shook her head.

'I've sent Ryan to the shops for more milk,' said Aasha.

Carrie blinked at her.

'And loo roll,' Aasha laughed.

Carrie winced. 'I'm not very good at all that.' Her voice was hoarse and tiny.

Aasha moved closer and sat gently on the bed. 'You're not very well,' she said.

'I sometimes think Ryan would be better off without me.'

Aasha shook her head. 'He loves you very much, Mrs Sanders. He just needs some help.'

A single tear ran down the older woman's translucent cheek and she turned away.

Aasha got up and crept to the door.

'Thank you,' Carrie whispered to the wall.

Ryan looks up at her now with his lovely grey eyes. It's as if he can see right to the very core of her.

'Let me draw you,' he says.

Aasha laughs. 'Shut up.'

'Seriously.' Ryan grabs a pad and some charcoal. 'Keep totally still.'

She's about to object but his fingers are already flashing across the paper.

'Don't make me look fat and ugly,' she chides.

He doesn't look up from his work. 'That would be impossible.'

As he smudges and shades Aasha knows that this is true happiness. If only she could stretch it like elastic and make it last.

But she knows she can't. Just as Ryan can't look after his mother for ever, nor can Aasha avoid her brothers.

A group of young boys had congregated outside the *madrassa*, chattering excitedly and flicking each other's noses with their copies of the Koran as they waited for their lessons. Lilly and Taslima skirted round them as they walked towards the Paradise Halal Butchers.

'What are you grinning at?' asked Lilly.

Taslima bit her lip. 'I think you finally got somewhere with Raffy.'

199

'About bloody time,' said Lilly.

'All the same, I saw genuine respect in his face,' said Taslima. 'He's decided to co-operate.'

'Which is fine and dandy,' said Lilly, 'except he doesn't have anything useful to tell me.'

Taslima wrinkled her nose. 'Not his fault.'

Lilly sighed. It was of course good news that her client was prepared to put his suspicions aside, but how much better it would be if he could give her some information that would help Lilly formulate his defence.

They paused outside the butchers where Mohamed was putting up a poster in his window.

*Aqeeqah* sacrifice.
£145 per lamb, £250 for two.

'Sacrifice?' asked Lilly.

'The traditional way to give thanks to God for the birth of a child,' said Taslima.

'What's wrong with a quick dunk in a font and a christening bracelet?'

'Nothing,' Taslima laughed. 'But lots of Muslims like to follow the Prophet, peace be upon him, and pay for someone to slaughter an animal.'

'Bloody hell,' said Lilly. 'That's pretty gruesome.'

Taslima laughed again. 'Not really. You give your cash to Uncle Mo, he does the business and the chops are delivered for tea.'

When Mohamed had finished he stepped back to admire his handiwork.

'Bit pricey,' said Lilly, entering the shop.

Mohamed scowled at her. 'This is not some conveyor belt, Miss Valentine.'

Lilly raised her eyebrows. 'I'm just surprised a religious celebration is something you could make money from.'

Mohamed narrowed his eyes at Taslima. 'Young lady, you would do well to find a master less ignorant than this one.'

Taslima's spine stiffened. 'I have no master but Allah.' She tapped the pound sign with her finger. 'Can you say the same?'

'What do you women want?' Mohamed growled.

'Do you know anything about an organisation called the PTF?' asked Lilly.

Mohamed missed a beat, then spoke slowly. 'I do not.'

'Have you ever heard of them?' she asked.

'I have not.'

He regarded both Lilly and Taslima with open animosity then turned away. 'If you'll excuse me I have a business to run,' he said.

Was it really possible that neither Mohamed nor Raffy had any knowledge of the PTF? Kash and Taslima were all too familiar with their actions so why weren't the men of the community? Mohamed was lying, Lilly was sure of it.

'Why will no one talk to us about the PTF?' she called. 'What are you hiding?'

Mohamed shook his head, locked the shop door and pulled down the closed sign.

'I'm not giving up,' Lilly shouted through the glass.

'If I do that Raffique will spend the next twenty years in prison.' She could see Mohamed's outline and could only hope he was listening. 'He's a young frightened boy,' she shouted, 'and he needs my help.'

She cupped her hands above her eyebrows and peered inside. 'Have you ever been to a prison Mr Aziz? They are the most soulless places on earth. Hundreds of prisoners crammed in together like animals. Your lambs might not be on a conveyor belt but the boys at Arlington surely are.'

She saw Mohamed's hand creep towards the lock.

'There are constant fights and beatings,' she added. 'Suicides are not unusual.'

The door opened a few inches. Mohamed remained inside but his voice floated out.

'Come,' he snapped. 'I'll give you five minutes.'

He left the closed sign in place and they made their way to the back room.

Lilly could see that the man's fury was spent. In its place was a weariness that aged him ten years.

'It didn't used to be like this,' he said. 'My generation were good, law-abiding people. We knew the meaning of the word respect.'

He reminded Lilly of her nan, who had shaken her laquered head in disgust at everything that happened after 1970. She used to speak fondly of painting her legs with gravy browning during the war – conveniently forgetting the thousands killed in the Blitz.

'These young folk care nothing for the sacrifices we made to come here.' Mohamed shook his head. 'Do you know I came to England with ten pounds in my pocket?'

Lilly had no idea where he was leading but experience taught her to let him continue. She nodded in encouragement.

'We tried to fit in, assimilate, as they say. We ignored the racists,' he continued, 'because we knew once this country saw what we had to offer they would accept us, that everything would open up for our children.'

Taslima looked as if she were about to speak but Lilly nudged her foot. There was a fundamental sadness emanating from Mohamed, but it could so easily return to anger with one wrong word.

'But what do they do?' said Mohamed. 'They throw it in our faces, too busy joining their gangs to apply for medical school.'

'You mean the PTF?' asked Lilly.

Mohamed wiped the back of his hand across his brow as if it contained a lifetime's toil. 'We don't speak the names.'

'Why not?' asked Lilly.

Mohamed circled his arm to encompass the room. 'This place might not look like much to you, but it's all I have.'

Something switched on in Lilly's brain. Mohamed was frightened. She had thought he was hiding something, that he supported the PTF, but now she realised he was frightened of them.

'Can you tell us anything about them?' she asked.

Mohamed shook his head but it was in weariness, not denial.

'If Raffy is to stand any chance, I need some information,' said Lilly. 'Nothing will lead back to you.'

Mohamed gave a small, humourless laugh. 'Do you think they are stupid?'

Lilly knew he was right and that it wouldn't take a genius to figure out who had spoken to her about the PTF, but she needed some help here.

'Think of Raffy.' She let the words hang in the air and didn't breathe.

The three of them stood in silence.

At last Mohamed exhaled. 'I hear things.'

'What sort of things?' asked Lilly.

'Not details,' he said.

Lilly swallowed her impatience and waited.

'They have been involved in putting pressure on some girls around here,' he said.

Taslima coughed and Lilly kicked her.

'Was *pressure* applied to Yasmeen?' she asked.

Mohamed sighed. 'I don't know, really I don't.'

Lilly believed him.

'Do you have any names?' she asked.

He looked at Lilly with heavy lids and again she waited.

'Abdul Malik,' he said. 'He delivers the chicken.'

Jack was still smarting when he arrived at the Clayhill Estate.

He'd left Northern Ireland to get away from all the bloody politics and now found himself in the midst of a sectarian war of a different kind.

Between worrying what this community or that newspaper would make of things, an honest copper couldn't get his job done.

Maybe he was an eejit not to have called the chief super last night, but it wasn't as if the senior officer cared less what happened to the girl. He was far more bothered about a whiff of bad publicity.

He slammed the car door shut and crossed the park. The glue sniffers were in their usual spot.

'Why aren't you lot in school?' he growled.

One of the boys looked up, his jaw slack.

'Have you no self-respect?' Jack shouted. 'Now go on, piss off.'

They stumbled away to find another rock to hide under.

As for Ryan Sanders, Jack wished he'd never laid eyes on the little shitbag. He was a nothing, a nobody, causing heartache and mayhem until one day he took up his rightful place in Arlington.

He climbed the stairs to the fourth floor. The place had its habitual stench and was covered in rubbish. He kicked a carton of chips across the stairwell. These people were animals. Chips and ketchup scattered across the concrete. Then Jack realised it wasn't ketchup, but blood.

No doubt some kids had been fighting. Would anyone have called the police? Not likely. They'd be in accident and emergency right now, having their heads stitched and swearing they'd had an accident on the swings.

By the time he reached the Sanders flat, Jack was furious. He would march in there and demand to see Aasha. If Ryan gave him any lip, Jack would slap him in handcuffs and if his face just so happened to scrape against the wall, then so be it.

He pulled back his fist and hammered as hard as he could on the door.

When it opened under the pressure Jack was taken aback. No one left their door unlocked on the Clayhill.

He listened to see if anyone was coming, half expecting Ryan to charge at him.

Everything was silent.

He pushed the door fully open and peered inside. The flat looked empty.

'Mrs Sanders,' he shouted. 'It's the police.'

Still nothing but silence.

He stepped into the hallway.

'I'm coming in now,' he shouted. 'Which room are you in?'

Maybe they'd gone out? But why would the door be open?

Jack's heart began to beat hard in his chest. The kitchen door was shut. What if Ryan was in there waiting? How easy it would be to pick up a knife and take Jack out.

The sensible thing would be to call backup.

He patted his pocket and swore. No bloody mobile.

Jack considered using a pay phone but God only knew where the nearest one was located and if it would work when he got there. Could he spare the time on a wild-goose chase?

No, Jack had to get in there, show Ryan who was boss and take Aasha home himself.

'Ryan,' he called. 'I'm coming into the kitchen.'

He stretched his fingers towards the door and took a huge breath. He pushed it open slightly and readied himself for the attack.

Sprung like a coil he kicked it the rest of the way with

his boot. It flew across and banged the wall behind. Jack heard a cry and pressed himself to the wall.

He waited a couple of seconds but no one emerged, only the sound of quiet keening.

'Ryan?' Jack said.

The response was more sobs.

Jack steeled himself again and leaned into the kitchen.

What he saw winded him like a boxer's punch.

The room had been ransacked. Dishes smashed, the table overturned. Among the debris Mrs Sanders was kneeling, tears pouring down her sunken cheeks, snot pooling under her nose. In her arms she cradled Ryan, his face broken and covered in blood.

The sound of a violin and the smell of cabbage floated down the corridor. Lilly sat outside Mr Latimer's office and waited to be called in. From time to time Mrs Baraclough looked up from her work to check Lilly was still where she should be or to glare at any passing pupils that dared to giggle with their friends.

Manor Park had been a bone of contention between Lilly and her ex-husband before Sam had even started at the school. The acres of manicured land, and the Great Hall with its vaulted Tudor ceiling, were enchanting. The children were delightful in their bottle-green blazers and hooped socks. Yet Lilly had never wanted Sam to attend. She had planned for him to go to the village school, where he'd hang out with local children and play on the green after tea. When it came time for him to transfer to secondary school he'd go on the bus with his mates and jostle for a place on the back seat.

Sitting in the corridor with its hushed whispers and dark wood panelling, Lilly berated herself for ever having given in to David.

She had deliberately not told him about the meeting. He would have made excuses, said Sam needed to toughen up. He'd tell her he'd survived public school, that it had been the making of him.

No doubt Mr Latimer would say the same thing.

Lilly stiffened her spine. Let him try.

Mrs Baraclough made an ostentatious show of checking her watch.

'Mr Latimer will be with you shortly.'

As if on a timer the head teacher appeared and led Lilly into his office. A floor-to-ceiling window afforded him views of the school playing fields and the rolling countryside beyond. In the distance a maintenance man trimmed the boundary hedge.

'I'm glad you could come in,' said Mr Latimer. 'Unpleasantness such as this is always difficult to talk about. Much better, I find, in person.'

'I'd say bullying was more than unpleasantness,' said Lilly.

'As I said on the phone, I'm not keen on the word "bullying".'

Lilly raised an eyebrow. 'Then what would you call it?'

'I don't find labels helpful,' Mr Latimer coughed nervously, 'in dealing with these incidents.'

'What sort of incidents are we talking about?'

'There has been some teasing and name calling, you know the sort of thing.'

Lilly nodded. She well remembered the sniggers over

her scuffed shoes, how the other girls impersonated her and referred to her as the 'gypo'. It still stung.

She swallowed hard. 'Anything else?'

'There have been some scuffles in the boys' changing rooms,' he said.

'Was anyone hurt?'

Mr Latimer pursed his lips. 'I'm afraid there have been some scratches and bruises. A bloody nose on one occasion.'

Lilly's eyes opened wide. 'A punch in the nose and you don't call that bullying?'

'I don't like that word.'

Lilly held up her palm to stop him in his tracks. 'You've made it very clear that you don't like it. But whatever you choose to call it, I'd like to know what you're going to do about it.'

'There have been some sanctions already,' said Mr Latimer. 'Demerits, lunchtime detentions.'

'But it hasn't worked, has it?' said Lilly. 'Why on earth haven't you called in the parents?'

Mr Latimer gestured towards her.

'Not me,' Lilly snapped.

'Then who?'

Lilly could barely control herself. Was this the man to whom she was entrusting Sam's education?

'The parents of the boys doing all this to Sam,' she said. 'I know you hate the word, but you need to speak to the bullies and their parents.'

Mr Latimer's face fell and when he spoke his tone was cold and calm.

'Miss Valentine, you appear to have missed the point entirely.'

'I'm sorry?'

'In this instance, it is *Sam* who is the bully.'

The end of the Bic biro disintegrated. Mark Cormack spat out the shreds of blue plastic into his palm. He'd been chewing for the best part of an hour, trying not to reach for a fag.

He'd decided that going cold turkey would never work. He would wean himself off gradually. First cut down to ten a day, then five. Then three. Then knock the whole rotten habit on the head for good.

A bloke in the pub had given him the tip, together with the name of a nag in the three fifteen at Chepstow.

Mark counted the ciggies left in the packet. Eleven. That meant he'd already smoked nine. Maybe he should have the last one and fuck off home to bed.

He was weighing up this option when the buzzer sounded.

He hit the intercom. 'Cormack.'

'We need to speak to you.'

Mark sighed. It was the Pakis. He'd left a message saying he had what they wanted. He should have known they'd be round to the office in a shot.

He buzzed them up and nodded to the mismatched chairs.

'Take a seat.'

The big, ugly one looked like he didn't fancy the sticky plastic but sat down all the same. The smaller one followed his lead.

Mark slid a manila envelope towards them. 'It's all there, photos, addresses, the lot.'

The big fucker took it and slid it into his pocket without opening it.

'We wondered if you'd be interested in earning some more money.'

Mark cocked his head to one side, noncommittal. It didn't do to seem too keen.

'This would be something a little more hands-on,' said the smaller man.

Alarm bells began to ring.

'I don't ever hurt women,' said Mark.

He might be a sad a old git with debts up to his arse-hole but his dad had taught him that only cowards hit women.

The big one put up his hand. 'We just want you to intervene, let her know she's being followed.'

'I don't know,' said Mark.

'It's worth another five hundred.' The Pakis got up to leave. 'Think about it.'

As soon as they left, Mark lit up a fag. He mulled it over, in a cloud of grey smoke. Five hundred would pay off a good part of what he owed. Or he could stick it on a tasty-looking mare called Fly by Night. If it came in at ten to one he could pay off all his debts.

He blew a smoke ring and decided how best to do it.

Lilly melted a bar of plain chocolate until it was viscous and glossy, then folded in a bowl of whipped double cream.

The cake she had baked already contained three hundred grams of Belgium's finest and did not strictly need a thick layer of topping but Lilly was in no mood for necessity. She smothered it over the sponge with a spatula until it was as high as the cake itself, then she licked each finger in turn.

Triple bypass on a plate.

She had no idea why she was making it. She had sent Sam to his dad's for the night, fearful of what she might say or do. She needed to process what Mr Latimer had told her before she tackled her son, or told David.

She couldn't quite believe it. Sam: a bully.

After the years she had spent trying to protect the vulnerable, she could hardly accept that he would do something so vile.

She reached into the fridge for a Flake and crumbled it over the cake like confetti.

Was it the school that had turned her son into a monster? The chamber choirs and lacrosse teams were all very nice but the arrogance on display by some of the pupils and their parents was astonishing. Some of Sam's friends considered swimming pools and holiday homes in Tuscany *de rigueur*. Had this made Sam jealous and spiteful?

Lilly shook her head sadly. She knew full well that the blame lay with one person only. And that person was her. She had brought Sam up as best she could but he had had to take his place alongside her work. He had never liked it. No matter how many times she explained that the children she worked for really needed her help, that they had no one else, he didn't want to share her. As he got older, he had stopped complaining about it, but Lilly knew he hated it all the same.

She checked her watch. It was seven o'clock and she hadn't heard from Jack all day. His mobile was where he had left it that morning – but there were phones in the station, weren't there?

She needed to speak to him, for him to give her a slow smile and tell her everything would be all right.

She opened the door to the dishwasher and spread her legs two feet apart. This was the only way she could bend forward to fill it. Not a pretty sight, she conceded. Her back and neck ached and she just couldn't reach.

She pulled out her mobile and scrolled for the number to the station. She had never called there except on work business and didn't feel comfortable about doing it now. For one thing, she didn't want him being teased for being on a tight leash, and for another she was known by a lot of the coppers as being 'on the other side'. She put her phone down. He was probably busy.

She decided to distract herself, and considered a bath. It was new, with one of those fancy whirlpools that turned a squirt of bubble bath into a cappuccino. The trouble was, she couldn't get in and out easily.

Lilly sighed and decided upon an indecently huge piece of cake and some reality television. For if there was one thing sure to take your mind off yourself it was an overload of cholesterol and the sight of a disgraced MP doing the chicken dance. She might even throw caution to the wind and have half a glass of wine.

Jack had a missionary zeal about limiting Lilly's alcohol intake but he wasn't here, was he?

She picked the most expensive bottle of Shiraz off the rack with a wicked cackle. Penny had given it to her as a thank you present, tied with an exquisite aquamarine bow and a hand-pressed card written in italics. God, that woman had style.

Lilly watched the blackcurrant liquid fill up to the half way mark and was about to add a slug more when she saw a light in the garden.

'Shit.' She flinched and knocked the glass over, spilling it over the counter.

As she reached for a cloth she saw it again. Definitely a torch. Her hand was shaking as she wiped up the wine.

This time she wasn't overreacting. Someone was out there.

The image of Mohamed, frightened and defeated, flashed through her consciousness. The PTF were dangerous, no doubt about it. If Lilly was right, then they'd killed Yasmeen.

She peered through the window but everything was now black. She couldn't decide if that was worse than the torchlight. At least with that, she knew where her tormentor was. Right now he could be anywhere. Maybe he was circling the house now, getting closer and closer.

Lilly grabbed her phone. She needed to speak to Jack.

'Child protection,' said a WPC.

Lilly tried to force the panic from her voice. 'Can I speak to Jack McNally?'

'I don't think he's here.'

Lilly swallowed. 'Are you sure? It's his partner and I really need to speak to him.'

'Just a mo,' said the WPC, and by the muffled scrapes Lilly assumed she had put her hand over the mouthpiece while she checked with colleagues.

'Sorry,' she said, 'he's been out all day and there's nothing in his diary.'

Lilly hung up and checked outside once more.

Where the hell was Jack?

She glanced along the purple stain left by the wine towards *his* phone.

It was not in her nature to invade the privacy of others. She didn't even like people looking at the newspaper over her shoulder and she afforded others the same respect. She had once found a journal kept by Sam, his spidery handwriting ordering any interloper to 'Keep Out'. She'd been desperate to know who he had a crush on and what he thought about his mother but she'd done exactly as asked and kept out.

Something scratched at the window. An overhanging branch?

There it was again.

Sorry, Jack. She grabbed the mobile and was met with a request for the password.

'Damnit.'

She typed in LILLY.

'Password incorrect.'

She typed in SAM.

'Password incorrect.'

Lilly thought furiously. What do men use as their passwords? Football teams? Penis sizes? What mattered to them?

She snapped her fingers and typed in FRANK.

'Welcome to network 3000.'

Now all she needed was some clue as to the case he was working on and where he might be.

She dialled instant messaging and listened to the chief super demanding Jack's immediate whereabouts.

'You and me both, mate,' she said.

She checked his last dialled numbers but didn't recognise any of them. MB was a regular, but that meant nothing to Lilly.

Why on earth did she think this would work?

As a last resort she went into text. There were plenty from the station and from voicemail but nothing that helped.

'Come on, Jack,' she shouted, and scrolled frantically. At last she found one from MB and pressed 'Read'.

When the words popped onto the screen Lilly had to lean against the fridge to steady herself. Her stomach felt as if it was lodged in the back of her throat.

I ENJOYED LAST NIGHT. U?

She read it. Reread it. Then she read it again.

A burning anger started low in her pelvis and snaked up to her face like a lighted fuse.

Bastard. Fucking bastard. He'd been out last night pretending to work when all the time he was . . .

When the fury reached her brain she exploded. With a scream she smashed her fist into the cake. She threw handful after handful at the wall. It slid down, leaving a slimy brown trail.

When Jack got home she would kill him.

An hour later Lilly was still in the kitchen. Every inch of her body ached and moaned. The realisation of what Jack had done was like a physical pain.

When she heard Jack's key in the lock she could barely move.

The first thing she noticed when he entered the room was how terrible he looked. His eyes were empty, his cheeks hollow. No doubt her own appearance was similar.

He glanced at the cake splattered across the wall but didn't say a word.

Instead he pulled out a chair and sank into it as if he had never felt so tired. He put his head in his hands.

'Lilly,' he whispered, 'I've done a terrible thing.'

Lilly couldn't speak. It was as if her brain had split in two, the connections lost.

'You're going to hate me,' he said.

She had an urge to run away, to avoid hearing the words, but her feet wouldn't move.

'You know the case I've been working on,' he said.

Oh God, he'd been having an affair with another copper. Lilly almost laughed at the cliché.

'Yes,' her voice was no more than a murmur.

'Well, I got it all wrong,' he said. 'The boy, Ryan, he wasn't what I thought at all.'

What was he talking about? What did this have to do with the text from MB?

'I thought he was just another little toerag, swinging the lead.' He looked up at her, his eyes bright with tears. 'I treated him like just another bag of useless shite.'

Lilly realised that what he was upset about had nothing whatsoever to do with her suspicions.

'I had a chance to help that kid but I blew it,' he said. He broke down, his shoulders heaving with each sob.

Lilly had never seen Jack so bereft, and despite herself, she reached out to touch him.

'Tell me what's happened,' she said softly.

So he told her about the lad who was truanting from school, who was bullying his mother, who had lured away a vulnerable girl.

'Only none of that's true,' he sobbed. 'If I had just opened my eyes for just one second I'd have seen what was right in front of me.'

Lilly stroked his hair. Whatever she had felt an hour ago was overtaken by the need to comfort Jack.

'His mum isn't the full ticket and he looks after her as best he can,' he said. 'And the girl came to him because she was frightened of her brothers.' He slammed his fist on the table. 'It was bloody obvious from the start.'

Lilly thought about Sam. Her lovely, sweet boy with a collection of teddies to rival Hamleys. The school bully.

'Things are never obvious,' she said.

'You'd have seen it in a jiffy,' he pointed a finger at her, 'because you're not some fucked-up cynic.'

'Neither are you.'

He pushed his knuckles into his tear ducts as if to stem another flow.

'Then why is Ryan lying unconscious in hospital?' he asked. 'Why is the girl missing?'

He wasn't looking for an answer, of course, but Lilly gave one all the same.

'Because, Jack, none of us are perfect.'

When he looked up at her his gratitude was palpable.

'You never judge,' he said.

She smiled at him. She knew then that she wouldn't tackle the text from MB now, not when Jack needed her support. She might be angry with him but she still loved him.

When her father left without a forwarding address but with a heap of unpaid debts, his name had never been uttered again. Elsa simply put her shoulder to the grindstone and took two jobs. Yet each night when she thought her daughter safely asleep, Elsa would lie on her bed and weep.

'Why does she care?' Lilly had asked her nan. 'He's a horrible git and she should be glad he's gone.'

Nan had stubbed out an Embassy Regal in her gilt ashtray on its jewelled stand and pulled Lilly into her arms.

'You'll understand one day, Lil.' She smelled of Hartnell's In Love. 'Feelings don't die overnight.'

Lilly suspected she was beginning to understand perfectly what Nan had meant.

'Have you been at the hospital?' she asked Jack.

He nodded. 'The poor kid has taken a terrible beating. They cracked his skull open like an egg.'

'And the girl?'

'We don't know,' he said. 'Ryan's mum said a group of men barged into the flat and grabbed her.'

'Did no one call the police?'

Jack frowned. 'This is the Clayhill, Lilly – what do you think?'

She nodded. Of course no one called the police.

'Apparently Ryan tried to stop them and took a swing at one of them. Broke his nose, by the look of the blood,' he said.

'It's got to be the brothers,' Lilly said.

Jack shook his head. 'Uniform went straight round but they've got a cast-iron alibi.'

'Then who?'

'A group of thugs who think they're above the law.'

Lilly felt as though she'd been slapped in the face.

PTF.

A shiver ripples down Aasha's spine and she pulls her knees tight into her chest.

It's not that she's cold – just very scared of what is going to happen next.

She had fallen asleep on Ryan's bed, exhausted by everything that had happened in the last few days with Imran and then with Ryan's mum. It had been a good sleep, deep and warm without any dreams to disturb her.

Suddenly, there was a bang in the hallway that woke her with a start. She could hear Ryan shouting. At first she thought his mum might have done something stupid again. The poor woman had seemed calmer when Aasha had taken in a cup of tea but you never could tell when people were sick. Their moods could change.

So she'd jumped off the bed, her heart in her mouth, terrified that once again the walls would be covered in blood.

When she got into the hall she saw two men pushing their way into the flat.

'Get the fuck out of my house,' Ryan shouted at them.

But one was three times his size, all pumped up from doing weights. He picked Ryan up by his T-shirt and slammed him into the wall. Ryan groaned and slid down to the floor. The other man was skinny with a weird twitch at the corner of his eye. It made him look even more mental than the big one.

Aasha screamed and ran to the kitchen to phone the police. Ryan might have a golden rule never to involve the authorities in his business but right now she didn't give a shit.

They followed close behind her and filled the tiny kitchen with their huge bodies.

'Don't make this any worse for yourself,' the big one told her. 'We're leaving.'

It was then Aasha realised that her brothers had sent them.

It was over. She was going home.

'Don't you touch her.'

Everyone turned to see Ryan in the doorway, the front of his favourite Lacoste T-shirt ripped.

The big one pointed at Ryan with a huge hand. 'Don't be stupid and you won't get hurt.'

Aasha took a tiny breath as she saw the baseball bat Ryan had by his side. She wanted to grab it, to stop things spiralling out of control, but she was so frightened she couldn't move.

'Don't,' she whispered.

The man looked from Aasha to the bat and back again.

'Worried about your boyfriend?' he said. 'Sweet.'

The other man laughed, his eye dancing manically.

'Come on.' The big one reached out to grab Aasha, his hand sweaty.

Ryan ran at him, swinging the bat and whacked him hard in the face. Aasha heard a crack like breaking wood.

'Little fucker,' the man roared, blood pouring from his nose.

The other man aimed a punch at Ryan but he dodged around until he was at Aasha's side, still swinging the bat to keep them at bay.

How long could he keep it up, Aasha wondered. She knew she should try to help, but she was paralysed by fear.

The big one wiped his nose with the back of his hand, smearing blood across his cheek. 'I'm going to make you wish you were never born,' he snarled.

He grabbed the edge of the kitchen table and upended it. Bowls and cutlery flew across the room. Aasha screamed again.

Ryan held the bat out like a sword. 'For the last time, I'm telling you to get out.'

The big one glanced at his friend and nodded.

For one second Aasha thought they were agreeing to leave, that Ryan had scared them off.

She was wrong.

They stepped forward, almost as if they'd rehearsed it. Ryan lashed out at the big one's bloody face. The bat didn't connect. Ryan swiped again, drawing an arc with the bat. When his arm was fully extended to his right and his own face was unprotected, the man with the twitch punched him square in the face. Aasha heard the air leave Ryan's mouth in a whoosh.

As he tried to gain his breath the man punched again. This time Ryan fell to the floor coughing and spitting blood.

The big one grabbed the bat from him. 'Get her out of here,' he ordered his friend.

The man with the twitch pulled Aasha roughly but

she didn't fight. She couldn't even lift her arms and she let him drag her from the kitchen. As she stumbled along the hallway she heard the horrible thud of the bat again and again and again.

When they got to a white Transit van her legs buckled. The man picked her up and threw her in the back as if she weighed nothing. Her shoulder bashed against the metal floor.

She rubs it now, knowing that if she could see it there would be a mark where it feels tender under her fingers. But she can't see. She's been locked in the back of the van, in total darkness, for what seems like hours.

She remembers a journey – she couldn't say how long – where she rolled and tumbled in the back. Then the van stopped. She'd braced herself, expecting the doors to fling open, to be thrown at Imran's feet. When they just left her in here she felt something like relief.

But it's been so long now, she's getting scared again, and the smell is making her feel sick. What if she needs to pee? What if the air runs out?

She holds her hands out in front of her and gropes for the doors or the sides. She waves in a circle, touching nothing but air, thinking how terrible it must be to be blind and have this nothingness every day of your life. Just that sickening smell.

She leans forward a little, then a little more. It is so disorientating, like being suspended in mid-air.

At last her fingers brush the side. The solid steel is so welcome she pats it like a dog.

Then she traces down, hoping for a handle.

The smell gets stronger and stronger until she gags.

When her hands are almost at floor level she touches hard plastic. It's a container of some sort. She follows its straight lines until something else makes her draw back. Soft, yet dense. Aasha can't think what it is. Gingerly, she reaches out again until her fingers meet its feathery lightness. She presses harder until she feels a firmness beneath. The smell, the touch – they are both familiar.

She strokes sideways, confirming the entire container is full of these objects. But what?

Then something scratches her finger. Hard and sharp. A beak.

Aasha recoils in horror and scoots away on her bottom until her back touches the stiff smoothness of another container. She tries not to cry and buries her hands in her lap. She doesn't want to touch them, she doesn't want to smell them, but she knows what they are.

She's been locked inside a van full of dead chickens.

# *Chapter Seven*

February 2009

'Those that make war against God and his people shall be slain.' The teacher is back at the mosque. 'This is the basis of Jihad.'

I am late for the discussion but a place has been reserved for me at the front now that I am known. I nod an apology as I make my way forward and the teacher nods back.

We are equals. Well, perhaps not equals, but I certainly have position.

A sister raises her hand. 'Does the noble Koran not tell us that whoever kills a human shall be regarded as killing all mankind?'

The teacher smiles patiently. 'This is a very good point,' he says. 'Does anyone here have an answer?'

I feel confident to have my say and gesture to the teacher with my eyes. Not for me putting up my hand like a child in school. The teacher gives me a nod.

'There is a duty upon every Muslim to live peacefully,'

I say. 'The word peace should be the most common of all words on the believer's tongue.'

'How then can we justify war or terrorism?' the sister asks.

'Because Allah requires us not to be the aggressor,' I pause for effect. 'But he does not expect us to do nothing while our enemies attack us.'

The teacher gives a modest smile but it is enough to spur me on.

'Any Muslim who is being prevented from following his true path has the right to defend himself.'

Over breakfast that morning I had the very same discussion with Yasmeen. When the news of a suicide bombing in Tel Aviv came on the radio she had shaken her head sadly.

'War is war,' I said.

'It's still horrible when someone walks into a café and blows up children sharing a Coke,' she said.

'What choice do they have?' I asked. 'Palestinian children are being murdered every day.'

'An eye for an eye,' she said. 'Since when did you become Jewish?'

I was about to throw an insult but Yasmeen batted me away.

'I understand where you're coming from. These are poor people without access to even basic food – we can't expect them to fight back in a traditional military manner,' she said. 'Terrorism is the only response available to the oppressed.'

I don't know where that came from, but it certainly shut me up.

I'm disappointed that she didn't come to today's meeting. I think she'd be impressed with how my standing has grown.

I asked her several times but she insisted she had somewhere else to go.

I turn my body slightly so that I am no longer answering only the teacher but addressing the congregation.

'Think of Chechnya, Palestine, Kashmir,' I say. 'Would Allah really expect us not to take action?'

After the meeting is over I don't need to hover for a word with the teacher. Instead he greets me warmly.

'You spoke well,' he says. 'With passion and conviction.'

'I feel very strongly,' I say.

He touches my arm with his hand. I feel the pressure from his fingers and the absence of his thumb.

The woman who spoke earlier approaches us. I want more time alone with the teacher but it would not be fitting to exclude her. The teacher shows a generosity of time and spirit that I would do well to emulate.

'I listened to everything you taught us,' she speaks quickly, 'and I'm convinced that we do need to take action.'

I want to point out that it was me and not the teacher who made that point. But I don't.

'I'm glad you have re-examined this, sister,' says the teacher.

I notice that the woman's hijab is not pinned neatly, that chestnut-coloured hair is peeping out.

'But what do you suggest?' she asks. 'What action can we take?'

He smiles at her, always so warm. 'We can pray, sister,' he says. 'Live our lives as Allah intended.'

'Don't we have a responsibility to do more than that?' she asks.

His smile is still intact. 'Some of us will be called upon to do more. Some of us will get involved in campaigns, take part in demonstrations.'

'Yes, yes.' She is excited. 'I can do those things.'

His eyes flick towards me. Briefly, but I catch it.

'And there are those of us who will be called upon to take more action still.'


Taslima watched Lilly wiping the smears of chocolate cake from the kitchen wall.

'Dirty protest?'

Lilly threw the dishcloth at her.

She'd asked Taslima to come round and discuss the PTF. Jack had left so early this morning Lilly hadn't had the chance to roll out of bed, let alone tell him her theory that the same men were involved in Yasmeen's murder and Aasha's disappearance.

To be fair, it would be better to work through it with Taslima before she presented it to Jack. And it would give her an excuse to avoid the issue of MB's text.

She stepped back to admire her handiwork. The paint-work was fucked.

'So you think the PTF took this girl?' asked Taslima.

Lilly rummaged under the sink for a tin of magnolia. After the cottage had been redecorated she'd insisted on keeping all the unused supplies. The bloody thing was right at the back and there was no way Lilly could reach.

'The only people interested in this girl were her family,' Lilly huffed, 'and apparently they had nothing to do with it.'

Taslima nudged Lilly out of the way and extracted the tin, together with a paintbrush.

'That doesn't mean it was the PTF,' she said.

'But it makes sense, you've got to admit,' said Lilly.

Taslima wrenched off the paint tin lid with a knife, dipped in the brush and made large rainbow strokes across the cake-stained wall.

'Are you sure you don't just *want* it to be the PTF?'

Lilly cocked her head to one side, taking in Taslima's artistic talents.

'Well, of course I want it to be them,' she said, 'and I want there to be evidence that they killed Yasmeen as well.'

Taslima laughed. 'All very neat.'

Lilly opened her arms to take in the mound of dishes in the sink, a pile of ironing Widow Twankey would be proud of and the stains on the wall. 'Welcome to my world,' she laughed. 'It would be nice if occasionally things went according to plan.'

Taslima finished the painting and put away the tin. She rinsed the brush under the warm tap.

'Then let's go and talk to the only person who seems to connect both crimes.'

Half an hour later they waved to Mohamed. If he was pleased to see them he certainly didn't show it.

'Another girl has been attacked,' said Lilly.

Mohamed busied himself cleaning a meat slicer, the circular blade already pristine and razor sharp.

'Her name is Aasha Hassan,' said Lilly. 'We think the PTF may have kidnapped her.'

Mohamed ran a cloth round and round the edge of the blade, his hand getting faster and faster. 'Why are you telling me this?'

'We wondered if you'd heard anything?' asked Lilly.

'Haram.' Mohamed ran the pad of his thumb against the blade, a thin line of blood immediately rising to the surface. 'I don't know anything.'

Lilly watched Mohamed put the wound to his mouth, covering his lips in a deep crimson stain.

'That looks deep,' she said.

He waved her away with his other hand and moved to the sink.

'Please,' he ran his thumb under the cold tap, 'just leave.'

The water ran red then pink into the basin until at last it ran clear.

'If you hear anything at all,' said Lilly, 'will you let us know?'

Mohamed reached for a box of tissues and began layering them onto his thumb.

'Perhaps,' he said. 'Now go.'

As Lilly and Taslima got into their car, a delivery van screeched to a halt outside the butchers.

'Didn't Mohamed say a delivery man was involved?' hissed Taslima.

Lilly nodded. They watched as he jumped out and made his way inside.

'Ouch,' said Taslima.

'Ouch indeed,' said Lilly.

230

The man had three strips of tape stuck to the bridge of his swollen nose and both eyes were black.

'How's the boy?' The chief super's tone was gentler than during their last encounter.

Jack had got up at six and spent two hours at Ryan's bedside before coming to the station this morning. He couldn't get Ryan's face out of his mind. His nose and mouth were nothing more than purple pulp, his eyes completely closed. The rhythmic wheeze of the ventilator mocked the boy this living corpse had been.

'He's still unconscious, sir.'

The chief fiddled with his cuffs. They were starched, white, perfect.

'And the girl?'

'No sign,' said Jack.

The chief puffed his cheeks and blew out the air. 'I don't need to tell you, Jack, that this hasn't gone quite the way we would have liked it to.'

No, thought Jack. You would have loved it if Ryan had been at fault and I could have returned Aasha to her loving family. The police could have been publicly seen solving a crime against a Muslim girl – conveniently offsetting the case they were pursuing against a Muslim boy.

'I don't think anyone wanted it to turn out this way,' said Jack.

'No.'

The chief looked at Jack expectantly. Jack didn't know what he wanted. There was nothing to tell. No leads. No clues. Just a half-dead kid and a missing girl.

'You're sure the family had nothing to do with this?' asked the chief.

'Alibi,' said Jack.

The chief looked relieved. Two honour attacks might just finish him off.

'But that doesn't mean they're not behind it,' said Jack.

He enjoyed watching the chief squirm.

'Then do whatever you have to do.' The chief straightened his tie. 'Double check, then triple check those alibis. Speak to everyone and anyone who had contact with these children during the last week.'

'That'll take a while, sir,' said Jack.

'I'll assign a couple of bodies to you,' said the chief.

Jack was astonished. He'd assumed the case would immediately be handed over to a DI.

'Are you putting me in charge, sir?'

The chief gave a curt nod. 'Let's find this girl.'

As Jack left the chief's office he shook his head to clear it. An attempted murder and a kidnapping. His time had come. In different circumstances he would have been over the moon, called up Lilly to crow and taken a bottle of wine home to celebrate. But Ryan's mangled features robbed the moment of any pleasure. Jack knew what he had to do. He would find whoever had done this to Ryan and Aasha and put them away, for a very long time.

When he reached the car park and unlocked his car his mobile bleeped. It was a text from Mara.

*What happened last night? I thought we had a date.*

Funny, Jack hadn't given Mara a second thought yesterday night or this morning. In the light of everything that had happened, his infatuation was beginning to look pretty juvenile.

He'd need to speak to her, explain that though he was flattered by the attention of such an attractive woman, their relationship was purely business.

He deleted her text. He'd call her later when he got a chance.


Aasha lies down on the floor of the van, hovering somewhere between asleep and awake.

The stench of the rotting birds is now mixed with urine. Aasha hung on for as long as she could, her bladder aching as she tried to hold it in, but hours ago she wet herself.

When the doors are finally opened, she's blinded by daylight flooding in and puts her hands over her eyes.

'Get out,' a man shouts at her.

She lifts her head slowly. She feels weak with fear and thirst. She hasn't had anything to drink since she left Ryan's and her tongue is thick in her mouth.

'Get out now or I'll shut the doors again,' he orders.

Aahsa pulls herself onto her knees. She still can't see his features, her vision is too blurred, but she crawls her way to him.

When she gets to the open door she feels a cool breeze on her face and the damp patter of rain. Without thinking, she sticks out her tongue, desperate for any liquid.

'Don't mess me around,' grunts the man, and pulls her out. She can feel grass under her feet instead of metal and she leans against the man, knowing if she doesn't she will fall.

He grunts again and leads her down a gentle slope. The grass is wet from the morning and it slicks her bare feet. She has to force herself not to bend down and lick it.

They reach a building. Aasha still can't see properly, her eyes are all grey and fuzzy, but it seems long and made of old-fashioned stone. Everything seems quiet. No traffic rushing past, just the scrape of the man's shoes on the doorstep and her own panic.

He unlocks the door and nudges her inside. Without the dazzle of daylight Aasha begins to regain her sight. In the hallway are a couple of pairs of muddy boots. A single waterproof jacket is hung on a peg. Everything else is space and silence.

Through the hallway and down a corridor the man jerks his head at a door. She sees now he is the man with the strange eye. The one who dragged her from Ryan's flat.

'Bathroom,' he says.

She goes straight to the sink, cups her hand under the tap and brings it to her mouth, sucking it down in noisy slurps.

After four greedy handfuls she turns to the man, unsure what to do now.

'You stink.' He wrinkles his nose at the dark stain at her crotch and thigh. 'Get cleaned up.'

Aasha looks around the room. It's empty apart from the sink, a chipped bath and an old toilet, brown with lime scale and worse.

'I don't have anything to wash with,' she says.

He pulls down his lip and surveys the room as though he were half expecting it to be full of scented candles and fluffy bathrobes.

'Wait here,' he says, then adds with a growl. 'Don't move.'

'OK,' she whispers.

She doesn't think she could move if she wanted to. Her head is banging and her arms and legs ache as if she has the worse bout of flu.

Moments later he returns with a bar of soap and an old towel, ripped at the edges and rough with age. Her mum turns linen in this state into floor cloths. 'Waste not, want not,' she says.

Tears spring into Aasha's eyes. She wishes Mum were here now, with her tired face and lined hands. She would give her daughter a hug and Aasha would smell the almond oil she uses in her hair.

'Why am I here?' she asks the man.

He snorts through his nose. 'You know full well what you've done to your family.'

She knows how angry her brothers will be. The terrible rage Imran whipped up on the day she ran away will have turned over and over in his mind until he will be ready to kill her. Ismail will join in, like he always does. Imran's shadow, that's what he is. That boy can't think one of his own thoughts.

What she can't understand is what she's doing in this place; why they haven't taken her home. Is this part of the punishment? And how long will it go on for?

'What happens next?' she asks the man.

His left eye spins uncontrollably. 'That's not up to me.'

*   *   *

The fingernails were laid in a line across the arm of the sofa. They stood out like tiny crescent moons against the brown leather.

Mum was always nagging Ismail about biting his nails. 'What girl will marry a man who wears his worry on his hands?'

He was tempted to point out that the girls round here were more bothered about the size of a man's BMW then the state of his cuticles.

'Women like a man they know will take care of them,' she said.

Ismail shook his head and laughed. Dad was bald, fat and frightened of his shadow. Wasn't that the reason Imran had had to take charge?

He tapped each nail with his knuckle and arranged them in a circle.

Imran sloped into the room and slouched at the other end of the sofa. He was wearing only jeans, his torso and feet naked.

'Are you stressed, bro?' he laughed.

Well, of course Ismail was stressed. They'd asked some specialist kind of nutters to grab Aasha and as if that wasn't bad enough, they hadn't actually brought her home. Ismail had spent most of last night tossing and turning, waiting for them to arrive. What could have kept them this long? He flicked the nails onto the floor.

'You need to learn to chill,' said Imran, and rubbed his bare chest. 'Or you're going to end up with a haircut like Dad's.'

Ismail was in no mood for teasing. 'Don't take the piss, Imran. You know full well what the problem is.'

Imran kissed his teeth and sauntered to the kitchen. His jeans were so low, the back pockets were almost at his knees. His Calvins glowed white against his hairless hips and back. He said he didn't wax but Ismail didn't believe him. Brothers on chemotherapy had more body hair that.

Ismail followed him into the kitchen.

'Where is she?' he hissed.

Imran reached for a box of Shreddies, tossed one in the air and caught it in his mouth.

Ismail's stomach growled. He hadn't been able to touch anything for breakfast.

At last he voiced his main concern. 'Do you think they've hurt her?'

Imran patted his six-pack and popped another Shreddie in his mouth.

'Relax,' he said. 'They've done exactly what we asked.'

'You've spoken to them?'

'Course I have.'

Ismail raked his fingers through his hair. 'Why didn't you tell me?'

'How was I to know you'd been working yourself up into a frenzy?' Imran shrugged.

'So what did they say?' Ismail asked. 'Where the hell is she?'

For a split second something flashed across Imran's face. The studied cool returned almost instantaneously. Too late. Ismail had seen the expression. Uncertainty.

'Things went a bit pear-shaped with the boy,' said Imran

'Ryan.'

'You friends now?'

Ismail ignored the dig. 'What about Aasha?'

'She's fine, bro,' said Imran. 'She just needs to lie low while things blow over.'

'I think they should bring her back now,' said Ismail. 'She's probably terrified.'

Imran slammed down the cereal box and squared up to Ismail.

'Remember why we did this in the first place.' He stabbed a finger inches from Ismail's face. 'That stupid bitch needs to learn a lesson.'

Ismail sighed. His brother was right. This whole mess was Aasha's fault. If she hadn't gone running off with some chavvy English boy none of this would have happened.

'What about Mum?' he asked. 'Can we at least tell her Aasha is safe?'

'These people aren't to be messed with,' said Imran.

'I know that,' said Ismail. 'I just want Mum to stop worrying.'

'We don't tell anybody anything.' Imran narrowed his eyes. 'You understand me?'

Ismail remembered the size of Abdul Malik's fists.

'Yes.'

The smell of disinfectant was hot at the back of Lilly's throat.

She loathed everything about hospitals: the harsh overhead lighting, the scratchy orange blankets and, of course, the smell.

Her mother had worked in a sewing factory for twenty

years, the fibres clogging up her lungs. When she could no longer breathe without an oxygen mask she went to St James's to die.

Each morning, before she took the bus into Leeds to sit on the edge of her mother's bed, Lilly sprayed the back of her hand with perfume. When the lifts doors opened and the nurses greeted her with cheery enquiries as to how she was getting on with her exams, Lilly pushed her nose into the skin of her hand and breathed in lavender and lemon.

Today she had nothing to stave off the stench and, worse still, her sense of smell was heightened by pregnancy.

A sister with happy eyes and a solid frame approached her. 'Are you looking for Maternity, love?'

Lilly was puzzled. Then she saw herself with her bulging lump and swollen ankles.

'No,' she laughed. 'Not due yet.'

The sister placed a firm palm at the point where Lilly's stomach met her pelvis. The gesture, though intimate, was not remotely intrusive. God, Lilly hoped she would get someone like this at the birth.

'The baby's head's down,' said the sister. 'He's just waiting for the right moment.'

Lilly put her hand over the sister's. 'Could you tell him that now is most definitely not the right moment.'

'I can tell him,' she laughed, 'but I can't promise he's listening.'

'I've already got one just like that,' said Lilly. 'I don't need another.'

The sister let out a low chuckle. 'So what can I do for you?'

'I've come to see the policeman visiting Ryan Sanders,' said Lilly.

The sister pursed her lips, all humour gone. 'That poor boy,' she said.

She led Lilly down the corridor to a private room at the end.

'Make sure you catch the animals that did this,' she said.

Lilly was about to explain that she wasn't a copper but thought better of it. After all, she certainly did want to see Ryan's attackers arrested.

She peeped through the window to see if she could attract Jack's attention. What she saw took her breath away.

The boy lay completely still on the bed, his face like smashed fruit. Tubes snaked up his nose and into his mouth. Jack sat on a chair beside the bed, his hand on the blanket, beside but not touching Ryan's. The room was entirely still and silent apart from the soft sigh of the ventilator.

Lilly watched them both, like characters in a tableau, until she felt the warmth of someone behind her. A thin woman with skin almost as colourless as Ryan's was also watching through the window. She could have been a corpse but for her hand, which fluttered across her bloodless lips.

Lilly guessed she was the boy's mother. 'Mrs Sanders?'

The woman looked startled, as if she hadn't noticed all twelve stone of Lilly and her shock of red curls.

'He's not going to die, is he?' she asked.

Lilly had seen enough head injuries to know it was entirely possible.

'Of course not,' she said.

The woman raised both hands to the window but she didn't let them touch the glass. Instead they hovered and shook in mid-air, each finger bloody and raw.

The movement made Jack look up and he nodded to Lilly. He murmured something to Ryan and made his way out of the room.

'Why don't you sit with him a while?' he asked Mrs Sanders.

Her fingers scraped wildly against her teeth but she didn't refuse, and let Jack lead her gently to her son's bedside. Lilly watched as he pressed her into the chair and crouched at her feet to speak to her. It reminded her of why she had fallen in love with this man and she was filled with regret and sadness about what she had discovered.

No one's perfect, no one's perfect, she told herself over and over.

He left mother and son together.

'Hi.' His eyes were tired but there was an energy to him that hadn't been there the previous night.

'How is he?' Lilly asked.

Jack shrugged. 'No change.'

'I've been thinking about all this,' said Lilly, 'and how the family all had alibis.'

'Bloody convenient,' said Jack.

'What if they didn't do it themselves?' she asked. 'What if they got a group to do it for them?'

Jack arched his eyebrows. 'What group?'

'When we were digging around to see if anyone else could have killed Yasmeen Khan we came across a local gang of men calling themselves the PTF.'

'Never heard of them,' said Jack.

'Nor had I,' Lilly agreed, 'but it seems they've taken it upon themselves to keep the Muslim girls in the area on the straight and narrow.'

'Girls like Aasha.'

Lilly smiled. 'Exactly.'

'So how do I find this PTF?' asked Jack.

'That's been the hard part,' said Lilly. 'People haven't been falling over themselves to finger them.'

'Isn't that always the way?'

'Naturally,' Lilly paused. 'But I have a name.'

A smile spread across Jack's face like sunrise.

'Abdul Malik. He delivers halal meat,' said Lilly.

'You,' Jack shook her shoulders, 'are the bloody best.'

'Maybe if I described him to Mrs Sanders she might remember him,' said Lilly.

Jack turned to the window. Ryan's mother sat rocking in the chair.

'I don't think she remembers anything much.'

Lilly nodded. Ordinarily she would have agreed that Mrs Sanders would not have made the best witness but this was no ordinary situation.

'He's very well built, huge really,' she said.

Jack smiled but she could tell he didn't think these details would be enough to have made an impact on someone like Mrs Sanders.

'More importantly,' she added, 'he's sporting a broken nose and two black eyes. Even Ryan's mum couldn't have missed that.'

Jack pulled on a white paper suit and tucked his hair into the elasticated hood. He had never understood how SOCO could work in this uncomfortable get-up.

He dipped under the yellow police tape stuck across the Sanders' door, and headed into the kitchen, rustling with each step.

'Well, if isn't Madonna.' The head of the forensic team carefully lifted shards of smashed glass with tweezers and placed them in a transparent evidence bag.

Nathan Cheney was an old mate. He and Jack had cemented their friendship on an all-night bender and it had survived the years on a diet of greasy curries and taking the piss. Jack's current healthy living regime was the source of much amusement.

'Could you pass the wheatgrass?' he asked his young assistant, who chuckled into her latex gloves.

'Will you ever stop?' Jack asked.

Cheney pushed his national health glasses up his nose. They were held together with a rough ball of Sellotape, which must have been uncomfortable. But then, this was a man with more metal in his ears, nose and lips than a scrap-metal yard. Each time they met, Cheney was sporting a new piercing. It was a fair assumption that comfort was not an item at the top of his list.

'Not while there's a hole in my arse,' Cheney laughed.

Jack knew when he was beaten. 'What have you got?'

Cheney pointed down the hall, the black, tribal tattoo encircling his wrist visible through the rubber of his glove.

'There are traces of Ryan's blood on the wall by the front door so I'd say he struggled with his assailants not to let them in.'

Jack nodded. Mrs Sanders said she heard shouting from her room but she was so frightened she stayed where she was.

'Somehow he ended up here with Aasha.' Cheney pointed to the cupboards at the far end of the kitchen.

Jack pictured the kids together, terrified and cornered.

'Ryan was attacked here, exactly where you found him.' Cheney kneeled at the edge of the pool of dark blood. 'The doc at the hospital told me there were very few defensive wounds to his arms, so I'd say he went down pretty quickly.'

Jack crouched next to his friend and touched the blood with his gloved finger. It hadn't yet dried but it was thick, viscous.

'They carried on hitting him when he was unconscious?' he asked.

'I'd say yes.'

Jack coughed back his anger. He needed to focus. 'Weapon?'

'Again the doc said he found traces of wood in Ryan's scalp, so I'm guessing a bat,' said Cheney. 'Whatever it was, they took it with them.'

Having no weapon was always a blow, but Jack had expected as much.

'What about Aasha?' Jack asked. 'Can we tell if she was hurt?'

Cheney shook his head and Jack heard the tinkle of his earrings inside the hood.

'I'm collecting blood samples but I can't say who any of it belongs to yet.'

'Thanks,' said Jack, and stood to leave.

'Where are you going?' asked Cheney.

'I don't know about you but I fancy a seaweed smoothie.'

He ducked outside, Cheney's laughter following him.

In truth, Jack needed some fresh air. He'd been at crime scenes before, seen plenty of bodies in his time. He wasn't some rookie that needed to throw up in private. But he had to admit that this one felt different. It could have all been avoided if only Jack had been doing his job properly.

He moved along the walkway, trying to process how he was going to find Aasha, how he was going to put away the men that had hurt Ryan.

The name Lilly had given to him was a good start, but Mrs Sanders wouldn't be able to identify him because she hadn't left her room. Jack tried not to dwell on what sort of person would hide under their duvet while their child was taking a beating. He reminded himself that she wasn't well, wasn't responsible for her actions.

He could, of course, just pull Malik off the street and demand some answers. But what was to stop him saying he had never even heard of Aasha or Ryan? Jack needed something to link them, something to link Malik to the scene.

When he got to the stairwell a rat scurried past, one of yesterday's discarded chips in its sharp teeth. Did no one ever clean up round here?

Suddenly it hit Jack hard, like a jab in the chest. Of course no one ever cleaned up. Not food, not dog shit. Not blood.

When he climbed the stairs yesterday he'd seen a fresh

trail of blood. He'd assumed kids had been fighting. He remembered what Lilly had said about Malik's face. What if during the attack Ryan had got in a punch and broken the bastard's nose? What if the blood in the stairwell was Malik's?

He ran back up to the flat and sprinted through the hall.

'All this jogging is impressing nobody,' said Cheney.

'Could you take a sample of some blood outside for me?'

Cheney nodded, reached for his bag and followed Jack.

He kneeled among the turds and ketchup and did his thing.

'This isn't going to be easy,' he said.

'Lucky for me you're the best.'

Cheney took out a cotton bud and began scraping. 'Flattery will get you nowhere.'

Jack laughed, not because it was empty flattery, but because Cheney was, despite the dog-on-a-string appearance, the very best. If anyone could nail Malik, he could. A glimmer of anticipation began to stir in Jack's stomach as they closed in on Ryan's attacker.


'I'm afraid there seems to be a problem.'

Lilly looked up at the prison officer. His shiny bald head was offset by a bushy black moustache.

'Problem?' Lilly asked.

'The prisoner hasn't been brought over.'

The hair on his lip squirmed like a small rodent. Under different circumstances it might have made Lilly smile but she had been waiting for Raffy in the hall of legal visits for nearly an hour. Her back was killing her and it wouldn't be long before she needed the loo.

'Can you get on the phone to his wing and tell them I need a conference with Raffy now?'

'They're fully aware of the situation.'

Lilly gave the man a hard stare. On closer inspection his moustache was full of crumbs and the ends were matted. Like a dead rodent, Lilly thought.

'My client is on remand and visits are therefore not limited.'

The guard smiled, the ratty rug tickling his teeth. 'They know that.'

Lilly counted to ten, telling this man that he was an idiot might make her feel better but it wouldn't help.

'Let me get this straight,' she said. 'Both you and I know my client is entitled to see me.'

'That's correct.'

'And the staff on his wing know he's entitled to see me.'

'That's correct.'

Lilly opened her palms. 'So why won't they bring him over?'

'Because he's not there.'

Lilly closed her eyes. It wasn't unheard of for inmates to be transferred around the prison without proper records being kept. The idea that the boys' movements were strictly monitored was a pipe dream. Lilly had once been caught in a lock-down during which each cell was frantically searched for a young lad who'd been released the week before.

'What are the chances of them finding him in the next hour?' Lilly asked.

The guard rubbed the edges of his moustache into two dirty dreadlocks.

'Oh, we know where he is.'

'Mary Mother of God,' Lilly stole one of Jack's favourite expressions, 'are you people incapable of basic communication? Why can't his wing liaise with wherever Raffy *is* and get him over here?'

A frown slid down the guard's face. 'You make it sound simple.'

Lilly threw up her hands in frustration. 'It is simple. A guard just tells him I'm here and they put one foot in front of the other.' She walked the first two fingers of her right hand across the table.

'That's just it,' said the guard, 'he can't.'

'Can't what?'

'Walk.'

Lilly sat back in her chair, nonplussed. 'Can't walk?'

The guard shook his head.

'I don't understand,' said Lilly.

'There's been an incident,' said the guard, 'and your client is in the hospital.'

Lilly had seen the inside of more prisons than the Krays. Men's prisons, women's prisons, high-security psychiatric units. She visited YOIs and secure units on an almost weekly basis. But she had never seen a hospital wing.

She was led through the bowels of Arlington, past the cell areas and outside to the exercise yard. Around twenty boys were playing football on a square of patchy grass, the goal area worn bare and muddy. They looked at her curiously but with only an hour's recreation every day they weren't going to waste it asking questions.

On the far side was another block. The same shape, style and brickwork as the main prison building, but a tenth of the size. A baby brother.

Lilly read the sign on the door.

'Welcome to Eagle Wing – Medical Centre.'

The guard punched in a security code and the door was released.

A nurse at the reception desk greeted them with a smile. She reminded Lilly of the sister she'd met earlier, all firm shoulders and a dependable face.

'What can I do for you, Lenny?' she asked.

'Depends what you've got in mind,' said the guard.

The nurse tittered. Clearly she didn't find the bald head and the moustache full of breakfast as repulsive as Lilly did.

'Seriously,' he said, as if they'd been joking around for hours, 'Miss Valentine wants to see Khan.'

'I'll see if that's possible,' said the nurse, and unlocked another door on the far side of the reception.

There was no way Lilly was going to be put off again. She'd already wasted the entire afternoon and she wasn't leaving without speaking to Raffy.

'This isn't an optional thing,' she said. 'My client has the right to a visit.'

The nurse pursed her lips. 'I know all about inmates' rights but I was thinking of you.'

Lilly raised her eyebrows.

'It's not always the right environment for a woman in your condition,' said the nurse.

'A few germs won't kill me,' said Lilly.

'It wasn't the germs I was thinking of.'

Jack knocked on Malik's door. The man lived in a rundown terrace in the heart of Bury Park. The front yard was empty except for a stinking dustbin and a few weeds that peeped through the cracks in the paving slabs.

Jack reminded himself not to get excited. This man might have nothing to do with any of this. An innocent man, whose name had come up in the wrong place. Jack had come to ask him some questions, nothing more. Thinking about arrests and generally getting ahead of himself would only cloud his thinking.

Cases like this were never solved easily. Today was unlikely to be an exception.

Still, his heart beat just that little harder when the door opened.

'Yeah?'

The man in the doorway was immense. His shoulders so square they almost touched the sides of the frame. 'A brick shit-house' was how he'd be described back home.

Jack flashed his badge. 'Can I have a word?'

Malik looked him up and down. If recently Jack had been feeling muscular, he didn't now. He felt like a stick man next to a giant.

'Come in,' said Malik.

He led Jack to the sitting room where Al Jazeera was playing on a forty-two-inch plasma flat screen. Surround sound pumped out the news from all corners of the room.

Malik snapped off the television with a remote. 'Is there a problem?'

Dried blood coated the strips of tape across his nose and a violent purple bruise underlined each eye.

'That looks sore,' said Jack.

'It's nothing,' said Malik.

Jack nodded as if massive facial injuries might be a part of everyday life.

'Do you know a girl called Aasha Hassan?'

'Nope.'

'What about her brothers, Imran and Ismail?'

'I seen them around.' Malik shrugged. 'They ain't part of my crew.'

'What about Ryan Sanders?' asked Jack. 'He part of your crew?'

Malik snorted. 'Never heard of him.'

'He lives on the Clayhill.'

'Shithole,' Malik ran his finger through his beard. 'Never go there.'

Jack couldn't take his eyes off the man's arms. The biceps strained against his T-shirt. His hands were huge, like joints of beef. He imagined what it would be like if this man were to wield a bat. He imagined what it would be like to be on the wrong end of that bat.

'Where were you yesterday?' he asked.

'Work.'

'All day?'

'Of course not.'

'What about the morning?' asked Jack. 'Before ten.'

Malik narrowed his eyes as if he were thinking. 'Here.'

'Alone?'

'With my boys.'

'They'll vouch for that, will they?' asked Jack.

'You know it.'

Jack did know it. A man like this would have friends who would swear he was on the moon if he told them to.

'Right then.' Jack turned to the door. 'If you could just give me the names of your friends I'll be off.'

Malik scribbled on a piece of paper and handed it to Jack.

'Thanks,' he said. 'Remind me how you said you hurt your nose.'

'I didn't say.'

Jack pocketed the names. 'Humour me.'

'Me and one of the boys were sparring.'

'Must have been a decent punch,' said Jack.

'He got lucky.'

'And that happened here?' Jack asked.

Malik folded his arms. 'I didn't say that.'

'Well, it wouldn't have happened at work and you said you spent the morning here.'

'Right,' said Malik. 'We were in the kitchen.'

'Got it,' said Jack. 'So not at the Clayhill?'

Malik frowned. 'What you talking about?'

'The accident,' Jack gestured to his own nose, 'it couldn't have happened at the Clayhill?'

Malik bared his teeth. 'I already told you, I don't go to that shithole.'

Jack paused for breath. The man was lying. Definitely

lying. But until the blood samples came back there was nothing even to place this man at the scene, never mind prove he had committed a crime. Jack could just imagine the chief's reaction if he was making a mistake.

Fuck it, he had to go with his gut.

'Abdul Malik, I'm arresting you on suspicion of the attempted murder of Ryan Sanders.'

'You're kidding me, man.'

'Nah,' said Jack. 'You're nicked.'


'Cunt scum, cunt scum.'

The boy's eyes were wild and wide. Saliva frothed at the corners of his lips.

'Cunt scum, cunt scum,' he screamed.

The nurse cupped his chin in her hand and looked deep into his eyes.

'You're all right, Robert. No one's going to hurt you.'

'Cunt scum, cunt scum,' his voice dropped.

'There now,' The nurse patted his cheek.

'Cunt scum, cunt scum,' he whispered.

Of the fifteen boys in the hospital wing it was obvious to Lilly that most of them had psychiatric problems. It was appalling. Like an asylum for children.

The nurse led Robert back to his bed where he knotted the sheet around his wrist and whimpered.

'Why isn't he in a proper mental hospital?' Lilly asked.

'The transfer would take longer than he's got to serve,' said the nurse.

Lilly watched the boy curl himself into a ball. 'But he's not well.'

'We do our best,' the nurse smiled.

It was a well-known fact among lawyers that at least half the adult prison population were damaged goods, drug- or drink-addicted, abused and depressed, but only the truly, frighteningly, insane ended up in Broadmoor. The rest muddled through and served their time in fear and disorientation.

That the same would be true for kids in custody shouldn't shock Lilly, but seeing them like this had back-footed her.

'I told you it wasn't nice in here.' The nurse glanced at Lilly's bump.

'I'll be fine.' She forced a smile.

'We put Raffique at the bottom,' the nurse pointed to the last bed. 'So he'd get a bit of peace.'

It was a small gesture, but it struck Lilly as inordinately kind in this difficult place. Like laughing at the jokes of a man with a silly moustache.

'I'm sorry.' Lilly put her hand on the nurse's arm. 'I was rude to you before and I shouldn't have been.'

The nurse gave a businesslike nod. 'We're both just doing our jobs.'

Yes, thought Lilly, but yours is a lot tougher than mine.

When she got to the foot of Raffy's bed he gave a tight smile.

'All right.'

Lilly bit her lip. For a boy of fifteen he seemed impossibly weary, the spark, the energy, the swagger, all gone. His body seemed slighter than the previous day, though he couldn't have lost mass overnight. There were scratches and bruises down both arms and his feet were swathed in thick bandages.

She perched on the end. 'What happened to you?'

'Skinheads,' he mumbled.

Shit. She'd told him to be careful, that bigging himself up with his 'brothers' would lead only to trouble.

'What did they do?'

'Pinned me down and slashed my feet.'

Lilly held her breath. Raffy's tone may have been matter-of-fact but it belied the horror of being held on the floor, with his arms over his head, while someone cut his feet with a makeshift shank.

'I'm sorry,' she said.

'Not your fault.' Raffy shrugged. 'And they'll get theirs, don't you worry.'

Lilly covered Raffy's hand with her own. 'I know you're tough, that you think can get through this.'

'I can.'

She squeezed his fingers. 'This is a terrible place, Raffy. It sucks the life out of everyone that comes here.' She nodded down the ward to Robert, still muttering on his bed. 'Look what this sort of life does to people.'

'I'm not some mental case,' he said.

'I know that,' she said. 'But you have got to let me help you, OK? You have got to let me try to get you out of here.'

He grunted.

'I'll take that as a yes,' she smiled. 'So tell me if the name Abdul Malik means anything to you.'

'He lives near me.'

'Is he PTF?'

'I don't know,' said Raffy. 'But he's bad news, if you get me.'

Lilly nodded. 'Could he have killed Yasmeen?'

Raffy screwed his eyes tight shut.

'You have to start giving me something, Raffy,' said Lilly.

He exhaled loudly. 'I don't know.'

'Raffy,' Lilly warned.

'Maybe.'

The maple syrup Lilly had poured over the spare ribs was blackened and bubbling in the oven, filling the kitchen with the smell of the Deep South.

Jack rubbed his hands together. 'It's a pity Sam is missing this.'

Lilly felt a stab of sadness. She'd arranged for Sam to spend a few more days with his dad.

'Is everything all right?' David had asked.

Lilly had assured him that she just felt under the weather, that she was tired. In truth, she was avoiding Sam or dealing with the situation. The more she thought about it, the angrier she became, and a stand-up fight would help no one.

'Is there any potato salad to go with those?' asked Jack.

'I thought you were sticking to the greens,' said Lilly.

Jack patted his stomach. 'I think the odd tatty wouldn't hurt.'

'Even a tatty smothered in mayonnaise?'

'I'd survive.'

She unveiled a deep bowl full of New Orleans' finest, which she'd assumed she would be eating on her own. Thank goodness she always over-catered.

'You are a very good woman,' he laughed.

As she laid the bowl on the table, with a completely unnecessary loaf of home-made bread, he caught the top of her thigh.

'I love you, Lilly,' he said.

She caught her breath. 'I know.'

He waited for a second for her to say it in return – but it stuck in her throat.

She busied herself with the ribs, transferring the sticky, sweet meat to a platter and adding a pack of hand wipes for good measure.

'Dig in,' she said.

He smiled at her and put four juicy ribs on his plate with a mound of potatoes and a thick slice of bread.

'I am starving.'

Lilly grinned. She hadn't seen him eat like this in months. 'We haven't done this in a long time.'

'Too long,' he agreed.

She watched him tear the meat from the bone, his lips slick with the sauce.

'How did you get on with Malik?'

Jack scooped a huge forkful of potato salad into his mouth and groaned with pleasure.

'I asked him all about Ryan and Aasha.'

'And?'

He covered his bread in a thick layer of butter and took a bite. 'And he said he'd never heard of either of them.'

'Is that it?' she asked.

'Just about.' Jack shrugged. 'But I threw him in the cells anyway.'

Lilly dropped her knife. 'You didn't.'

'There's a chance his blood is all over the scene,' said Jack. 'I'll know tomorrow.'

'And what if it isn't his blood?' Lilly asked.

'Then I'm in deep shit.'

Lilly stared, open-mouthed, but Jack just helped himself to another dollop of potato salad.

'You think he did it?' she asked.

'I think he's lying about something.'

Lilly let a smile spread across her face.

'I know what you're thinking.' Jack pointed his knife at her.

'Oh, yeah?'

'You're thinking that if this guy is part of the PTF, then there's a chance he did Yasmeen.'

She couldn't deny it. The sight of Raffy, in the medical centre with all those other poor kids, was branded upon her mind's eye. She had to try to get him out of there.

# *Chapter Eight*

March 2009

'Are you on that thing again?' Yasmeen stands over me, trying to look at the screen of my laptop.

Instinctively I try to shield the page I'm viewing.

'What are you so embarrassed about?' she teases.

'Go away.'

'You're so secretive these days.'

I pause. I'm not secretive or embarrassed, just careful. As the teacher regularly points out, 'Not everyone will understand our path.'

I decide I *will* trust her. Although the path I have chosen is the right path, God's path, it is often lonely. Perhaps Yasmeen will walk with me.

I move aside and let her see the website I have been posting on.

Pakitalk – the social networking site for young men and women of Pakistani descent.

'A chat room.' Yasmeen is incredulous. 'You spend all these hours in a chat room.'

I feel the heat rush to my cheeks. I should have realised that she wouldn't understand.

Yasmeen's eyes flash. 'I'm surprised that someone with your intelligence would want to waste it on something like this.'

I shake my head, flustered. 'It's not what you think.'

She puts her hands on her hips, challenging me to explain myself.

'This is my duty,' I stutter, 'a *wajib*.'

'Reading the inner thoughts of sex-starved teenagers is not a duty.'

She is making it sound so pointless, so dirty.

'Come on then,' she taps the keyboard. 'Let's see what Banglaboy has to say about the war in Iraq.'

I try to push her hand away.

'Or what about Niqab Ninja?' she says. 'Any interesting opinions on Guantanamo Bay?'

I slam the computer lid down, crushing her fingers.

'Shut up,' I shout.

She tries to prise her hand out but I press down with all my strength. I know I'm hurting her but she is too proud to show it.

'You're a joke,' she says, tears in her eyes.

I press down even harder and she takes a sharp breath. If I carry on her fingers might break and I wonder if I'd be prepared to do that.

'Pain is part of any war,' says the teacher. 'We must not be afraid to receive it or give it.'

At last her chin begins to tremble. 'Please,' she whispers.

I release her immediately. I have made my point.

When she has gone I go back to my work.

Pakitalk is not one of my favourite websites. In fact, of the fifty or so I post on, I don't like many of them. But this is something we all do.

When the teacher asked if I would consider joining a group of Muslims who wanted to take things to the next level, I took my time to answer for the sake of seeming thoughtful. In all honesty, I didn't need to consider anything because I was desperate to start turning my beliefs into actions.

'Islam is not just a religion, it is a political system,' he said. 'And like all systems it must reach out to as many people as it can.'

'The crowds at the mosque are growing every week,' I pointed out.

The teacher smiled. 'We must think far bigger than that.'

He is right, of course. We need to raise the consciousness of every Muslim so that they can come to see that our way is the right way. But how? We are so few.

'We already have the perfect tool to reach thousands, if not millions, of our brothers and sisters,' he said.

I waited patiently while he pulled from his bag a slimline laptop.

'The weapon of the future,' he said. 'The internet.'

Now a handful of us spend every free moment surfing. We seek out forums with any connection to Islam, however tenuous. And we post.

By Freedomfighter on 28.2.09 at 22.25
Wake up, brothers and sisters. All around the world

261

Muslims are being slaughtered or starved. How much longer will we continue to allow this?

By Islamist on 1.03.09 at 03.05
Chechnya, Palestine and Kashmir are Islamic issues and every Muslim must try to solve them. Will you ignore these genocides until it is the turn of British Muslims to be cleansed?

Sometimes I post well into the early hours. Often I'm abused or ridiculed, but I continue none the less.

I once complained to the teacher and he nodded patiently.

'Not everyone is ready to hear.'

'Then why do we do it?' I asked.

'Because the dream of an Islamic state may be a dream but it is not an illusion.'

'Sometimes it feels that way,' I said.

The teacher pointed into the distance. 'It is just out of sight, but it is on its way.'

So I fight on, hoping that Allah sees, that he is pleased with my efforts, that he will lead me where I can be most useful.

'You do not have to say anything . . .'

Jack read the caution slowly, enunciating each syllable. He had barely slept, tossing and turning into the small hours. Lilly had literally kicked him out of bed around five.

'Go to the station,' she mumbled from under the duvet, 'before I kill you with my bare hands.'

He'd kissed her head and jumped into his car.

He prepped the interview room and waited. And waited.

'Shall I wake him up?' the custody sergeant yawned. It had been a quiet night and he was clearly looking for something to keep him awake.

'Not till seven,' said Jack. 'I don't want to give him any excuse to say he can't be questioned.'

So Jack let him sleep, wash, eat a slice of toast and have a chat with his brief. At eight o'clock he pulled on a tie and got Malik into the chair opposite with a camera pointing at him.

'You know why you're here?' said Jack.

Malik shifted in the chair, his bulk took up the space of two men and his solicitor was forced into the corner next to the wall. He stared Jack down.

'No comment.'

Jack nodded. 'Then let's run over it one more time. Someone went to the Clayhill Estate and attacked Ryan Sanders. He was beaten unconscious and remains in a coma. His friend Aasha Hassan, was kidnapped and remains missing.'

The butcher stroked his neck, the muscles bulging. 'No comment.'

Jack breathed deeply. He had promised himself that he would stay calm.

'I put all this to you yesterday and you said you hadn't heard of either Ryan or Aasha.'

'No comment.'

'You said you hadn't been to Ryan's flat on the Clayhill Estate.' Jack pretended to check his notebook. 'That you never went to that shithole.'

Malik leaned back in his chair and Jack wondered if it would take his weight. The man must be close to seventeen stone, every ounce solid muscle.

'No comment.'

'Now I was tempted to believe you, but here's the funny thing,' said Jack. 'A heap of your blood was found at the scene.'

Malik's solicitor coughed. 'You said a smattering of blood was found at least fifty metres away.'

Jack waved away the discrepancy. 'Your client said he hadn't been there, now why was that?'

Malik sniffed loudly, drawing mucus into his mouth.

'If there was any reasonable explanation then why not give it?' Jack continued.

Malik swallowed the mouthful of mucus. 'No comment.'

Jack resisted the urge to gag. 'See, I don't think you have a reasonable explanation because I think you *were* there and you *did* beat an innocent kid to within an inch of his life.'

They glared at one another, the room silent around them.

'I'll tell you something else I think,' said Jack. 'If Ryan dies you'll go down for murder.'

Something flitted across Malik's face. Jack wasn't sure what, but it was a reaction. He pressed harder.

'You love this tough-guy image, don't you? All your mates looking up to you?'

Malik cocked his head to one side.

'But there are lots of tough guys in prison,' said Jack, 'and they don't like kiddie killers.'

Malik opened his mouth to speak and Jack thought he'd got him. If he could get him denying and defending he could tie him in knots.

'No comment.'

Jack smoothed down his tie. He hated ties with a vengeance, wearing them strictly for funerals and giving evidence in court, but he'd seen a DI on a murder case make exactly the same gesture whenever he became agitated. It gave frustrated fingers something to do and the long stroking motion had a calming effect. Jack had mused on why this type of tactic wasn't part of every copper's training. Maybe it was if you were fast-tracked. Either way he'd adopted it himself for difficult interviews.

'As for a young girl going missing, well, some might get the wrong idea about that.'

Malik ran his finger through his beard. It occurred to Jack that this was a stress mechanism like his tie. This one was good.

'No comment.'

'Cards on the table,' said Jack. 'If you tell us where the girl is, any judge is going to give you credit for that.'

'No comment.'

'But if things carry on and Aasha is kept away from her family, they're going to throw away the key.' Jack tossed something imaginary over his shoulder. 'And you'll end up collecting your bus pass inside.'

Malik leaned forward, his hands pressed into the table. He snarled so close to his face that Jack could smell the toothpaste on his breath.

'No comment.'

\*   \*   \*

Taslima hurried down the hospital corridor.

'Is everything all right?'

Lilly nodded. 'I'm having a scan. You don't mind being here, do you?'

'Shouldn't Jack be with you?' Taslima asked.

'He's arrested Abdul Malik.'

Taslima's mouth made a perfect 'O' shape.

Lilly laughed.

'Do you think he'll admit anything?' Taslima asked.

'I doubt it,' said Lilly.

Taslima's face fell.

'Don't worry,' said Lilly. 'Hardly anyone ever confesses.'

'Then what's the point?'

Lilly held up a finger. 'To see if he'll trip himself up, give something away.'

Lilly's name was called and she went through to the ultrasound room. Taslima helped her on to the bed and wrinkled her nose when Lilly pulled up her top and exposed the tight skin of her belly, covered in stretch marks.

'Don't look so horrified. Your time will come,' said Lilly.

Taslima gave a thin smile.

The sonographer covered Lilly's bump in cold jelly and began pressing the wand against her. The monitor jumped into life. There on the screen was the baby, curled tight, his hand in his mouth. The steady heartbeat filled the air.

'Beautiful,' Taslima whispered.

And it was. Very beautiful. Lilly felt a tear trickle down

her cheek. She and Jack were the parents of this perfect little soul growing inside her, but she couldn't even be sure they would still be together by the time he was ready to join them.

'Everything's fine,' said the sonographer.

If only that were true, thought Lilly.

The chief super called Jack up to his office. To his dismay, DI Bell was already there, leaning on the window, coffee in hand.

He took a sip. 'How's it going, Jack?'

'Fine, thanks,' Jack replied.

'I meant the case.'

Jack didn't answer. Who the hell did the DI think he was, cross-questioning him? This was Jack's case and he intended to discuss it with the chief, not his monkey.

He placed himself with his back to DI Bell. 'Sir.' He spoke directly to the chief super.

'Has Malik told us anything?' asked the chief.

Jack shook his head. 'No comment all the way.'

'You've applied some pressure, I assume?'

'As much as I dare.' Jack ignored the sighs from behind. 'As you know, this whole thing is very sensitive and we don't want any whiff of undue pressure.'

'Performing a robust interview is hardly brutality,' said the chief.

'There's a fine line,' said Jack, 'and I'm standing well back from it.'

DI Bell approached the desk. 'Then we should let him go.'

'What?' said Jack.

'You don't have anything concrete on him,' said DI Bell. 'Without a confession you have to let him go.'

Jack loosened his collar and smoothed his tie, determined not to lose his cool. He had deliberately ignored the gossip about Bell but could see now that some of it was true. But he had kept control with Malik and he could do it with Bell.

The chief super tapped his desk with the tip of his nail. 'What exactly have we got on him?'

'Bugger all,' said DI Bell.

The chief waved him away. 'Jack?'

'We know he was close to the scene,' said Jack. 'His blood was found in the stairwell nearest to the Sanders' flat.'

'It's at least fifty metres away,' said Bell.

'Have you been over there with a tape measure?' Jack snapped.

The chief held up his hand to stop them. 'Anything else?'

'He lied about it when questioned,' said Jack.

'But not under caution,' DI Bell pointed out.

Jack could feel his temper beginning to swell. He turned to face Bell. 'Why are you so keen for me to let this animal go?'

'I can see how easily this could be turned against the Force,' he answered.

Jack let out a cold laugh. 'Are you sure you're not just worried that I might have picked up the real killer of Yasmeen Khan?'

'Now you really have lost the plot,' DI Bell laughed

back. 'Have you been taking tips from that girlfriend of yours?'

'Enough.' The chief super slapped his hand against his desk. 'This is getting us nowhere.'

Jack needed to think fast. He knew he didn't have enough evidence to charge Malik and that the chief super would do anything to avoid bad press. But he wasn't ready to give up. The man was involved, he could feel it.

'Give me an extension, sir,' he said. 'Let me hold him another twenty-four hours.'

'To do what?' asked the chief.

'He didn't act alone,' said Jack, 'which means there is someone out there holding Aasha.'

'You have absolutely no idea about that,' said DI Bell. 'And in a community like this, no one is going to talk to you.'

Jack didn't take his eyes off the chief. 'I have some names.'

Bell snorted. 'What names?'

Jack pulled out the piece of paper that Malik had scribbled on.

'He gave me the names of some mates who can supposedly give him an alibi.'

Bell snatched the paper. 'And?'

'And if these men are prepared to lie for Malik, maybe they're involved in all this.'

The chief continued tapping, the noise chipping away at Jack's brain. If he could just have a little more time he could find Aasha and Ryan's attackers, he was sure of it.

At last the chief nodded. 'I'll get the extension.'

Jack couldn't contain a smile.

'Twelve hours,' said the chief.

Jack's smile slipped.

The chief pointed to his watch. 'The clock is ticking.'

Aasha sits cross-legged on the floor, her back against the cold stone of the wall. From time to time the man unlocks the door to let her use the bathroom or to pass in some food.

Other than that she is alone in this room with its tiled floor and bare walls. There are no windows and a single bulb hangs from the ceiling. Sometimes she falls asleep but she has no way of knowing what time of day it is.

She pulls her knees up into her chest and waits.

She thinks about Ryan. He was just trying to help her by letting her stay with him. He couldn't have known just how much trouble Aasha was bringing to his door.

Aasha's mum has always been quick to pass on the disaster stories of her friends' children.

'Auntie Shahida called today.' She would shake her head and sigh, before launching into a tortured story of ungrateful children failing their A levels or marrying beneath them.

Aasha had never done the smallest thing to bring shame to her family. She laughs out loud at the irony.

She prays that Ryan is all right. She makes a pact that if he is OK she will never do anything wrong for as long as she lives. She will get the best results in her class, study medicine at university and Mum will have something to brag about to all the neighbours.

The key rattles in the door and Aasha is on her feet before the door is opened. Though she is desperate to get out of this prison cell she feels the familiar stab of fear.

'Come on,' the man grunts, 'bathroom break.'

Aasha nods and follows him down the hall. Sunlight streams through the windows, dust dancing on the beams. It feels good after the sickly half-world of the electric bulb.

He lets her into the bathroom and stands outside. He allows her to shut the door but she knows he guards it from the other side. She gets about five minutes then he gives a knock of warning and opens it once more.

She quickly fills the bowl and splashes water over her face. As she wipes it with the cardboard stiffness of the towel she looks through the window. Outside there is a field, and another field beyond that. Aasha is a townie and has never been this far into the countryside. It seems to go on for ever, though that can't be true.

She listens carefully. At first she thought it was totally silent but she's started to pick up other sounds. The odd car in the far distance which means she must be within walking distance of a road. Not that she could get to it because the window is locked.

Sometimes she catches something else, like a baby crying or something.

There it goes again. Aasha stands perfectly still and concentrates. Not a baby, but an animal bleating.

She once read an old book called *The Silence of the Lambs* where some FBI agent mentions hearing her uncle

271

killing the baby lambs on his farm. Well, they wouldn't have been silent, would they? They would have been bleating like the animals outside.

She tries not to think about sharp knives, and blood and screaming.

Her thoughts are interrupted by the man's phone. In the quiet of the house it makes her jump. She listens at the door. The man is speaking in Urdu.

'What's going on?' He sounds cross but scared as well. 'Has he said anything, do you think?'

There is a pause while the person on the other end speaks, and by the sound of footsteps, the man is pacing up and down the hallway.

'I'm telling you now,' the man shouts, 'I'm not going to gaol.'

Aasha presses her ear to the door. The man is panting as if he's totally stressed by what he's being told.

'So what shall I do with the girl?' he growls.

What the answer is, Aasha has no way of knowing, but she is not as stupid as Imran says. She knows that some of the options are very bad. She's heard the stories about girls that were sent 'back home', forced to marry cousins they had never met. Girls that were in school one minute, then never seen again.

She moves back just as the door flings open, without the usual knock. The man scowls at her. He is so angry she fears he might beat her, and she flinches.

'Out,' he barks at her.

She scurries down the corridor, back to her cell. She's almost glad when he shuts her back inside.

*   *   *

Lilly hurried towards the station. Jack hadn't been able to tell her over the phone what had happened during Malik's interview and she was frantic trying to guess the permutations of what could have happened.

The best-case scenario was that he had made a full confession and implicated himself in Yasmeen's murder. But as Lilly had explained to Taslima, that wasn't very likely.

When she saw him leaving the car park she beeped her horn for him to cross the road and jump in.

'How did it go?' she asked, though his face told her everything she needed to know.

'He didn't say a word.'

Shit. To be fair, if Lilly had been his lawyer she would probably have advised the same thing.

'Did you have enough to charge him?' she asked.

Jack shook his head. 'Without forensics or a witness I can't place him at the scene.'

Lilly felt her heart plummet. She knew how badly Jack would take it. He had been desperate to put things right.

'When did you release him?' she asked.

'I didn't,' he said. 'I got an extension on the custody limits.'

Lilly let out a low whistle. 'That must have taken some fancy footwork.'

'Let's just say I have twelve hours and not a second longer.'

Lilly instinctively checked her watch. It was impossible. They both knew it. They looked at one another.

'I'm not ready to give up yet,' said Jack. 'Are you?'

'Not fucking likely.'

'Then we need to move fast,' said Jack, 'collect as much evidence as we can.'

'Where do we start?'

'I have a list of Malik's close friends. Uniform are checking them now.'

'What about us?' Lilly asked.

'I'm going back to Aasha's family to see if there's any link between them and Malik,' said Jack.

'I'll do the Khans,' said Lilly.

Jack threw open the car door. 'If anyone has so much as spoken to this bastard on the bus I want to know.'

She had been about to tell him about the scan, show him the grainy photograph of their unborn baby, but somehow it seemed all wrong.

'OK?' he asked.

'Let's do it,' she said.

Ismail sat on his hands. He'd bitten his nails right down to the quick but he still felt an urge to bring them to his lips.

His brother had taken up his usual position, lolling on the sofa. How could he be so relaxed? Did it not worry him that they might spend the rest of their lives in prison? Probably not. He could spend his days lifting weights and watching TV – identical to what he did now. But Ismail had plans. College, a good job, maybe run his own little business. He wanted to get his end away with a ton of English girls before his parents introduced him to some nice girl from Kashmir. Or lose his cherry, at the very least.

And what about Aasha? Didn't Imran care that their

sister was locked up somewhere and they had no way of finding out where?

A quick glance at his brother told Ismail the answer. Imran didn't give a shit about Aasha, never had done. Ismail wasn't convinced he gave a shit about anyone or anything apart from himself.

Mum perched on the very edge of her seat, listening to every word the policeman said.

'Abdul Malik is a very dangerous man,' McNally told them. 'The young lad he attacked is in a serious condition.'

Tears welled in Mum's eyes and Ismail had to turn away. This whole mess was killing her. He imagined how she'd feel if the police found out he and Imran were involved. It didn't bear thinking about. And what if they were arrested and taken to court? The shame would probably finish her off, which was stupid when you considered that this all started because Imran said Aasha had shamed the family.

'I'm sorry,' Mum murmured. 'I don't know him.' She looked over at her sons, desperation glinting in her tears.

'Nah,' said Imran. 'Never heard of him.'

Ismail didn't trust himself to speak and just shook his head.

The policeman frowned at them. He was one of those white men you just couldn't read. He seemed so polite and ineffectual, yet Ismail could sense something behind that.

'That's strange,' he said. 'Malik admitted that he did know you.'

Ismail risked a glance at Imran. What had Malik been

saying about them? Imran met his eyes and the warning was very clear.

'He must be mistaken.' Imran shrugged at Jack.

The policeman smoothed down his tie, a horrendous, polyester thing that he must have got cheap.

'He was quite clear that he knew you.'

Ismail's stomach flipped and bile stung his throat. He leaped to his feet and ran to the kitchen, retching into the sink.

Mum was behind him in seconds, rubbing his back. He wiped the back of his hand across his mouth, a string of mucus stretching between them.

'Everything all right?' The policeman was standing in the doorway, Imran by his side.

'We've all been very upset,' said Mum.

'Of course,' the policeman said, but he stared hard at Ismail.

Imran shot towards Mum and took her arm from Ismail's back.

'Why don't you show Sergeant McNally out and I'll take care of Ismail?'

She smiled at him gratefully and led the policeman away. When they were safely out of earshot he took a handful of Ismail's hair in his fist and hauled back his head. He yanked hard, making Ismail cry out.

'What the fuck do you think you're doing?'

Imran twisted the hair, his knuckles digging into Ismail's scalp. Ismail could feel the roots ripping away from the skin. 'What do you mean?'

Imran pushed Ismail's head down into the sink so his nose was almost touching the vomit.

'This crap,' he hissed. 'Like some sort of batty boy pussy.' He let go of Ismail and snorted in disgust. 'You may as well crawl down to the station and tell them everything.'

Ismail took a swipe at his tears. His scalp was screaming. 'That policeman said Malik told them about *us*.'

'He's lying,' said Imran.

'How can you be sure?' Ismail sobbed.

'Because Malik's a true Muslim brother.'

'But what about Aasha? What's going to happen to her?' asked Ismail.

'Malik will sort it out.'

'From prison?' Ismail shook his head. 'Maybe we should talk to that policeman. Explain that we never meant for any of this to happen.'

Imran grabbed his chin. 'Listen to me. If you go to the police Malik will kill you.'

'But what about Aasha?'

'That bitch is the reason we're in this mess.' Imran squeezed until Ismail's chin stung as much as his scalp. 'And if I hear you mention one word of this to anyone, I'll kill you myself.'

Anwar showed Lilly and Taslima through to the sitting room. He was anxious and agitated.

'Is Raffy OK?'

'Let's sit down,' Lilly suggested.

Saira and her mother had already taken chairs at the edge of the room. Saira held her mother's hand. Anwar gestured to Lilly and Taslima to sit, then took his place opposite. He was fidgeting and biting his lip.

'What's happened?' he asked. 'The prison called an hour ago and said there's been an incident. We've been trying to contact you.'

Lilly took a deep breath. She was here to discuss Malik but obviously the situation at Arlington was all the Khans could think about.

'I saw him yesterday,' she said. 'He's been moved to the hospital wing.'

'Why didn't they inform us sooner?' asked Saira.

'Prison communication is glacial,' said Lilly. 'A day's delay is not bad.'

She glanced at Mrs Khan, still silent and unmoving. Saira squeezed her mother's hand so hard her knuckles were white.

'The governor said there had been a fight.' Anwar shook his head. 'What has my brother done now?'

'Absolutely nothing,' said Lilly. 'He was attacked by another inmate.'

Anwar stood up and began to pace. 'You saw him at court, Miss Valentine, totally out of control.'

'He was provoked by the guard,' Taslima pointed out.

Anwar flapped his arms. 'There's always some reason why he loses his temper. His behaviour is never his fault.'

Saira gently replaced her mother's hand in her lap and approached her brother. She led him back to his place and sat close to him, patting his leg.

'Calm, Anwar,' she whispered.

Lilly was taken again by how maternal this seemed, as if Saira had taken on the role of mother.

'I don't believe this was Raffy's fault,' said Lilly. 'It was a racially motivated attack.'

278

Anwar's eyes opened wide. 'He was attacked because he's a Muslim?'

'A Muslim, a Sikh, a Jew,' said Lilly, 'black, brown or yellow, these people don't care.'

'How can such things take place in prison?' asked Anwar.

'Come on,' Saira spoke in a hushed tone, 'these things happen every day out here so why not in prison?'

Anwar nodded, the truth of it weighing visibly and heavily.

'So what now?' he asked.

'He's recovering well,' said Lilly, 'and the other boy will be charged with assault.'

Anwar blew through his nose.

'OK then.' Lilly paused. She had to ask about Malik but she needed the Khans to focus. Under normal circumstances she would have let them calm down for a day or so, but she didn't have time. She sneaked a look at her watch and gulped. Minutes and hours were ticking away. Soon Malik would be released and any chance of linking him to Yasmeen's murder would be lost. She nodded slightly to Taslima to steer the conversation away from Raffy.

'Actually, I wanted to talk to you about something else as well,' said Taslima.

Anwar and Saira looked up at her expectantly.

'We've been trying to think of anyone who might want to hurt Yasmeen,' she continued, 'and someone's name has come up.'

'Who?' Anwar and Saira spoke as one.

'Abdul Malik.'

No one said a word.

'The police think this man is involved in another honour attack,' said Taslima.

Anwar covered his mouth. 'Another girl has been murdered?'

'Kidnapped,' said Lilly. 'They're desperately trying to find her.'

'I can't believe it,' Anwar muttered.

'That's why I want you all to think very, very carefully,' said Lilly. 'Whatever you can tell me about this man might not only help Raffy's defence but also save another girl.'

'Abdul Malik,' Anwar rolled the words around his tongue. 'Sorry, I've never heard the name.'

Lilly's heart sank. 'He delivers meat to the Paradise Halal Butchers.'

Anwar turned to his mother. 'Do you know him, Ma?'

Mrs Khan didn't respond.

'We don't use it,' said Saira.

'But he's your uncle,' said Lilly.

Saira gave a tight smile. 'Uncle Mohamed is a very good man in lots of ways, but his meat is tough.'

Lilly almost laughed out loud. 'Blood is thicker than water,' her mother used to say, 'but it isn't cement.'

'Malik's very distinctive,' said Lilly. 'He must weigh seventeen stone, about six two.'

'He has a beard.' Taslima stroked her chin.

Lilly willed them to recognise the description. 'In the last few days his nose has been broken. He has black eyes.'

'Sorry,' said Anwar, 'no.'

Lilly and Taslima said their goodbyes and left the Khans.

They were no further forward in placing Malik at the scene.

Jack punched the kitchen wall. 'Damn it.'

Lilly and Taslima jumped.

'Sorry,' Jack shook the pain from his fist. 'I just can't believe no one has even heard of this guy.'

'Do we believe them?' asked Taslima.

'Good question.' Jack sucked his knuckles. 'The Hassan boys are hiding something. The younger one started puking when it got too close to home.'

'The Khans seem to be telling the truth,' said Lilly.

'Though I thought Anwar was a bit quick to respond,' said Taslima.

Lilly nodded. He had been quick to deny any knowledge of Malik and quicker still to blame Raffy for starting the fight in prison. Then there was Mrs Khan, utterly unengaged in her son's fate.

'I think there's something they're not telling us,' she conceded.

'If I had my way I'd nick the lot of them and shove them in a cell until they were ready to talk,' said Jack.

'Don't let something as small as the Human Rights Act stop you,' Lilly laughed.

Jack slapped his forehead with his hand. 'Someone must know this man.'

'The only person who's been willing to mention him is the uncle,' said Lilly.

'Then let's go back there,' said Jack. 'See if there's anything else.'

Lilly and Taslima exchanged a look.

'He's going to be very unhappy,' said Lilly.

Jack grabbed his coat. 'I don't care if he's crying into his tea.'


'No, no, no.'

The old guy stood in the doorway to his butcher's shop, blocking Lilly and Taslima.

'Please, Mohamed,' said Lilly. 'It's important.'

He shook his head and turned the sign to closed.

'It's always important with you,' he hissed. 'Now go away.'

Jack couldn't wait around any longer. His extension was seeping away. With the Khans and the Hassans refusing to play ball, this guy was the only connection Jack had. What was wrong with everyone? Did they like having Malik stomping around their neighbourhood telling them what they could or couldn't do?

'Five minutes,' Lilly begged.

'Leave now,' said Mohamed, 'or I'm calling the police.'

Jack pushed forward and jammed his foot in the door. 'Guess what, sunshine? I am the police.'

Mohamed checked Jack's badge carefully, then let them in. The shop was in darkness, the fridges humming in the background.

'Tell me about Abdul Malik,' said Jack.

Mohamed threw up his arms. 'I've told these two all I know. I hear things, whispers, nothing concrete.'

'And what do these whispers say?'

Mohamed looked around him as if someone might be listening in the shadows. 'That he's involved in some things around here.'

'Bad things?'

Mohamed nodded. 'Family stuff, when girls disobey their parents.'

'Honour attacks.'

Mohamed sighed.

'A girl called Aasha Hassan has gone missing,' said Jack. 'Was Malik involved?'

A silhouette floated across the window as someone walked past the shop. Mohamed froze.

'Was Malik involved?' Jack repeated.

Mohamed craned his neck, watching as the figure outside moved away. 'People think so.'

Jack's head began to pound. 'What the hell do you mean?'

'People come in here to buy meat and they gossip.' He waved at Lilly. 'What you solicitors call hearsay.'

'Then why don't they come and tell us?' Jack roared. 'Don't they care what happens to Aasha?'

Mohamed's eyes darted from the door to Jack and back again.

'A few think she got what she deserved,' he said.

Jack exploded. 'She's fifteen, for fuck's sake.'

Mohamed stared at Jack until Lilly stepped between them.

'What about the others?' Her tone was deliberate. 'You said some people thought Aasha deserved it but what about the rest?'

Jack took a lungful of air and exhaled slowly. He knew Lilly was trying to defuse things, that he'd gone too far. But it was impossible not to.

'Some people are saying that Malik and his cronies

283

are out of control,' said Mohamed. 'That none of us are safe.'

'Tell me about these cronies,' snapped Jack. 'Who are they?'

Mohamed shook his head. 'I don't know.'

Jack felt rage taking over. He had to get out of there before he did something he'd regret. He stormed out of the shop, crashing the door behind him.

Moments later, Lilly and Taslima joined him.

'Jesus Christ, Jack,' said Lilly. 'You've got to calm down.'

'How can I,' he roared, 'when all I come up against is this wall of silence?'

'The PTF are bullies,' said Taslima. 'Everyone is frightened.'

Jack stabbed his chest with his thumb. 'I've lived in communities run by the paramilitary. Trust me, you can't let these people dictate things. Someone has to take a stand.'

'Not everyone is brave enough,' said Taslima.

At that moment Lilly's mobile rang.

'Hello?' She paused, listening, her face impassive.

'Right,' she said, 'thanks.'

She snapped her phone shut.

'Let's thank our lucky stars that someone is brave enough to take a stand.'

'No riddles, Lil. My brain is aching,' said Jack.

Lilly smiled. 'Mohamed has just given me the name of one of Malik's little friends.'

'You are joking.'

'Nawed Jalil,' said Lilly.

Jack pulled out Malik's scribbled note and tapped it

triumphantly with his thumb. Nawed Jalil was on the list.

'Come on, you beauty.'

Jack hadn't wanted to stop for a coffee, but Lilly had insisted. It would take less than five minutes, and anyway, they needed to gather their thoughts and decide what to do.

They took seats at the sticky table in a café and Lilly stirred heaped teaspoons of sugar into her cup. Jack hovered outside, calling the station for Jalil's address.

'He's not always this bonkers,' Lilly assured Taslima.

Taslima gave a shy smile. 'Passion is a good sign.'

Lilly smiled back but it felt tight on her face. She couldn't help wondering who else Jack had been getting passionate about.

Jack pushed his mobile into his pocket and dived into the café. He remained standing and grabbed his coffee. He took a sip and wrinkled his nose.

'Full fat?'

'They were all out of soya,' Lilly winked.

He snorted and drained his cup. 'Right, I'm off.'

'Hold on,' Lilly held up her hand. 'You can't just pole up at his house.'

'Why not?'

''Cos he'll take one look at your ID and shut the door.'

'I'll just nick him,' said Jack.

Lilly rolled her eyes. 'You have no evidence whatsoever to arrest him on.'

'I'll worry about that later.'

'Jack,' Lilly put her hand on his, 'stop for a second.

You don't have time to get this man to the station, get him booked in and everything else. By the time you get round to interviewing him, Malik's extension will have run out.'

Jack's shoulders slumped. 'So what do you suggest?'

'I don't know,' Lilly admitted. 'If we watch him he might lead us to Aasha.'

'We could spend the rest of the day following him to McDonald's and back,' said Jack. 'I'd rather take my chances going round there myself.'

'I don't think that would be wise.' Taslima spoke in a small voice. 'If he's involved in these crimes he's hardly likely to help you with your enquiries, and even if he's not, we've seen how this community react to the police.'

'Well, I have to do something,' said Jack. 'At least this way we won't be any worse off than we are now.'

Taslima moved her cup forward in a slow, deliberate motion. 'Sorry, but I think it will be worse. If your extension expires while you're chasing Jalil then Malik will be released and I don't think that bodes well for Aasha.'

Jack opened his mouth, then closed it. They all knew Taslima was right.

'This is impossible,' said Jack.

'I could speak to him,' said Taslima.

Lilly and Jack exchanged looks.

'How would that help?' asked Jack.

'We've already established that you can't do it,' she said, 'and if Raffique Khan's pregnant lawyer turns up making waves the result will be much the same.'

Lilly and Jack waited.

'But I'm an insider,' said Taslima.

'But what would you say?' asked Lilly.

'That I've been sent by the Hassan brothers to get Aasha out of the country.'

'Isn't that a bit far-fetched?' asked Jack.

Taslima raised her eyebrows. 'Do you know how many Asian girls are whisked away each year? I'll say the family know she's caused nothing but trouble and want to put this all behind them by marrying her off in Pakistan.'

'What if he checks up?' asked Lilly. 'Calls the Hassans?'

'I'll say the police are round there now, speaking to them, and that it's urgent we get Aasha out.'

Lilly played it over in her mind. The plan was hardly flawless, but perhaps it could work. With time running out perhaps they should try.

'I say we give it a go,' she said.

Jack sighed and ran his hands through his hair. 'I say we don't have a choice.'


As the threesome went along the street past his car, Cormack slid down in his seat and hid his face in the shadows. He'd been following the woman all day but she'd been haring around from one place to the next. Cormack was knackered just keeping up.

When the man had turned up, Cormack had nearly given up. He was plod. No doubt about it. And Cormack had no intention of getting into a Q & A with a copper. What he needed to do had to be far from prying eyes.

After a while, though, it became obvious that the man wasn't paying attention to anything around him. He was as stressed out as a punter before a race. So Cormack kept up the tail but at a safe distance. Besides, the Pakis had promised him a pony when he got this part of the job done. God knows what all this was about, but it must be serious for them to be flashing cash like that around.

When all three got in the same car, Cormack decided to call it a day. He let them pull away and reached for a fag. The one good thing about days like today was he'd barely even thought about smoking. Maybe that was the trick. Keep himself busy.

He puffed contentedly and put his key in the ignition. He'd catch up with the woman soon enough.

# Chapter Nine

April 2009

> Allah is Our Lord
> Mohammed is Our Leader
> The Koran is Our Constitution
> Jihad is Our Way
> Martyrdom is Our Desire

I smile at the words that I diligently typed out, printed and stuck on the wall beside my bed. When I wake in the morning they are the first thing I see. They never cease to surprise me with their exquisite clarity. They are a gift from Allah, as is the person who gave them to me.

I reach for my laptop, eager to get back to www.mujahidtoday.

I discovered it in the course of my posting work and it soon became clear to me that many of the forum members were not teenagers swapping gossip.

Regulars, like Light of Jeddah and Peacekeeper, left forthright and often stinging messages on any political subject. They were bold in support of the *Ummah* and always bumped any threads I began.

A week ago I got into a long debate with Kalid42 about the co-existence of religions.

Re: The One True Religion . . . by Khalid42 at 9.25
on 2.4.09
I believe that we can live side by side with our non-Muslim brothers and sisters. The prophet (pbuh) didn't instruct us to live apart. I choose to integrate and love all my brothers and sisters.

This was an argument that came up often so I typed in my standard response.

Re: The One True Religion . . . by Believer at 9.27
on 2.4.09
We will not need to live apart when everyone submits themselves to Allah and it is the duty of every true Muslim to spread his wondrous word.

Re: The One True Religion . . . by Khalid42 at 9.30
on 2.4.09
Can we not all live in peace and allow each person to choose?

I was about to explain that there would never be peace until the world accepted Allah, when someone else joined in.

Re: The One True Religion . . . by Fighting4Islam at 9.32
   on 2.4.09
Choosing another religion is rejecting Allah – the worst
possible sin. How can we walk by and ignore that?

I watched with fascination as the new poster poured
scorn on each suggestion that Muslims should just live
and let live. His views were shouted down by others
calling him 'extremist' but they seemed crystalline to me.
I clicked onto his member profile.

Name: Fighting4Islam
Age : 22
Location: the front line
Way of Life: Allah is Our Lord
Mohammed is Our Leader
The Koran is Our Constitution
Jihad is Our Way
Martrydom is Our Desire.

I hope Fighting4Islam is on line. Our exchanges have
become the highlight of each day. There is great wisdom
in his words and bravery. His refusal to compromise is often
seen as arrogance or stubbornness but I see it as purity.

Despite the fact that it's so early in the morning the
forum is buzzing. Someone has posted a link saying
Hamas have intercepted UN trucks containing aid and
distributed it amongst their followers.

The Zionist apologists are out in force.

> Re: UN trucks intercepted . . . by Khalid42 at 6.05 on
>    9.4.09
> Why are we surprised that a terrorist organisation such
> as Hamas would do this? They have brought nothing but
> fear and violence to our brothers and sisters in Palestine.

I skim the responses until I find what I'm looking for.

> Re: UN trucks intercepted . . . by Fighting4Islam at 6.15
>    on 9.4.09
> Don't rely on mainstream Western media to tell you the
> truth. Those bringing fear and violence to Palestine are
> Israel and her supporters.
> They want to demonise Hamas because they know the
> truth . . . Hamas build hospitals, schools and mosques
> here. That is their main work and that is why the people
> of Gaza love them.

I reread Fighting4Islam's post to check I'm not mistaken.
But no, there it is '. . . Hamas build hospitals, schools
and Mosques *here*.'

My fingers flash across the keyboard.

> Re: UN trucks intercepted . . . by Believer at 6.20 on
>    9.4.09
> Are you in Palestine, brother?

I wait for the answer. Outside the world is turning. Cars
on their way to the station for the morning commute.
The electric whirr of a milk float. Even in my house a
shower is running in the bathroom.

But in my room it is as if the air has been sucked out. As if I am floating in the vacuum of space. Waiting.

Re: UN trucks intercepted . . . by Fighting4Islam at 6.25
   on 9.4.09
Yes.

'Are you sure about this?'

Lilly and Jack looked behind them to the back seat of his car, where Taslima was sitting.

She nodded her head, a slight smile playing on her lips.

As she reached for the door handle, Lilly realised that even if Taslima wasn't having second thoughts about their plan, she was.

'Hold on.' She grasped Taslima's knee. 'We need to go over this again.'

Jack nodded but Lilly could feel his impatience. Time was flying away. Even so, this wasn't something they could rush.

'I tell Jalil that Aasha's family have sent me to take her out of the country,' said Taslima.

Lilly breathed deeply. It sounded so easy and yet there were so many things that could go wrong. She tried not to recall her old boss's face when a previous case had attracted hostile attention. Rupinder had received a beating so severe she had spent six weeks in ICU. Even after the scars had healed, she never returned to work.

'What if he turns nasty?' she asked. 'This man was involved in a horrendous attack on a child.'

'My instinct tells me that was Malik,' said Jack.

'That's as maybe,' said Lilly, 'but Jalil was still part of it. And let's not forget Yasmeen.'

'What about her?' asked Jack.

Lilly rolled her eyes. 'I'm pretty sure this lot killed her, remember.'

Jack opened his mouth to speak but Taslima got there first.

'I understand your point, Lilly, that this man may be dangerous.'

'Exactly.'

'I've dealt with violent people before,' Taslima said. 'Don't worry.'

But Lilly was worrying. She knew that her own brand of enthusiasm often carried people along, often into trouble.

She turned to Jack. 'Can't we wire her up or something?'

'A wire?' Jack laughed. 'This isn't an episode of *Spooks*.'

Lilly put up her hands in surrender.

Taslima fished out her phone and pressed a key. Lilly's own phone sprang into life.

'Hello.'

Taslima giggled. 'It's me. I'll keep it on and then you can hear everything.'

'You're good.' Jack wagged his finger at her.

She opened the car and stepped outside.

Lilly watched her walk up the path to Jalil's house and was filled with sisterly love. As an only child she had longed for a sister. Another girl who would share styling tips for their stupidly curly hair, who would gossip about boys and concoct the best mix of foundation and concealer to cover a love bite. The complete opposite of Taslima, in fact, and yet there it was.

As Elsa would have said, 'Feelings are feelings.'

Taslima's slender hand reached out to ring the bell and Lilly's stomach lurched.

'Do you think we're doing the right thing?'

'She'll be fine,' said Jack, but there was no certainty in his voice.

With less than eight hours left to keep Malik inside, time was running out.

Taslima half hoped that no one would answer the door. In the comfort of the car she'd been clear in her mind that this was the best opportunity for them to find Aasha, but as she'd approached the house, some of her bravado disappeared. By the time she rang the bell she was shaking. She checked her phone, which lay in her closed bag. The line was still open with Lilly and Jack. They would hear if she got into any trouble.

When the door opened she murmured a swift *dua* that Allah would show her the way and smiled.

'Nawed Jalil?'

The guy was in his early twenties, dressed in an Adidas tracksuit. His beard needed a trim and his left eye twitched.

'Who wants to know?' he asked.

'Taslima Hassan,' she said. 'I'm Aasha Hassan's cousin.'

A mixture of conflicting emotions raced across his face, confusion and fear among them.

'I don't think I know the name,' he said.

Taslima didn't let her smile slip. 'Sure you do. Can I step inside?'

When he closed the door behind her and she knew Lilly and Jack could no longer see her, she felt a stab of panic. When he turned briefly to lead her into the kitchen she rechecked her phone for reassurance.

'Aasha's family sent me,' she said.

'Why?'

This was the crux of it. Everything depended on whether she could carry off the lie.

'Malik's locked up and they're very nervous,' she said.

The look on Jalil's face told Taslima that he was equally concerned.

'They think it will be better for everyone if Aasha is removed from the situation,' she said.

'Removed how?'

'Taken out of the country,' Taslima continued, 'for a long holiday.'

The relief poured from Jalil's eyes to his mouth and a crooked smile spread across his face.

'Back to Pakistan?'

Taslima nodded. 'They have someone interested in marriage.'

The man exhaled as if he had been holding his breath for an interminably long time and finally Taslima's heart began to slow.

Whatever the holes in her story, Jack had pointed out that Jalil would want to believe her. He was right.

'You know what's happened to Malik,' she said, 'and the police are round at my cousins' right now. If we move quickly then they won't be able to make the link.'

'You want to take the girl now?'

Taslima rolled her eyes dramatically. 'We fly out tonight.'

'Tonight?' Jalil repeated.

Come on, thought Taslima, you know you want rid of her. What could she say that would tip him into her direction? She remembered Jack mentioning that one of Aasha's brothers had been distressed and vomiting at the very mention of Malik's name.

'If they arrest Aasha's brothers I'm not convinced they'll keep it buttoned.'

'Imran's sound,' said Jalil.

'It's not him I'm worried about.' Aasha gave him what she hoped was a knowing look.

Jalil frowned. She'd hit the nail on the head.

'I told Malik we didn't need to meet up with them,' he said.

Taslima had him. 'Look, it doesn't matter what he tells the police if Aasha's not around to make a statement.'

Jalil gave one short nod. He had clearly made up his mind.

'Right then, let's go.'

Lilly put her hand over the Bluetooth sensor and smiled at Jack.

'You were right,' she whispered. 'She's bloody good.'

They'd patched Lilly's phone through Bluetooth so that they could hear Taslima on speaker phone. The sound was muffled and crackled wildly in her bag.

'Does she keep a bag of crisps in there?' asked Jack.

Lilly pictured Taslima's bag. The slimline diary, the leather-bound copy of the Koran and the second phone for emergencies. There was certainly no food or rubbish.

They'd sat, rapt, at Taslima's attempts to get Jilal to divulge Aasha's whereabouts. Lilly cringed at the idea that sending Aasha away would be the end of all their problems. Surely anyone with half a brain would realise that there was Ryan in the equation?

But Taslima had banked on Jilal being desperate, and a desperate man asks few questions.

When they emerged through the door, Lilly couldn't quite believe it. The plan had worked. Taslima was a genius.

Jilal led Taslima to a battered Ford Focus and they got inside. Like a complete professional Taslima's eyes didn't so much as flicker towards Jack's car.

'Bloody fantastic,' Jack whispered, and started up the engine.

Was it really going to be this easy? Would Jilal simply take them to Aasha? It hardly seemed possible.

The Ford raced out of Bury Park.

Jilal's voice came through the speaker but the words were unclear as they fought with the car's engine and the noise of the road outside.

'What's he saying?' Lilly whispered.

Jack shrugged.

Taslima's voice in response was louder, unnaturally so, no doubt to compensate for the background noise. Lilly prayed it wasn't obvious to Jilal.

'The plane leaves around seven,' she said. 'Will there be enough time?'

Jilal's answer was monosyllabic – Lilly guessed at a solitary 'yes'. She did a quick calculation in her head. Wherever Aasha was being kept couldn't be more than an hour's drive. With any luck this would all be over very soon.

The car bore left onto the dual carriageway and quickly picked up speed. Clearly Jalil wanted to put an end to all this too.

The traffic was heavy, lorries and vans all steaming their way out of Luton to the motorway. Jalil's car began weaving impatiently, overtaking a juggernaut on the inside lane.

Jack followed behind, narrowly avoiding being forced off the road.

'Christ,' he muttered, and Lilly put her finger to her lips.

As they approached a line of traffic cones – a flimsy barrier between the cars and half a mile of waterlogged ditches housing uncovered pipes – everyone jockeyed for position as the road narrowed to one lane. A taxi and a stretch limo tried to force their way in front of Jack. Jack kept his foot on the pedal, not giving an inch.

The electric windows of the limo came down and a gang of women dressed for a hen party began waving and shouting at them. By the look of them, they'd already started drinking at breakfast.

Lilly gesticulated to her watch to show that they were in a hurry.

A plump woman in a pair of bunny girl ears leaned out. She held a bottle of Lambrini in one hand, a cigarette in the other. A learner plate hung round her neck on a string and flapped in the wind.

'Got a light?' she squealed.

Another woman in a white cowboy hat trimmed with marabou roared with laughter.

Jack ignored them and kept his eyes ahead. The limo signalled to be let in. Jack ignored that too.

'Let us in, you miserable fuckers,' the bunny girl slurred.

'You tell 'em, Jade!' the cowgirl shrieked.

The bunny girl leaned out even further so that her breasts hung over the side, barely covered by a crop top emblazoned with the words 'Porn Star'.

'You need your leg over, mate, then you might not be so uptight.'

Lilly glanced at Jack, saw the muscles of his jaw working up and down. He couldn't let the limo come between Jalil and him, but the limo was now close enough for them to reach out and touch. If he didn't ease back they would collide.

'Jack?' Lilly whispered.

'Yes, mate,' called the cowgirl. 'Come in here and we'll release your tensions.'

Jack gritted his teeth but kept his foot flat.

'How about a quickie before I get married?' Bunny Girl hiccuped. She threw both her arms wide as if to embrace Jack. 'Shit.' She let go of the bottle and it arced into the air, spraying cheap wine over Jack's side window. It landed with a thud, then a crack, on his windscreen.

Lilly instinctively covered her face with her hands and Jack slammed on the brake. His car slid to a halt, batting traffic cones aside in its wake. As the car behind screeched to a stop, its horn blaring, the limo accelerated away, as did Jalil's Ford.

'Are you OK?' Jack panted.

Lilly waved wildly at the phone sensor. Jack grabbed it, turned it off and shoved the handset up his jumper.

'Are you hurt?'

She was shaking uncontrollably and her neck felt strained, but no, she wasn't hurt.

'We've lost them,' she said.

Jack nodded and slapped the steering wheel with his palms.

Taslima scrabbled into her bag and turned down the volume on her phone. Although faint there were all sorts of noises coming from it and she was terrified Jalil would hear.

'What was that?' he asked.

Taslima shrugged. Behind them a group of women were leaning out of the windows of one of those stupid stretch limos, screaming and singing.

'I think it's that lot,' she said.

Jalil checked in his rear-view mirror. 'Slags,' he declared.

She couldn't see Lilly and Jack but assumed they were behind the limo. She had no idea where they were and searched the horizon for something familiar. How long had they been driving? Forty minutes? An hour? How many miles from Luton were they?

'Is it far?' she asked.

He looked at her sideways. Perhaps she was asking too many questions, making him suspicious.

'I'm just anxious about the flight,' she added.

'Don't worry,' he said. 'We'll be there soon.'

DI Bell cracked his knuckles, something the old man had told him to stop throughout his childhood. Admittedly, it didn't fit in with his image as a smooth operator, but somehow it released tension.

And he was feeling the tension.

The Khan case was going to be the making of him, the platform from which he would rise to the upper echelons of the Force. It would give him a level of credibility that he could use to his advantage. In a couple of months he would apply for a transfer to the Honour Attacks and Forced Marriages Unit. Their profile and allocated resources was growing and Bell could make a real name for himself. Comments on Radio Four, interviews in *The Times*, he could see it all now.

He had it all planned out.

Then Jack fecking McNally swanned in with this case of a missing girl.

Not only was it taking the wind right out of his sails, there was an outside chance that the body Jack had locked up for it might have had something to do with the Khan murder.

He pulled on his jacket and smoothed down the fabric. He was destined for the highest ranks. It had been expected since the day he had joined and he had spent all his career mapping it out, working towards it. There was no way he was going to let it all collapse.

He trotted downstairs to the custody suite and checked the white board.

| Cell | Name | Offence | Time in |
|------|------|---------|---------|
| 10 | Abdul Malik | SAO | Extension |

'How long's left on the clock?' he asked the custody sergeant.

The sarge checked his watch. 'Six hours.'

DI Bell scowled. Jack's time was running out. Had he managed to find anything?

'Has McNally called in?' he asked.

'Nah,' said the sarge. 'But that's Jack all over.'

Typical. McNally was the worst sort of copper, all unfinished paperwork and bleeding heart. Certainly not the type to crack a serious case in six hours. A soft touch.

And yet he'd heard all the stories. Only a few months earlier, Jack had been involved in a shooting and had taken out some kid at close range. So not that soft.

'Give me the keys to ten,' Bell said.

The sergeant raised an eye.

'I just want to check if he's ready to talk,' said Bell. 'See if there's anything that can help Jack.'

The sarge reached for the phone. 'Let me get his brief.'

Bell placed his hand over the receiver. 'Not an interview,' he said. 'Just a quiet chat in his cell.'

'Absolutely not.' The sarge shook his head. 'You know me, everything done by the book.'

Bell buried his hands in his pockets, fighting the urge to crack his knuckles.

'In normal circumstances I'd agree, but there just isn't the time.' He could see the sarge wavering.

'If I can get anything out of him that will help Jack nail this bastard then it's got to be worth it.'

'You won't be able to use anything he says,' said the sarge.

'Not directly,' Bell agreed, 'but I might get something we can use another way.'

The sarge touched the pocket where he kept his warrant card.

Bell made a last-ditch attempt. 'Will you be happy when we have to let that monster go?'

The sergeant reached behind him and tossed a set of keys to Bell. 'Ten minutes, and I didn't see anything.'

Bell peered through the hatch of cell ten. Malik was positioned on the floor doing push-ups, his shoulders like pistons. Christ, the man was strong.

Bell unlocked the cell and stood in the doorway.

Malik continued without looking up. The smell of his sweat filled the room.

'Can we speak?' Bell asked.

Malik placed one hand behind his back, taking the weight of his entire body onto the other. He grimaced at the floor, but showed no signs of stopping.

Bell closed the door behind him and moved to the bed. The enormity of the other man and the sheer animal energy of him was like an assault. Bell tried to hold back his fear.

'Sergeant McNally is sure you attacked Ryan Sanders,' he said. 'He even thinks you might have killed Yasmeen Khan.'

Sweat poured down the butcher's face and pooled on the concrete below his chin. He panted with each move.

'He's out there now trying to find Aasha,' said Bell.

At last Malik stopped. He gripped the bottom of his T-shirt, pulled it up to his face and wiped it dry. When he let it drop, the wet stain turned Bell's stomach.

'I'd say finding Aasha was the key, wouldn't you?'

Malik didn't look at him but lay down on his back and began a series of sit-ups, each lift punctuated by a sharp whistle of air.

Bell watched him for a second, then left.

'Anything?' asked the custody sergeant.

Bell passed back the keys. 'Not a word.'


When Jalil's car pulled off the main road and down a dirt track, Taslima felt relief flood over her. Throughout the journey he had hardly spoken and she was terrified that he would change his mind.

'We're here?' she asked.

Jalil nodded.

Taslima glanced in the wing mirror but there was no sign of Jack's car. To be fair, she expected Jack and Lilly to stay well back. They wouldn't want to give away their presence until they were sure this was the right location.

'Is Aasha on her own here?' Taslima asked.

'When I'm not here,' said Jalil.

'No other girls then?'

Jalil frowned. 'We're not running a hotel.'

Taslima blushed. 'I just thought maybe you were helping other families like ours.'

'Well, you thought wrong.'

'What about Yasmeen Khan?'

'Never heard of her.'

Taslima watched his expression carefully. She was almost sure he was telling the truth.

They turned left through iron gates and arrived

outside an old farmhouse surrounded by fields and outbuildings. The sun was still shining and birds were singing. Under normal circumstances Taslima would have felt enchanted.

'A farm?' asked Taslima.

Again the man just nodded and unlocked the large oak door. Taslima checked her phone was still switched on. An animal bleated nearby and she turned to the sound.

'What's that?' she asked.

Jalil sighed. 'Let's just get on with it.'

He led her down a corridor, each door along it locked, until they came to the very end.

'Aasha's in there?' Taslima asked.

Jalil produced another key. 'Well, it isn't the Queen of Sheba.'

In the gloom and airlessness of a room without windows a young girl was huddled in the corner. When she lifted her face to the open door and saw Taslima standing there she couldn't hide her surprise.

Taslima stepped into the room. 'Hello, Aasha.'

The girl pursed her brow and Taslima's heart skipped a beat. Would Jalil suspect they didn't know one another? Surely the look on Aasha's face said it all.

'Get up now,' she blustered, 'we're leaving.'

She widened her eyes, trying to signal to Aasha that she needed to play along, but the girl didn't budge.

'Who—'

'Come on,' Taslima almost shouted. 'We can't waste time talking.'

'Hang on a minute.' Jalil held up his hand. 'I thought you two knew each other?'

Taslima turned to him and grinned. 'Of course we do. I'm Aasha's auntie.'

Jalil screwed up his mouth. 'I thought you said you were her cousin.'

'Auntie, cousin,' Taslima waved her hand at him, 'it's all the same, no?'

Briskly, she walked across to where Aasha was still sitting. 'Now get up, young lady. We have a plane to catch.' She held out her hand to Aasha to pull her to her feet. With her back to Jalil she mouthed the words 'Trust me' and prayed that the girl would.

Aasha seemed bewildered and her eyes glistened with tears as she looked at Taslima's outstretched hand.

Taslima stood in the same position for what seemed like for ever when at last Aasha held out her own hand and their fingers touched.

'Good girl,' said Taslima. 'There's nothing to worry about.'

Aasha nodded but there were still tears in her eyes.

'I need the toilet,' she murmured.

Taslima turned to Jalil and raised her eyebrow.

Jalil's left eye spun in circles. 'This way.'

Sweat made Malik blink. A salty trail of it ran down his face. He wiped his hands across his eyes but they were soaking too, as was his T-shirt.

Working out in his cell wasn't easy but he needed to stay focused. The police could place him at the Clayhill Estate by the blood from his nose, but he would come up with an explanation for that. Without any witnesses they couldn't disprove it. The boy wouldn't be saying anything for a long time, so there was only the girl to worry about.

As long as Jalil held firm there was no way the police would find her. Then when Malik got out of here, he'd get rid of her himself.

It hadn't been part of the deal but it was the only way.

No witnesses.

He inhaled through his nose, sweat rattling in his nostrils. He wished it were anyone but Jalil with the girl. They'd met in prison, of course. Malik had been doing a lump for GBH and Jalil had been on remand for some road-rage thing. The brother wasn't stable at the best of times, but under pressure he was a liability. Sometimes at night he would punch the wall till his knuckles bled.

A black brother on a transfer from Brixton got them into reading stuff about Afghanistan. Surrounded by low-life junkies and paedophiles, Malik could easily understand how you had to keep these people under control. You had to impose order.

On the out, he and Jalil set up the Luton branch of the PTF. Malik liked the kudos it gave him in the community, how people came to him with problems that needed solving unconventionally.

Jalil liked being part of it but he was still a grade A nutter. Malik generally only used him as extra muscle.

He screwed his eyes shut as another rivulet poured into them. They stung like hell. He reached for the blanket on his bed to wipe his face. As he pulled it towards him he heard a clunk as something heavy and metal hit the concrete floor of the cell.

When he cleared his eyes he looked down. It was a

mobile phone. He glanced at the door and back again. It must have been hidden in the folds of the bed.

He hooked it with his foot and dragged it to him. As he turned it over in his fist he wondered how it had got there. The DI was one stupid mother if he had dropped it.

Frankly he didn't care. It was a gift from Allah. He stabbed a number and brought the phone to his lips.

'It's Malik.'

'Oh man, am I pleased to hear from you.' Malik could imagine Jalil's eye doing somersaults. 'When did they let you out?'

'They didn't.'

Jalil was incredulous. 'Then where are you ringing from, man?'

'Forget about that, brother, and listen to me carefully,' said Malik

'OK.'

'The police are trying to find the girl.'

'You're not joking, brother. They're at the Hassans' place now. If they start chatting we're all in trouble.'

'Don't worry about the Hassans. They won't say anything.'

'I hope you're right because I didn't like the look of the young one,' Jalil was gabbling. 'He looked like just the type to lose his nerve and I don't know about you but I am not ready to do time for this.'

'Nobody is doing time,' Malik growled. 'The Hassans know what will happen if they squeal and there is nobody else but the girl who can give the police what they need.' He paused to let this information sink in.

'We just need to make sure the police don't get anywhere near the girl.'

'That's under control, brother,' Jalil laughed. 'Where she's going they won't ever find her.'

Malik stopped short. 'What do you mean?'

'Her family are sending her away, man,' Jalil lowered his voice. 'There's some auntie here now to take her.'

Malik shook his head. How could the Hassan brothers have organised that without their parents' agreement?

'That doesn't sound right to me.'

'She said the family sorted it.' His voice was tinged with panic. 'She said she was flying out tonight.'

Malik's eyes were throbbing and he dug the heel of his hand into their sockets, one after the other.

'Use your brain, brother. Don't you think the police will have put a stop on the girl's passport? Don't you think every airport will have a picture of her?'

'So who's that woman?' Jalil was breathing heavily. 'Who is the lying bitch?'

'Listen to me,' Malik's voice was barely above a whisper. 'You need to deal with this and you need to deal with it now.'

Taslima was pacing outside the bathroom door waiting for Aasha to finish.

It was almost over. In minutes they'd walk outside and with any luck Lilly and Jack would be waiting at the end of the drive. By now they probably had backup. She considered texting but was fearful that Jalil would see her. She didn't want to risk detection when they were so close to freeing Aasha.

She tapped lightly on the door with her knuckles. 'Aasha, are you ready?'

The door opened and the girl gave a nervous smile.

Taslima smiled back. 'Don't worry, you're safe.'

'Safe,' the girl repeated.

She opened her mouth as if she were going to say something else then stopped, her eyes following something behind Taslima.

Then they opened wide.

'What's wrong?' Taslima asked.

She didn't hear the girl's reply. Instead she heard a crack and felt an explosion at the back of her neck that sent her reeling forward.

'Oh.'

She felt the shape of the sound on her mouth, then nothing.

Just black.

# *Chapter Ten*

May 2009

> Re: Time for action . . . by Fighting4Islam at 10.30 on
> 3.5.09
> Salaams to all my brothers and sisters.
> I have asked myself time and time again when will I
> be called upon to take action and today Allah has
> answered me.
> So I ask you humbly to make a *dua* for me.

It has been a week since Fighting4Islam has been on the
board. I've missed his solidarity and scanned the posts
for any sign of him.

When I read his latest message I'm happy to hear
from him and tap out a response.

> Re: Time for action . . . by Believer at 10.34 on 3.5.09
> It's good to hear your voice, brother.
> I will ask Allah to keep you safe and strong for the long
> struggles which lie ahead.

His reply comes quickly.

> Re: Time for action . . . by Fighting4Islam a10.36 on
> 3.5.09
> I feel Allah's strength within me, my friend, but it is for
> you and other good Muslims to continue the struggles
> ahead without me.

I have to take a deep breath. Can he really be saying
what I think?

> Re: Time for action . . . by Believer a 10.40 on 3.5.09
> You can count on your friends here in the UK to help.
> We are collecting as much money as possible to send
> out aid to our brothers and sisters in Gaza.

When he responds I feel the blood rushing in my ears.

> Re: Time for action . . . by Fighting4Islam at 10.42
> on 3.5.09
> Jihad is Our Way
> Martyrdom is Our Desire

I can't speak or work for the rest of the day. My mind
moves between manic thoughts and total paralysis.

Later, at supper, I can't sit with my family as they
stuff their faces with chapatti as if nothing is wrong.
Yasmeen is yapping like a terrier about some book she's
read about Fidel Castro. I want to shove her face into
the dahl to make her stop.

In the bathroom I splash my face with water, trying

to cool my anger, but it burns so deeply inside me I know nothing can help.

In bed that night I surf the news. Two suicide bombers entered a market square in Sderot and blew themselves up. Sixteen Israeli shoppers, including a handful of foreign aid workers, were killed. More still were injured.

I imagine Fighting4Islam in those final moments. As he enters the square, he can hear women chatting in Hebrew as they prod and poke lemons piled high on a barrow, their citrus tang filling the hot air. A child stops in front of him to pick up a ball, his curly hair swinging against his cheek. Fighting4Islam feels a stab of regret for the chubby toddler, but reminds himself of the hundreds of children less than an hour's drive away, their homes bombed-out shells, their fathers scrambling through rubble for wives and babies.

He takes a position in the centre of the square, the weight of the explosives heavy under his coat. He lets his finger stroke the Koran in his pocket and whispers his final goodbye.

I can't work or sleep, so I spend those dark hours praying.

I am sad beyond measure to have lost so great a brother, but through my prayers, my sorrow soon turns to pride.

I ask Allah to bless Fighting4Islam, to lift him high, with all the other heroes, and take him to paradise.

Then I beg him to show me my own path, to show me the way. When it will be my time to take action?

\* \* \*

Jack inspected his windscreen while Lilly punched Taslima's number into her mobile.

Jack looked up from the crack in the glass. 'This should hold,' he said.

Lilly nodded as she listened intently to the phone.

'Anything?' Jack asked.

She shook her head.

The last thing Lilly had heard were some strange animal sounds and a muffled conversation.

'You sure?' asked Jack.

Lilly held her phone to Jack's ear. 'Nothing. Not even voicemail.'

'Shit.'

The enormity of their situation was pressing down on Lilly. Taslima was with a dangerous man and they had absolutely no idea where he was taking her. The young woman was utterly alone.

'I'd better call the chief for backup,' said Jack.

'And what can they do?' asked Lilly. 'Drive around aimlessly?'

'Well, we can't just do nothing.'

Lilly racked her brains. There had to be another way to contact Taslima.

She snapped her finger. 'She has another phone.'

'You're kidding.'

'I've seen it in her bag,' said Lilly. 'She keeps it for emergencies.'

'So call it,' shouted Jack.

Lilly sighed. Here came the ridiculous part. 'I don't have the number. She never gave it to me.'

'For God's sake, why not?'

Lilly threw up her hands. 'Well, I don't know. Maybe she runs an escort agency, maybe she works for MI5.'

'Shit.'

'Can we get someone to find the number?' Lilly asked.

'Which phone company?'

Lilly groaned. On the telly, surveillance units could track down details at the touch of a button, but this wasn't the telly, was it?

Think, woman, think.

If someone wanted to get access to Lilly's number where would they find it?

At home of course, in an untidy pile of unpaid bills.

'Her flat,' said Lilly. 'We might find it there.'

Jack bit his lip. 'Tell me you at least know where she lives.'

Lilly rummaged in her bag. Taslima's CV was still crumpled at the bottom, covered in chewing gum. She pulled it out and thrust it under Jack's nose.

He gunned the engine. 'Christ, you never mentioned she lived on the Clayhill.'

'To be honest, I never even looked at it.'

Taslima tried to open her eyes but it was as if she were underwater and the pressure fought against her. There was a humming in her ears and a dull sensation at the base of her skull.

In the distance was a shape, a figure perhaps, and a noise floated towards her, the edges blurred. She tried to focus, to sharpen the pictures and sounds.

The shape loomed closer, a gooey figure, but definitely a figure. A girl perhaps?

'Faaaah.' Words oozed from the girl's mouth. 'Faaaah.' What was she saying? Did it matter?

Taslima tried to repeat the sound but her tongue lolled, useless and wet, picking up a familiar taste from the air.

'Faaah.' The girl's lips undulated in a fascinating dance.

As darkness began to seep from the sides and the girl floated away, Taslima decided it didn't matter at all.

A pitbull growled in the square below. Lilly watched as its owner, a teen in a Dayglo tracksuit and box-fresh Nikes, struggled to keep it under control. It pulled its massive squat body, straining against a spiked collar. The boy heaved in the opposite direction, the lead taut between them.

'Shit.'

Behind her Jack was desperately going through his ring of skeleton keys as he tried to open Taslima's door.

He grabbed a short brass one and stabbed it into the lock. There was some movement but only halfway.

'This is a fecking nightmare,' he said.

That about summed it up. Lilly's young assistant was at the mercy of a man they suspected of a brutal attack.

Jack growled in frustration. 'Step back,' he barked.

Lilly did as she was told while Jack kicked out at the door with a fury he rarely showed. As his boot connected with the wood, the door flew off its hinges with a crack.

'Thank Christ the council don't spend any money on this shithole.'

Lilly nodded. She hadn't been to the Clayhill in over a year but it hadn't improved. An endemic drug problem and a pervasive sense of hopelessness kept the estate in the top ten places in the UK where you were most likely to encounter violent crime.

How the hell had someone as intelligent and well-educated as Taslima ended up here?

'I'll take the kitchen,' said Jack. 'You do the sitting room.'

Lilly normally hated being told what to do, particularly by her partner, but right now she felt like she was drowning, that no matter how hard she swam, the waves kept pulling her under, and she was just glad he was taking charge. Was this the side to him that had appealed to the woman in his texts? Did she like his protective nature in a way Lilly never had?

She forced herself to let it go. Now wasn't the time.

She lumbered down the hall towards the sitting room, but when she stepped inside she felt as though it were she and not the front door that had been shattered. On the tiny sofa, nesting among embroidered cushions and ornate throws as a Pooh Bear. Sam had had exactly the same one as a baby and had gurgled whenever Lilly pulled the string between his legs and a tune tinkled out. How many nights had she stared into the dark of the early hours with that bloody music in one ear and her ex-husband's snore in the other?

From the bear, Lilly's eyes were drawn to the activity centre where crabs and starfish in primary colours dangled seductively, a tiny blue sock abandoned in the corner.

'You never said she had a kid,' Jack called from the kitchen.

Because she never told me, Lilly thought. Why was that?

She remembered the night on the phone when Lilly

318

had heard a child crying. Taslima had said it was a neighbour. Why?

She shook her head to clear it.

Taslima, living on the Clayhill, with a secret baby. It didn't make any sense.

'There's nothing through there.' Jack poked his head in the room. 'To be honest, she's a bit of a neat freak.'

'I'll try in here,' Lilly approached a set of cupboards in the corner of the room.

On the top were photographs of Taslima with someone who looked like her. They smiled out with the same exquisite cheekbones. A sister? Taslima had never mentioned one, but then again, she had never mentioned a bloody baby.

The drawers were impeccably tidy. One housed hand cream and alcohol-free perfume, the other a small stack of letters, bound with an oversized paper clip. Lilly flipped through them but there were no bills. These were personal, handwritten in bright blue ink, signed off with clusters of kisses.

'You may as well know I've called the pol-is.'

Lilly looked up. A black woman stood in the doorway, her hands on more than ample hips. The grey in her hair marked her as at least in her fifties, but her face was entirely unlined, her eyes bright.

'We are the police,' said Lilly.

The woman's eyes flashed. 'Is dat right?'

Jack came from the bedroom and flashed his badge.

'So what do you want,' the woman's eyes were no less angry, 'that you come here flinging a girl's door open?'

'We need her mobile number,' said Lilly.

The woman crossed her arms over enormous breasts. 'You break down her door to give her a call?'

'It's very urgent,' Lilly explained. 'There was no other way.'

'She's a good girl,' said the woman. 'A very good girl.'

Tears sprang into Lilly's eyes. This was her fault. She had been so set on finding out who killed Yasmeen and proving Raffy's innocence she had lost all sense.

'I know that and I can't tell you how sorry I am that I got Taslima into this.'

The woman frowned.

'If I could turn back the clock I would,' Lilly could hear herself gabbling. 'I would never have let her do anything this dangerous.'

Lilly began to cry, her words choking her.

'I wouldn't even take on this stupid case because, as usual, it's brought me nothing but trouble.'

The woman crossed the gap between them and put a soft hand on Lilly's shoulder. The gesture was so comforting Lilly felt herself melt like chocolate.

'I'm sorry,' she murmured, but Lilly could feel herself unravelling.

Her insistence on handling this case was at the heart of all her problems. Jack was so pissed off with her he'd been having an affair. Sam had turned into a bully because he was starved of attention at home. Lilly was terrified because some nutter was stalking her and now Taslima, lovely, funny, clever Taslima, was in dreadful trouble and it was all her fault.

'I'm sure we can sort this out,' the woman stroked Lilly's hair, 'but you're going to have to tell me who is this Taslima.'

'Faaah, faaah.'

The girl's words bled into Taslima's ears, forcing her out of the cosy black space.

She opened her eyes and everything was the same, though the girl was nearer and that smell stronger.

And there was a thudding at the back of her neck. It was the only part of her body Taslima could feel. Her arms, legs and feet were all deliciously blank, like someone had cut them off.

The girl reached out to Taslima and touched her. She could see that was what she was doing but she couldn't actually feel it. The sensation, or lack of it, made Taslima want to laugh, but something in the girl's face told Taslima it wasn't funny.

The girl's eyes flicked between Taslima's face and to something behind her. Taslima tried to understand, grasped at what she saw on the girl's face.

And that smell again. What was it?

The woman led Jack and Lilly next door to her own flat and introduced herself as Evelyn Roberts.

She scooped up a yoghurt-coated two-year-old and held him to her bosom.

'This is Rogon,' she said. 'Zahara's baby boy.'

Lilly exchanged a look with Jack. He was as confused as she was.

'Zahara,' Lilly repeated.

'That's right.' Mrs Roberts wiped a thick finger under the child's sticky chin.

'Maybe we've made a mistake,' said Jack. 'Come to the wrong address.'

Lilly shook her head. Rogon was unmistakably Taslima's son, with the same smile and cheekbones as his mother and the woman in the photograph.

If Taslima lied about having a family, was it really that hard to believe she lied about her name? But this was all so confusing. Lies and secrets. Lilly's head was spinning and she felt sick. It made her want to lie down.

Yet whatever her name was, it was the same brave young woman out there and in need of help.

'Do you have a mobile number for Taslima?' asked Lilly. 'I mean, Zahara.'

Mrs Roberts handed the child to Lilly. He beamed up at her, leaving a vanilla trail across her jacket with his chubby fist.

'I'll get my book,' Mrs Roberts reached into a kitchen drawer. 'Which one do you need?'

Jack stepped outside to call the station with Taslima's second number. God knows what the chief super would say when he explained what they had done. That he'd been careering around trying to find Aasha with his pregnant girlfriend in tow and that Jack had involved someone else in their crazy scheme. That that someone was a vulnerable Asian woman.

Lilly couldn't bear to listen and stayed with Mrs Roberts and Rogon.

'Do you have any idea why she used a different name?' Lilly asked.

Mrs Roberts shrugged. 'It don't often pay to ask too many questions,' she said. 'I usually find people have their reasons.'

'But don't you think she owed it to you, to tell the truth?'

'You sound just like her, always saying she's going to pay me back for minding her boy.' Mrs Roberts kissed Rogon's head. 'Zahara don't owe me nothing. She needed help, I gave it.'

Lilly felt a stab of guilt that she could never just let people be themselves. Unlike Mrs Roberts, she felt the need to uncover stones and peek underneath.

When Jack came back inside the colour was bleached from his face.

'How did it go?' she asked.

Jack gave a weak smile. 'Well, I haven't been promoted.'

'Can they find Taslima for us?'

Jack opened his hands, palms to the ceiling. 'They're trying the networks now. If there's a signal they might be able to locate it.'

'How close can they get?' she asked.

'A couple of square miles.'

Lilly sighed and bit her lip.

'She's going to be all right, isn't she?' asked Mrs Roberts.

'Of course,' said Jack, but Lilly couldn't look at him. They both knew there was no way he could promise that.

At last his phone bleeped with a text and he showed it to Lilly.

*The number you gave is currently active in St Stephen's Green.*

'Where the hell's that?' she asked.

'A village on the other side of Harpenden.' Jack checked his watch. 'We can be there in twenty minutes.'

Lilly jumped to her feet and they headed for the door.

'Take care now,' said Mrs Roberts. 'And bring Rogon's mama back safe and sound.'

Lilly didn't trust herself to answer.


Fear. That's what was on the girl's face. The sort of fear that, no matter how hard you tried, you couldn't escape.

Taslima knew how that felt. She couldn't remember where or why but she recognised terror that sickened you to the very core.

She turned instinctively to see the cause, her body begrudging the order to move, hard, cold tiles pressing into her lifeless shoulders as she attempted to turn her head.

From her place on the floor all she could see was a bare wall and a closed door.

Again she fought the urge to laugh. Who could be frightened of that?

But there was something else. A cloud forming in the tiny gap between the two. She would have thought nothing more of it, closed her eyes and given herself up to the wonderful darkness, but for the smell. Like the distant memory of her own fear it galvanised her. What was it? She breathed in a deep lungful, desperate to reach the far recesses of her brain.

It was hot. It hurt.

Suddenly, her eyes opened wide. She knew exactly what it was and what the girl had been trying to tell her.

'Faaa.'

Fire.

She struggled to sit, her arms barely able to take her weight. The numbness that had been so seductive now gave way to the ripping fingernails of pain. The base of her neck erupting in agony.

Groaning, she pressed her hand under her hijab to what felt like a fireball. When she brought it back to her face, her vision, although still blurred, had cleared enough for her to see her fingers stained red. The pain was so excruciating, she had expected white-hot lava.

'We have to get out of here,' said the girl, her words still muffled as though she were behind glass.

Taslima knew she couldn't speak but nodded.

She tried to push herself to her feet but her hands couldn't get purchase, sliding across the wet floor. She seemed to be sitting in some sort of puddle.

Again, she brought her fingers to her face but this time the liquid was clear. She sat mesmerised by the feel of it on her skin, the way it evaporated like . . . petrol.

The thought slipped towards her, gently at first, then gathering momentum, increasing its mass, until it hurtled towards her like a freight train.

Outside the door, not four feet away, there was a fire – and she was sitting in a pool of petrol.

She scrambled to her knees, her sodden trousers clinging to her legs. She looked around wildly at the bath, toilet and basin.

Where on earth was she and what was she doing here?

Somewhere in the back of her mind, like a long forgotten dream, she recalled arriving here. She could smell the fresh grass of fields and hear the sound of animals.

The girl interrupted her with a wide-eyed scream. What had been a whisper of smoke was now billowing under the door, filling the room with a thick, choking fog.

'What are we going to do?'

Taslima tried to think but it was as if her mind was a room full of people all talking at once.

Who are you? Where are you? What's happening? Each question piled on top of another in an unanswered tangle.

'My brain hurts,' she said, because it did.

The girl began to sob and beat her hand against the window. 'It's locked.'

Taslima looked from the window lock, to the door and back again. Behind the door she could hear the roar of flames that would soon make their way inside the bathroom.

The girl began to wail, the sound pressing deep into Taslima's head, like a sickening migraine.

'We're going to die,' the girl screamed.

Jack screeched through the main street in St Stephen's Green, the wheels of his car mounting the pavement.

'They could be anywhere,' he shouted.

Lilly didn't answer but kept her eyes peeled for Jalil's car, or Jalil himself. Jack had called the station for more details put the police had only the name of the village.

'It was definitely St Stephen's Green?' she asked.

'And the outskirts,' Jack answered.

Lilly groaned. That could stretch well into the outlying countryside.

Jack reached a crossroads. 'Which way?'

'God knows.'

'This is hopeless.' He smacked the side window with his elbow.

Lilly squeezed her eyes shut, trying not to think about what might be happening to Taslima and Aasha.

'Someone must have noticed them,' said Jack.

Lilly looked around her at the pretty village, much like her own. The whitewashed pub, with a scarlet headband of hanging baskets, nestled in the dappled shade. The post office stood proud with its glisteningly clean windows, the door held open with an old iron horseshoe.

Jack was right. In a place like this where everyone knew everyone, someone must have seen them.

'Let's ask,' she said.

He crunched the car into reverse and shot back up the high street.

'You take the shop,' he slammed on the brake, 'and I'll do the pub.'

Lilly was about to point out that a group of extremist Muslims were hardly likely to be found sharing half a lager in the Spotted Dog but Jack had already disappeared.

She hauled herself out of the car and approached The Old Village Shoppe. A woman in her sixties was already at the door, her thinning, yet overly red hair framed by the window behind her, which was completely covered with posters advertising local fetes, dog groomers and amateur dramatic productions.

'You can't leave it like that.' The woman pointed to Jack's car, parked with two wheels on the kerb.

'Sorry,' Lilly shrugged. 'I don't have the keys.'

The woman let out a theatrical sigh and went inside. Lilly followed.

The shop was a cramped hotchpotch of newspapers, croissants and boxes of tea, the counter piled high with charity collection tins, the village magazine and discount chocolate.

'Can I help you?' the woman barked.

Lilly attempted a smile. Mrs Singh ran the off-licence In Little Markham with a similar lack of warmth, but no detail of anyone's life passed her by.

'I'm trying to find someone,' said Lilly.

The woman looked unimpressed. She sniffed and began rearranging a shelf of cigars.

'Some people actually,' Lilly explained. 'A guy called Nawed Jalil.'

The woman shook her head. 'The name doesn't ring a bell.'

'He has a friend called Abdul Malik and a few days ago they would have had an Asian girl with them, about fifteen years old.'

'Sorry,' said the woman.

'And today they would have had another woman with them in her twenties, wearing a hijab.'

'A what?'

Lilly circled her head with her finger. 'A black head-scarf.'

'Oh, one of them things.' The woman gave a little snort. 'Bleeding ridiculous, if you want my opinion.'

Lilly reined herself in from pointing out that indeed she did not want this woman's opinion.

'Have you seen anyone in the village wearing one?'

'No.'

'Are you sure?' asked Lilly.

The woman cocked her head to one side. 'This isn't bleeding Afghanistan. We don't get that sort here.'

Lilly gritted her teeth, nodded her thanks and stumbled outside. Jack was crossing the road towards her.

'Any luck?' she asked.

He shook his head. 'You?'

'Nope.'

'Shit.'

'I wish you'd stop saying that.'

'Sorry.'

She waved away his apology. She was being unreasonable again and she knew it. Perhaps it was the stress, perhaps it was the text, perhaps a culmination of everything, but she couldn't stop herself so she turned to the window and read one of the posters.

'*Christmas Will Be Late This Year.* An uproariously funny comedy from the St Stephen's Players.'

Somehow she doubted a bunch of retired accountants pretending to be Santa's helpers would ever be hilarious. Similarly, she doubted that an organically reared goat, as described in the next poster, would ever be the perfect gift for the birth of a child.

'Come on,' she snapped. 'We're wasting time.'

But when she got to the car she stopped in her tracks.

'I thought you didn't want to waste any more time,' said Jack.

She put up her palm for quiet. Something was tickling the back of her mind. Something she'd seen before.

'That's it.' She hurried back and tapped the window.

'I don't think tickets to a musical can help us now,' said Jack.

She rolled her eyes at him and tapped the next poster along. 'I saw something just like this in Paradise Halal.'

'And?'

'And Malik delivers the meat there,' she said. 'Perhaps this is something to do with him too.'

'Bit of a stretch,' said Jack.

'What else have we got to go on?' asked Lilly, and shot back into the shop.

The woman glanced up at her. 'Have you moved your car yet?'

'What?'

The woman flapped her hand at Jack's car. 'I've told you already, you can't leave it there.'

Lilly took a deep breath. Now was not the time to lose her temper. 'The poster in the window about the meat,' she said. 'Is it halal?'

The woman narrowed her eyes. 'You're not from Health and Safety, are you? Because it has absolutely nothing to do with me.'

'No,' said Lilly, 'I'm—'

'People ask to put things in my window all the time and I charge them a few quid. Everything else is down to them.'

'I understand that,' said Lilly.

'If they've done anything wrong then I'm not responsible.' The woman wagged a finger. 'If you're not from Health and Safety, you're not a bleeding lawyer are you?'

'Yes, but—'

'Well, listen to me. I've done nothing wrong.' She jabbed her chest with her thumb. 'Not liable. It says so in the small print. So you stick your writs and your summonses where the sun don't shine.'

'Will you stop talking and listen!' Lilly shouted.

The woman pulled a face. 'Charming.'

'Please,' Lilly evened her tone. 'I'm not here to cause any problems for you. I just want to know where the farm is on the poster.'

'Well, why didn't you just say that?'

Taslima put her hands to her temples to calm the traffic of her thoughts.

Who was the girl? What were they doing here?

She didn't have any answers but one thing she did know: she didn't want to burn to death in this unknown place.

'Allah will show us the way,' she said.

'Allah?' The girl was hysterical now. 'Are you mad?'

Taslima just smiled. Though right now she had no idea what it was, she knew that she had survived something terrible, and that she had done so by trusting in God.

She made a *dua*, apologising for its brevity, and waited. The paint of the door began to bubble and crack as the flames licked through.

'Do something!' the girl screamed.

Taslima nodded and went to the window. The lock was secure and the frame solid with layer upon layer of paint. She looked around the bathroom for something to break the glass. Nothing.

The room was now filled with smoke and the girl began coughing wildly.

Taslima ran her finger around the frame to see if there was any give, but it was firm.

The girl's coughing turned into a strangled wheeze and Taslima shouted, 'Hold on,' as the girl began to sink to the floor.

Taslima pressed against the glass. It felt heavy, unbreakable. She pulled off her hijab, the pain at the base of her neck nearly cutting her in two.

'Give me strength,' she prayed.

She wound the hijab around her hand and took a deep breath. Then she made a fist and punched.

The jolt of agony running from her hand to her shoulder made Taslima gasp. It felt as if the entire limb were in a vice.

She checked the glass but there was no sign of even a hairline crack.

She held her hand to her chest, tears running down her face. The girl was now sprawled beside the bath, her head to one side.

Taslima steadied herself, took another lungful of air and smoke, then punched again with all her might.

There was a hideous snapping sound and Taslima screamed. The glass remained intact but her knuckle was broken.

Her head spun both with pain and lack of oxygen. She could barely make out the girl through the smoke. They would both be dead within minutes.

She was so tired, so confused. Perhaps it would be OK. She would slip away quietly and sleep. She began to feel her knees bend and her shoulders slump. The darkness beckoned again.

'No.'

Her own words jolted her back to life. She would not give up, she was better than that.

She positioned herself, legs akimbo, back straight. She wound the bloodied hijab around her other hand. Then she closed her eyes, pulled back her fist and thrust it at the glass.

She heard the smash, together with her own screaming. When she dared look she saw her entire hand had passed through the window. She pulled it back inside, wincing as sharp splinters lacerated her skin through the material of her hijab. She could feel the stickiness of blood pouring down her arm but bit her lip as she pushed out the rest of the broken glass.

She bent to the place where the girl lay and shook her.

'I did it,' she said. 'We're getting out of here.'

The girl stirred, murmuring gently.

'Come on,' Taslima said and pulled her to her feet. The girl leaned heavily against Taslima and another spasm shot through her.

'Are we going home?' the girl whispered.

'*En sh'Allah.*'


The address the woman gave to Lilly was ten minutes outside the village. Jack drove at breakneck speed through tight country lanes. Lilly held on to the edge of her seat.

As they careered around a hairpin bend at seventy Lilly prayed they weren't too late.

'There,' Lilly pointed to an iron gate in the hedge that flanked miles of single-track road.

Barely slowing, Jack pulled in, the side of his car scraping against the gatepost.

When they sped along the dirt track leading to the farm, the tyres hit a pothole with such force Lilly was propelled sideways into Jack, their shoulders clashing, the suspension heaving. Lilly's hands flew to her bump.

'Sorry,' Jack shouted but she didn't reply. Couldn't reply.

Instead she stared straight ahead.

'Mary Mother of God,' said Jack, and Lilly knew he had seen it too.

The farmhouse was ablaze.

Orange and red flames licked the windows and doors while plumes of poisonous black smoke swirled skywards. The fire greedily sucked in the surrounding air and belched out a roar in return.

Lilly covered her mouth with her hand. 'They're inside.'

Jack pitched open his door and ran towards the building. Lilly followed him, the feverish heat assaulting her.

As they neared the front door it spat at them in anger.

'I'm going in,' said Jack, and pulled his leather jacket over his head. 'Call the fire brigade.'

'Don't!' Lilly screamed, but he was already on his way, face bowed by the heat.

He kicked out at the door, which gave way easily under his boot. Inside, Lilly could see everything was clouded by smoke. Jack bent as low as he could and went in. In less than a second she could no longer even make out his outline.

'Jack,' she shouted, 'this is madness.'

If he called back she couldn't hear him over the crash of the flames.

He was fast, she told herself. Hadn't he been training all these months? He'd find Taslima and Aasha and be out of there in seconds.

She scrabbled for her mobile and dialled 999. Help would be here soon. Everything would be OK.

No sooner had she held the thought than there was a throaty rumble from deep within the house, then a whoosh that she felt as well as heard. It knocked her off balance with its dizzying intensity. As she scrambled to her feet, she felt the heat scorch her skin and smelled her hair singe.

A window exploded outwards in a spray of glass and wood, and the entire ground floor was engulfed in flames.

'Jack!' Lilly's screams were like wire in her throat. 'Jack, are you OK?'

She stumbled back, her arms held protectively in front of her face. Tears poured down her cheeks. 'Jack, where are you?' She fell to her knees, weak from the blistering heat. 'Jack,' her words were no more than a scratch.

Sobbing, she held her stomach. 'Don't leave me.'

In the maelstrom of fog and flame a black shape catapulted towards Lilly. She turned her back, anticipating a flying piece of wood. She had to get away. There was nothing she could do for the others.

She crawled on her hands and knees, her belly low

to the ground. Her nails dug in the scorched earth. Behind, she felt something hurtling towards her. She curled into a ball, bracing herself. It landed at speed, glancing off her shoulder, rolling sidewards. She turned to look.

'Jack?'

He lay on the floor, his face black, his eyes streaming, gulping air.

'The girls,' he forced out the words, 'they're at the back. On the roof.'

Lilly allowed herself a second to touch his arm before she raced around to the back of the house.

She scanned the roof, her hand shielding her eyes. At this side of the building the fire had reached the first floor, and orange fingers clamoured out of every window. At the very top, above what looked like a small bathroom window, two figures were pulling themselves towards the apex.

Lilly cupped her mouth. 'Taslima.'

Both figures looked in her direction. Through the charcoal clouds Lilly saw it was her. The other girl must be Aasha.

'Hold on,' Lilly shouted. 'The fire crew will be here any second.'

She checked behind her but there was still no sign of the engines.

The roof groaned and shuddered, tiles sliding down and detonating on impact with the ground below. Then a crack began to appear, sucking away the very fabric of the building. A hole gaped. Lilly realised the roof was about to collapse.

Taslima and Aasha clawed their way higher, flames hot on their heels.

Lilly could hear sirens in the distance. Come on, come on, she willed them.

'They're here,' she shouted, but her words were drowned out by an enormous rip, as if a giant sheet were being torn in two. The roof gave way, tumbling into the depths of the inferno. Only the very frame remained, like a fragile skeleton, the girls perched like terrified birds.

Behind Lilly, the engines arrived, lights flashing, sirens blaring. A fireman put his hands on her shoulders.

'Step back, love. It's going to cave in.'

Lilly shrugged him off. 'My friend is up there, and another girl.'

'Bloody hell,' he muttered.

'Bring a ladder,' Lilly shouted. 'Get them down.'

He shook his head and pointed to the walls, which were fast beginning to disintegrate. 'There's nothing to lean it against.'

Lilly put her hands in her hair, feeling the brittle ends where her curls were burned. 'You have to do something.'

He turned to his colleagues and shouted something to them. Within seconds they arrived with a net.

'Who's the one nearest to us, love?'

'Aasha,' said Lilly.

The fireman held up a megaphone. 'Aasha, can you hear us?'

She nodded, her face illuminated a strange orange by the fire.

'I want you to jump out as far as you can.' He paused. 'Do you understand that? Jump out.'

337

Aasha looked towards Taslima. It was impossible to say if they spoke but Aasha steeled herself, then dived. She seemed to be suspended in the air, the burning building crashing around her, before she hurtled downwards and landed with a thump in the middle of the net.

The fireman gave a tight smile then turned to Lilly. 'What about the other one?'

'Taslima,' said Lilly.

Again he lifted the megaphone. 'Taslima, I need you to do the same for me.'

Lilly waited for her to turn around, to push back with her hands and jump to safety. Instead, Taslima crawled further up the roof.

'Taslima,' the fireman shouted, 'you need to stop climbing and jump.'

Taslima didn't respond but continued to make her way upwards until she was at the chimney. Then she clung to it.

Aasha was brought to Lilly, wrapped in a silver blanket.

'I don't think she can understand you,' she said. 'She got a whack on the head and she doesn't seem to have any idea what's happening.'

'Taslima,' the fireman shouted. 'There isn't much time.'

Taslima wrapped her arms even tighter around the chimney.

There was another sickening heave and the walls began to crumble. Any moment now, Taslima would be propelled into the fire.

Lilly snatched the megaphone. 'Taslima, you listen to me right this second. Just stop buggering about and jump.'

Bricks began raining down and Aasha screamed.

'We can't stay here,' shouted the fireman.

'Please,' Lilly begged. 'I can get through to her.'

She looked up at Taslima. Without her hijab her hair streamed around her head like a wild waterfall.

'Taslima, I know you're very frightened but you have to do this.'

Taslima didn't move.

'After everything you've done for me I will not let you die. I cannot do without you and neither can Rogon.'

At her son's name, Taslima looked up.

'That's right, Zahara, I know all about your beautiful little boy,' Lilly's voice caught, 'and trust me, he needs you.'

Taslima couldn't breathe. The flames and the smoke and the noise swirled around her. She imagined that this was exactly like hell would be.

It wouldn't be long before the very face of evil himself came for her.

She had been sure that getting out of the bathroom had been the right thing, that she wanted to escape, live to fight another day. Now up here on the blazing roof, the bricks of the chimney unbearably hot beneath her hands, she wasn't certain of anything.

She looked up at the sky. It looked so cool, stretching out into for ever.

From down below a shout pierced her thoughts. The voice was a woman's. Oddly familiar. She could scarcely make her out through the shrouds of smoke.

'I will not let you die,' the woman screamed.

Taslima was sorry. The woman obviously cared but

339

she just didn't have the strength. Though she couldn't recall the details, Taslima knew she'd been fighting for a very long time. She was sapped.

'I can't,' she whispered, a single tear wetting her cheek.

Then the word. The one word that Taslima did remember.

Rogon.

'I know all about your beautiful little boy,' the woman shouted.

The memory of him caught Taslima like a punch. She doubled over with the force of it.

He was eighteen months old. His eyes were like midnight. He was the reason she got out of bed each day.

The woman's words filled the air. '. . . he needs you.'

Once more, Taslima put her trust in Allah.

And jumped.

'You are so dead,' Imran sneers into Aasha's face as soon as she crosses the threshold.

After everything that's happened, she's surprised that she still feels a stab of fear in her belly.

'Got nothing to say now?' he growls.

Aasha looks at the floor. The doctor had suggested that she stay in hospital overnight but Aasha had begged her mum to let her come home. Now she wondered if hospital would have been better.

Imran's eyes flash. 'Or are you hoping your little boyfriend will come around to save you?'

Her eyes fill with tears at the thought of Ryan.

Imran grabs her chin and forces her to look at him. 'Don't you cry for him, you little slut.'

'Enough.'

It's Mum in the doorway.

Imran doesn't let go. 'She needs to know what she's done.'

His grip is so tight Aasha can hardly breathe.

Mum moves towards them. 'She knows what she has done, Imran.'

'Does she?' he snorts. 'Does she know the shame she has brought us all? Do you?'

Aasha feels her knees begin to give way. After everything she's been through, will they send her away? She doesn't know if she can bear that.

'I know exactly what Aasha has done,' Mum says. 'And I know exactly what you have done.'

Imran glares at her. 'Someone has to keep this family in order.'

Aasha expects Mum to crumple but instead she reaches over and pulls Imran's hand from her face.

'I am your mother,' she says, 'and don't you ever speak to me like that again.'

He stares at Mum with an intensity that makes Aasha shiver, but Mum doesn't back down. She stares right back at him.

Aasha holds her breath, waiting. At last Mum speaks.

'Things are going to change around here,' she says.

# *Chapter Eleven*

5 May 2009

I arrive the mosque as if in a dream. In the days since Fighting4Islam left us, life has seemed unreal.

I have tried to focus on the forums, on my work, but everything seems so trivial. I know now that I want to make a difference. A real difference. I am just waiting for Allah to show me the way.

I slip off my shoes and enter the meeting.

The sister who spoke to the teacher the last time I was here is on her feet.

'We must raise our voices,' she is saying, 'and show the world that Islam is not to be trifled with.'

Something in her body language annoys me. Maybe it's the way her chin tilts upwards. Or the way her hip thrusts to the side. Once again I notice the tendril of hair that escapes from her hijab.

'How can we show we are serious in our intentions if sisters cannot obey the simple rules set down for them?'

Everyone turns to me.

'We must live completely in Islam.' I take control of the crowd.

The sister at least has the dignity to concede and sits down.

I point my finger to the sky. 'And make no mistake, we must be prepared to die that way.'

Later, as I walk home, I begin to open my eyes. I begin to notice things around me.

Women are everywhere, chatting, shopping and laughing. I have been so consumed with hatred for the *kuffar* that I have failed to notice my own people have taken a wrong turn.

It takes my breath away. Bare heads. Lipstick. Painted toes.

While my face has been turned towards Palestine I have failed to notice evil much closer to home.

I make a *dua*. Allah has shown me my path.

The nurse applied cream to the blisters on Lilly's forehead. The pain made her wince.

'Is it bad?' Lilly asked.

The nurse gave a half-smile. 'I've seen sunburn worse than this.' She reached behind her for a mirror and held it up.

Lilly groaned. The blisters looked like the late onset of acne, or a nasty batch of chicken pox, but that was not the worst of it. It was her hair. What was often frizzy and out of control now resembled an old bird's nest. She pulled at a tendril but there was no spring in it, like a dried-out clump of grass.

'What in God's name am I going to do with this?'

The nurse laughed. 'Get a bob?'

Lilly sighed. She had had long hair since childhood. While all her school mates were getting Purdy cuts and perming their fringes, Lilly had retained Pre-Raphaelite curls to the base of her spine.

'Like an angel,' her dad used to say.

Elsa had whinged about the time it took to wash and had raked a vicious wire comb through it each morning. But Lilly didn't care. She had kept it long and luscious. Over the years she'd trimmed it to shoulder length but it had still been her crowning glory. Now look at it.

She thanked the nurse and went to find Taslima. She still couldn't think of her as Zahara. She needed to ask her so many things. Find out why she had lied.

But when she arrived at the ward Lilly swallowed her questions. There would be time for answers, but not now.

Taslima lay very still, her head no longer swathed by her hijab but a thick cap of white bandages. Her right hand had also disappeared under a white dressing.

'Hi.' Lilly dropped gently into a chair at the side of Taslima's bed.

Taslima tried to speak, but her voice was little more than a choke that erupted into a coughing fit.

Lilly poured a glass of water from a plastic jug and held it to Taslima's lips. She watched her trachea move as she swallowed.

'Thanks,' Taslima whispered.

'Do you know who I am?' Lilly asked.

Taslima smiled. 'Things come and go, but not you.'

'And not Rogon.'

'Definitely not him.'

Lilly bit her lip and reminded herself that now was not the time.

'Why didn't you tell me about him?' she asked.

Taslima gave a small shrug that made her wince. Lilly wondered if the wound to her head hurt or the reason for all the lies.

'I had to leave home,' she said. 'Start again.'

'And that's why you changed your name?'

Taslima nodded. 'My husband is not a good person.'

Lilly gulped back her tears. Taslima was not the first woman to leave everything behind to escape domestic violence. And she wouldn't be the last.

'But why keep Rogon a secret?' Lilly asked.

'If my husband found us he'd take him,' said Taslima.

'You could get custody.'

Taslima shook her head against the pillow. 'A piece of paper wouldn't make any difference to a man like him. If he finds Rogon he'll take him back home and I'll never see him again.'

Lilly did understand. Wouldn't she do anything to protect Sam? To keep him with her?

She stroked Taslima's hand, the bandages rough to the touch.

'Everyone's getting hurt. You, Raffy, everyone. Sometimes I think I'm cursed.'

'That's nonsense,' said Taslima. 'I knew what I was doing was dangerous and the attack on Raffy had absolutely nothing to do with you.'

'Sometimes it feels like I make matters worse.'

Taslima's eyes flashed. 'Without you I wouldn't have a job and Raffy would have no one on his side. I'm proud that we tried to help Aasha.'

Lilly couldn't help a smile. 'We did, didn't we? And she's safe.'

'And so are lots of other girls that the butcher and his nasty gang would have set their sights on,' said Taslima. 'Justice has prevailed.'

'I'll drink to that.' Lilly held up the glass of water. 'Justice for Aahsa and Yasmeen.'

'Ah,' said Taslima.

Lilly frowned. 'What?'

'They didn't kill Yasmeen.'

Lilly slumped back in her chair, water sloshing over the rim of the glass onto her trousers.

'Sorry,' said Taslima. 'Jalil had never heard of her.'

Lilly rubbed the water with her other hand, succeeding only in spreading the stain so she looked like she'd wet herself. She gave a weak smile.

'Let's not worry about that now.'

Lilly sat with Taslima until she fell asleep, then made her way back to A and E. It had always been a long shot that the PTF had been responsible for Yasmeen's death, but she couldn't hide her disappointment. Raffy's case was back at square one.

She needed to find Jack; remind herself that his case at least was a complete success.

She searched for ten minutes until the nurse who had laughed at her hair informed her he'd gone up to visit Ryan.

Wasn't that just like Jack? Any other copper would have gone straight back to the nick to celebrate. Instead, Jack was visiting the victim. She smiled. He was a good man.

When she arrived at Ryan's room her smile faded.

Jack was by Ryan's side, but another woman was in the room. She was a tall blonde. Slim. Her bleached hair was expertly blown dry, fake tan just the right side of golden. She put a hand on Jack's and whispered something in his ear with glossy lips. He whispered something back, their intimacy palpable.

Lilly felt the room tilt. It had to be her. The woman in Jack's secret texts. And the way they were together told Lilly all she needed to know.

She turned on her heel and fled.


Jack smiled at Mara.

'I'm sorry,' he said.

'Don't be,' she sighed. 'I always knew you were one of the good guys.'

He'd been surprised to find her at Ryan's bedside, reading something to him while the ventilator kept time. He had watched for a while, listening to her voice.

At last she'd looked up and given a small surprised smile.

'Is he any better?' Jack asked.

'The nurses say he might be able to hear.' She didn't answer his question.

Jack's eyes filled with tears.

'I got the men that did it,' he said.

'I knew you would.'

They sat next to one another in silence and watched Ryan's lifeless face. Jack could smell Mara's perfume. It was delicious.

'I can't believe I didn't guess what was really happening to Ryan,' she said.

'How could you?'

'The scruffy clothes, stealing things, always hungry,' she said. 'Classic symptoms of neglect.'

Jack shrugged. 'Hindsight is a wonderful thing.'

Mara nodded but he knew she didn't accept that. She had let the boy down and he knew exactly how much that hurt.

She moved very close to him. Close enough to kiss.

'You want to call this thing between us off, don't you?' she whispered.

'I'm sorry,' he whispered back.

She left seconds later and he knew he wanted nothing more than to find Lilly.

'I hear you've had a good result,' said the chief.

Jack nodded into his mobile. He hadn't been able to find Lilly and had stepped outside to call her when the chief caught him.

'I suppose you could say that,' said Jack.

'I'm not saying your decision to send in a civilian was a good one.'

Jack thought about Taslima up on the roof, a burning building collapsing around her.

'Not my finest idea,' he said.

'But a good result is what matters.'

Jack almost laughed. At least the chief was predictable.

'Better get your backside down here, now,' said the chief.

'I just want to check Lilly's OK,' said Jack.

'Don't be ridiculous, Jack. Malik has to be charged in the next twenty minutes and I'm assuming you want to be the one to do it.'

Jack checked his watch. 'I'm on my way.'

Lilly rummaged in her fridge and snapped off a cube of mint Aero. Her hands were shaking.

The woman – that woman – had knocked her completely off balance.

She swallowed the sweet coolness of the chocolate and took another cube.

She had been so tall. So blonde. So not like Lilly.

But wasn't that the point?

Jack was sick of the real version. The messy, awkward, pregnant one. Instead he'd gone for an entirely different model, with smooth fingernails, painted ice pink.

Where Lilly liked to think she had depth, the other woman was like cinder toffee. Sweet yet brittle.

She popped the rest of the bar into her mouth and was hunting for another, when a dark shape shot past the kitchen window.

Lilly caught her breath. Had it just been a bird? Perhaps it was the little chaffinch that had been knocking on the glass? Not very likely this time of night. It was almost ten and, apart from their resident owl, who let out a comedy hoot as if on cue, the birds were asleep. She peered outside and berated herself.

The PTF had not killed Yasmeen. Both Malik and Jalil were safely in custody.

She was being silly. Dark or not, it was a bird.

Jack let himself into the custody suite.

He'd been sorry to miss Lilly but couldn't wait to see the look on Malik's face when he read out the charge.

Result.

'If it ain't Inpector Morse,' the custody sergeant grinned.

Jack high-fived him. 'Let's get that bastard out of the cell.' He rubbed his hands together.

The sarge reached around for his keys. 'I'm going to enjoy this,' he said. He clanked open the lock to cell ten and pulled the door.

Malik was performing squat lunges.

'All right, sunshine, let's be having you,' said the sergeant.

Malik looked up, his face slick with sweat, and smirked. 'Time to let me go, is it?'

Jack snorted. 'Hardly.'

Malik's face darkened.

'We've found Aasha and she's told us exactly what you've done.' Jack knew he was smiling. 'You're bang to rights on this one.'

Malik nodded and got slowly to his feet. Jack had expected a bigger reaction. It was almost disappointing.

The huge man stretched his arms behind his head and rolled his head as if he were limbering down in the gym. He leaned over to the bed as if he were going to use it as ballast.

'Don't mess us about,' said Jack.

Too late, he saw Malik's hand graze against something silver. Too late, he saw Malik's hand swinging towards him, crashing something hard and metal into his face.

Jack staggered backwards, his cheek split.

The sergeant flew past him, into the cell. He swung at Malik, trying to push him to the ground. Malik swung back, landing a sharp blow to the sergeant's stomach.

Blood dripping down his face, Jack threw himself back into the cell and tackled Malik by his legs. The huge man lost his balance and toppled forwards, taking the sergeant with him. Then Jack pounced on his back, forcing his knees into Malik's spine and the heel of his left hand into his neck so that his cheek was flat against the floor.

Malik grunted but Jack didn't release the pressure. Instead he used his other hand to pull his right hand behind his back. He grasped for the metal object. It was a mobile phone.

'What the hell?' Jack shouted.

He held a tissue to his cheek. Blood was pissing down his face and it stung like hell.

'You'll need a stitch in that,' said the sarge.

'Never mind a fecking stitch,' said Jack. 'How did your man end up with this?' He dangled the mobile phone between his thumb and forefinger.

'I searched him myself,' said the sarge. 'He must have had it up his arse.'

'Jesus.' Jack dropped the phone on the desk. 'Is that even possible?'

The sergeant chuckled. 'You'd be surprised what they can get up there when they know they're going inside.'

Jack picked up a biro and poked at the phone. He knew packing drugs was common, but a phone?

'He had no idea I was going to arrest him so unless he's in the habit of keeping a spare one up his jaxy, it didn't get in here that way.'

Jack hooked it towards him with the nib and flipped it open. He pressed phone ID.

'This is Bell's phone,' he said.

'Bloody hell,' said the sarge. 'He went in to speak to Malik. He must have dropped it.'

'Dropped it!'

Something about all this didn't smell right. In fact, it stank like the station house toilets the morning after a party at the Bengali Tandoori. Coppers didn't drop their phones around dangerous suspects, especially those for whom the clock was ticking.

And why had Bell been in the cell with Malik?

'Why did he want to speak to him?' Jack asked.

The sergeant shrugged. 'He said he wanted to help you out.'

Now Jack could not only smell the bullshit, he could taste it.

Bell was desperate to see Raffy Khan go down and ride his coat-tails to promotion. He had been terrified that Malik would turn out to be Yasmeen's killer and ruin his plans. But surely he wouldn't deliberately jeopardise Jack's investigation? Surely he wouldn't put lives at risk?

Jack stalked out of the custody suite and rushed up the stairs to Bell's office. He pushed hard on the door and it hit the wall behind. The office was empty.

Anger made Jack's face burn and his cheek tormented

him. He was so incensed he directed his fury at Bell's desk and upended it onto the floor. Papers, pens and coffee cups scattered across the room.

He remembered how the signal on Taslima's phone had suddenly gone dead, as if she'd been found out. As if someone had alerted Jalil. Being ambitious was one thing, but how could Bell have stooped so low?

Jack kicked the papers on the floor.

Were there any lengths the man wouldn't sink to?

The answer appeared to Jack on the floor, in the disarray of memos and phone notes. A note from Cheney in forensics.

Dear DI Bell,

R V Raffique Khan

Further to your request of a search of the DNA data base, I confirm that we have found the identity of the father of Yasmeen's child.

His name is Rory Freeman, a member of the extreme left-wing organisation Socialism Today, with a string of public order offences to his name. But more interesting are the three years he served for stabbing his pregnant wife.

Regards,

Nathan Cheney

It was dated two days ago. This was crucial information in the Khan case and Bell was sitting on it.

Lilly felt sick. She had polished off another mint Aero and a family bag of M&Ms. She burped ruefully.

'You OK?'

Jack smiled from the doorway.

'What happened to you?' she gasped at the sight of his bruised and bleeding cheek.

'Malik didn't want to miss the final of *Strictly Come Dancing*.'

Lilly sighed. She'd been ready to have it out with him. Tell him that she knew all about his bottle blonde. But the sheer exhaustion in his eyes, coupled with the injury, made her shy away. After a day like today he needed to rest.

'You should go to bed,' she said.

He nodded. 'I just wanted to give you this.' He handed a letter to her.

She read it. 'Should you be doing this?' she asked.

'It's a complete breach of police protocol,' he said, 'but I'm past caring.'

She reached for her coat.

'Where are you going now?' he asked.

'To ask the Khans if they've ever heard of Rory Freeman.'

Anwar gasped.

'Is everything OK?'

Lilly imagined how she looked with her blistered forehead, her singed hair, her smoke-stained jacket. Saira and Mrs Khan stared at her in horror.

'There was a fire,' she said.

Mrs Khan screamed something in Urdu. It was the first time she had shown any emotion – that in itself startled Lilly.

'Raffy dead?' Mrs Khan's accent was strong but there was no mistaking her fear.

Lilly realised how this must look. She had arrived unannounced, late at night, looking like shit, talking about a fire. Of course the poor woman feared the worse.

She shook her head furiously. 'No, Mrs Khan, Raffy's fine.'

Saira led her mother to the sofa, where the woman sat, shaking uncontrollably.

'It's OK,' Saira soothed. 'Everything's OK.'

Lilly bent low and took the old woman's hand. 'The fire was at a farm. The PTF tried to kill the girl they kidnapped.'

'Not Raffy?' Mrs Khan's eyes were stricken.

'No,' Lilly whispered, 'not Raffy.'

Anwar slumped next to his mother. Lilly noticed he too was shaking.

'I'm sorry to have given you all such a fright,' said Lilly.

Anwar nodded and gave her a weak smile.

'It's just that some very important information came my way and I needed to speak to you about it,' she said.

The Khans looked up at her wearily. She couldn't blame them.

'Does the name Rory Freeman mean anything to you?'

'No,' said Anwar.

Lilly looked into his eyes. 'Give yourself a second to think about it.'

Anwar couldn't return her gaze and instead stared at his hands.

'Never heard of him.'

He's lying, Lilly thought.

She looked at Saira, who was also playing with her fingers in discomfort. Only Mrs Khan met Lilly's eyes.

'Who is Roree?'

Lilly gulped. 'He is the father of Yasmeen's unborn child.'

A strangled noise came from Anwar's throat. He coughed to clear it.

'It's possible that he killed Yasmeen,' said Lilly.

The Khans sat in complete silence.

'The police have tried to suppress this evidence and I want to go to court in the morning to explain the situation to the judge.'

'Raffy coming home?' asked Mrs Khan.

'I can't promise that,' said Lilly, 'but I will be requesting bail whilst we find out why the police have utterly ignored an obvious suspect. That's why it's important you tell me anything you know about this man.'

Anwar stood up. 'Like I said, we've never heard of him.'

It was obvious Lilly was expected to leave.

Lilly nodded curtly and headed for the door. 'I'm sorry to have bothered you.'

When Lilly got back into her car she stifled the urge to scream. What was wrong with these people? Raffy was fifteen and about to go down for a crime he didn't commit. What were they covering up for that was worth letting him rot in gaol?

All around her were families hiding secrets. Secrets that they would keep hidden whatever the cost.

She had pushed her key into the ignition when her phone rang. She expected it to be Jack, but it was a number she didn't recognise.

'Lilly Valentine.'

No one spoke but Lilly could hear the caller breathing.

'Who is this?'

Again no one answered.

Lilly's heart began to beat hard. She looked around her. Was anyone there? Was she being watched? She stabbed central locking. The buttons clicked. No one could get in.

Lilly forced herself to sound braver than she felt. 'Could you tell me who you are, please.'

More breathing.

'If you don't tell me who you are I shall hang up,' Lilly gulped. 'And I shall report this number to the police.'

More breathing.

'Right,' said Lilly.

'Saira,' said the caller, as Lilly was about to snap her phone shut. 'It's Saira Khan.'

Lilly's heart quietened. 'Saira? Why on earth didn't you say anything?'

'I wasn't sure I should.'

'And now?'

'Now I'm just trying to consider Raffy,' said Saira.

Lilly paused. Saira clearly wanted to tell Lilly something but felt she shouldn't.

'You sound torn,' said Lilly.

A sob sounded in Saira's throat.

'It's always hard when you feel you have to make a choice,' said Lilly.

'And how do you know what is right?' asked Saira.

Lilly sighed. How did you know? 'You don't know for sure, but there are some things that can never be right.'

'Like what?'

'Like letting Raffy take the rap for something he didn't do.'

The girl sniffed into the phone.

Lilly knew she had to tread carefully but she needed the information. 'So what do you want to tell me, Saira?'

'I want to tell you,' she stumbled over her words, 'I mean, I want to say that I do know Rory Freeman.'

Lilly closed her eyes. She'd been right.

'And you knew he was Yasmeen's boyfriend?'

'I suspected – well, we all did.'

'Did she say anything to you?'

'No, she could never have admitted that. It would have killed Mum,' said Saira.

Lilly bit her lip. Yasmeen had been young and impressionable, Rory violent. If she had felt able to confide in her family perhaps this tragedy could have been averted.

Secrets and lies. They never did anyone any good.


Mark Cormack slammed the CD into the player. He was desperate for a fag and his hand hovered over the packet.

Not a moment too soon, Paul McKenna's voice floated around the car, urging him to think positive thoughts. Cormack closed his eyes and listened.

The trouble was, Paul bleeding McKenna hadn't spent all day trying to get the woman on her own. He hadn't wandered up and down the corridors of Accident and Emergency, side-stepping some stroppy matron. In the end, she'd stalked right up to him, her nostrils flaring, a bowl of what looked like piss, slopping in her hands.

'Can I ask what you're doing here?' she'd barked.

'Waiting for the missus,' he said. 'She knocked herself out opening the garage door. Claret everywhere.'

The nurse raised an eyebrow.

'In fact,' said Cormack, 'I'll pop down to the shop and get her a box of chocolates.'

Now he was pissed off. He hadn't got the job done. And, God, did he want a fag.

Tomorrow he would do this thing.

# Chapter Twelve

Lilly pulled her robe around her. Outside the sun was shining but in the cell area of the Crown Court the air was stale and cold.

'I'm going to tell the judge that Rory Freeman is the most likely person to have killed Yasmeen,' she told Raffy, 'and that the police have deliberately covered that up.'

She thought he might lose his temper, start a rant about their corruption. That the whole thing was institutionalised racism. Instead he just sat in his wheelchair, his feet still encased in bandages. He looked very young.

'I'm going to say that the police must investigate further and that your case should be dismissed.'

'Will he agree to that?'

Lilly smiled. 'I don't know for sure, but he'll certainly want more information about Freeman and I'll ask for bail in the meantime.'

Raffy's eyes widened. 'I'm going home?'

'I hope so.'

He seemed in shock, as if he couldn't take in what she was telling him.

'Saira is going to give evidence about Freeman,' she said.

'Saira?'

Lilly nodded. 'Even though she can't say he killed Yasmeen, she can say her sister was troubled, that something wasn't right between her and Rory.'

A shadow flashed across Raffy's face. 'I don't think she should get involved.'

'She wants to,' Lilly smiled.

'You don't understand . . .'

Lilly held up her hand. 'I understand that she's kept quiet this long because of her desire to protect your mother and the family.'

Tears filled Raffy's eyes. Lilly touched his hand.

'Now she wants to protect you.'

When Raffy looked up Lilly saw fear in his eyes.

'Anyone but Saira,' he whispered.

Lilly understood that after what had happened to Yasmeen he wanted to keep his other sister far away from all this. He wanted to prevent this horror from touching her.

'I know how you feel about Saira,' she said, 'but just trust me.'

Lilly made her way up to court room one. The stairs seemed twice as steep. She held the rail with one hand and put her other in the small of her back. It had been aching since she arrived, in short uncomfortable waves.

For God's sake, she was heavily pregnant, she should be at home with her feet up.

'Bad day at the office, dear?'

Taslima was waiting for her at the top of the stairs. She had a hijab on but the dressing peeped through. Her right hand was also fully wrapped.

'What on earth are you doing here?'

'Nice to see you too, boss,' Taslima smiled.

Lilly lumbered over and hugged her assistant, hard.

'I mean you should be tucked up in bed.'

'Stop fussing.' Taslima waved her hand. 'Anyway, you don't look marvellous yourself.'

Lilly laughed. What with her blisters and frazzled hair, and now Taslima wrapped up like a mummy, they looked ridiculous. No wonder the guy in the corner was staring at them. Wait till Raffy was wheeled into the dock – then he really would have something to gawk at.

As the man realised she'd spotted him, he picked up a paper and buried himself behind it.

'I can't believe the police didn't tell us about Freeman,' said Taslima.

'How did you know about that?'

'Jack told me.'

When the man thought Lilly wasn't looking, he stared at her again. Something in his gaze troubled her. He no longer seemed to be enjoying the show, rather he seemed to be appraising her, as if he were working something through in his mind. Perhaps she was just edgy about the hearing.

'When did you see Jack?' she asked Taslima.

'He's here,' said Taslima, and pointed to a figure at the far end of the corridor.

Lilly looked up at Jack and nodded. He did the same. There was going to be a pitched battle between Lilly and the police, and she knew he couldn't be seen to be taking her side. It suited Lilly this way. She didn't want to be distracted by thoughts of the blonde and her texts.

She risked another glance at the man. He was doing something with his phone, holding it out in front of him.

'You OK?' Taslima asked.

Lilly wasn't sure. Something about the way the man was holding out the phone bothered her.

'Nothing,' she said, 'just my back killing me.'

Taslima put an arm around Lilly's shoulders. 'Let's do it.'

Cormack took a quick photo of the woman. She was standing with the other one outside court.

This was absolutely not an ideal place to do this, but there was no way he could wait any longer. He sent the picture to the Pakis, to show them he had her in his sights. And to give them the opportunity to call it off.

Within second he received a reply.

*Do it.*

'Court rise.'

Lilly pushed herself to her feet. A sudden burst of pain shot into her spine and she gasped.

Taslima put her hand over hers.

The judge pursed his brow at Lilly's dishevelled appearance. 'Miss Valentine?'

Lilly bowed awkwardly, wincing in pain. 'Your Honour.'

He looked up as the guards wheeled in Raffy. His eyes went from Raffy, to Lilly, then to Taslima, his expression growing ever more puzzled.

'Miss Valentine, are you and your client well?'

Lilly thought about it. Raffy had been attacked by a Nazi, Lilly herself had been almost burned alive and as for Taslima, the image of her clinging to the chimney was branded on her brain.

'I think the saying goes, Your Honour, that we are as well as can be expected.'

'Very good. I'm assuming that your appearance and today's emergency listing reflects that you have something urgent to tell the Court.'

Lilly nodded. 'Your Honour, I wish to make an application that the case against the defendant be dismissed.'

The judge frowned. 'Miss Valentine, I can see that things are strained. Are you sure this application is well advised?'

Lilly leaned heavily against the advocates' table. She was so exhausted she could barely stand.

'I am certain, your Honour.'

'I am not prepared to waste time on an ill-conceived request, Miss Valentine,' the judge said.

'Nor am I,' said Lilly.

They stared at one another for a moment.

At last the judge opened his palms. 'Then begin.'

Lilly took a deep breath. She needed to be measured; not let her emotions get the better of her.

'Your Honour is aware that my client is the only suspect the police investigated in connection with the death of Yasmeen Khan.'

'I'm sure they looked into any other possible suspects.'

Lilly shook her head. 'Raffique was the only person they chose to interview.'

'No doubt the other lines of enquiry proved fruitless.' Judge Chance took off his glasses and frowned. 'We've already had this discussion, Miss Valentine, and you will recall that I gave the police a week to provide the documentation in question.'

'Well, that's just it, Your Honour.' Lilly held up a finger. 'I think there was only ever one line of enquiry.' She took a drink of water to steady herself. 'I think the police decided that this was an honour killing by a member of the Khan family and looked to the most likely son.'

She turned to Raffy, dwarfed by the dock. 'They chose the one shouting his mouth off.'

The judge pursed his lips. 'I very much hope that you have dragged us all here today for something more interesting than a critique of police motivation in this case.'

Lilly heard Kerry sniggering to the side.

'I'm afraid that those motivations are at the heart of this case,' said Lilly. 'They are the reason the investigating officer not only failed to investigate but actually suppressed evidence in respect of another suspect when it came to his attention.'

'That is a very grave accusation, Miss Valentine.'

'It's not one I make lightly,' said Lilly, and held out a piece of paper. 'This is a letter from Dr Nathan Cheney to DI Bell confirming that the father of Yasmeen's baby had been identified by his DNA and that he had a list of previous convictions as long as your arm.'

'Where did you get that?' Kerry tried to grab the letter.

Lilly held it out of reach. 'And more importantly, that one of those convictions was for trying to kill his pregnant wife.'

'Is this true?' the judge thundered at Kerry.

'I know absolutely nothing about this,' stammered

Kerry. 'And I object strongly to having evidence sprung on me like this.'

Lilly let out a laugh. 'And I object to not being told that the victim's lover had a history of violence against women.'

The judge held out his hand for the letter. The usher plucked it from Lilly and passed it over. The judge read it in stony silence. Lilly wished to God she could sit down but there was no way she was going to ask.

When he had finished Judge Chance laid the letter carefully in front of him. 'This is very serious indeed.' He stood. 'I will adjourn for ten minutes, during which time the Prosecution must take instructions.'

When the judge had retired, Kerry leaned over and hissed. 'Where did you get that?'

Lilly shrugged. She wasn't about to land Jack in the shit.

'This is police property.' Kerry bared her teeth.

'So arrest me,' said Lilly.

Kerry glared at Lilly.

'If I were you, love, I'd spend your time working out what you're going to say next,' said Lilly.

Kerry spun on her heel and pulled out her phone.

Lilly headed to Raffy.

'I don't want you to make Saira say anything,' he scowled.

'I'm not making her do anything.'

'Seriously,' he said, 'I'm fine where I am. I can front it out.'

Lilly patted his arm. 'You don't need to.'

The judge returned to court, his face dark.

'Miss Thomson,' he frowned at Kerry, 'this is a very grave matter indeed.'

Kerry leaped to her feet as if stung. 'Your Honour, I recognise that, but I must point out the irregular nature of this private letter being shared with all and sundry.'

'I'd take your point, Miss Thomson, if the letter were being bandied around at the pub, but this is a court of law and we are all here to see that justice is done.'

'And justice must surely preclude the use of stolen correspondence.'

Lilly pulled herself to her feet. 'With all due respect, the Defence should have been made aware of this correspondence in the first place. How we got it is an irrelevance. Now what have you got to say?'

'Sit down please, Miss Valentine,' the judge admonished.

'The Americans would say that fruit of a poison tree is poisoned itself,' said Kerry, grasping at straws.

Lilly threw up her hands. 'This is Luton, not New Orleans. Now what have you got to say?'

'Sit down, Miss Valentine,' the judge shouted. 'Frankly, you look like you need to.'

'Thank you, Your Honour,' Kerry said. 'I was beginning to wonder if Miss Valentine remembered we were in court.'

Lilly sat back in her seat. Her cheeks blazed.

'Thank you.' The judge gave her a cold stare.

Kerry smirked at Lilly. 'As I was saying, this piece of correspondence cannot possibly be taken into account. It is inadmissible.'

'I think you'll find that is my call,' said the judge.

'Of course, Your Honour,' Kerry stuttered.

He held up the letter. 'And frankly, I am all ears as to what you've got to say.'

Kerry opened and closed her mouth like a fish in a net.

'Miss Thomson?'

Kerry cleared her throat. 'The police do not believe that Rory Freeman is a suspect.'

Lilly couldn't believe it. 'You have got to be kidding.'

The judge glared at Lilly. 'Miss Valentine, I will not tell you again.'

Lilly glared back and folded her arms across her chest. There was absolutely no way she would allow the police to gloss this over.

'Miss Thomson,' the judge continued, 'what investigations have the police actually done into Mr Freeman?'

'Sweet FA,' Lilly whispered from the corner of her mouth.

Kerry ignored her.

'Your Honour, I couldn't say what exactly has been done. You'll appreciate that I'm not the officer in the case.'

'Then get him here,' interjected Lilly.

The judge lifted his thumb and index finger. He gestured to the gap between them. 'I'm this far away from having you removed, Miss Valentine.'

'I agree, Your Honour, it's outrageous,' said Kerry.

The judge nodded. 'The behaviour perhaps, but the sentiment is understandable. Have the officer brought over here to explain himself.'

'But he could be anywhere,' Kerry said.

The judge smiled. 'I can wait.'

Lilly slotted a handful of coins into the vending machine and chose a Twix.

'How can you even think of eating?' asked Taslima. 'Aren't you nervous?'

Lilly shrugged. Heightened emotion rarely suppressed her appetite. In fact, she usually ate more if she was stressed. She pushed in another handful of coins and chose a Mars bar as well.

'I thought you were sticking to one bar a day.'

Lilly could smell Jack behind her: the leather of his jacket and the lemon of his aftershave.

'Pregnant women need more calories,' she replied.

He chuckled to himself. 'You'll certainly need the energy when Bell gets here.'

'Not a happy bunny?'

'More like the big bad wolf.'

Lilly snapped the Twix in half and pushed one into Jack's mouth.

'Well, I ain't little Red Riding Hood.'

It was now or never.

Cormack watched the woman pacing the foyer. She had the other one in tow, like they were stuck with bleeding glue. She didn't look like she'd put up a fight, but you never knew.

At least the copper had buggered off.

He looked around. No one was paying any attention so he reached into his back pocket.

'Is there anything more sickening than a bent copper?'

Lilly and Taslima strode down the corridor from the foyer to the court room.

'I mean, everyone wants to win,' said Lilly, 'but hiding evidence is the lowest of the low.'

Taslima was incredulous. 'I still can't believe it.'

Lilly was about to point out that, after all these years, there was very little she wasn't prepared to believe, when she saw the man out of the corner of her eye.

He was fiddling with his mobile again. Then she remembered. It was the estate agent. Or at least that was what he'd said. It hadn't sounded right at the time, and the fact that he was here now made it even less likely. So why had he been taking pictures of her office? And why was he taking pictures of Lilly today?

She felt her pulse quicken.

'What's wrong?' asked Taslima.

Lilly nodded at the man. 'He's been following me.'

'Why?'

'I don't know,' said Lilly. 'I thought it might be something to do with the PTF.'

The man walked towards them, his eyes narrow.

Lilly looked around wildly for Jack but he was back in court.

When the man was feet away, Lilly put up her hand. 'What do you want?'

The man stopped in his tracks. Lilly could feel Taslima shaking beside her.

'Just tell whoever sent you, that I know what they're up to,' she said.

The man drew his bottom lip into his mouth.

'Tell them that they cannot intimidate me,' she said.

The man watched Lilly intently. Then, very slowly, he reached into his back pocket.

Lilly took a step back, her hand still out in front of her. What did he have? A knife? A gun? Lilly felt a scream form in her throat. She knew she should run but the man's eyes held her to the spot.

He moved forward swiftly, bringing the weapon out in a flash. Lilly braced herself.

'Zahara Khan,' he growled, 'this is for you.'

He released Lilly from his glare and held something out in front of him. Lily's eyes darted to the object.

Not a knife. Not a gun. It was a brown envelope.

The man waved it at Taslima and tentatively she plucked it from him.

The toilet lid was cold and hard.

Taslima moved her weight as she turned the letter over and over in her hands. She recognised the writing on the envelope immediately. Despite all the deceit, the secrecy, the hiding, they had found her.

'Taslima,' Lilly knocked on the toilet door, 'let me in.'

After the man had given her the letter, Taslima had sprinted to the ladies' toilets and had locked herself in. She didn't know how long she'd been in there but she did know that Lilly had been shuffling around outside for most of it.

At last, Taslima opened the door. Lilly stood over her, concern etched around her eyes.

'Is it from him?' she asked.

Tears filled Taslima's eyes. 'It's over.'

'Don't say that,' said Lilly. 'I'll get every order in the book to keep him away. Hell, you can move in with me.'

Taslima smiled sadly. 'You are a true friend.'

'I mean it,' Lilly smiled back. 'I've dealt with worse than your ex-husband in my time.'

Taslima got up and hugged Lilly.

'We'll get a panic button,' said Lilly, 'patched straight through to the nick. Jack can sort it out.'

'Lilly,' Taslima whispered into her ear, 'when I said it was over, I meant it.'

Lilly shook her head.

'He's been deported.'

'What?'

Taslima couldn't contain her tears. 'He's been sent back to Pakistan.'

'Oh my God,' said Lilly. 'How?'

Taslima held up the letter. 'My mum says he committed some sort of fraud on his original application.'

A smile slid across Lilly's face. 'So you and Rogon are safe?'

Taslima could hardly believe it. All those times he had beaten her and threatened to take her son away, she had prayed for Allah's protection. She had thought he'd forsaken her but she should have known better.

She tossed back her head and laughed through tears. 'I'm going home.'

Back in court, Lilly couldn't force the smile from her lips. Taslima was free.

She could feel the hatred wending its way to her from Bell and Kerry, but she stuck her nose in the air.

Burying evidence was bad policing and they knew it. Nothing they could say would dissuade her. Soon her client would be exonerated and everyone would see that she had been right all along.

Bullies and their ilk, whether they be criminals like

Taslima's ex-husband, or the PTF, or part of the estab-lishment, could not be allowed to prevail. And when she got home tonight she would deal with Sam. He needed to know that she was disgusted with his behaviour, that she would not tolerate it. But he also needed to know that she loved him all the same. They would work this out. Together.

The judge entered and Kerry was on her feet.

'So what have you discovered?' he asked.

'Your Honour, I've taken instructions, and the police are, as we speak, attempting to contact Mr Freeman.'

Lilly got up. 'That's all very convenient but what happens in the meantime? My client's fifteen and languishing in prison.'

'With all due respect,' Kerry sighed, 'the defendant is in a young offenders' institution, not Alcatraz.'

'However you dress it up, these are not places fit for children,' snapped Lilly.

'I'm sure the defendant is being well taken care of.'

Lilly pointed at Raffy in his wheelchair. 'Does he look well cared for to you?'

The judge put up his hand. 'Enough. What we need to ascertain is how long the police investigations will take.'

'I'm guessing around ten years,' said Lilly.

'Enough,' the judge barked. 'Miss Thomson?'

'There has been some difficulty finding Mr Freeman's whereabouts,' said Kerry.

'Which is police speak for we have no idea where he is or how long it will take us to find him.'

The judge stared hard at Lilly and dropped his voice

to little above a whisper. 'Miss Valentine, I cannot allow you to interrupt any further.'

Lilly shivered. Sam hated it when she used the trick on him and now she knew how it felt. Give her shouting any day.

'Sorry,' she mumbled.

'Excellent.' The judge turned back to Kerry. 'Tell me, if the police investigation were to be prolonged, how would the Prosecution feel about bail for the defendant?'

Kerry turned to Bell, who nodded.

Lilly exhaled. At least they were being reasonable about bail.

'We would be absolutely opposed to any application for bail,' said Kerry.

Lilly gasped.

'On what basis?' asked the judge.

'On the basis that there is no reason whatsoever to believe that Raffique Khan did not commit this offence. Speaking with Mr Freeman is a matter of crossing the Is and dotting the Ts.' Kerry pulled herself up to full height. 'There is nothing to suggest that Mr Freeman is a suspect.'

Lilly opened her mouth to speak but stopped herself in time. She bit her lip so hard it hurt.

After what seemed like hours, the judge turned to her. 'Miss Valentine?'

'Your Honour, this is ridiculous,' Lilly burst out. 'Rory Freeman was the victim's boyfriend. She was having his baby.'

The judge cocked his head to one side. 'That doesn't mean he killed her.'

'But we know he was violent to his ex-wife, when she was pregnant.'

'Indeed, though that doesn't mean he was violent to Miss Khan, does it?' he asked.

'Your Honour, he's the most likely candidate, isn't he? If it wasn't for the honour killing angle he'd have been suspect number one and Raffy would be at home doing his homework.'

The judge paused and closed his eyes. Lilly had a thousand more things to say but she kept quiet.

'If there was any evidence whatsoever that Mr Freeman behaved badly towards Miss Khan I would be minded to grant bail while that were investigated.'

'But there is none, is there?' asked Kerry.

Lilly couldn't hold back a smile.

'Your Honour, I would like to call Saira Khan as a witness. She can tell the Court of her fears about the relationship between Mr Freeman and Yasmeen.'

'Very well, call her in.'

The usher went into the corridor and called Saira's name. There was no answer. He called again.

'Without a witness I suggest we adjourn this hearing,' said Kerry.

'One second, Your Honour,' said Lilly, and scuttled to the door.

As she passed the dock, Raffy shook his head.

'Don't worry,' she whispered. 'Leave it to me.'

She hurried into the corridor. Don't let me down, Saira. Don't let Raffy down.

There was no one there.

She could hear raised voices at the security gate.

'If you don't take it off, you ain't getting in,' said a security guard.

Lilly rounded the corner and saw Saira arguing at the X-Ray machine.

The guard was gesticulating to her coat. He wanted her to put it through but she was resisting.

'Let her in,' Lilly called.

'No can do,' said the guard.

Lilly put her hands on her hips. 'This young woman is needed by Judge Chance right now.'

The guard put her hands on her own hips.

'Fine,' said Lilly. 'I'll go up there right now and tell him you won't let this vital witness into court.'

'I didn't say that,' said the guard.

It was a fair point, but Lilly was in no mood for fairness.

'I'll tell everyone that the most high-profile murder case in ten years can't go ahead because you won't let this woman in.'

'Oh, for God's sake,' the woman threw up her hands, 'do what you like. I'm just trying to do my job.'

Lilly motioned to Saira, who hurried after her.

'I'm going to put you straight in the box,' said Lilly, 'and you can tell the judge that Yasmeen was scared of Freeman.'

Saira nodded. Lilly could see the tightness of her mouth and the beads of sweat above her lip.

'Don't be nervous,' she smiled, trying to reassure the young woman.

Lilly led Saira into court and directly to the witness box. Raffy whispered his sister's name but she didn't look at him. She looked terrified. Small, despite the thick coat wrapped around her like a protection blanket.

The usher offered her an array of holy books upon which to swear. She hesitated. Glanced at her brother. Picked up the Koran with a shaking hand.

'I swear to tell the truth, the whole truth and nothing but the truth.'

The judge spoke gently. 'Miss Khan, would you like to sit down? Take off your coat, perhaps?'

Saira gave one shake of the head. 'No.'

He raised his eyebrows to Lilly. His look said it all; are you sure about this witness?

Lilly stuck her chin in the air. What choice did she have?

'Miss Khan, could you tell us about your sister, Yasmeen?'

Saira swallowed visibly. 'What would you like to know?'

'Were you close?' Lilly shrugged.

'We were family.'

Lilly paused. She knew Saira was reluctant but this was going to be painful.

'Did she talk to you about things?'

'Sometimes.'

'Boys?'

Saira coughed. 'Sometimes.'

'And what did she say?'

Saira shook her head distractedly. 'That she hoped to marry one day.'

'Did she tell you she was having a relationship with Rory Freeman?'

Saira flinched. 'I knew.'

'And what effect did that relationship have on Yasmeen?' Lilly asked.

'She changed.'

'How?'

'Her moods were unpredictable. She argued with everyone.'

Lilly nodded, as if this was exactly what she wanted, then slipped in the most important question.

'Was she frightened?'

Saira paused. Lilly could see she was still shaking.

'I think so, yes.'

Lilly took her seat and let Kerry cross-examine. She prayed she had done enough to secure Raffy's bail.

'Miss Khan, you say you think your sister was frightened?'

Saira nodded.

'Did she tell you that?'

Saira shook her head.

Kerry smirked. 'So what exactly did she do to make you think that?'

'She became very secretive,' said Saira.

Kerry leaned on the advocates' table. It groaned under her weight. 'Couldn't that be because she knew what she was doing would not have her family's approval?'

'I suppose so.'

'Because Yasmeen did not have the approval of her family, did she?'

'No.'

'Her brothers, for instance, would have been furious, no?'

Saira's eyes darted towards Raffy. 'Yes.'

'Is it possible that it was the fear of discovery, and not Mr Freeman, that she was afraid of?'

Saira glanced again at Raffy. He had buried his head in his hands. Saira opened her mouth to speak. Her lips trembled.

Kerry frowned. 'Is it fair to say that if Yasmeen's affair and pregnancy with a non-Muslim had been discovered she would have been in very serious trouble?'

Tears sprang into Saira's eyes. They sparkled against the black of her irises. 'She knew she should not have behaved that way,' she said

Kerry nodded. 'And she understood the consequences?'

The tears ran down Saira's face. 'She understood.'

There was silence in the court.

Lilly could hear only the blood rushing in her head. She'd called Saira as a witness to help Raffy – but she had not only ensured bail would be denied, but was also confirming that Yasmeen's death had indeed been an honour killing.

From the dock, the silence was punctuated by a sob.

'I'm sorry, Raffy,' Saira whispered. 'I have to tell the truth. Allah demands it.'

Lilly watched the girl shiver. Despite the heat and the ridiculously thick coat, Saira's shoulders shuddered.

Then she turned to Raffy. He was still sobbing, his head bobbing in his hands. Hadn't he tried to tell her not to put Saira on the stand? Hadn't he begged? Lilly had ignored him and now the case was on its knees.

Kerry sat down, satisfaction oozing from every pore.

Lilly began her redirect without knowing what on earth she could possibly say.

'Miss Khan, you say Yasmeen was frightened of discovery?'

Saira swiped at her tears with the back of her hand. 'Yes.'

'What would she anticipate would happen?'

'I don't know,' Saira stuttered. 'She would have had to stop seeing that man, for a start.'

'And the baby? What would your brothers have made of that?'

Saira shook her head as if bewildered. 'They wouldn't have believed it of her.'

Lilly remembered Raffy having just that reaction when he was arrested. He could not believe it of Yasmeen. 'She's a good girl,' he'd said. He'd been shocked. Horrified.

'Raffy didn't know Yasmeen was pregnant, did he?' asked Lilly.

'No.'

'He didn't know about Rory Freeman, did he?'

'No.'

Lilly nodded. It was as if the clouds were clearing after a tropical storm. Her mind, like the air, sharpened.

'Raffy didn't kill Yasmeen, did he?'

Saira bit her lip. Her hand involuntarily reached out to touch the Koran.

'No, he did not.'

Lilly's heart beat hard in her chest. There was only one person in the Khan family who had known about Yasmeen and that person was in front of her. A person who couldn't bear to see her own flesh and blood betray her religion and dishonour everyone around her.

Hadn't Raffy been trying to tell her this all along? Hadn't he said his sisters were the sword of the prophet? Lilly had thought he was talking about Muslim sisters generally, but he had meant something much closer to home.

She stood as tall as she could and asked the only question left.

'Miss Khan, could you tell us who did kill Yasmeen?'

Saira held the Koran against her. 'I did.'

The court was filled with gasps. Even the judge looked shaken.

'Are you a member of the Purity Task Force?' Lilly asked.

Saira snorted. 'Those meatheads are nothing but a bunch of thugs.'

'So you acted alone?'

Saira was still clasping the Koran to her chest. 'Allah is always with me.'

Lilly nodded. It was over. Saira Khan had killed her sister.

'Miss Khan,' she said, 'do you understand what you're saying?'

Saira's face changed instantly. Gone was the fear.

'I understand perfectly.'

Lilly swallowed hard. 'Then could you tell the Court what you did.'

'Yasmeen had already told me about Freeman. That she was having an affair with him,' said Saira. 'She promised to end it.'

'And?'

'I didn't believe her. She was still scurrying around

like a rat in the shadows, so I challenged her.' Saira let out a laugh but there was no humour in it. 'She said that she couldn't end it, that she was carrying his child.'

'So what did you do?' asked Lilly.

'I did what Allah intended. I took action.' She paused as if to ensure she remembered the detail correctly. 'I ground up the medication and put it in her drink. Then I waited.'

Lilly was incredulous. 'You sat and watched your sister die?'

'I sat with her and prayed.'

Lilly looked at the judge. 'I think, Your Honour, we all need a moment.'

The judge nodded and turned to DI Bell.

'Perhaps you would accompany Miss Khan to the cells for further questioning.'

Bell had lost his composure, eyes wide, mouth gaping. He look winded as he got to his feet.

Saira gave him a look of pure hatred. 'Keep your distance.'

Bell furrowed his brow. Didn't the girl realise what was going to happen now?

Saira suddenly seemed stronger. In control. She shrugged off her coat and Bell stopped in his tracks. Kerry screamed.

Strapped around Saira's waist was a suicide belt.

Lilly smelled the sharp tang of urine from someone in the room.

'Everyone, stay back.' Saira's voice rang out across the courtroom.

Bell retraced his steps. Everyone stared at the

authoritative look on this young woman's face and the pouches of explosive attached to a tangle of black wires.

Slowly, Lilly felt Taslima rise to her feet.

'*Assalamu alaikum*, sister,' she said.

Saira gave small laugh. 'Don't try that comrade stuff with me.'

'It's a sad world when one Muslim can't greet another,' said Taslima.

'It's a sad world where Muslims are butchered in their beds,' Saira spat. 'It's a sad country where decent Muslims dare not practise their religion without being ridiculed or attacked.'

Taslima nodded. Took a tiny step towards Saira.

'We all share your anger but this is not the way, sister.'

Saira bared her teeth. 'So what do you suggest? That we sit back and let the religion we love be disrespected?'

'We try to change things,' said Taslima. 'One step at a time.'

'I won't do it.' Saira patted her chest with the flat of her hand. 'I won't stand by while this legal system supports torture and detention without charge.'

'But there must be other ways than this. Better ways.'

Saira screwed her eyes tightly shut and shook her head. 'Wake up, sister. We've marched and demonstrated. We've sent aid. It's time for direct action.'

Raffy was still sobbing in the dock.

'What's the matter, brother?' Saira snarled at him. 'We've all heard you spouting the political stuff. Declaring war on the streets of Luton. Well, here I am, a soldier.'

'These people are innocent civilians.' Taslima spread her arms. 'They are not a legitimate target.'

'You're wrong, sister. This courtroom, with its police and judges, is the heart of the state.'

Taslima pointed to Lilly. 'But some of us are here to help your brother.'

'Even Valentine is part of the corrupt process. You all are.'

'What about our children?' Taslima asked. 'Have you thought about them?'

'Allah will provide for the faithful.'

'And your own family? Do they deserve to die?'

'I will see them again in Paradise,' said Saira.

Taslima shook her head. 'The holy Koran tells us that we may not take another life.'

Saira's eyes blazed and she held up the book in front of her like a talisman to ward off evil.

'Fight and slay the pagans wherever you shall find them. Just as the prophet, peace be upon him, did then, so shall we.' Then Saira closed her eyes and began to pray.

Taslima flashed Lilly a look. There was nothing more she could do.

Lilly couldn't breathe. Her mind whirled. Would she never see Sam again? And what of the unborn child, kicking her now. Would she never get to see his smile?

Saira's voice carried around the court, the words in Arabic melodious, beautiful. At odds with the horror of what was about to happen.

Lilly looked wildly around her. No one dared move. It was as if no one believed Saira would actually do it. But Lilly had watched her throughout the exchange with Taslima and had seen deep into her heart, and there was nothing there. The girl talked of religion and politics but there was nothing but darkness and hatred. Lilly had met murderers before, however they dressed up their reasons, that was all there ever was. She had killed her sister and would kill them all.

It was up to Lilly.

The girl's voice echoed, rising in a crescendo. Lilly knew there were only moments left. She wouldn't even make it across the courtroom in time.

She glanced at Jack, sitting rigid next to Bell, in the seat nearest the witness box. She knew he was thinking exactly the same thing. Saira had to be stopped.

He held up three fingers. One, two, three.

Lilly grabbed for the jug of water. The glass was heavy and dull in her hand.

She held it aloft and threw it as hard as she could. It arced through the air, spraying water across the table. Again Kerry screamed. The jug hit Saira square in the face, knocking her backwards. The jug landed with a thump on the carpet.

Without a second's hesitation Jack leaped towards her, grabbed the jug and brought it crashing down into Saira's face. It smashed. There was an explosion of glass and blood.

The bomb squad swept the court for further devices but Lilly knew they wouldn't find anything. Saira had turned herself into a weapon. That was all she needed.

Lilly stood outside in the sunshine, enjoying the breeze on her face, surveying the police scurrying about like ants.

'You were unbelievable,' she told Taslima.

She gave a modest smile. 'You were pretty great yourself.'

'We make a damn fine team.'

Jack appeared from the building. 'It's clear.'

'Raffy?'

'Someone's taken him back to the nick to ask a few questions,' said Jack. 'He'll need to explain how those tablet boxes came to be in his locker.'

'Perhaps Saira put them there,' said Lilly.

'Perhaps,' Jack agreed. 'Or perhaps he guessed what had happened and hid them.'

'So he was covering up for Saira all this time?' asked Taslima.

'Which is an offence,' Lilly pointed out.

Jack nodded. 'But he's served a lot of time in prison already, so either way he'll be out in an hour or so.'

Lilly nodded. The boy could go home to his mother and elder brother. With each other's support maybe they could rebuild their lives.

'Let's get our stuff,' she said, and walked towards the door.

When she put her foot on the first step she knew she wouldn't be able to make it. The pain in her back had worsened, snaking its way around to her pelvis. She let out a guttural moan.

'I'll run up,' said Jack.

Lilly snatched his arm. 'Don't go anywhere.'

'What?'

Another wave of pain overtook Lilly's body.

'I think I'm in labour.'

She sucked down the gas and air as the ambulance tried to wend its way through the police barrier.

'Sorry,' shouted the paramedic, 'this whole area's been cordoned off.'

'Shit,' Jack shouted.

Lilly held the mask to her face, feeling the plastic mouthpiece imprinting itself deep into her skin. Another contraction ripped through her like a wave crashing onto rocks.

'I'm going to die,' she screamed.

Jack pushed the hair from her face. 'Not on my watch.'

She took another gulp from the canister; braced herself for another contraction.

'Try to relax,' called the paramedic.

Lilly struggled to sit up. 'Relax? I'm about to give birth to a pumpkin – how the fuck can I relax?'

The paramedic chortled to himself. 'Give me the drunks on a Saturday night.'

Jack pushed her back down onto the stretcher. 'Keep calm, Lilly.'

'Don't you start.'

He smiled and kissed her cheek.

It was then that she knew she had to ask him about the blonde. Ridiculous, in an ambulance, about to have their baby. But she had to.

'Jack,' she panted, 'I saw you at the hospital with a woman.'

A shadow passed across Jack's face. 'I can't think who that might be.'

'Don't lie to me, Jack. I saw the texts.'

He winced. 'I'm sorry.'

She didn't want to, but Lilly could feel tears streaming down her cheeks.

'Do you love her?'

'God, no. It was never anything like that.'

'Then what?'

He shook his head as if to clear it. 'Stupidity, a flirtation, nothing.'

'Did you have sex?'

'No.'

'Did you want to?'

He didn't answer. Didn't have to.

He took her hand gently and kissed it. 'Can you forgive me?'

She was about to answer when pain coursed the length of her torso.

'Oh my God.'

The paramedic climbed into the back and rolled up his sleeves.

'What are you doing?' Jack asked. 'We need to get to the hospital.'

The paramedic smiled. 'No time for that, my friend. This baby's coming now.'

## In Conversation with Helen Black

*If you were stranded on a desert island, which book would you take with you?*

*Trainspotting* by Irvine Welsh. The first time I read it I was blown away and every journey through it since has brought something new.

*Where does your inspiration come from?*

Everywhere. Literally. The newspapers and radio are rich fodder, as are overheard conversations. Almost daily, I see or hear something and think 'that would make a great story'. I have to be very careful that the latest sparkle doesn't derail the project I'm working on.

*Have you always wanted to become a writer?*

I always enjoyed writing but never saw myself making a living from it. To be honest, before I had my children I was far too busy saving the world and downing tequila slammers. But once I had babies I had the sudden urge to do something creative and started writing my first book *Damaged Goods*.

Now, I can't imagine not writing.

### What's the strangest job you've ever had?

Well I've done all the usual grotty numbers: waitressing, cleaning, pot washing in a pub. And I did a stint at a fizzy drinks factory that opened my eyes as to why orangeade and electric wires do not mix.

But by far the strangest experience was when I trained in the City. The hours, the money, the strong personalities all made for a dizzy mix. Like day care for the terminally ambitious.

### When you're not writing, what are your favourite things to do?

Like my main character, Lilly Valentine, I love to cook. I'm at my happiest surrounded by cookery books and a fridge full of good ingredients.

I also love bubble baths, so hot they can give you a heart attack. Up to my neck in Chanel No 5 wouldn't be a bad way to go, would it?

### What is a typical working day like for you? Have you ever had writer's block? If so, how did you cope with it?

I do the school run, then take an hour or so to walk in the countryside with a friend. When you spend a lot of time at a computer you need fresh air and a few laughs.

Once home I eat, then work until it's time to collect the kids from school. Some days will be spent researching, some writing, some editing. Either way it's important to put in the hours.

I'm not sure I believe in writer's block. All writers get stuck and the challenge is to come up with the way around a problem. Often I just move on and come back later. Forward motion is hugely important when you've 90,000 words to produce.

### Do you have any secret ambitions?

Lots.

Each New Year I write a list of all the things I'd like to do. Turning the Lilly Valentine series into a television programme is high up there. As is living somewhere sunny.

### What can't you live without?

Books. Roast chicken. Silence.

### When you were a child, what did you want to be when you grew up?

When I was ten, my mum took two photographs of me. One was outside number ten Downing Street, the other was outside RADA.

I had big plans.

**Which five people, living or dead, would you invite to a dinner party?**

Irvine Welsh because he sounds like a riot.
Nigella Lawson to share the cooking.
Julie Burchill to spice up the conversation.
Fatboy Slim to bring the music.
JK Rowling to talk me through how she did it.
And my dad. Because he always did love a party.